A TIME OF OSTRICHES

PUBLISHED BY SIMON PRIM

THE PRIM PRESS

CORK

2022

A TIME
OF
OSTRICHES

BOOK ONE

by

S.K. FRANCIS

2022

First Edition

Published in Ireland by The Prim Press
www.theprimpress.ie

ISBN 978-1-3999-0730-9

SET IN CASLON CLASSICO 11 PT

PRINTED AND BOUND BY
THE IMPRIMERIE FABRIK & CO

A TIME OF OSTRICHES

A TIME OF OSTRICHES

PRINCIPAL CHARACTERS
ARRANGED IN FAMILY GROUPS

THE BALESTRAS

LAURA BALESTRA, *Estella and Solomon Cansino's daughter*
ISAAC BALESTRA, *her late husband*
MARGUERITE (RITA), *her eldest daughter*
COLETTE (COCO), *her younger daughter*
TEDDY, *her son*

MARCO BALESTRA, *Isaac's brother*
ALLEGRA BALESTRA, *Marco's wife*
GUISEPPE (SEPPY), *their eldest son*
NORA, *their eldest daughter*
YVONNE, *their middle daughter*
SYLVIE, *their youngest daughter*

THE CANSINOS

ESTELLA CANSINO
SOLOMON CANSINO, *her husband*
LEONARD, *their older son, Laura's brother*
MIRIAM, *Leonard's wife*
BOBBY, *their younger son, Laura's brother*

THE D'ARAQUYS

VIOLETTE D'ARAQUY, *Estella's younger sister*

PHILIPPE D'ARAQUY, *her husband*

JOSETTE (JOSIE), *their daughter*

CLEMENT (CLEMMIE), *their son*

THE ARDITTIS

LUCIA ARDITTI, *Allegra Balestra's cousin*

RAPHAEL ARDITTI, *her husband*

LUCA, *their eldest son*

ANNETTA (NETTA), *their eldest daughter*

GABRIEL, *Raphael's father*

THE SUTTONS

DANIEL SUTTON, *a young Scotsman*

RUTH, *his younger sister*

HAROLD, *his father*

PEARL, *his mother*

THE CARASSOS

SOFIA CARASSO

EZRA CARASSO, *her husband*

EMMANUEL (MANU), *their son*

A TIME OF OSTRICHES

BOOK ONE
1938 - 1940

Cieux, écoutez ma voix ; terre, prête l'oreille.

I

PART ONE

CHAPTER I

The train, with its distinctive blue and white livery, moved easily through the landscape, the blinds of the sleeper carriages lowered. The sky was grey, and the mountains hidden in mist, and on either side of the tracks, bright orange poppies ran hem-like. A kite hovered above terraced vines, swooping down on its prey only once the train had passed, and somewhere else, a dog howled. Morning was everywhere.

And in the last carriage, a man rolled over in his bunk and pulled the sheets higher about his chin. Without opening his eyes, he knew exactly where he was, and he sighed with contentment. The rosewood panelling and ivory marquetry were as familiar to him as his own home, and the hand reaching towards the side table did not fumble. He weighed a heavy, gold watch in his fingers for a moment before clipping it around his wrist, then lay there, listening to the clatter of the rails, and the knocking of stewards as they made their way along the corridor. When they reached his door, however, he sat up and snapped the lamp switch, and when the man in the braided cap and cuffs entered the cabin, he might have been awake for hours.

As he did every morning, Marco Balestra gently stroked his chin, his short, thick fingers making a fan across his face. The thought of his new electric razor pleased him, and he remembered how thrilled his wife had been when she bought it. His thumb smoothing his well-trimmed moustache, he watched the steward as he poured coffee, and felt suddenly displeased. Something was wrong.

'No newspaper?' he said, reaching for the fur coat he had arranged across his feet the night before, and draping it about his shoulders.

'*Certo*, Signore Balestra,' smiled the steward, gesturing to the table, where a copy of *Le Matin* had appeared as if by magic. He tucked a fur sleeve behind Marco's pillow, and handed him a tray with his coffee and two breakfast rolls. The gentleman was a regular on the Simplon and the steward knew his ways. 'A little ham, like always. And a tomato.'

Marco Balestra nodded. 'I eat a tomato every day of my life,' he said, and the efficiency with which this had been brought about today cheered him.

The steward busied himself laying out fresh towels and soap. 'I hope Signore wasn't disturbed at Domodossola,' he said, speaking to the mirror. Marco Balestra was slicing his tomato, and did not respond. 'A gentleman with an irregular passport, and the Swiss causing the usual fuss.' He lowered his voice, still confiding in the mirror. 'Refugee,' he said, much as one might share a medical complaint.

'Europe's a mess,' said Marco Balestra, opening the newspaper and glancing at the headlines. He did not generally trouble himself with current affairs.

The steward adjusted the heating wheel. 'Many foes, much honour,' he said, because that was what everyone said in Italy these days.

And the gentleman, who had turned to the financial pages, nodded.

Marco Balestra was not a particularly wise man, but he had the appearance of one. With his French newspapers and his English tweeds and his Italian brushed felt hat, he was the embodiment of a European gentleman, and he moved through life with ease. He kept his curly hair cut short, and found he liked the speckling of grey around his temples as it suggested authority. He was not as tall as he would have liked, but then neither was Napoleon or Charlie Chaplin, nor Mussolini for that matter. Life was what it was, and fortunately for Marco Balestra, his was good.

Outside the window, the grey-green countryside had been exchanged for the suburbs of Milan, and the sky was smaller now, cut into squares and rectangles that fitted neatly between the buildings. He dressed with care, enjoying the unfolding of his well-pressed shirt, choosing a white silk handkerchief to match, preferring a plain necktie. Because he was always cold, he wore a long-sleeved cotton vest beneath his shirt, and today, a waistcoat too, undeceived by the glittering efforts of the sun. Had he thought about it, he would have said he found Milan a damp, uninviting city, whose monumental facades and vaulting arcades could not hide the fact it had been built on marshland. But he didn't, and instead he blamed his sinking stomach on the ham. He folded his newspaper, pressing it flat, and slipped it into his briefcase. He checked his pocket for his passport (Greek, he was born in Corfu), and then his wallet for something to tip the steward, and then again for his passport, as you couldn't be too careful these days. Then he pulled his coat around him and sat back, his head resting on the lacquered wooden panel, his stomach rumbling softly to the clack-clack of the wheels on the rails.

◆　　　◆　　　◆　　　◆　　　◆

THE WINTRY SUN FELL IN SHARDS through the vast iron and glass arches of the Stazione Centrale, bouncing off the bronze chandeliers, and causing the mosaics which lined the walls to glow like church windows. Marco lingered for a moment on the steps, feeling his mood brighten, then swung himself onto the platform, looking around for someone to carry his luggage.

The steward, Marco's generous tip still warming his pocket, appeared beside him and, with the enthusiasm that always surrounds a wealthy man, sent bags and porter scurrying towards the front of the station. Marco strode behind, his fur coat swinging about his stocky frame.

The Piazza Doria was bathed in sunlight, orange-painted trams turning wide circles beneath a criss-cross of clicking wires. Marco had forgotten to telegram his arrival time to the office, and now he saw with dismay the long line for taxis. He frowned and lowered his hat, watching as the porter unknotted the rope which held his bags, then removed his glove and held out a hand towards Marco.

'*Ecco*,' said Marco, vaguely repulsed, and he dropped a coin into the man's palm. The man studied it for a moment, turning it over so that Il Duce faced down, then slung his rope across his body, and turned away. Marco looked towards the piazza, thinking how much he disliked this country. Even the most perfunctory of encounters seemed charged with some kind of— what was it? Hostility? Ungraciousness? Allegra had been right to insist that he close the office.

Once again he had the feeling that something was wrong, and he remembered their fight before he left last night. Allegra had accused him of being in love with his sister-in-law, and when he had laughed and called her ridiculous, she had shut herself in her dressing room and refused to say goodbye. It had been made worse by Nora and Yvonne taking their mother's side, and even Sylvie, his favourite, had seemed to hesitate. But then she had followed him out to the car and clasped her arms around his neck, whispering to him not to worry, and to send all their love to Auntie Laura, who must still be feeling so sad. Marco felt the knot in his stomach return, and the injustice of the whole thing filled his body like air in a balloon. Nobody understood how difficult it had been for him since his brother died, trying to keep everyone happy, the responsibility for the business on his shoulders alone. He turned up his collar, shrugging deeper inside his coat.

A blast of tram horns on the other side of the square caused him to look up. A car was weaving its way across the piazza, a woman leaning out of the driver's window and waving gaily in his direction. Marco braced himself: it was Lucia Arditti, his wife's cousin, and as usual she was making a scene.

'*Presto, presto,* don't just stand there!' The car screeched to a halt yards from where Marco was standing and a woman in a lambskin coat launched towards him across the rails. Seizing his suitcase, she ran back towards the car. 'How are you, *mi amore*? Good journey?'

Marco smiled. 'Lucia Arditti, what a surprise!'

'Allegra told me you were coming, I thought I'd spare you a taxi ride.' She flung open the rear door and two small faces peered out. 'Boys, say hello to Uncle Marco! Watch out, mind your heads!' and she thrust his suitcase onto the ledge behind them.

Marco held out his arms to embrace her, but she pushed him away. 'Get in, get in, you'll have me arrested!' she said, running around the front of the car. She gestured towards the tram drivers. 'You won't believe how inconsiderate people are these days,' and she slammed the car into gear and sped out of the station.

'Lucia Arditti, what a surprise,' Marco repeated. Steadying himself against the dashboard, he gazed at her, thinking she had aged since he last saw her. 'You look wonderful, how is it you never change?'

'As charming as ever,' she beamed, 'no wonder my cousin is on the telephone every two minutes wondering what you are up to.' She spoke the clean, precise Italian of a loyal citizen, but frequently lapsed into French, as was the habit in those circles. 'I said to her, I'll go and see him, but it is for my own pleasure, not as a spy. *La pauvre* Allegra, she does get herself worked up.'

She turned back to the road, swerving to avoid a cyclist. 'Indeed, if anyone should be upset it's me. Not once have you called me to say you were in Milan! And according to my cousin, you are here all the time!'

'Hardly.' Marco twisted to look at the two boys. 'How smart you both are,' he said.

'Luckily for you, I'm very forgiving,' continued Lucia. 'And by the way, you'd have been standing there forever, Graziani took all the taxis to Abyssinia, didn't you hear?' She laughed, and patted his knee. 'Do you mind if we go via the Duomo? I promised Robespierre and Charles Laughton here that I'd drop them. The Count of Monte Christo is coming with the maid.' She glanced at him. '*Carnevale*,' she added, when he did not reply.

'Of course it is.'

She chattered on, giving him news of the family and bits of gossip she had heard, some of which was true, some not. Marco listened with disinterest. It saddened him that Allegra had not forgotten their row, he ought never to have left like that. Perhaps he would send one of the office girls to Rina to choose something pretty to give her. And he would call her, just as soon as he got to his desk, and tell her he was sorry. He sighed, adding his wife to the ever-lengthening list of things to sort out.

They slowed down as Lucia turned onto the Via Mengoni, and pulled up opposite the cathedral. She jumped out, shouting to the children to follow and berating the maid for waiting on the wrong corner. Marco remained where he was, peering up at the wedding-cake spires of the Duomo and remembering the time his darling Sylvie had dressed up as Claudette Colbert for a talent contest and a woman had told her she should be a photographic model. He took his wallet from his pocket and opened it, and when Lucia climbed back in the car, he handed her the photo like a ticket for a bus.

'Very pretty,' said Lucia, nodding her head. She thought of her own daughter, with her gangly limbs and cross, anxious face. 'That's the kind of daughter I thought I would have,' she said, 'one I could dress up and show off to people. But Netta hates all that.'

Marco smiled. 'I'm sure she's adorable just the same.'

Lucia thought about this and shrugged.

They watched as a group of young boys marched across the piazza, heads held high, arms lifting and dropping with each step. The swinging tassels of their caps were like many tiny pendulums, and their black silk shirts gleamed unnaturally in the bright sun. 'Shorts, at this time of year,' murmured Lucia, shaking her head. '*Cosa fare*, they will freeze to death.'

CHAPTER 2

The Milan office of Balestra Brothers was in a large colonnaded building on the Corso Littorio. Lucia Arditti stopped the car opposite the brass-plated doors, and continued the story she had been telling about Count Ciano, whom Marco had once met, and Lucia had not. It was something to do with golf, and Marco's mind was elsewhere, but still he nodded and smiled and occasionally ended her sentences, with the ease of a man who does not mind being bored. When at last she finished, he reached across and took her hand, kissing it affectionately.

'Lucia, it has been a joy to see you, I cannot tell you how much you've cheered me up,' and she forgot that he had a stock of such phrases and flushed with pleasure.

'Will you be at the Carassos later?' she asked, watching as he gathered up his things. 'It's their last At Home, everyone will be there.'

'Everyone?'

She nodded. 'I'm taking a young man who's staying with us, a Mr Sutton, perhaps you know the family?' Marco shook his head and Lucia said, 'shops,' so that he would think he should. 'Poor fellow, he'll probably hate it, but I promised his mother I'd take him about a bit, and the Carassos always have such interesting people. Lord Perth was at the last one, apparently.' She picked a piece of lint from the brim of Marco's hat and dropped it out the window. 'Do say you'll come.'

Marco smoothed the front of his waistcoat, adjusting the buttons so that they strained less across his chest. 'I might pop my head in,' he said, 'I'm supposed to be seeing my sister-in-law, we have a mountain of paperwork to go through.' He glanced sidelong at Lucia. 'I'm here to work, you know, whatever you and my wife might think.'

'And you *will* be working.' said Lucia. She thought for a moment. 'You mustn't indulge her, you know.' She meant Allegra. 'I've told her, lose that weight and you'll find you lose your troubles too. That side of the family are all the same.'

Marco smiled. 'Dear Lucia.' he said. His fingers were on the door handle. 'Where would any of us be without you?' He glanced around, looking for his suitcase. 'No, no, stay where you are, I can get it,' and he opened the door and swung his short legs onto the pavement. Suddenly Lucia lunged forwards, grabbing at his sleeve.

'Must you close the office?'

Marco turned back, lowering his head to look at her. 'Excuse me?'

'The office. Must you close it? I know it's nothing to do with me, and the circumstances are difficult, your brother dying so unexpectedly— but is closing it the answer?' Lucia hesitated. 'People might think it disloyal.'

'Disloyal? To whom?'

She wavered. 'To Il Duce.'

'Oh Lucia, is that why you came to meet me?' He sat down again, clearly irritated. 'To tell me I'm disloyal?'

'Of course not,' she said quickly. 'It's just that everything is so—' she searched for the right word, 'so unsettled these days. If you could only wait a while, things are sure to improve.'

'Wait for what?' She was still holding his sleeve, but now he pulled it free. 'I've offended you. I shouldn't have said anything.'

'I'm not offended.'

'Yes you are.'

Marco tugged at the knees of his trousers. 'If what you're worried about is the Arditti contract—'

'It's not about that.'

'Then what is it about?'

Lucia sighed. She wanted to tell him how difficult it had been here these past months, how on edge everyone was. Everywhere you looked there were articles about the *patria* and references to Jews as 'recent guests,' something like this would only make it worse. But instead she said, 'Nothing, nothing at all. I'm just being an interfering old woman. You know I can't help myself.' She shivered, gesturing to the open door. 'Do go, you're letting all the warm air out.'

He climbed out, closing the door and then immediately opening the one behind in order to retrieve his suitcase. Lucia watched him in the rear mirror. 'That's a very nice hat, by the way. Is it a Borsalino?'

Marco put a finger to the brim and tilted the angle slightly. 'My sister-in-law gave it to me.'

'It suits you, it makes you look taller. When I saw you at the station, I thought, something is different about Marco Balestra, and now I see it's the hat. It gives you stature.'

'That's what Laura said too.'

Lucia nodded, watching a group of small children dressed as dwarves follow an even smaller Snow White along the colonnade. One of them dropped his neck scarf, but where Lucia would usually have leapt out of the car to retrieve it, now she just sat there as a gust of wind caught it up and blew it into the road.

'Did you hear she has cut her hair? Your sister-in-law, I mean. Such a shame, her hair was the thing you always noticed about her.'

'Laura's cut her hair?'

Lucia put her hand to her chin to show how short it was. 'Apparently she didn't tell anyone, she just went out and did it. They say her mother burst into tears when she saw it.' She thought about this. 'It's funny, isn't it, how sometimes it's the small things that seem most significant?'

Marco nodded, and they reflected upon this, as if therein lay the answer to some essential mystery.

WHEN AT LAST LUCIA DROVE AWAY, lurching into the afternoon traffic like a salmon leaping upstream, Marco stood for a moment on the pavement. He dreaded going up there, to the office full of his brother's things, and he glanced towards San Ambroeus, where Isaac had always taken his morning coffee, the easy warmth of the Venetian chandeliers and mirrored panelling almost winning him over. But then duty got the better of him, and, pushing at the door with its brass plaque, he stepped inside.

He sighed. It was all so familiar to him, the entrance with its colourful mosaic floor, the white marble walls snaking around a central lift shaft. A glass partition ran the height of the staircase, and he remembered how Isaac had hated this, said it gave the building a flimsy feel, as though it might be dismantled at any moment and packed away. And yet here it still stood, and it was Isaac who had gone.

Marco picked up his suitcase and started up the stairs, glancing through the door of a small bureau on the first floor landing as he passed. The concierge leapt to his feet.

'*Buongiorno*, Signore Balestra.'

'*Buongiorno*, Paolo,' said Marco, pausing and trying to remember something about the concierge's life that might suggest interest. He could not. 'Busy?'

'Always, sir.'

'Good, good,' said Marco. He continued up the stairs. The concierge would be out of work by the end of the month, it was better to keep his distance.

'Will you be with us long, Signore Balestra?' asked the concierge of the empty stairwell.

'I don't know,' said Marco, although his return was booked for Tuesday.

Another brass plaque, just like the one outside, glowed in the dimness of the second landing. *Fratelli Balestra*. Marco ran his finger around the edge, thinking he must remember to have them kept for him. Hardly a sentimental man, he seemed to be accumulating a number of such souvenirs. He frowned, his shoulders slumping, then he straightened himself up and pushed open the door.

At the sound of his entrance, a woman in her mid-forties with dyed black hair and an unromantic face, quickly stood up. She had been waiting for him all morning, but nevertheless his arrival seemed to fluster her.

'Good morning, Sybille,' said Marco, giving her one of his best smiles. He glanced around the room, with its mahogany bookcases and herringbone parquet, leather armchairs and Persian rugs, checking everything was as it should be. 'Ready to work?' he asked.

She nodded and hurried ahead of him into the adjoining office, kicking open heating grids and sending up rushes of warmth into the still air. Marco settled himself in his brother's chair, adjusting the seat so that he was at the right height, plumping the cushion. A list of that morning's telephone messages was on the desk, and he glanced down it, noting that Allegra had called twice and feeling pleased. 'I'll return my wife's calls first,' he said.

Sybille was checking for ink in the two fountain pens Marco had taken out. 'Your wife has not called, Signore,' she said.

'I thought—' he glanced back at the list then stopped, realising his mistake. 'You mean Signora Isaac, then,' he said, more sharply than he intended. The woman nodded. 'Well, perhaps call my wife anyway, she'll like to know that I've arrived safely. And then afterwards I'll speak to Signora Isaac.'

He braced his hands against the edge of the desk, cracking his knuckles and looking directly at the woman. 'How does that sound?'

Sybille said she would see if she could get a line.

Marco waited for her to leave, then sighed and looked around the room. His brother had collected paperweights, bright, colourful orbs of glass that were dotted around the surfaces of his office. Marco reached out and picked one at random, curling his fingers around it as he leafed through a pile of papers: there was a new buyer for their cotton poplins, an agent in Alexandria had increased his commission, a company his brother had invested in had patented several new dyeing techniques. After a while he looked up to find Sybille standing in the doorway. 'My wife?' he asked, but she shook her head and said the number was busy.

He returned to flicking through the papers, but almost immediately he looked up again. Sybille had not moved. 'Was there anything else?'

She gazed at him, her hand moving to her face as if she were about to cry. Marco frowned. Since his brother had died, he seemed to spend all his time managing people.

'Come and sit down,' he said. He waited until she was still and then leaned forwards.

'This is difficult, I know,' he began, 'you have worked as hard as anyone to keep this office open, but with the political situation being what it is, and without Isaac, there's really no choice—' He stopped, for Sybille was looking at him in distress, her eyes like wet pebbles. He tried to think of something to divert her, a joke or some funny observation, but the only thing that came to mind was Lucia's golf story, and so he said nothing.

'It's just all so sudden,' she said after a while.

Marco nodded sympathetically. He watched as she searched her sleeves for a handkerchief, waiting until she had composed herself. Her gaze, when at last she lifted her head, was on the bookshelf behind him, and when he turned he saw she was looking at the photographs of his brother's family. Marco sat back, still cupping the paperweight, like a ball he was about to throw. 'Actually,' he said, 'Isaac was talking of closing the office for some time.' Sybille's attention was back on Marco. 'It was only because of his wife that he held off. She likes it here, she didn't want to move again.' He paused. 'I don't need to tell you how hard it was under the sanctions −' The woman was shaking her head, and so he stopped. For a moment the room was quite silent, the only sound the faint rumbling of his stomach. He gazed at her helplessly, for he hated it when anyone was upset.

'I'm sorry,' she murmured.

Her head was lowered and he felt a rush of pity for the woman, for himself, for everyone in this rotten country. On a whim he leaned forward, holding out the paperweight. Tiny glass flowers encircled a brightly coloured dragon fly. 'Here,' he said, 'to remind you of my brother.'

'I couldn't−'

'Isaac would have wanted you to have something.'

She hesitated, then smiled weakly, taking it and holding it in her lap like a small animal. 'Thank you.'

'And you mustn't worry. I have everything in hand and I'll make sure you're well looked after. You have my word on that.'

'I'm not worried,' she said.

'Good.' He grinned and looked at Sybille with renewed enthusiasm. 'Then how about we try calling my wife again? She ought to be off the line by now. And perhaps the other Signora Balestra too, only make sure you tell me which one it is I'm speaking to or I'll be getting myself in trouble!'

CHAPTER 3

The guests were beginning to arrive at the Carasso villa, the cool night air causing the women to hug their fur coats and the men to stamp their feet like horses in a field. Wide marble steps led up to the entrance, and every time someone rang, a uniformed butler opened the glass doors and the silence of the evening was broken by the noisy warmth of inside, a volume dial turning up and down. Two housemaids in frilled aprons stood behind the butler, arms held out, and as each guest removed their coat, they draped it across one or the other. Electric lamps blazed on all the surfaces, throwing sharp patterns onto the ceiling above, while straight ahead a staircase curled around an enormous sculpture which seemed to have grown there. Carved oak doors opened onto a series of rooms, and the guests drifted from one to the next, pulled by some invisible force.

Sofia Carasso stood at the far end of the drawing room, her back to the fireplace and her coiled grey hair reflected several times in the mirrored wall behind. She was tall, with wide flat cheekbones and a long nose, which she tilted upwards as if balancing something. She wore a silk dress just a shade darker than her hair, and around her neck three strands of pearls that clattered as she moved. In one hand she held a glass of champagne, and the other she used to greet her guests, arranging them around the rooms with casual precision. And all the time she smiled wearily, as though the effort of being herself were almost too much to bear.

'Darling Sofia,' said Marco Balestra, who had just arrived, seizing both her hands and kissing her. 'Four times,' he reminded her, when she pulled away too early, '*A la belge*!'

'Marco, I'm so glad,' said Sofia, leaning back to get a better view. 'I heard you were in Milan, but I wasn't sure you'd have time for our little entertainments.'

'How could I not have time for Sofia Carasso? Seeing you is one of my few pleasures in this dreadful city.'

'Not for much longer. I leave on Sunday for Brussels. My *winter of discontent*–' she paused, so that he might appreciate the prettiness of the phrase, '–is over, the apartment is finished, and my darling son come to take me home. Tell me, have you seen it, the house? We're practically neighbours now, do you approve of my husband's grand design?'

'Approve? I am humbled,' said Marco with fervour. 'Il Duce could learn a lot from Ezra Carasso. Such elegant simplicity, one gets so tired of all these triumphal arches and flying buttresses. I tell you, every time I come to Milan, I recognise it less. Whoever thought Fascism required so much aggregate and cement?'

Sofia smiled. 'Marco Balestra, as delightful as ever.' She rested her elbow on the chimneypiece and looked past him to where more guests were coming in, 'I can't think why everyone says such awful things about you. Just yesterday I was obliged to defend you against a positive tirade.'

Marco laughed. 'Ah, what can I say? Apparently I'm disloyal for wanting to preserve what's left of my brother's business for his poor family.' He pushed his hand inside his waistcoat as if about to declare an oath. 'Trade requires stability in the Mediterranean, don't tell me Filippo isn't saying the same thing.' (Filippo was Sofia's brother-in-law, and the owner of this villa.)

'Filippo is a man of the Party, he says and thinks exactly what he is told.' Sofia glanced sidelong at her reflection in the mirror, and then adopted a rigid half-smile, so that the lines around her mouth receded. 'They're in Cortina, skiing, or he'd tell you himself. My sister took the children out of school for the month, no one seems to mind if it's sport.' She lowered her voice. 'Which perhaps shows how unthinking this country has become.'

'Everywhere except here,' said Marco.

'And soon not even here.'

'Alas, the lamps are going out all over Milan.'

Sofia squeaked with pleasure. 'I believe you're quite my favourite guest, Marco Balestra. We must see more of each other in Brussels, I can't think why we never do.' She took a sip of her champagne, then waved to a waiter to approach. 'Here, fill it up. No one serves anything but prosecco these days, but as I told Ezra, I don't mind them dubbing the films, I can get used to Nazionale cigarettes, but I draw the line at replacing champagne with vino spumante.' She patted her hair, as if such heroism had involved a physical struggle. 'Do you know Dr de Perreira? I'm expecting him later, I'm told he's quite the oracle on Madrid. He was in Rome visiting King Alfonso, and is only here for a day, we're lucky to get him.'

'There's a de Perreira related to my sister-in-law,' said Marco.

'Laura? I had no idea she had such connections. How is she, by the way? I invited her tonight, you know, I've invited her to all my little *soirées* whilst I've been here, but she never comes. Of course, I understand, I'm sure it's the last thing she feels like doing. But I should hate her to think we'd abandoned her.'

Marco set his glass on the chimneypiece, pushing it around the marble ledge like a piece on a chessboard. 'I'm sure she doesn't,' he said.

'One feels so helpless.' She put her hand on Marco's glass to stop him moving it. 'When I first heard, I thought someone would have organised a little rota — you know how it is, everyone chooses a day, then sends the maid with a *lasagne* or *polpette*, so that there isn't the worry of mealtimes. But your brother died in the summer, when most people were away, and by the time I arrived in October her family were here and there was no need. I sometimes worry we let her down.'

Marco shook his head. 'She has a cook,' he said.

'I just wonder if we might have done more.' And she bowed her head, so that her long nose was no longer balancing something.

For a moment neither of them spoke, each following their own train of thought, until at last Sofia roused herself, looking up and resuming her usual expression of weary serenity. She smiled, scoping the room as the beam of a lighthouse scopes the sea, then settling on the jardin d'hiver where an interesting group had gathered.

'I'm also expecting a fellow countryman of ours,' she said, peering to see if he had arrived yet. 'Roger Hallemans. He's going on somewhere afterwards, so won't stay long, but he promised he would put his head in. Do you know him? I'm never sure how I feel, there's something rather *superficiel* about him,' she used the French word, for she considered it a French trait, 'but he is very amusing. The last time we saw him he had everyone in stitches with a story about King Leopold being dragged off to England to find a wife!' Sofia began to laugh. 'You must get him to tell it.'

'Hallemans, you say?'

'He's very wellconnected,' said Sofia. 'You must know all the same people.'

'Well we both know you,' said Marco. 'What is it they say, that there are only six degrees of separation? Well, I tell people that in Brussels it's just one —' He hesitated for effect. 'Sofia Carasso.'

Sofia laughed and turned to greet some new arrivals, chatting briefly and urging them to join a game of Mahjong that was being played in the far corner, promising to follow in just a minute. Then a waiter wanted to know whether he should open more champagne (he should) and one of the maids hurried forward to ask whether the cook should serve the caviar yet (she shouldn't). Several telegrams were brought in on a silver tray, which Sofia read and then dropped into the fire, because she could hardly be expected to reply in the middle of a party. And then a woman in a red velvet cape gave a long and meandering explanation as to why she must leave so early, the simple version of which was 'opera tickets'. At last she turned back to Marco. 'I've just had rather a good idea,' she said, 'would you like to hear it?'

'Go on,' said Marco smiling.

'Quite brilliant, in fact. It's about your sister-in-law. You remember that the new house is divided into apartments? Well, we're at the top and I was hoping that Manu would take the one underneath. If I'm honest, it was the main reason I agreed to the whole project, I was perfectly happy where we were before. Anyway, Manu told me yesterday that they want to stay where they are. I can't think why, it's far too small now they have the baby, but he's quite determined. He's being very stubborn about it, and you know what it's like — perhaps you don't, your children are still young —' She shrugged and held up her hands, her rings glittering.

'And so your nest is empty?'

Sofia sighed gratefully. 'Yes. Ezra said all along that Manu wouldn't want it. And it turns out he was right.'

'Poor Sofia.'

She took a sip of champagne, eyeing him over the brim of the glass. 'Well it just came to me,' she looked at him expectantly, 'what about Laura?'

'Laura?'

'Yes. Now that you're closing the office she has no reason to stay in Milan, and Brussels is so civilised in comparison, none of the marching and sabre-rattling that goes on here. A change is just what she needs. What do you think?'

'I think you're very sweet. But she plans to go to Manchester, all her family are there.'

'Yes, yes, I know, but nobody ever *wants* to go to Manchester —' She thought for a moment then touched her fingertips to Marco's arm, leaning closer so that her breath was warm against his cheek. 'I think you should tell her about my apartment and suggest she come to Brussels instead.'

Marco said nothing, reflecting upon this idea for a moment. There was something rather appealing about Laura being in Brussels, and he wondered why he had not thought of it before. And then he remembered Allegra and saw that it was impossible.

'Sofia Carasso, you're too adorable,' he said, 'and it's a wonderful idea, really it is. But the family seem set on her going back to England and I'd hate to interfere. The mother hasn't forgiven me for taking Laura to the cinema last time I was here, apparently it's not the done thing. In Manchester.'

'Well she's not *in* Manchester.'

'Not yet, no.'

Sofia frowned. 'Then what if I ask her? What if I just call her up to see how she is and happen to bring up the apartment? I wouldn't even mention your name.'

Marco thought about this, experiencing a sudden exhilaration which he supposed was the champagne. 'I suppose it couldn't do any harm.'

'Harm? It's by far the nicest apartment in the whole of Brussels. Apart from my own, of course.'

Marco grinned. 'Then I think it's a wonderful idea. No, really, I do.'

'Then the matter's settled,' said Sofia. 'It will ease my conscience to do something and who knows, she might even like the idea and then Ezra will be happy too. He's convinced we'll end up with a hoard of unwashed German refugees.' She laughed and raised her glass, touching it to Marco's. 'And now come with me,

I've monopolised you long enough and there's a number of people I think you should meet.' And she thrust him towards the middle of the room, as if she were launching a small boat.

◆   ◆   ◆   ◆   ◆

LIKE ACTORS IN A PLAY, THE guests moved about the rooms, their lines delivered with well-rehearsed ease, their gestures familiar. The principal roles were played by a group of men who had gathered in the jardin d'hiver and where Marco now drifted as if carried on a tide. The floor was of honey-coloured marble and the two exterior walls which gave onto the garden were glass, and could slide away completely if a lever was pulled. A large lozenge shaped sofa filled the centre of the room and all around it were placed armchairs and stools, upon which were balanced the pick of Sofia's invitations. A young man in fashionably wide flannel trousers and a cabled sweater stood to one side, and for the moment all eyes were on him. This was Sofia's son, Manu.

'What I don't understand,' he said, weighing each word as he spoke it, 'is how Mussolini and that brute Hitler suddenly got so friendly. One minute Italy's lining up with France and Britain to oppose him, and the next it's quite the opposite.'

An older man in a cravat adjusted his position on a low sofa. This was Paolo Varinetti, the middle-aged son of a famous industrialist and a fixture of Milanese society. 'What Il Duce is doing for us now is what any parent does for a child, he's looking out for our future. He wants Italy to be great again, as in the times of the Roman Emperors, when we ruled all Europe. Is that so terrible?'

'The League of Nations seems to think so.'

The older man waved a hand dismissively. 'Don't talk to me about the League of Nations! It's merely the plaything of the decadent English, a stick with which they might beat poor Italy.'

'Ah yes, *Italia contra mundum*,' said Manu, smiling as his mother bore down across the rug. Even from the next room she could sense when her son was making trouble.

Signore Varinetti had opened his mouth to reply but Sofia was too quick for him. 'Look who's here!' she said, clapping her hands. 'Marco Balestra!' She presented him to the room as if he were a cake she had iced herself. 'Marco, you must tell Signore Varinetti about your latest business venture, he'll be quite enthralled. Marco has invested in a company in Poland that makes artificial silk, everyone's talking about it.' Marco expressed surprise. 'Oh, Marco, no one has any secrets these days! Besides, the future's rayon, or so my husband keeps telling me,' and she smoothed her expensive silk dress and looked about herself contentedly. 'Am I not right?'

'*Sofia ha sempre ragione*,' someone said, misquoting one of Il Duce's slogans. 'Sofia is always right.'

Nodding, satisfied that she had effected a diversion, Sofia turned to ask an elderly man with a monocle about his journey that evening, and whether he had found the villa easily. He replied that he had and they chatted for a minute or two about how difficult it was to park in Milan, now that the middle classes had discovered motoring. Manu was required to give his opinion on the new Simca, which Marco Balestra had just bought and which Varinetti was rather tempted by, while Sofia moved chairs and filled glasses with all the grace and hospitality for which she was renowned.

Raised voices in the drawing room caught her attention, and she turned and glided back across the thick rugs towards a high table set with her sister's gold Meissen tea set. Two men were talking in animated Spanish, one tall, one short, and beside them Lucia Arditti squawked and flailed her arms, so that the young man accompanying her had to step back to avoid being struck. Sofia immediately perceived that the shorter of the two men was Dr de Perreira and she swooped down upon him possessively.

'I'm so happy you could come,' she declared, her pearls clattering as she reached for his hand. Dr de Perreira was small, with a broad chest and stocky legs, and wore a velvet suit edged with gold brocade, the jacket of which buttoned all the way up to his chin. He had an elaborately curled moustache, over-bright cheeks and his hair was as black and smooth to his skull as if it had been painted on. He bowed, pressing his damp lips to the back of Sofia's hand, then continuing to hold her fingers as he straightened up. His reputation as a seducer of beautiful women was not without foundation and he treated her to one of his most ardent smiles, the ends of his moustache lifting like the horns of a charging bull.

'Forgive me, I'm terribly late,' he said, 'the King kept me talking, he so misses his beloved country. I came straight here, I haven't even been to my hotel. And then I met my cousin Leonard Cansino, fresh off the boat from Egypt, just the moment I walked through the door.'

'They haven't seen each other for twenty years, not since Mr Cansino was a boy,' said Lucia breathlessly. She had changed her dress and wore a red crepe suit with a white collar, that made it look as if her head were resting on a dinner plate. 'This is Daniel Sutton,' she added, thrusting forward a youth of about eighteen, with schoolboy hair and a face he had yet to grow into. 'I hope you don't mind my bringing him along. I promised his mother I'd show him the sights and when I got your invitation I thought, what better way to see Milan?' She giggled and squeezed the young man's arm, so that he nodded and repeated 'thank you for having me,' several times.

'I wasn't aware I was in the guidebook,' said Sofia, adding 'welcome, welcome, do help yourself to tea.' Her fingers were still in the possession of Dr de Perreira and she left them there, nodding to a waiter to bring champagne and tossing her head when everyone said what a treat it was.

'You must have a glass,' insisted Lucia, when Leonard Cansino continued to pour himself tea.

'I don't drink,' said Leonard. He had a kind face, with thinning hair that he combed backwards and the type of skin that burned in the sun. He was holding his coat and hat, as he did not intend to stay long, and beneath the lights of the glass chandeliers, his suit seemed dull and threadbare. 'I just stopped by to thank you for my sister's invitation.'

'Your sister?' asked Sofia.

'—Laura Balestra,' interjected Lucia.

'Of course!' said Sofia. 'How sweet of you to come in person. And all the way from Egypt too!'

'Oh, no, I didn't—' he stopped, for Sofia was smiling, and added, 'You've always been so kind, inviting her.'

'Well now you are here you must join us. Especially as it seems you are related to most of my guests.' She smiled. 'I have Marco Balestra next door.'

'Ah, Marco,' said Leonard (in fact, it was in the hope of seeing Marco that he had called by). 'Perhaps I'll just say hello.'

'If you're staying you must have a glass of champagne,' insisted Lucia, handing him one. 'Daniel will drink your tea.'

'The English and their tea,' said de Perreira, letting go of Sofia so that he might use both hands to twist his moustache. And he followed his hostess across the room, chattering about the time the British Ambassador caught the measles and all his medications had to be administered in a cup of Earl Grey.

'Doesn't he remind you of a guinea pig?' whispered Lucia, mimicking the moustache twisting as they followed after. She glanced at Daniel Sutton. 'Be careful with that teacup,' she said.

CHAPTER 4

In the jardin d'hiver, the conversation was back to Europe. There were several newcomers, including the well-connected Roger Hallemans, who was midway through a long and complicated joke about the League of Nations, and Sofia's husband Ezra, who stood smoking with his son and Varinetti. Marco had settled himself into a deep armchair, but leapt up when Leonard came in and made a great fuss of how happy he was to see him and what a lot they had to discuss. Then he sat back down again, his elbows pushed out against the sides like wings, his expression one of fixed amusement.

A rise in shrillness indicated Hallemans had arrived at his punchline: 'The Chinese were too yellow, the Ethiopians too black and the Spanish too red!' he exclaimed, slapping the sofa joyfully, as though it were a horse that had just carried him over a particularly challenging fence. Everyone laughed and Ezra Carasso, seeing his wife brandishing her prized guest, hurried towards them and shook the doctor's hand. Dr de Perreira waited as Sofia introduced him to the room, watching as each guest was brought forward and repeating their name with such familiarity, it was as if they had known one another all their lives.

'Daniel's mother and I were at school together in Lausanne,' said Lucia, still hovering at the doctor's side. 'He has been staying with me for two weeks. It is so important, don't you think, that young people travel and see the world.' She lowered her voice. 'He's at school in Bristol,' she added, as if this explained everything.

De Perreira puffed out his barrelled chest, his neck disappearing into his collar. 'Bristol, really?' He looked around. 'How charming,' he said, meaning the marble, the glass walls, the lozenge shaped sofa.

'It's the same architect as the Santa Maria della Grazie,' said Lucia. 'Not Bramante, obviously — the one restoring it.' She glanced at Daniel. 'Where they have the Leonardo, remember?'

Daniel nodded, his fingers buttoning and unbuttoning his tweed jacket.

'We keep saying we'll go, don't we,' Lucia continued, 'and we simply must before you leave. Have you seen it, Mr Cansino? I'm sure you have.'

'Actually, I haven't,' said Leonard.

Lucia gasped. 'But it's one of our greatest treasures, Mr Cansino! How could you have missed it, especially with your sister living here all these years?'

'I don't really know.'

'Well how lucky I asked. You must come with Daniel and me, we shall make it a project. How about tomorrow? Seize the day, as they say. Perhaps Dr de Perreira will join us too.'

'Sadly I'm leaving on the first train,' said de Perreira, 'I must be back in Paris by the evening.'

'And I promised I'd take the little ones to the carnival,' said Leonard.

'Ah, but that's perfect,' said Lucia addressing him in the same tone she used for her children. 'Bring them with you to Santa Maria, and then afterwards we'll all go to the carnival together. It'll be fun. Besides, it's not like the Pinacoteca which takes all day, this is one painting, two if you count the Sforza; we'll simply put our heads inside the door and then be on our way.' And with a rapturous smile she patted his hand to suggest the matter was closed.

'Really, I— I don't think I can,' tried Leonard again, but Lucia had already forgotten him and was leaning over the back of the sofa listening to Dr de Perreira, her thin arms making dents in the green velvet.

'It seems to me,' said de Perreira, with the air of a man quite certain of his own brilliance, 'that the greatest danger facing Europe is the English sense of fair play. They appear to have confused politics with cricket!' He paused to consider his audience. 'Such arrogance, with their Pacts and their Formulas, thinking they can lay down the law and the world will say, "Thank goodness for those good gentlemen of England." Of course, France isn't much better these days, all those little Bonapartes with their dreams of turning the world French.' He gazed around, his chest heaving, the gold brocade glinting and flickering with each breath. 'Democracy is finished in Europe,' he declared and he glanced towards the dark windows, as though watching it depart.

'Hear, hear,' said Paolo Varinetti.

'Little Bonapartes,' repeated Marco. 'That's very funny, "little Bonapartes", I like that.'

'Of course, only once they lose Gibraltar will the English wake up to this,' continued de Perreira. 'Without it, their precious Suez will be worth nothing to them.'

'I don't think anyone's suggesting we'll lose Gibraltar,' murmured Leonard Cansino. Sofia eyed him, ready to intervene should the conversation stray from the convivial.

'If Franco wins, how can it be held?' Hallemans smiled and bit the end off a cigar, revealing two rows of perfectly straight white teeth. 'The Doctor is right, democracy in Europe is finished.' He gazed directly at Leonard. 'Ask your Mr Eden, isn't that why he resigned?'

'Oh, that was such a shame,' said Lucia, fussing with the cushions of the sofa. 'He brought a little glamour to the whole business, don't you think?' She folded her hands in her lap and looked around. 'He reminds me of Ronald Colman.'

'In Spain we call him *El Gancho*,' said de Perreira.

'Mr Eden resigned because of Il Duce,' said Leonard, 'because he can't be trusted.' He was agitated and fidgeted with his hat as he spoke, turning it round and round like a wheel. Sofia frowned and stepped between the chairs.

'Do let me take your things,' she said.

'No, no, I mustn't stay, I promised I'd be home early.'

'Oh, what a shame,' said Sofia. She stood back, so that the way to the door was clear.

'Don't be ridiculous, Leonard, you can't leave yet!' exclaimed Marco. 'You must make the most of your last weeks of freedom.' He addressed the room: 'Mr Cansino's wife is having a baby.'

Two red spots appeared on Leonard's cheeks and he nodded. 'In June,' he said, and it was clear this was a source of great happiness.

'I love babies,' declared Lucia, swinging her legs back and forth.

Sofia frowned. 'Dr de Perreira, you must tell Signore Varinetti about your adventures in Madrid. He is a loyal supporter of General Franco, he knows the pilot who first flew him into Spanish Morocco,' and she arranged the two men in a corner of the room and then remained there, keeping guard.

Lucia continued to chatter about babies, offering all sorts of advice to the blushing Leonard, while the others listened in silence, their reflections motionless on the dark window.

'Will I open?' said Ezra, wandering over to the brass lever and trying to remember how it worked. 'Ah, there we are.' The two panels slid apart and the chill night air rushed in.

Everyone murmured appreciatively, for the room had become rather stuffy, and Lucia pushed Daniel Sutton forwards so that he might see how the mechanism worked. Marco loosened his tie and said something amusing to Leonard, who smiled and shuffled his feet, as his shoes were new and they pinched. Roger Hallemans checked his watch.

'Did you know that the Duke of Wellington is one of the largest landowners in Spain?' de Perreira was saying in the corner. 'Obviously not the same Duke of Wellington as finished off Bonaparte, but it's interesting, don't you think? The Bourbons cast a long shadow over history, only when we accept that can we begin to rebuild Europe.' Varinetti nodded, quite sure that the doctor was saying something fascinating, but uncertain as to what it was. 'Revolution and restoration,' de Perreira continued, and he held up his two small hands as if the secret to each were clutched within.

'Revolution and restoration,' repeated Sofia, turning back towards the sofas where the conversation had begun to lull. 'Dr de Perreira was just telling us about Spain,' she announced.

'I was explaining my theory of the natural order of things,' said de Perreira, adjusting his trousers so that the braid ran in a straight line down each side. He sighed and looked lovingly at the assembled faces. 'Above me, my King. Above my king, God.' And he lifted his small black eyes towards the ceiling.

'Some people think democracy is the natural order,' said Manu.

De Perreira affected not to hear him and kept his gaze on the ceiling. Lucia continued to swing her legs, and after a brief silence Roger Hallemans stood up and began to pick his way through the chairs.

'Surely you're not leaving already?' said Sofia, hurrying after him. 'Do stay a little longer or everyone will think we've bored you.'

'How could anyone be bored in such company?' he said mechanically. 'If I weren't obliged to put my head in at the embassy, I would stay, I assure you. It's a terrible chore.'

He bowed and smoothed his waistcoat, and Leonard Cansino, who had been hovering behind him, sidled around the lozenge-shaped sofa and sat down next to Marco. Sofia followed

Hallemans towards the hall, thanking him for coming and asking after his wife, enacting the same ritual she would enact with all her guests that evening. In the jardin d'hiver, de Perreira slowly lowered his head.

'Did you see that Italian soldiers are being trained as flame-throwers?' said Ezra Carasso, thinking to get the conversation going again. 'Boys of eighteen are being sent off wearing fireproof suits and gas masks.'

'Their poor mothers,' said Lucia and she clutched at Daniel Sutton, as if holding him back from some abyss.

'Their poor victims,' said Manu, who had been staring out at the garden.

Lucia looked at him in dismay. 'You're quite right,' she said, adding, 'how awful everything is.'

No one could think of anything to say to this, and for a moment the guests were silent. Then Marco leaned forwards. 'So your father is in shops?' he said, addressing himself to Daniel. 'Might I know him?'

But before Daniel could answer, Dr de Perreira loudly cleared his throat and began to recount his party piece of the death of his dear friend Primo de Rivera. When he got to the part where the red and white tulips were strewn around the corpse's head and feet, his audience sighed, enchanted. 'We felt as though Spain herself had died,' he finished and everyone nodded in delight, for it wasn't every day that you heard such stories.

THE WAITERS NO LONGER HURRIED to fill up the empty glasses, but instead gathered them on trays and carried them clinking down the stairs to the kitchen. In the hall the maids ran back and forth to the cloakroom, aprons flying as they swept up the limp bodies of coats and shawls and delivered them to their owners. Someone had taken the wrong hat and someone else had mislaid their keys, and there was a flurry of activity as each was restored to its rightful owner. The butler drew the long brocade curtains in the drawing room, throwing the garden into darkness, so that the guests had to light matches to find their way to the gate. And in the jardin d'hiver someone struggled with the lever, bringing the glass walls back together with a comforting thump.

Sofia was standing at the front door, kissing cheeks and saying how she wished these things were not always so frantic. As she talked, she leaned against the marble side table, for she was tired now, and every so often she would press her fingers to her temples as if resetting a button that kept her awake. Her husband watched her in adoration.

Marco was one of the last to leave and was standing by the stairs with Leonard, gazing at the large bronze sculpture there. Lucia had offered both men a lift home, but it was late now and she was nowhere to be seen, so Marco said he would walk out and find a taxi instead. Leonard became flustered and said in that case he would take the tram and that it was probably faster at this time of night and then just as they were agreed, Lucia appeared, pulling the English boy after her, and said would they mind if she didn't drop them after all, Daniel was exhausted and needed to get to bed. And slowly, their voices clear where before they had been muffled, they drifted towards the front door.

'I had such a lovely time,' gushed Lucia, pushing Daniel forwards and urging him to say 'thank-you' in Italian. 'You always invite the most interesting people, Dr de Perreira was a joy.' And she turned to Leonard adding, 'How lucky for you that you came.'

Leonard, who still hoped to have a word in private with Marco, said it was. He edged out onto the steps, waiting for them to follow.

'I shall see you next in Brussels,' said Marco, holding Sofia's hands and swinging them.

'Our loss is your gain,' Lucia trilled. Exhilarated by the cold air, she leaned back inside. 'You looked so pretty tonight,' she said to Sofia.

'Pretty?' demanded Ezra, his hand on the door, 'Pretty? *Elle est magnifique!*'

Sofia smiled serenely and Marco laughed, thinking he must remember to use this line himself. Lucia nodded, repeating 'Yes, *magnifique, magnifique,*' as she walked backwards down the steps, and everyone waved and shouted goodbye as the doors closed against them.

'THIS WAY,' SAID LUCIA PULLING Daniel onto the grass. 'Those little stones will ruin my heels. Mr Cansino,' she called, for the two men had walked ahead, 'I'll see you at ten o'clock at Santa Maria, don't be late. It will be our little pilgrimage!'

'Ten o'clock!' Leonard responded and glanced at Marco. 'I was hoping she'd forget.'

'Lucia Arditti never forgets anything.' Marco yawned, the warmth of his breath making a cloud as he exhaled. He turned towards San Babila, where he was sure to find a taxi. 'It doesn't seem just this morning that I arrived,' he mused, meaning in Milan, 'I feel as though I've been here for weeks,' and he turned up his collar to keep out the damp night air.

'I wanted to ask you something,' said Leonard, 'about Laura.'

Marco was looking up and down the Via Monforte in case a taxi were to pass.

'I know you're seeing her tomorrow,' continued Leonard, 'and I just wanted to ask if you might reassure her about everything? She's not been very good this week, I think she told you, and it's difficult to get her to see the positive side of anything. I think if you were to encourage her, explain how it will be a new start for her and the children, she'd feel better.

She values your opinion, you know. She always listens to you.'

'This is about leaving Milan?' asked Marco. He felt in his pocket for some change, peering at it in the dim light of the street and counting the coins with his forefinger.

'Well, yes, and about coming to Manchester.' Leonard stopped and put a hand on Marco's arm. 'I think I might have found a house for them, with a big garden and lots of space for the children to play. The rent is very reasonable, but unless we put a deposit down straight away, the owner won't hold it. I've tried to talk to Laura about it, but each time I do she gets upset—' Leonard thrust his hands deep inside his pockets. 'I think if *you* thought it was a good idea, she'd feel more hopeful.' He grimaced at Marco, who was staring straight ahead. 'Would you mind?'

Marco rubbed his cheek, thinking of his earlier conversation with Sofia. 'I'm not sure what I could say.'

'You could just say you saw me tonight and I told you about the house, and that you think it's a good idea.' He hesitated. 'I'd so appreciate it. We all would.'

Marco peered at the empty road. He was fond of Leonard, but even the briefest of encounters with him felt exhausting. 'You worry too much,' he said, smiling and patting the younger man on the shoulder. 'You really don't need to. Everything will work out, you'll see. Ah, there's a cab,' and he raised his hand as a motorcycle turned the corner, its sidecar rattling. 'I really do hate this country,' he said, as it slowed and came to a halt by the two men. Marco climbed inside, grumbling as he arranged himself on the metal seat.

'Then you'll talk to Laura?' said Leonard, leaning over and tucking Marco's coat inside the door.

'I'll talk to Laura,' said Marco.

CHAPTER 5

The tram stopped on the Corso Vercelli, and Leonard stepped down, walking quickly through the empty streets until he came to the familiar dark outline of the Casa Grandolini. The top floor, with its wide windows and low-hanging roof, was in darkness, and he frowned, wishing he hadn't stayed so late. He pushed at the front door, and let himself into the entrance hall, the blue and gold ceiling glowing dimly in the light of the concierge's window. The elevator stood open at the foot of the staircase, but Leonard hurried past, his footsteps echoing on the wooden steps as he bounded up the three flights to the top. Removing his shoes, he let himself into the apartment and locked the door behind him, tugging the curtain across the entrance, and checking for any gaps.

From where he stood, Leonard could make out the shadowy bulk of the tiled Dutch stove, and he tiptoed towards it, laying his coat on top of others that were drying there. He stood for a moment, his hands resting on its porcelain surface, absorbing the warmth. He knew he should go straight to bed, but he didn't feel in the least like sleeping, and so he stayed there, leaning on the stove, thinking about the evening. He had been so intent upon talking to Marco that he had barely paid attention to anyone else, and now he thought about Dr de Perreira, and that Hallemans character, and he wished he had made more of an effort. It was as his father always said, he never saw an opportunity until it was too late to take advantage of it. No doubt that was why he was over thirty and still living with his parents. He sighed and rested his forehead against the chimney, imagining what he might have done differently. Men like Marco made life look so easy, they always knew what to say, how to behave. 'What's wrong with me?' he asked himself, the stove red-hot against his skin. 'Why do I make everything so hard?'

A door opened at the end of the corridor.

'Is that you, Leonard?'

'Yes, Mamma.' He hurried towards her, his feet padding on the narrow carpet. The door opened wider, and the space was immediately filled by the pillar-like shape of Estella Cansino. A helmet of yellow hair framed a face that had once been delicate, but was now painted that way, with rouged cheeks and powder that stopped at her neck. She wore a black dress that reached almost to the floor, and around her neck were looped strands of heavy jet beads. The fingers which clutched the door frame were covered with rings, and she could tell you a story about each one: how she had lost it once, or where the stones had come from, or who she was going to give it to when she died.

'I thought you were asleep,' whispered Leonard, placing his hands on her rounded shoulders and kissing a soft cheek.

He looked beyond her at the room, with its cherrywood bed and piles of satin eiderdowns, littered with wrappers from an empty box of *marrons glacés*. Two thin novels lay uncut on the table, next to a jigsaw he had started with her before he left for Egypt. And by the window where the light was best, her dressing table, its surface covered with pots of face-cream and the contents of a large vanity case.

'I was waiting for you,' she said, turning and shuffling into the room, 'you know I can never settle until you're home.' She sat down heavily on a blanket box at the end of the bed, her short legs with their tiny feet hanging beneath her skirt like weights.

Leonard began to gather up the sweet papers from the bed, dropping them into a bin full of tissues and pencil shavings.

His mother watched him. 'Did you eat something?' she asked, for Leonard's digestive habits were a source of continual worry to her. 'I hope it wasn't one of those parties where they just hand around a few *bruschetta* and imagine they've given you dinner. I'll never understand this fashion for not feeding people.'

Leonard had not in fact eaten, but he knew better than to share this with his mother. 'You won't believe who was there?' he said. 'Dr de Perreira.' He paused. 'Cousin Max. He was visiting King Alfonso in Rome. Don't you find it incredible that we have a relative who's personal physician to the King of Spain? Such a shame Laura didn't come, it would have cheered her up. Sofia Carasso looked decidedly put out when she saw me talking to him, I think it's probably very bad manners to be related to the guest of honour!'

'Sofia Carasso has far too many airs and graces. Besides, why shouldn't we be related to someone like that, Leonard? I really don't see why you should find it incredible.' She fiddled with a corner of the eiderdown, twisting it around her fingers.

'Incredible was the wrong word,' said Leonard. 'He told a wonderful story about Primo de Rivera, and knew everything about what's happening in Spain. Everyone thought him quite brilliant.'

'He always tells that story.'

Leonard murmured a reply, and continued to move around Estella's room, picking up bits of paper and embroidery thread and arranging all her bottles and compacts into straight lines. He knew he should ask what was wrong, but for as long as he did not know, he was absolved of the need to find a solution. He placed six small velvet slippers in pairs under the window ledge, then drew the curtains, so that three children appeared to be hiding there.

'She gave Nina the evening off,' said Estella, still twisting the eiderdown. 'I said, just this once, could we have a proper Friday night, with candles and challah and everyone together?

It's hardly too much to ask, is it, after all this time and when you've been away so long? But Nina does fish on Fridays and of course we can't upset Nina by changing her plans, so Laura gives her the night off instead. And when I asked who was going to make dinner if Nina wasn't here, Laura said she didn't care, she wasn't hungry.' A fat tear squeezed from one of her carefully drawn eyes and slid down her cheek, leaving a narrow track in the powder. 'I'm just trying to help, Leonard, that's all I'm doing. But everything I say is wrong—'

'Mamma, I'm sorry,' said Leonard, sitting down beside her and taking one of her putty-coloured hands in his. 'Laura doesn't mean it, really she doesn't. And she knows that you're doing everything you can for her, we all do.'

'But I don't think she does,' she whispered, turning to face Leonard, her large face glittering with tears. 'Sometimes I think she doesn't even know I'm here.'

'Oh Mamma, you mustn't think that, it's not true.' He felt in his pocket for his handkerchief. 'You're just feeling upset because it's been a difficult evening. You take too much on yourself Mamma, you know you do, Miriam's always saying you ought to do less.'

'Miriam's a good girl.' She sniffed, rallying a little. 'She made me a sandwich before she went to bed and brought it in with one of those little red drinks I like.'

'The bitters? I forget you love those. We're going to have to try and find some for you in Manchester, aren't we, you'll miss your little *aperitivo* in the evenings. Poor Mamma, what a time of it you've had.'

'Nobody knows,' she sniffed

'I do, Mamma, I know. But it will be better soon. A change of air and something different for Laura to think about, that's what's needed.' He lowered his voice, for the walls in the apartment were thin. 'She misses Isaac so terribly, but for the children's sake she must focus on the future. It's the only way.'

'Dear Isaac,' murmured Estella, pressing the handkerchief to her spilling eyes, 'I miss him too, you know. He was much more than a son-in-law to me, there will never be anyone to replace him. I think she forgets that, Leonard, she thinks it's just the children and her who have lost something, but really it's all of us. He made our happiness complete. And now he's no more and —' Her voice had begun to rise, and Leonard looked at her in despair.

'Try not to upset yourself,' he pleaded.

Estella put her hand to her chest, her breath coming in shallow gasps. She leaned forwards, her voice a whisper. 'I think of him all the time, you know. I find myself asking, what would Isaac have done? What would he have us do? But I don't always know the answer.'

'Oh Mamma—'

'I have this dull ache which never goes away,' said his mother, gathering force. 'And sometimes I worry it's something serious, that perhaps I'm going to drop dead like that Sylvia Dellal — they didn't find her for three days, you know! What if nobody found me?'

'Of course we'd find you Mamma.'

'I'm a burden, that's the truth,' whispered Estella, crushing the handkerchief in her lap. 'Laura used to telephone me every day, I always knew what she was doing, who she was seeing, and now I might be in my room all day and all night and she doesn't come in. And then Marco Balestra calls up and she's ready to go straight out and meet him. The only reason she didn't was because she didn't want to go to that party. What have I done wrong, Leonard? Why is she so angry with me?'

'Laura's not angry.' Leonard leaned forward, rubbing at his calves. 'She's just very sad.' He shook his head, as if trying to free himself of difficult thoughts. 'It's so hard for you Mamma, I know that. It's so painful to see Laura without hope or thoughts for the future. That's why it's important she has a change of surroundings, a change of atmosphere, so that she can return to a more normal state of mind.' He took his mother's plump hand in his. 'Dear Mamma, I hate to see you like this, you're quite worn out. How about I go to Cook's tomorrow and fix our return? Perhaps it was a mistake to stay this long.' He moved his thumb back and forth over her dimpled knuckles. 'Shall I do that? Shall I go to Cook's tomorrow?'

Estella did not answer.

'Mamma?'

She gave a little sob. 'This is the worst thing that's ever happened to me,' she murmured, and it was clear that she had said these words many times in her head. 'Worse than my mother dying, worse than Papa losing the business.'

Leonard gazed helplessly at the back of his mother's trembling yellow head. After a while Estella stopped sobbing and looked up.

'Go to bed Leonard, it's late.'

'I'm all right, I'd like to stay a bit longer with you.'

Estella nodded. They sat in silence, the only sound the faint hiss of the heating system as the warm air eased through the floor vents. 'I think there's a plate of cheese from lunch,' said Estella at last, 'and some of that egg mayonnaise you like.'

'Are you hungry?' asked Leonard. 'Would you like me to bring you something?'

'I was thinking of you. I shouldn't imagine the aunties ever let you go to bed without eating.'

'I think my system is still recovering from the constant attentions of the aunties. I must be the only European who comes back from Egypt needing to lose a few pounds.'

'Nonsense, you're skin and bone.' She leaned forwards and pinched his cheek, as she used to do when he was a child. Behind her glasses, her eyes once again brimmed with tears. 'You're a good boy, Leonard,' she said. 'I don't know what I'd do if I didn't have you and Miriam, I don't know how I should manage.'

'Well you *do* have us,' said Leonard. And his heart swelled at the thought that it should be he, Leonard, upon whom his mother depended.

THERE WAS A TAPPING AT THE door, and it opened to reveal the dark, tousled head of Leonard's eldest niece, Marguerite.

'I thought I heard you,' she exclaimed, pushing the door wider and leaping into the room. Her pink dressing gown was belted tightly around her waist, the quilted collar tucked inside itself and making a ruff under her round, smiling face. Olive green eyes looked from one to the other, taking in the familiar elements of her grandmother's room.

'Rita! What are you doing still up?' asked Leonard.

'Close the door,' said Estella.

Rita giggled. 'I was reading, I can't sleep. Did you have a wonderful evening, Uncle Leonard? I wish I might have come with you, Mammy says Sofia Carasso is famous for her parties.' She bent down so that her grandmother might straighten her collar. 'Was Uncle Marco there? He called up and spoke to Mammy earlier and said he was going, but you never know with Uncle Marco.' She glanced at Estella. 'Granny thinks he's *inaffidabile*, don't you Granny?'

'Uncle Marco was there,' said Leonard, frowning at Rita and waiting for his mother to reprimand her. She did not.

'Go on, tell us everything!' Rita dropped to the floor, resting her chin on the wide shelf of her grandmother's lap. 'We want to know all about it, don't we Granny? Papa always came to my room when they got back from parties.' She gazed up at her grandmother. From this angle Estella looked like a cannonball, her large breasts resting on her belly and forming a single round mass, and Rita felt a stab of delight at the thought of recounting this tomorrow.

'There was a cousin of ours there, a very important doctor

from Paris, Dr de Perreira. And Sofia's son from Brussels. And lots of other interesting people, but no one you know. I really think you should be in bed, Rita, you have school tomorrow.'

'I have school every day, Uncle Leonard,' said Rita. 'Even Sundays if there's Piccole Italiane.'

'Yes, well, that's another matter,' said Leonard, who disapproved of all these marching groups. 'It's still important that you get enough sleep. Auntie Miriam says you often have your light on long past everyone else has gone to bed. How will you do well at school and make everyone proud if you don't get enough sleep?'

'But everyone's already proud of me. And I'm near the top of my class for most subjects.' She stretched out a foot and traced the outline of one of the roses in the carpet. 'Some people simply don't need as much.' She thought for a moment. ' "*There will be sleeping enough in the grave.*" Who said that? I forget.'

Estella shuddered.

'Bed, Rita,' said Leonard.

'Benjamin Franklin, that was it. Teddy has a book about him, he said all sorts of clever things. Did you know he only went to school for two years? I wish I didn't have to go to school.'

'Well you do,' said her uncle.

'What about Lucia Arditti, was she there? She goes to everything. Papa used to say she'd turn up for the opening of a jar.' She giggled, ignoring her uncle's disapproving look. 'Her daughter's in my class, Annetta Arditti. It's like one of those tongue-twisters — Annetta Arditti, Annetta Arditti. Actually she's rather dull.'

Despite himself, Leonard smiled, and Rita took this as a sign to keep repeating 'Annetta Arditti, Annetta Arditti', only breaking off when her grandmother leaned forwards and pressed her plump finger against Rita's lips. 'Enough,' she said.

The girl grinned, revealing a glimpse of the intransigence that her father had encouraged and that her mother was afraid of. Estella sighed and tipped forwards off the blanket box, standing up and swaying slightly. Her dress was caught up in itself and she tugged it loose then tottered the few steps towards the door. Leonard slid off the bed and held out his hand to Rita, who gazed up at him from the red and blue roses of the Persian rug. Her thin legs, with their covering of downy hair, seemed out of place amongst all that colour and she carefully tucked them inside her dressing gown so that only her toes showed. These she flexed back and forth like a diver about to spring from a board, then slowly, deliberately, stood up. Estella glanced at her bare feet. 'Slippers?'

Rita shrugged and Leonard leaned over and kissed the top of her curly head. 'Are you hungry, would you like something to eat? We were going to see if Miriam had left us anything.'

'She made a ginger cake. Your favourite, with the syrup that she pours on afterwards. We haven't been able to have it while you were away because she said it wasn't fair.'

'And she was right, it wouldn't have been,' said Leonard.

'I said we just shouldn't tell you, but Auntie Miriam thinks you'll find out everything. And so we've only had boring Madeira cake the whole time you were in Egypt, haven't we Granny? Apart from Teddy's birthday, when we had a chocolate one from Cucchi. I can bring it in if you like, the cake.' She knew her granny often ate her meals in her room.

'If you're going to eat cake, I'd prefer you did so in the kitchen,' muttered Estella. 'Nina barely has time to do my room as it is.' She opened the door.

'Come on then.' said Leonard, bowing and holding out his arm to Rita. He opened the door, and Estella hurried away down the hall, a monolith of black on two tiny castors.

THE KITCHEN, LIKE THE REST of the apartment, was in darkness but when Estella snapped on the light, she saw with satisfaction that the trays had been made up for breakfast and a pan of

water stood ready on the stove to make tea. It must have been
Miriam. She felt a rush of affection and began noisily opening
cupboards and lifting lids, muttering all the while about the
lateness of the hour and how no one should have to suffer a
life like hers.

'Shall I take it into the lounge?' asked Rita, for Estella
had found the cake and was cutting it into thick slices.

'Drawing room, drawing room,' grumbled Estella, as
Rita went out, for along with 'settee', 'pardon' and spoons above
the plates, this came from Miriam.

'Will we have it with butter?' asked Leonard, opening
the cupboard under the window. 'Miriam found me some
Empire Slightly Salted in that little shop in the Galleria. Now
where's she put it?'

'I think the children finished it,' said Estella, gathering
up the crumbs from the tin and pushing them into her mouth.

'Finished what?' asked Rita, coming back in.

'The special butter Miriam bought,' said Leonard.

'It's in the cold cupboard. I saw her put it there, she told
everyone it was just for you.'

Rita crouched next to her uncle and peered into the
small box-like cupboard. It was open on the other side and the
night air cooled their faces.

'Well, it's gone— never mind,' said Leonard, standing up.

Estella handed him a pile of plates, 'They're like
gannets those children,' she murmured.

The injustice of this stung Rita. 'Uncle Leonard, we
didn't eat your butter.'

Leonard shrugged. 'It doesn't matter.' And he picked up
a packet of the usual Italian butter and put it on a plate. Estella
took it and shuffled into the next room, where she lowered
herself into her favourite chair and looked around with
impatience for the others to join her. Rita lingered in the
kitchen, feeling that something terrible had just happened.

'Come on Rita, you're the one who had to eat,' complained Estella after a minute, banging the table.

'Come and sit down, Rita,' said Leonard, 'it looks delicious.'

'Goodness knows I'm used to going to bed on an empty stomach these days. Ah, there you are at last, sit down.' Estella reached a forefinger towards the cake plate and slid it towards her granddaughter. 'Help yourself,' she said, watching beadily as the girl picked up one of the hefty slices Estella had cut. 'I'll just have a little one.'

'Let me, Mamma,' said Leonard, passing her two good-sized pieces on the flat of his knife, 'you've barely eaten all day.'

As if she did it only to please him, she sighed and then stabbed at the butter, cutting a thick corner. That was another thing she had to put up with, scraping the butter. Estella glanced at Leonard, who was folding back his cuffs and then at her granddaughter, who was cutting her slice into squares and arranging them around her plate. 'Come on, eat up,' she said.

Leonard, feeling cheered, shifted on his chair and began to tell a story about one of the aunties in Egypt swallowing an orange pip and becoming convinced that she would die of peritonitis.

Rita giggled. 'Just one pip?'

'Just one pip! I think she thought a tree would grow inside her. She only calmed down when a cousin called for a tangerine to be brought and then ate it whole — skin, pips and all. When he didn't drop dead, she thought she might survive too.' He sighed. 'You would so love the aunties, the tales that go round are just too funny for words.'

'That must be Virginie, she always was a silly girl,' said Estella, licking a trace of syrup from the side of her hand.

'Is it true they won't let you lift a finger when you're there, that you're treated like royalty?' asked Rita.

Leonard nodded. 'Only don't tell Miriam — I like her to

think I'm suffering when I'm not with her. If I hadn't missed you all so much, I should probably never have left. I might have got rather fat though.' He patted his stomach and Rita giggled.

'Auntie Miriam says you're competing with her,' she said, taking a bite of cake and pushing at her hair with her wrist.

'Does she now?' said Leonard. He reached across and tucked a curl behind her ear. 'I shall have to have a word with her, slandering me like that. It's a serious business, eating for two.' And once again he rubbed his stomach.

Rita gave a shriek, clamping her hand to her mouth before anyone could tell her to be quiet. 'But Uncle Leonard, you're only one,' she whispered with delight. Leonard feigned surprise, looking around the room as if he had lost something.

'Don't get her all excited, Leonard.'

Leonard leaned across to Rita, miming dismay, and the girl widened her dark green eyes and tried her utmost not to laugh. It was so rare these days that grown-ups were silly around them. She gazed happily at her uncle and he continued to clown around, looking under his chair, lifting Rita's plate, until Estella finally lost patience and rapped the table with her knuckle.

'Leonard, please do stop,' she cried. And Leonard's face suddenly altered and he became serious again.

'Sorry Mamma,' he said.

Rita smothered a laugh and tried to catch his eye, but Leonard just ate his cake in silence.

'I think I should like to go to Alexandria,' said Rita after a while. 'I should like to be looked after like that.'

'We'll see,' said Estella.

'Mammy says if Uncle Bobby's out there, we might go and visit him.'

Estella looked up. 'Why would Bobby be there?'

Leonard glanced at his mother. 'You know that Bobby's going, Mamma, he's really looking forward to it. One of us needs to, and I'll have the baby, remember.'

'Your father travelled all the time when you children were small, I don't see why you shouldn't.'

Leonard began to protest, then changed his mind. He turned to Rita. 'Well, maybe once you're all settled in Manchester, you'll go for a holiday. The aunties and uncles would love to meet you all, they hear so much about you. Perhaps you'll go this summer.'

'We go to Cortina in the summer.'

'You used to, Rita, I don't think you will this year.'

'Mammy said we would.'

'Yes, but she has so much on her mind at the moment, she perhaps hasn't thought it through. It would be very impractical, you'll be in Manchester by then, Cortina's a long way from Manchester. Besides, you'll need time to settle in the new house, there will be lots to do to make it feel like home. Did I tell you that I spoke to the owner about putting a swing on one of the trees and he said he didn't mind in the least? It will be lovely for you children to have a garden, there are apple trees and roses and the biggest magnolia tree you've ever seen, right outside the front door. That's how I knew which house it was when Bobby first told me. The bus to the office goes straight down Palatine Road and in April there's one house that's completely hidden by pink flowers. When Miriam saw it she said it looked like it was all lit up with bright candles. She always puts things better than I do, I just said pink flowers.'

'We go to the Sempione, we don't need a garden,' said Rita.

Leonard nodded, his kind face losing some of its enthusiasm. 'Bobby had a good look around and he said there's a set of chairs and a table in the shed, so in summer you can eat outside. And Mammy can sit out with her coffee too. It will be good for her, you know. It will be good for all of you. And Miriam and I and Granny and Grandpa are just around the corner, we'll be able to pop in all the time and check on you. '

'We don't need checking on,' said Rita pushing her plate away.

Leonard glanced at his mother, but she ignored him for she was still upset about Bobby going to Egypt. Leonard sighed and wondered when everything would stop being so complicated. Only with Miriam did it seem that he could relax and be himself; with everyone else he was constantly made to feel that he had failed.

'Well, I hope we do go to Cortina,' said Rita, standing up and pulling at the belt of her dressing gown, 'we have all our friends that we see each summer. Some of them we've known since before Teddy was born, that's how long we've been going there. I shouldn't like to go anywhere else.' Her full pretty mouth had become pinched and hard and Leonard felt a surge of frustration.

'I think,' he said slowly, 'that you should really leave such decisions to Mammy. It's still very soon and going back to a place that reminds her of Papa might be hard for her. You know how difficult even *Carnevale* has been.'

'It's just as soon for us as it is for Mammy,' said Rita. She hated it when her uncle spoke to her as if she were a baby. It was fine to use that tone with Teddy, or even Coco, they didn't mind being treated as younger than they were. But she would be fourteen in July, she was practically a grown-up. She shoved her chair back under the table, catching the edge of the rug and exposing the dull, unwaxed parquet beneath.

Leonard bent down and flicked the rug back into place. 'I didn't mean that it was easier for you, Rita, of course I didn't,' he said, trying to keep the irritation from his voice. If Miriam were here she would have put her arms around the girl and told her how proud everyone was of her, and how wonderful she had been, always staying so cheerful and never moping or feeling sorry for herself. But she was not, and so he pointed to his niece's empty plate. 'Take your things into the kitchen,' he said.

Rita did as she was told. 'I'm going to bed,' she said from the doorway. She turned away quickly, wanting them to understand that she was cross with them. It was always the same, grown-ups were kind and funny and made you feel you were their friend, but then if you said something they didn't like, they changed and became mean. She expected it of Granny, she was always getting upset and telling everyone what to do, but Uncle Leonard was supposed to be fun. Tears began to fill her eyes but she blinked them back, and she hurried down the hallway towards her room, the floorboards squeaking beneath her tread.

CHAPTER 6

Rita's bedroom was at the end of the corridor but she did not get that far. The dining room blinds were open and moonlight spilled like water across the table and out through the door, so that the hallway seemed awash. A puddle outside her mother's room was full of tiny quivering shapes and she stepped in it, watching as the shadows rose over her bare feet and stretched up her ankles. 'It's all wrong,' she said to herself, looking at the floor, the walls, the closed doors, for they were no longer familiar to her. And when she pushed open the door to her mother's room, she might have been fleeing something.

Inside it was dark and it took a moment for her eyes to adjust, for the curtains were a heavy velvet and her mother liked that they were drawn tight. The bed took up most of the room, with its intricately carved legs and delicate fretwork, and Rita stumbled towards it. 'It's all wrong,' she repeated, slipping under the sheets and lying perfectly still. She could just make out the murmur of her mother's breathing and she wondered if she had taken one of her special pills to help her sleep. Rita was not supposed to know about these, but she had overheard Granny telling Leonard, and now, lying beside her sleeping mother, this too was not as it should be. Before, when her father was alive, they only had to cough or turn over in bed and their mother would wake up. '*Comme une grosse grenouille*,' Papa used to tease, for he had read somewhere that bullfrogs didn't sleep either. Rita sighed, wishing things could be like before. Before that holiday in Vittel, when their father had tipped forwards off his chair, coughing dark red blood across her sandals and causing everything to change.

Once again tears pricked her eyelids, and Rita brought her knees up to her chest, her dressing gown tangling about her middle. She and Coco had made a promise not to cry, so that they could be strong for Mammy just as Papa would have wanted, but in the last few weeks, Rita found it harder and harder to keep. Everyone had made such a fuss of them at first that it was easy to be brave, and she had been proud of how nice they looked in their smart clothes, and how pretty Mammy was, in her best black coat and the hats with all the net. But after a while, people drifted away, and now when they saw a familiar face, it was as though nobody knew what to say. Friends of her parents, people who had come to lunch at the apartment when Papa was alive, would cross the road to look in a shop window, or, if they were already upon them, discover they were late for an appointment, or that their tram was just leaving. And her mother would seem not to notice, or, worse, would blink and say, 'Of course, of course, you must hurry,' as if she believed them. But Rita felt abandoned.

The sheets were cool against her face, and she pulled them higher, her fingers tracing the silken ridges of embroidery. Sometimes, when there was nobody at home, she came and lay here in the middle of the day, imagining she could smell her father's hair oil on the pillow, or the lavender-scented soap he always used, that her mother had stopped buying now. Sometimes she would open the door to his wardrobe, where all his suits still hung, their lifeless forms punctuated with little bags of cedar shavings that kept off the moths. She would choose him a shirt and lay it on the chair, and then take out the box of cufflinks from his drawer and find her favourite ones, gold with a pearl inset, and fit them to the cuffs. And she would imagine him standing there, fresh from his bath, saying that was just the shirt he would have chosen, and how handsome he was going to be today. He would not say, like Granny or Uncle Leonard, that she was a big girl now, and that it was in her that her mother would find hope and strength for the future. Her father wanted only that she choose him a shirt.

There was a window open, and the curtains swelled faintly in the night breeze and then slackened again, their weighted hems slithering on the polished floor. If they left Milan, what would they do with all their father's things? Would they be boxed up for the refugees, given in bundles to the men who stood on street corners and who Miriam always hurried past with a quick nod and a '*scusi*'? She couldn't bear to think of her father's beautiful suits standing out in the cold.

She heard a tap running in the bathroom next door, and she listened as Leonard hummed softly to himself as he washed his face and got ready for bed. She imagined him taking his razor from its case on the shelf (he said there was nothing nicer than going to bed cleanly shaven) and lathering his cheeks, but then she heard the click of the door and his footsteps going back along the corridor. She thought of calling out to him goodnight, but she knew that if he found her here he would send her back to her own bed, so she kept quiet. Life was a series of such calculations these days.

Laura sighed in her sleep and turned onto her back, pulling the eiderdown with her so that Rita was left with only the thin sheet. She lay there with her eyes open, longing for the warmth of her mother's body but afraid to disturb her. Before, it had been Papa they had to mind, for he hated being woken up, would barricade himself behind pillows so that stray legs could not kick him, or small bodies roll into his space. But now it was Laura who must be protected, who needed her sleep if she was to get better, who had been surrounded with an invisible wall that the children were not supposed to cross. And it was Rita who lay awake.

Pushing herself upright, Rita slid across the mattress until her head lay on the pillow next to her mother's, and she could feel her breath on her face. Laura's arms were folded across her chest, like the Cycladic figurines they had seen in Greece, and Rita put her hand on one of her mother's arms, easing it towards her so that it lay across her shoulder. As if spring-loaded, the other arm immediately opened too, and Rita felt herself gathered up and pulled in. For a moment, she was afraid to move, but then she heard her name, and when she turned her head her mother's eyes were open, glittering in the dark at her. Her newly short hair clung to her face, and she looked very small against the white expanse of pillow.

'Rita darling, are you sick?'

'I didn't mean to wake you,' said Rita. Her throat felt tight, and she was seized with an urgent need to explain something, but she didn't know what it was. She held her breath, feeling oversized and clumsy next to the delicate form of her mother. 'I'm sorry,' she whispered.

'I wasn't asleep,' said Laura, for it seemed to her she had not been. She ran her fingers over Rita's hair, stroking it flat against the pillow, then sighed, a long, empty release of air. 'Is everyone in bed?'

'I think so. Granny and Uncle Leonard were talking, we had cake.'

'That's nice.'

'They were talking about Manchester.' She hesitated, trying to make out her mother's face in the darkness. 'Do we really have to go, Mammy? I don't want to live in Manchester, can't we stay here like you said at first?'

'Oh Rita, please don't start,' said Laura, turning away and gazing at the dark room.

'But why must we? We never had to do anything we didn't want before. Papa always said that as long as we were kind and didn't hurt anyone, nothing else mattered. I don't see why that has to be different now.'

'It's different because we're on our own now. I am on my own.' Laura removed her arm from beneath her daughter's shoulder. 'I must think what's best for all of us, even if it's something that we don't really want. And I need you to help me by not arguing about every little thing.'

'I *am* helping you,' said Rita, rising up on one elbow and leaning over her mother. Laura's eyes were closed and she looked as if she were made of very fine porcelain, the kind that you can see through when you hold it up to the light. Except that looking at her mother now she saw nothing at all.

'Well I need you to help me more,' said Laura, 'by trusting me to do the right thing and—'

'—but I don't want to go to Manchester. I couldn't bear it,' interrupted Rita. 'I hated it when we were there for Uncle Leonard's wedding. It was cold and grey and Coco and I had to wear two vests all the time, even under our bridesmaid dresses. And Papa didn't like it either, he said it made him bone-cold. I don't want to live somewhere that made Papa bone-cold, especially now.'

'Papa was brought up in Greece, everywhere was cold to him.' Laura spoke quietly and without emotion. 'Uncle Marco's the same.'

Rita said nothing, remaining propped on her elbow but no longer looking at her mother. She was thinking of how simple life had been before, and how easy it had been to be happy. Their world had been like a beautiful bubble, and it felt like nothing could ever touch them because they were in this magical, perfect place. Mammy had laughed all the time then, and gone to parties and worn pretty dresses and there had always been someone ringing up to chat or to ask them out. And nobody ever wondered how she was doing at school or told her she must work hard to make Mammy proud, because Rita was clever and popular and there was no need. Rita frowned, imagining what her father would make of all this. He would be so disappointed in them.

'Let's make a plan, Mammy,' she said. Laura remained motionless and Rita thought she might have fallen asleep again. 'Mammy?'

'I heard you.' Her voice was faint, as though coming from some faraway place.

'That's what Papa always used to say, do you remember? "Let's make a plan." '

'That is what I'm trying to do, Rita darling.' She lifted a hand to her daughter's face, tracing the softness of her cheek. 'It's all I think about from the moment I wake up, because everyone says that once we have a plan it will all feel better. But what if it doesn't feel better? Or what if it does and then —' The words trailed off and she covered her face with her hands. Rita watched, feeling that pitiless detachment a daughter reserves for her mother. If it had been the other way round, and it was her father who had to pick up his life and start afresh, she was sure he would have been stronger, less afraid. He would never have lain in bed for days on end refusing to see anyone, making everyone around suffer and despair. What was it he had always said to Rita? To be successful in life you must have character. He had spelled it out for her, in her autograph book, all capital letters and underlined to emphasize its importance. CHARACTER. She gazed in silence at her mother and wondered if she had any.

Outside the window, the night shifted and stirred. An owl hooted in a nearby tree and somewhere else a telephone was ringing, so that it was as if the two were in conversation. A loose shutter in the apartment below swung on its bracket, tapping against the wall of the Casa Grandolini like a visitor demanding to be let in. A car changed gear as it turned the corner, the straight, wide length of the Via Elba — a temptation to the most staid of drivers. And in a courtyard somewhere a woman was singing that Trio Lescano song Miriam loved, the one about the flies, so clear that it was as if she was in the room with them. Down the hall, Estella was snoring.

'Please don't make us leave,' said Rita, turning on to her side so that she was facing away from her mother. 'Please, Mammy.'

Laura sighed and let her hands fall from her face. 'Go to sleep, darling,' she said. She reached across and pulled the eiderdown across her daughter's shoulders, tucking it around her and kissing her lightly on her cheek. Then she lay back on the pillow and closed her eyes.

CHAPTER 7

Marco Balestra had enjoyed himself at the Carassos, and the next morning found him propped over his coffee in the hotel dining room, waiting for his head to clear. On the table in front of him was a pile of newspapers, and every so often he would pick one up and read a few lines, because it was too early to smoke and he had to do something when sitting on his own. The maître d', in swallowtail coat and striped trousers, flitted back and forth, keeping a constant eye on him. Gentlemen like Signore Balestra, he informed his staff, always appreciated the extra effort.

Breakfast was over and the tables cleared when at last a woman in a fur-trimmed coat and cropped hair came hurrying through the main doors of the hotel. She wore almost no makeup, and her cheeks were sallow, but despite this she was easily the most elegant creature to have crossed the front hall that day. Glancing this way and that, as if unsure what she was looking for, her eyes skimmed the faces scattered around the lobby, tugging them after her. At the entrance to the dining room she paused, smiling graciously as the maître d' threw himself into her path, and they crossed the floor together, partners in a waltz.

'Marco, I'm so sorry, I'm horribly late.' She dropped onto the chair opposite him, unbuttoning her coat and glancing around. 'Are we staying?' she asked Marco. And when he nodded, she stood up again, and peeled off her outer layers, still chattering about the terrible traffic, and how there was never anywhere to park.

'Laura darling, I was beginning to worry about you,' said

Marco, helping her with a sleeve. 'I'd have called you up but I didn't want to get Estella. I'm afraid I drank too much champagne last night to speak to your mother.'

Laura smiled. 'Teddy keeps telling her she doesn't have to shout, and she says yes, yes, I know, but then the telephone rings and she forgets and starts shouting again. English tea, please, no milk,' she said, for the maître d' was waiting.

'Coffee,' said Marco.

Laura glanced at her watch. 'Only Americans order coffee after midday,' she whispered. 'What a disappointment you'll seem.'

Marco shrugged. 'I suspect only Americans pay these prices,' he replied, and they both laughed. He gazed at her for a moment. 'It suits you,' he said, gesturing to her hair. 'You're starting to look your old self again, I'm glad. We were all rather concerned about you.' He reached across and put a hand on hers, and she smiled and remained very still, so that he shouldn't think she was uncomfortable with the gesture.

Their order arrived, along with a trail of white-jacketed waiters, who were laying up for lunch. All around them linen cloths were shaken out and smoothed across the Oriental tables, then laid with cutlery and glasses delivered from trays held at shoulder height. A maid dusted the leaves of the potted plants, and another swept beneath the chairs, while another did battle with a long wooden pole that opened slits in the glass roof above their heads. The maître d', like a sailor checking his ropes, moved from place to place making tiny adjustments, every so often snapping his fingers and bringing waiters scurrying to replace a dull knife or a broken wick. 'We're like the eye of a storm,' said Laura, sipping her tea. And Marco laughed, just as a quartet struck up a bright air and the first diners arrived, shopping bags and briefcases swinging as they stepped in time to the tune.

'Sofia Carasso called me this morning,' said Laura, when they had at last finished with Allegra's health, and the children's studies, and whether or not to see *Snow White* now all the songs were dubbed in Italian. 'Did she tell you she was going to? Has she spoken to you?' She picked up a jug of hot water and poured it into the teapot, stirring the leaves and frowning.

'About what?'

'About her idea.' She closed the hinged lid and then opened it again, peering inside. The steam rising from the pot brought a flush to her cheeks and caused her face to shine. 'Would you ask for some more hot water? I've made it too strong.' Marco turned and gestured to the waiter. Laura stared into her empty cup. 'She wondered if I'd considered moving back to Brussels.' She looked up. 'It rather took me aback. That's why I was late, it wasn't the traffic. Although it was difficult to park but in the end I left the car with the doorman, he said he would put it in a side-street. Of course, I told her it was impossible, everything is arranged.'

Marco watched as a waiter hurried forward with a jug of water.

'Have you eaten? Shall I order you something?'

She shook her head. 'All I ever seem to do is eat,' she said. 'Eat and sleep.'

'That sounds good to me,' said Marco.

'So you think that was the right thing to say then, to Sofia Carasso? That we've made our plans and it's settled we're going to Manchester?'

'Is it settled?' Marco ran his fingernail along the edge of the linen cloth. 'I thought you were still undecided.'

Laura was silent. 'I'm sorry I've been bothering you so much,' she said at last. 'Allegra must be tired of me calling you up at all hours. Is she? Of course she is, anyone would be. I'll stop, I promise, only I haven't known where else to turn. Leonard gets so upset with me when I can't make up my mind and Mamma and I never seem to stop bickering.' She fiddled with her napkin. 'Oh Marco, I just feel I'm letting everyone down.'

'You're not letting anyone down. And nor are you bothering me, you couldn't possibly. All I want is what's best for you and the children.'

Laura nodded, her head bowed.

Marco glanced around, his gaze lingering on a platter of oysters at a nearby table. He waited for Laura to continue.

'What about Allegra? Would she mind if we were in Brussels, do you think?'

'Allegra? She'd be thrilled.' He kept his eyes on the oysters.

'I mean, I'm not saying we would, and really, if it weren't for Sofia Carasso calling up, I'd never have thought of it.'

'Of course.' He waited for her to continue, and after a while she did.

'He's found us a house to rent, did he tell you? Leonard has. Just around the corner from them, he's terribly pleased about it.'

'I think he mentioned it, yes.'

'He's gone to such trouble over it.'

'I'm sure.'

'It has a big garden and fruit trees and lots of spare rooms for visitors to come and stay. He thinks it's perfect for us.' She looked at Marco hopefully. 'The children have never had a garden, not one of their own, it would be so nice for them.'

'And you?' Marco considered his fingernails. 'Would it be nice for you?'

Laura sighed. 'I thought it would.' She looked away. 'Except that when Sofia described her apartment, well, it sounded so much more what I'm used to. Has she told you about it? It's only just finished, apparently, but even though it's brand new and probably not at all like the Casa Grandolini, it felt familiar. It felt like the kind of place Isaac would have chosen for us. You must have seen it, have you? Is it the kind of place Isaac would have liked?'

'I suppose it is.'

'Leonard would understand that, don't you think? He might even be slightly relieved. He'll have his own family soon, he can't be worrying all the time about me. And I know Brussels, I have friends there. To go back to Manchester would be to start all over again, whereas in Brussels I'd feel— as though I were just picking up after a spell away.'

'Dear Laura,' said Marco, once again reaching out and taking her hand. He cupped her fingers inside his, her skin soft like the kid leather with which his tailor lined his trouser pockets. 'I'm sure Leonard will worry about you wherever you are, that's what he's like.' He smiled. 'But he also wants what's best for you — and if he thinks you'll be happier in Brussels, I'm quite sure he'll support you.'

Laura smiled, but the sadness which had suffused her features did not lift.

'I'm so tired, Marco.' She tipped back her head and gazed at the glass ceiling of the dining room.

'Are you sleeping? Because if you're not, you must get something for it. Allegra has all sorts of potions she takes.'

'Oh I sleep, it's not that.' He was still holding her hand, but now she gently withdrew it and sat back. 'Do you ever get an urge to just lie down? Wherever you happen to be? I do, all the time. I got it last week, waiting outside the children's school, it took all my strength not to lie down in the middle of the pavement, right there amongst all the bicycles and baby carriages. I told Leonard about it and he said I probably have an ear infection. I don't have an ear infection.'

'Of course you don't. Although it's still probably best if you don't start lying down on pavements.' He grinned.

'I won't.'

'I'm glad to hear it.'

'I'm just so tired.'

He nodded in sympathy and she turned away, her gaze

skimming the dining room and lingering on a waiter filleting a Dover sole. Marco pulled at a thread in his napkin.

'Sometimes I think people are comforted by what has happened.' She glanced at Marco and then turned back to watch the waiter. 'I don't mean that they're happy that Isaac died, or that the children and I are alone, no one would wish that. But we had so much, we had such a store of happiness all to ourselves, that perhaps it seems fair we should suffer. It reassures people there's justice in the world. Oh, look how beautifully he's done it.' She was talking about the fish.

Marco did not speak, for there was something terrible in her words.

'Oh Marco, I don't mean you, of course I don't,' said Laura, taking his silence as a reproach. 'I don't mean anyone that I can think of particularly, it's just how it feels sometimes.'

He nodded, and for a moment they sat in silence. She was remembering all the tiny humiliations: the mothers at the school gates who went silent when she approached, or who, when they did speak, saw no need to filter their curiosity; the fathers who heartily patted Teddy's head, as they would a dog they were fond of, and offered skiing trips or long hikes as proof of their own vitality; the suggestions of a quiet family dinner 'as soon as you're up to it,' the embarrassed references to parties to which she had not been invited, the condolence letters signed by both husband and wife, as if to remind her how alone she was now. And behind all these things, a kind of glee, like the thrill one gets reading a newspaper article about some murder or terrible accident. Because unless you have suffered something of a similar magnitude, grief such as hers meant nothing. It's value was purely anecdotal, to be offered around like sugared almonds, all the sweeter for the fact that, having happened to Laura Balestra, it could not possibly happen to them.

'Ignore me, I'm being silly,' she said.

Marco leaned forward. 'That's the spirit. No, nothing else,' he said to the maître d', who had approached the table. 'Unless the *Signora—* ?'

Laura pushed away her cup with a quick smile. She waited until the man had moved away, then said, 'I should go, they'll be waiting for me.'

They stood up, gathering their things and looking around the busy dining room. The maître d' arrived with Laura's coat and Marco took it and held it out for her. 'Have you read any Coué?' she asked, slipping her arms into the sleeves. 'Has Allegra? It's all about how we make our own happiness.' She smiled at him over her shoulder. 'Conscious autosuggestion, he calls it. Don't look like that, you should try it.'

'Should I?' He pinched the brim of his hat and set it on his head. Laura reached up to straighten it.

'*Tous les jours, à tous points de vue, je vais de mieux en mieux.*' She laughed. 'It's in French.'

'Of course it is.'

'You're making fun of me now!' The diners at the next table looked up.

'I promise I'm not.' She had dropped one of her gloves and Marco bent to pick it up for her. 'So you're thinking about it then, the Carasso apartment?'

She took the glove, smoothing the leather fingers. 'I don't know, it's all a bit sudden,' and she sighed and the old, undecided Laura reappeared. But then almost immediately she brightened, adding 'Although it would be such a treat to move somewhere new like that, I've always loved the Avenue des Nations.'

'It's quite the smartest street in Brussels,' said Marco, for it was on this wide, elegant road that he too had a house.

'I'd need to bring all our furniture, there isn't a stick there. Leonard has been telling me to sell everything — the house he's found is furnished — but the children would hate that.

Besides, I don't think I'd like to live with other people's furniture. How spoilt I sound.' She flushed guiltily. 'Do you realise, Marco, if I did decide to take it, it would be the first decision I'd made on my own since I agreed to marry your brother.' She smiled, and in her beautiful eyes with their dark rims Marco glimpsed a memory of complete happiness. 'Imagine that.'

'I'm imagining it.' He grinned. 'How does it go, *à tous points de vue* —?'

Laura laughed. '*Je vais de mieux en mieux!*'

'Better already! Come on, let's find your car.'

She shook her head. 'I'm meeting the children at the Duomo, it's probably quicker if I walk from here.'

'And if you'd like me to have a word with Leonard I'd be happy to.'

'No, he'll only think you'd talked me into it. Would you like to join us? Teddy would love you to see him, he's very proud of his costume. He's the Scarlet Pimpernel, and he really does look like a young Leslie Howard.'

'You're kind but I really must get on.' He patted his briefcase. 'Allegra will be furious if I delay my return.' He looked around importantly lest all this sitting around chatting should suggest he was not a busy man with work to do. 'Whatever happens, you can count on my support. You know that, don't you?'

Laura nodded. 'I couldn't manage if I didn't have you, Marco,' she said, suddenly serious.

'Nonsense, of course you could.' He took her arm and they wove their way through the lunch tables, people looking up as they passed.

When Leonard and the two children arrived at Santa Maria della Grazie, with its drum-shaped dome and terracotta brickwork, Lucia Arditti was already there. She was standing at the entrance to the museum, and as they approached she frowned, pointing to a notice pasted onto the Chapel door. 'Chiuso?' said Leonard, and Lucia threw up her hands in disbelief. The children, who were both sulking at having been made to come, suddenly brightened, swinging on their uncle's arms and giggling.

'*Carnevale, carnevale*!' chanted Coco, the older of the two, eager to get to the Duomo for the parade, and Leonard looked at her sternly. The ringing of a bicycle bell on the other side of the piazza caused everyone to look round.

'There's Daniel,' said Lucia and she waved to him, 'I sent him to buy *chiacchere.*'

She fussed as Daniel stood up his bicycle then watched as he shook hands with Leonard, adding '*E i bambini, e i bambini,*' so that, embarrassed, he shook hands with Teddy and Coco too. Then she retrieved a large paper bag from the bicycle basket and handed it to the children.

'Just one,' said their uncle, 'you don't want to spoil your lunch.'

'Ah, but they're like puppies at this age!' said Lucia. 'They need to be fed every few hours, am I right? Take another, I've tried all the bakeries in Milan and these are the very best. Mr Cansino, you too.'

'Sadly I'm not a puppy,' said Leonard, peering into the open bag.

'Nor I,' said Lucia, popping a pastry into her mouth. 'Here, Daniel, take the bag or I shall finish the lot.'

'Is it closed all day then?' Leonard glanced towards the entrance.

'Yes. *Sabato Grasso*. Silly me.'

'What a shame. Though Miriam did wonder, didn't she, children? Never mind, we can come another time, I don't suppose it's going anywhere.' And he took another chiacchere to show what a good time he was having.

'But you are going somewhere, Mr Cansino! And Daniel too. No, we absolutely must see it today. Wait here, I'm sure if I explain the circumstances they'll take pity on us.'

'Oh no, please don't trouble yourself,' said Leonard quickly. 'The children don't mind in the least. Really, I'd prefer to come when it's open.'

'Two minutes,' said Lucia brightly, hurrying away.

Leonard rubbed the sugar from his fingers. 'Dearie me,' he said, glancing guiltily at the children. He felt he had compromised them in some way. Daniel Sutton grinned and sat down on a nearby bench.

'She does it all the time,' he said, rolling down his socks to free his trousers. 'No one minds really.'

Leonard brushed the seat with his hand and sat down too. 'Really?'

The boy nodded. 'It was the same at the Cimitero. The Famedio was closed for restoration work but she convinced one of the stonemasons to let us in.' He took a camera from his jacket pocket and unwound the strap, hanging it around his neck. 'She said I couldn't come to Milan without seeing Alessandro Manzoni.'

Leonard gazed across the piazza to where the children were kicking up piles of paper confetti. 'Did she also tell you *I Promessi Sposi* was the greatest novel ever written?'

Daniel nodded.

'Italians always say that, especially in Milan. Teddy, come here, I promised Mammy I'd keep you both clean! So she took you to the cemetery?'

'Yes. We saw Ascari too,' he said, adding, 'The racing driver?' when there was no response.

From behind there came the scrape of iron bolts on stone and they turned to find Lucia standing triumphantly in the open doorway. Beside her was a young man in the long white robes of the Dominican friars.

'I've been telling this kind man all about your cousin and the King of Spain,' she announced. 'He would be honoured if you'd like to visit the Leonardo, he says any friend of King Alfonso is a friend of the brotherhood.'

'Oh, but I'm hardly—'

'Fra Guiseppe is a great supporter of the monarchy, all Catholics are. You wouldn't believe how many priests — good men of the church, just like the brother here — have been murdered since the uprising. I told him you'd be sure to give your cousin their best wishes. Come along children, hurry inside.'

Lucia stood back to allow them into the dim hallway beyond. There was little chance of Leonard seeing de Perreira again and he felt he should make this clear, but when he tried to explain Lucia shushed him and urged him ahead.

'He's very happy to be of service,' she whispered. 'These poor men feel quite helpless, there's not much else they can do. Except pray, of course. There,' she smiled, as they were led through a small wooden door, 'now don't tell me that wasn't worth it.'

The refectory was a long narrow chamber, with high walls and a vaulted ceiling. Wooden panelling lined the four walls and on the two longer sides rows of windows filled the room with cool grey light. Beneath these windows ran a thick band of painted scrollwork, with looping garlands and curled ribbons, parts of which were hidden by the framed canvases which hung below.

Refectory chairs were arranged at intervals on the bare floor, all facing in the same direction, and amongst them were placed easels set with glossy oil paintings. Her arm hooked inside Leonard's, Lucia led him towards the far end of the room and stood gazing upwards. Fra Guiseppe waited by the door.

'Look children,' she gestured to Teddy and Coco to sit down, 'isn't this the most beautiful thing you have ever seen? Daniel, come closer, your mother will be so pleased you saw it.'

Everyone did as they were instructed. Leonard gazed at the faded paintwork and then at the walls around. All the pictures were smaller copies of the Leonardo, so that it was like being in a hall of mirrors, with the same image reflected in all directions. He rubbed the back of his neck and murmured admiringly, as one ought to in the presence of something magnificent.

'The first time I saw it,' said Lucia, 'I wasn't much older than Coco here, and I thought it rather overrated. They say the paint started peeling within twenty years of Leonardo finishing it, something to do with painting onto dry plaster rather than wet. Or is it the other way round?' She glanced towards the door, but the brother had disappeared. 'Perhaps you could look that up, Daniel, there should be a guidebook somewhere. Anyway, I didn't come again for many years and the next time was just after I had Luca. He was the most dreadful baby, always screaming and carrying on. But when I brought him in here he became quite calm.' She laughed and flicked her hair. 'He was just a baby, of course, and it was probably all the bright colours, the restorer had used some sort of glue to fix them. Since then I've always loved it. Do look at Freddy, he's mesmerised.' She meant Teddy.

Teddy turned around. 'Don't you think that one looks like Coco?' He pointed to a figure in blue and pink.

Lucia peered from Coco to the painting. 'A little, yes!'

'That's the Apostle John,' said Daniel, who had found a printed sheet and was reading it.

68

'It doesn't look a bit like me,' said Coco, frowning and twisting at her plaits. Teddy was always making fun of her in front of people. 'Tell him it doesn't, Uncle Leonard.'

'Don't fuss, poppet,' said Leonard.

Coco gasped. 'But he said I look like a man—' Her bottom lip quivered. 'You can't take his side!'

Leonard sighed. 'I wasn't taking anyone's side. Teddy, come and sit down again. Nobody looks like anybody. Let's just sit quietly and enjoy the painting, or Signora Arditti will think we don't appreciate all the trouble she went to.'

Coco stared at her uncle in dismay. Teddy always got away with everything, that was what happened when you were the youngest. And she turned and walked to the far end of the room, wishing she could go further.

Lucia grinned. 'I do love it when other people's children argue. It makes me feel so much better about my own.'

'They're usually very well-behaved,' murmured Leonard.

'It says here,' said Daniel, still peering at the printed sheet, 'that the very last figure to be painted was Judas. That's Judas there, the one with his back to us. "*Perlustrato*"? What does *perlustrato* mean?' He glanced at Lucia, who strode over and took the sheet from him.

'Ehm... scoured,' she said, 'Leonardo "scoured" Milan for the face of Judas.' She looked up. 'How depressing to be chosen as the model. For hundreds of years people are going to look at your face and see it as the depiction of wickedness. Don't you find that sad, Mr Cansino?'

Leonard said he did.

'It's probably sadder to actually *be* Judas,' said Teddy.

'Very true.' Lucia glanced towards the door, where Fra Giuseppe had once again appeared. 'We're having such a nice time,' she said.

'I could take a photograph of everyone in front of the painting, if you like.' Daniel had taken out his camera. 'As a souvenir.'

'What a good idea,' exclaimed Lucia. 'Although according to this,' she held up the printed sheet, 'it's "tempera", not a painting at all. Children, come over here next to me.' She held out her arms. 'Mr Cansino, you too. How's that, Daniel? Do you have enough light? Not that I'm an expert, I've never taken a good photo in my life. Perhaps we should ask Fra Guiseppe to take it, then we could all be in it. No? Oh all right, as we are then.'

'Will you send it to us?' asked Coco, after the shutter clicked and Daniel had put the camera back in its case. 'Do you have our address?'

'I'll give you mine,' said Leonard. 'Most likely they'll just be around the corner. I have a card somewhere,' and he began to pat his pockets. 'I'd be much obliged to you, if it comes out well.'

'Is Mammy meeting us at the Duomo?' asked Coco, taking Leonard's hand and swinging it happily. She turned to Lucia. 'I'm going as Lucie Manette. From *A Tale of Two Cities*, have you seen it? It's Mammy and my favourite film, we've seen it tens of times.'

'Tens?' asked Leonard.

'It's true,' said Teddy. 'Granny says if they make her watch it one more time, she'll chop her own head off!'

'I'm sure she didn't say that,' said Leonard.

'Ah, now that's who you remind me of!' Lucia tapped her forehead. 'Elizabeth Allan, not that silly Apostle John. Of course!'

Coco beamed.

They were moving towards the door. Lucia began telling a story about the time she dressed all the children as French Revolutionaries, and Leonard was looking for his umbrella, which he was sure he had with him, but now couldn't find. When at last everyone had left, and Fra Guiseppe was closing the door, Daniel stepped back inside and took one last picture of the empty room.

'Did you know Bonaparte and Josephine had their honeymoon in Milan?' said Coco, as they waited in the hallway.

'And that Josephine was a widow when they met, with two children?' She looked at Teddy. 'That's like Mammy marrying Il Duce!' She giggled and Teddy stared at her for a moment, then began giggling too.

'On the sheet it said Bonaparte's army was stationed here after he invaded Italy,' said Daniel, catching up with them. 'They climbed ladders to scratch out the eyes of the Apostles.'

Coco stopped and gazed at Daniel in horror. 'Why?'

'They didn't like the Church,' said Lucia matter-of-factly. 'Revolutionaries never do,' and she smiled and chattered about Spain and the Terrors and what a nice man Dr de Perreira was, until they were through the wooden door and out into the sunny piazza.

CHAPTER 9

They took the Number 16 tram to the Piazza Cordusio then followed the stream of people surging towards the cathedral. Leonard, always nervous in crowds, insisted that the children hold his hands and he tugged them into his sides as if they were dogs he was keeping to heel. The bells of the cathedral were ringing and everywhere people laughed and pointed at one another and threw handfuls of tiny confetti that stuck to their feet and settled like hoar frost on their hats and sleeves. Teddy saw a friend from school and waved excitedly and Coco danced and spun on Leonard's arm, so that three times he had to stop and pull his glove back on and tell her to calm down. The sky was polished lapis.

Miriam was waiting for them in front of Motta, a bag containing their costumes on the pavement next to her. Teddy threw himself upon it and began pulling out scarves and capes and petticoats while Miriam, bending stiffly, laughed and protested that she had everything in order. Coco refused to get changed on the street so Miriam suggested they use the bathrooms inside the shop and Leonard said if they did that, they must buy something. Teddy, fixing the elastic of his hat, said he would have a double scoop of pistachio, and then Coco thought she would like one too, so that rather than getting dressed they joined the queue for ice cream which was surprisingly long given it was March.

'This is nice,' said Miriam, lacing her fingers through Leonard's and smiling up at him. Her cheeks were pink from the warmth of the shop and her blonde hair shone beneath the brim of her green felt hat. Pregnancy suited her, giving a fullness to her features that made her look even younger, so that she was often mistaken for the children's sister rather than their aunt. She sighed happily and leaned against Leonard, watching through the steamy window as a band began to tune up across the way. Leonard agreed that it was nice, resting his chin on top of her hat, and he was filled with such a sense of well-being that, almost immediately, he began to worry.

'Where's Rita? I thought she was coming with you.'

'She saw some friends by the Galleria, she's going to come and find us later. Oh, Leonard, she looks so pretty, she let me dress her as Lady Blakeney, and she's the image of Merle Oberon.' She smoothed his lapel. 'I know you find her a bit wilful sometimes, but she's a wonderful girl. There's such a spirit about her. I didn't know Isaac that well, but I do feel she's the most like him. She will do something special with her life, you watch.'

She smiled, gazing at her husband with such sweetness that Leonard, who would never have allowed Rita to go off alone, felt she had done just the right thing.

'Well I'm glad she came along,' he said. 'They've had to grow up so fast these last six months, it's good to remember they're just children.'

'I wouldn't say that to her today,' said Miriam.

Leonard thought about this, but suddenly the band outside the window struck up a noisy foxtrot and everyone on the street was dancing, Miriam tapping her heels on the mosaic floor. Coco watched in delight, forgetting her desire for ice cream and clutching Miriam's arm.

'Come with me so I can get changed,' she pleaded, pulling at the bag. 'We're wasting time, I want to go outside.'

'Go, go,' said Leonard, 'Teddy, you go too. And make sure you all stay together.' Miriam looked at him fondly, wrinkling her nose in the way she did when he fussed too much, and causing tiny creases to appear on her otherwise smooth brow.

'We'll be quick,' she promised.

Leonard turned back to the queue. All around him people laughed and chatted.

'Isn't this wonderful,' said a woman in front of him, and Leonard agreed.

Just then, the door to the shop opened and one of the dancers strode inside, a thin man in an open necked shirt, a cigarette in his mouth. He was breathing heavily from his efforts and he looked around the crowded room then strode to the front of the queue where he was rewarded with applause and a kiss from one of the servers.

'He works here,' someone said.

Leonard watched. A streak of sweat ran from the man's collar to half way down his shirt and his shoes were worn and grey with dust. He had dark curly hair that fell over his eyes and a wide unsmiling mouth but when he put out his hand to a woman in furs at the front of the queue, she did not hesitate. She slid towards him as if on skates and suddenly he was flinging her around the overcrowded tables so that everyone had to draw in their knees or lean forwards to make room. The woman laughed, her head flung back, her feet barely touching the floor, her crocodile handbag swinging from her elbow like a metronome. Leonard thrust his hands deep into his pockets and inched forward with the queue.

'Isn't this wonderful?' repeated the woman in front of him, for the band were playing faster and the people sitting at the tables were clapping their hands in time.

At last the music ended and the couple stopped spinning and everyone applauded so that the man who worked there made a deep bow and the customer, flushed and breathless, wafted the reveres of her coat to cool herself.

'Still waiting?' Miriam had put on fresh lipstick and rearranged her hat, and Leonard felt sure that if she had been standing in the queue, the man would have danced with her.

'I think we should go, I don't want Laura to be fretting. And we should probably find Rita.' He took Miriam's elbow and steered her firmly towards the door.

LAURA WAS STANDING ON THE steps in front of the Duomo, watching some children by the almond seller's cart. They had laid out all their money on the pavement and the *venditore di mandorle* was waiting, his hands hovering over the wooden scoop, to see if they had enough before he filled a bag. Laura was hoping that they would not, so that she could give them the coin she had already taken from her purse and which was pressed inside her glove. She was feeling happy since her meeting with Marco and the world seemed lighter and a little more deserving than it had before. The blackened saints on the cathedral facade gazed down benevolently, the fountain splashed, the beggars on the steps might be about to burst into song. A car on the other side of the piazza backfired and hundreds of startled pigeons rose into the air like extras in a Busby Berkeley movie. The man gave the children their nuts.

'Laura! You've been waiting. Oh, I knew we'd been too long, the children wanted to change. Where's Marco? Surely he didn't let you come on your own?'

Leonard broke onto the scene with his usual agitation but Laura only laughed, looking past him at the children. 'Leslie Howard, what are you doing in Milan?' she cried, throwing her arms wide, and Teddy flung himself at his mother so that she stumbled backwards and Leonard had to catch her elbow.

'Careful, Teddy' said Leonard.

'And you brought Marie Antoinette, how adorable,' continued Laura, hugging Teddy then standing back to admire the layers of petticoats and silk scarves in which Coco had draped herself. She glanced at Miriam, who had slipped her arm through Leonard's and was smiling gently. 'Did Rita come?'

'She's with some friends by the Galleria,' said Leonard, 'I'll fetch her.'

'She finally agreed to be Lady Blakeney,' said Miriam, giving Leonard's arm a squeeze as he turned to go.

'I'm so pleased,' said Laura, 'how perfect everyone looks,' and she gazed beyond their little group at the busy piazza.

Leonard returned a few minutes later having found not only Rita, resplendent in Laura's yellow silk dress, but Lucia Arditti's daughter Netta too. A thin, sullen looking girl with a heavy jaw and deep-set eyes that gave the impression she was always tired, she was wearing sky blue tights and a cape of the same colour.

'She's a bluebird,' said Rita, pointing to a yellow beak on a piece of string that hung around Netta's neck, 'from *Sleeping Beauty*.'

'What a good idea,' said Miriam.

'Why don't you two go off?' said Laura, turning towards Leonard. 'Have a little time to yourselves, I'll stay with the children.'

'Are you sure?' Miriam, glanced at Leonard. They had barely spent a minute on their own since Leonard had arrived. 'We could go to Cova, Leonard, I haven't been there yet.'

Leonard shook his head. 'Everywhere will be so busy today,' he said. He turned back to Laura. He wanted to ask if she and Marco had talked about the house, but Laura was in one of her polite, breezy moods and was giving nothing away.

'Teddy's been telling us about his list,' said Rita.

'Teddy has a list?' asked Leonard.

'Of all the girls who are in love with him,' said Rita. She glanced at Netta, who shuffled her thin blue legs. 'Apparently they like his eyes.'

'I have flowers in my eyes,' Teddy said. 'See?'

Leonard looked, and it was true; the coloured parts of Teddy's eyes were crinkled like the petals of a flower.

'See,' said Teddy, turning this time to Netta. The girl agreed nervously and pulled at the elastic around her neck so that Miriam felt obliged to put her hand on it, afraid it would snap.

'So go on, tell us who's on this list,' said Rita. Coco giggled.

'I'm not going to say,' said Teddy, as if it was a matter of honour to him. 'Besides, it's embarrassing. It's not that I want them to like me, they just do.'

'When you're older,' said Leonard, bending down so that his face was level with Teddy's, 'it won't seem like such a problem, take it from your poor old uncle. You'll be glad for the slightest bit of interest from a pretty girl.'

'Oh, they're not pretty,' said Teddy and everyone, even Netta this time, laughed. 'I mean it,' he continued, 'not one of them is pretty.' He smiled, unsure as to what was so funny.

Rita considered this for a moment. 'Well who is pretty, then?' She raised her chin, mimicking the voice of the wicked stepmother in *Snow White*. 'Who is the fairest one of all?'

'Alas for her!' said Leonard, playing along.

'Rags cannot hide her beauty!' added Coco.

'Well, Mammy first of all,' said Teddy, ignoring them. 'And Coco and Auntie Miriam. And perhaps even you too, Rita, when you're not wearing make-up.'

'And Netta too,' said Leonard, so that she shouldn't be left out.

Teddy glanced at Netta with her lank brown hair and too big chin. He felt everyone's gaze upon him and he shrugged and said nothing.

'Teddy!' repeated Rita, clearly delighted.

'That's not very kind, Teddy.' Leonard turned to Netta,

who was twisting the edge of her cape. 'I think he's embarrassed,' he said kindly.

'No I'm not,' said Teddy. His eyes had taken on that glassy, unblinking look that always preceded tears.

Leonard looked at him in surprise. 'Well, you should be—' he began, but Laura cut him off.

'Enough now,' she said and she pulled Teddy towards her. He pressed his face into her coat and instinctively the other two children moved towards their mother. 'Netta has brothers and sisters,' she said firmly. 'She understands how families tease one another.' And that Leonard could not possibly understand this was more than clear to him. Miriam slipped her arm through his and squeezed it again, but Leonard did not want her support and pulled away.

Netta muttered something about 'only brothers', and Laura laughed and said, 'exactly.' and then Rita said 'four brothers,' and Laura laughed again and said, 'poor you!' Coco found some confetti in her pocket from earlier and, one by one, arranged the coloured squares around the collar of Teddy's coat and Teddy, recovered now, waited until she had finished and then shook himself violently. Laura glanced at Leonard, who had his hands pushed deep inside his pockets and was looking the other way.

'Really, I insist you two have some time together,' she said, 'I won't be able to enjoy myself if you don't. Do go, you'll have fun.'

'If you're sure?' said Miriam, glancing at Leonard.

'Of course I'm sure!' She shook her head in exasperation, then added, more softly, 'take your wife to Cova, Leonard. She deserves a treat. You both do.'

Leonard looked from the hard smiling line of his sister's mouth to the noisy milling crowd in the piazza. He felt Miriam's fingers in the crook of his elbow. 'All right,' he said.

'Uncle Leonard's a bit scary sometimes,' whispered Coco as they watched them walk away.

Laura gazed up at the facade of the cathedral, the vast blocks of dirty pink marble rising into the cloudless sky. A pigeon was trying to land on one of the stone slaves, upon whose cowed heads rested (apparently) this entire edifice and it beat its wings loudly against the stone as it dropped and then flew up again. 'Not really,' she said.

ON THE STEPS, NETTA HAD SPIED her brother and she waved, pointing him out to Rita as he slouched across the piazza. Luca was tall and gangly, with the same heavy features as Netta, except that on him they were beautiful. He wore the thin-lapelled black suit of all disenchanted Italian youth and a crumpled white shirt. Behind him, wheeling a bicycle, was Daniel Sutton. Netta glanced towards Rita, then ran to meet them. Her small, worried face had taken on a lightness and vigour and it was clear that it was because of the young English boy.

'You look ridiculous, Netta,' said Luca, following his sister up the steps. 'Aren't you too old for dressing up?'

'I was looking after the little ones, they wanted me to,' she said.

'Well come on then,' said Luca, noticing Laura Balestra and thrusting his hand at her. 'Pleased to meet you,' he said, with practised politeness, then turned back to Netta. 'I said I'd meet you and I have. Either you come with me now, or you can wait for Lucia.' (He always called his mother by her first name). 'I'm meeting people and I can't hang around all afternoon with a bunch of kids.'

'Just stay a little,' began Netta, 'it's too early to leave.'

'Actually, there's nothing really happening,' said Rita, pulling at one of her dark ringlets. She had dropped her hat and shawl and was suddenly a pretty girl in a summer dress. 'It might be fun to go somewhere else.'

'Fine with me,' said Luca dismissively.

Rita looked at her mother. 'May I?'

'But everything is only just starting,' said Netta, 'they haven't even done the parade yet, we can't miss that. Just wait a bit longer, Luca.'

'Oh darling, of course you can't,' said Laura, laughing gently.

'But why not?'

'Because we're spending the afternoon as a family and because you're too young to go off like that and because—' She stopped, for Rita was glaring at her with such outrage that she felt anything she added would only make things worse. 'Netta can stay with us if she wants to,' she said to Luca. She smiled at Netta.

'If you don't mind, I might stay too,' said Daniel Sutton.

'As you wish.' Luca raised a hand and stepped backwards, his eyes on Rita. Then he turned and sauntered away.

'So, what does everyone want to do first?' asked Laura. 'We could go for ice-creams, we could watch the Commedia, what do you think?' She looked around, as if nothing were too much trouble. 'Mr Sutton, is there something particular you would like to see? My brother tells me you're only in Milan a few more days, I do hope you have managed to see all the sights. We often get overlooked in favour of Rome and Florence, but really, we have treasures of our own here, don't we Rita?'

'If there are such treasures in Milan,' said Rita, 'why are we leaving?'

Laura held her daughter's gaze, surprised by the challenge. 'Because there are other things to consider as well,' she said and she was not afraid to look straight at Rita, glowing in her yellow dress. 'Mr Sutton, have you been to the top of the cathedral? The views are quite startling, it's one of my favourite places in the world. We used to go on Sunday mornings when everyone was at High Mass, it's rather magical to hear the sound of hundreds of people singing beneath your feet. And no queues for the lifts at that time either!'

'Do you remember when we saw the Savoia-Marchettis?' said Teddy, stroking the fur hem of his mother's coat. 'SM81s,' he added, glancing at Daniel.

'Teddy wants to design aeroplanes when he grows up,' said Coco. 'He's very good at drawing.'

'Or I might be a pilot,' said Teddy.

'You could be both,' offered Daniel. 'Like the fellow who invented the Spitfire.'

'I'd like that,' said Teddy, for the Spitfire was one of his favourites.

'My housemaster says if we do have to fight Germany, it will be the aircraft designers who'll win it for one side or the other. That's what he thinks.'

Laura shuddered and fiddled with her earring, which had caught in her scarf. 'Coco, can you help me with this,' she said, and she turned away so that Coco could disentangle it.

'I can take him,' said Rita suddenly. She looked at Daniel, inclining her head as though challenging him to something. 'Unless you mind heights?'

There was a boldness about her and Daniel blushed. He shook his head, meaning, no, he didn't mind heights.

'Come on then.' Rita swished her yellow skirt, enjoying his discomfort. 'I'm an excellent tour guide.'

Laura quickly opened her handbag. 'Let me give you some money for the lift,' she said. 'It's only two lire. Netta, here you are too, I'm sure you've been up lots of times but it's always fun to show it to someone.'

Rita looked at her. 'Yes, of course, come too if you want.'

'Off you go then,' said Laura. 'We'll wait for you here.' She smoothed Netta's hair encouragingly and pressed her forwards.

Rita turned away. 'Last one there's a rotten egg!' she cried and she set off, squealing and pulling Daniel after her. Netta remained where she was, staring fiercely at the ground. All the joyfulness of earlier had disappeared from her face and it was closed off and heavy again.

'Do hurry, they're going without you,' said Laura. She pushed the girl forwards, watching as she walked away along the front of the facade, a blue speck lost in all that baroque glory. She had the feeling that something unkind had just happened, but was unsure what it was, and so instead thought how enchanting Rita had looked standing there, and felt glad.

CHAPTER 10

The café was full when Leonard and Miriam arrived, the glass doors giving onto a bright salon full of rosy-cheeked customers pressed against the long bar or perched at the marble-topped tables. Waiters in starched white shirts and shiny cummerbunds threaded the room, glancing at their reflections in the mirrored walls and solemnly repeating orders as if they were complicated mathematical equations, whilst in the garden, closed at this time of year, men in long coats were smoking. At the piano, a woman with blonde hair and thighs that spilled either side of the piano stool, played jaunty tunes, leaning forwards as people squeezed by, beads of sweat gathering in the creases of her powdered neck. When she saw the young English couple, she waved, missing several bars of the song, though she knew neither of them.

Miriam gazed with delight, pulling off her hat and pretending not to hear when Leonard said it was too busy and they should go somewhere else. Laura had often spoken of Café Cova, for she and Isaac used to come here all the time, and Miriam had longed to see it before they left Milan. She took Leonard's hand, manoeuvring sideways through the tables and joining the throng around the bar where cakes and tiny *panini* were arranged on silver trays. An elderly gentleman stepped aside to let her past, smoothing his grey moustache and bowing at the radiant young mother, remembering his own wife at that age and patting Miriam's shoulder with affection. Leonard signalled to the barman, a tall man with white gloved hands that fluttered like doves, so that he too bowed and performed a series of intricate moves that resulted in Miriam and Leonard sitting atop stools at one end of the long bar, drinking lemonade.

'Italians love mothers,' said Miriam triumphantly. Her hands rested on the mound of her belly. 'I shall miss that when we go home. Not once have I stood up on the tram, it's not like that in England.'

'Well, you don't know yet,' said Leonard, half-smiling to hide the irritation he had been feeling since they left the Duomo. He unhooked one of the newspapers that was hanging beneath the counter and rested it against the brass rail.

'Oh look, *panini con tartufo*! Laura said that's the speciality here! Do you think I can just help myself?' She leaned across the bar and took a pale soft roll, holding it to her nose and then biting into it. She chewed slowly, already nostalgic for this moment, then offered it to Leonard. He shook his head.

'I'm not hungry.'

'Do try, Leonard.' She continued to hold it out to him but he had turned his attention back to the newspaper and so she ate it herself. 'I could get a taste for truffles!' she said, for everything delighted her today. 'Did you know they use pigs to find them, Teddy told me. Apparently they go crazy for the smell and so they take the pigs into the woods where truffles grow and when they start digging and pawing the ground, they know that's where to look. Oh!' She put her hand to her mouth. 'Does that mean they're not kosher?'

'Probably,' said Leonard. It was easy to be unkind when he was in a mood like this.

'Oh dear,' said Miriam, and stared ruefully at the crumbs in her napkin. It had been one thing after another since she had been in Milan. Nobody here seemed to care about such things and although Nina had been instructed not to serve pork or shellfish during their stay, bits of prosciutto and salami turned up in everything. Even the minestrone soup she had been eating all winter turned out to have a ham bone boiling away at the bottom of the pan.

'Actually, truffles are fine,' said Leonard after a while.

'Really?' She was pushing at the crumbs with her fingertip, so that at first they were a star shape, then a flower, then a small heap. 'Shall I take some back for Mamma then? As a treat? I can give them to her with her little red drink tonight, she'll love that.' She hesitated, her fingers resting lightly on the brass rail, then leaned forwards suddenly and kissed Leonard's cheek. 'That's for nothing,' she said, when he looked at her in surprise.

They sat in silence, Leonard reading and Miriam listening to the piano player and watching the other customers as they chatted and moved around the bar. For all she chirped and praised, she was weary of Milan, weary of waking each morning to such sadness, falling asleep each night to much the same. She worried that grief, like the milk everyone told her she must drink, might pass from her to her baby, that it might even now be growing inside bones and fingernails. She sighed and took another *panino*.

Beyond the window, the sky was beginning to darken, and the door to the café opened only outwards, as people gathered up their things and went home. Leonard closed the newspaper, returning it to its hook beneath the bar. 'So. Will we head back?'

Miriam nodded and began buttoning up her coat. She had wrapped two rolls inside a fresh napkin and she slipped them in her handbag. 'Thank you for bringing me, Leonard. I know it wasn't what you felt like, but I had such a nice time. Here, let me.' She took the bill from its silver tray, looking it over then opening her handbag and feeling around for her purse.

'I insist,' she said. 'It will make me happy.'

Leonard smiled. 'Well then thank you,' he said,

wondering, as he often did, why someone as sweet-natured as Miriam should choose to be with him. He wanted to tell her how much he had missed her, how empty his life was without her, but instead he said:

'Did Laura seem different to you? Just now, when she was standing on the steps with the children. Did you not think there was something strange about her?'

'Laura? I don't think so.' The buckle on her shoe was undone and she raised her foot towards Leonard, for she could no longer reach it herself. He glanced around self-consciously, then bent down to fix it, still thinking about his sister.

'I'm going to talk to her tonight. I've been here a week now and we still haven't sat down and talked things out. Sometimes I think she's avoiding me.'

'I don't think she's avoiding you.' She took his arm so that he could help her down off the stool.

'No, I know she isn't. I don't mean it really, it's just that I'm worried that she'll keep finding excuses and we'll end up doing everything in a hurry at the last minute. Laura's not the most practical of people, you've probably noticed that. She hasn't needed to be.'

'I think you worry too much,' said Miriam, 'Laura is stronger than you think.' She was still holding his arm, her fingers gently squeezing.

'Perhaps,' he said.

◆　　◆　　◆　　◆　　◆

WHEN THEY GOT BACK, LAURA and Estella were waiting for them in the dining room. Laura had made tea in the silver pot and laid the table with the best linen and porcelain while Estella, who thought such things should be kept for special occasions, was complaining about how much extra work it would cause.

'How pretty everything looks!' said Miriam. 'Like something out of a magazine.'

'I wanted to make it nice,' said Laura, adding, 'they've gone to tea with Marco,' for Miriam was looking around for the children.

'I don't think I've been in here without Teddy making me dance,' said Miriam, pulling out a chair and sitting down heavily. 'It's not that I don't like Carlo Buti, but there's always such a fast beat and I'm not as light on my feet as I was. Shall I pour, or would you like to, Mamma?'

Estella nodded, adding 'She makes it very weak,' so that Miriam said she didn't mind how it came.

'I'm sorry you had to wait for us, there was no tram for ages and Leonard wouldn't hear of us walking to the main stop. Leonard, what's keeping you?'

'I'm just changing,' said Leonard from across the hallway. Moments later he joined them, having replaced his jacket with a sweater that Miriam had knitted for him, his tie still neatly knotted underneath. 'What's the occasion?'

'No occasion,' said Laura.

'Oh,' said Leonard, sitting down.

Miriam glanced at him as she passed out the cups and repeated how nice it was not to have to dance to Carlo Buti. When nobody joined in, she embarked upon a description of Café Cova and how busy it was and how fortunate they had been to be able to sit down. She remembered the rolls she had brought for Estella and she looked around for her bag. 'We brought you a little present,' she said.

'You did?' said Estella, her eyes lighting up. 'I love presents, how exciting!'

But when Miriam produced the two rolls from her bag, she only said 'Nice.'

'We met the English boy who's staying with the Ardittis,' said Laura, to change the subject. 'Sutton, his name is — Mamma, don't we know some Suttons? I thought Papa might have done business with them, they're in shops somewhere further north.'

'Shops?'

'I do think English boys have the most beautiful manners, I should be very happy if Teddy turned out like that. Tall too and a proper haircut, unlike all the floppy-haired Italian boys. I think Rita was rather taken with him.' This last was not true, but Laura said it anyway. 'He's not even eighteen but he was terribly self-possessed. I suppose that's what boarding school does for you.'

'I think I might take a nap,' said Estella. 'Miriam dear, give me your arm, would you? My mother, you know, used to go to bed after lunch every day and not just for a nap. She would undress and get right under the covers and it was quite forbidden for anyone, even Papi, to disturb her.' She sighed, leaning on the back of the chair and pointing a finger at her handbag so that Miriam might pass it to her. 'I never once saw her with shadows under her eyes. She was very beautiful, everyone said so.'

Leonard stirred his tea, his spoon clinking against the side of the cup. Estella shuffled out, the floorboards creaking as she went.

'She meant me,' said Laura, glancing in the long mirror that hung above the sideboard, 'that bit about the eyes.'

'You don't have shadows,' said Leonard.

'I don't know how Miriam does it,' said Laura, sighing and tracing the patterns of the damask cloth with her fingernail. 'She's so kind and sweet natured, she puts me to shame the way she is with Mamma. If she hadn't been here these last few months, I don't know what we would have done. She's wonderful with Rita too,' and she began to recount some incident but Leonard was not listening and so she stopped. He put his hand on hers.

'I've been wanting to talk to you,' he said.

'I know.'

'All you need to do is give me your dates and I'll do everything else. I've been thinking that it might help speed things up if you sign a '*bon pour pouvoir*' then I can deal with the banks as well. I asked Papa and he said there's a branch of the Comptoir de Paris in London, so it should be quite straightforward. I know you hate to think about all this, which is why you mustn't trouble yourself with it.' She had an eyelash on her cheek and he reached forwards and gently took it, showing it to her on the tip of his finger. 'Make a wish,' he said, but he blew it away before she could think of one. 'I don't mind, really I don't. It will be a relief to me to feel useful. I see Mamma and Miriam doing so much and I want to be able to do something too. You're not alone, you must see that.' She tried to speak, but he held up his hand. 'I don't want you ever to feel that you have to face the future by yourself, or that we don't share your concerns or interests. Because we do. All of us. I couldn't bear it if you thought that.'

'I don't, of course I don't,' said Laura.

Leonard nodded and waited to see if she would continue. She didn't. 'I'm sorry if I'm irritable sometimes,' he said.

'You're not.'

'It's just because I feel so helpless.'

'I understand, really.'

He nodded. 'I feel quite sure that with time,' he emphasised the word 'time', so that she shouldn't think he was rushing her, 'with time you can rebuild a new life of interest and usefulness. Even of joy.' He frowned and began stirring his tea again.

Neither spoke. After a while, Laura stood up and walked over to the window. 'I just don't know if I can do it in Manchester,' she murmured. There, she had said it.

Leonard peered at her from under his eyebrows.

'Not yet, anyway,' she said. She paused. 'Please don't be cross with me.'

'I'm not cross.' Leonard's head was lowered, as if it were suddenly too heavy. He remembered a dream he had when he was in Egypt, about Laura being ill and the doctor coming. He had seen them all so clearly and when he woke up he could not work out whether it was the lying in bed that was real or the dream. He rested his elbow on the edge of the table. 'What do you mean?' he said at last.

Laura sighed. 'My life is here.' She gazed around the room, noticing, as if for the first time, the curved backs of the chairs, the shine of the parquet, the way the gold thread in the curtains was dull in some places and brilliant in others. 'It isn't in Manchester any more, it hasn't been for a long time.'

Leonard's gaze was still on the table. 'But the house— You were happy about it, you said it was what you wanted. I don't understand what's changed.'

Laura shook her head, the permanent waves of her now short hair bending and then springing back. 'Nothing has changed,' she said, her fingers kneading at her dress. 'You know I always hated it there, those low skies, all that rain. It was bad enough when we were children, I don't know how I'd bear it now.'

'That's my home you're talking about,' said Leonard.

She looked at him in surprise, for he had spoken sharply. 'I know it is,' she murmured. 'I didn't mean—' She broke off.

'What about Mamma, have you thought how she'll feel?'

Laura rested her forehead against the cool window. 'She'll probably be relieved.' A car accelerated somewhere and she looked down. Leonard said he hardly thought so and he stood up and began pacing back and forth, his shoes squeaking on the waxed floor. She put out a hand to stop him, adding, 'You know how it gets when we spend too long together.'

'She adored Isaac.'

'I know she did.'

Leonard cleared his throat. 'We could find somewhere further out, if you preferred. Palatine Road was just a suggestion. There's no reason it shouldn't be Hale, or even Bowdon. Then you might not feel so—' What did she feel? He didn't know.

Laura pressed her hands against the window-sill, her fingers splayed. She felt the space between herself and Leonard widen still further, his incomprehension like a river forcing its way between two banks.

'This is your time now, Leonard, yours and Miriam's and this little baby's. I know how worried you've all been about me, but I've been feeling calmer recently. Really, I'm much better.'

Leonard looked around the dining room as if there were something here that he could blame. 'So are you saying you want to stay here? On the Via Elba?'

'I don't know. Rita thinks we should.' She knew if she mentioned the Carasso apartment he would get worked up about that too, and tell her what a terrible idea it was. 'In any case, we'll stay here until the summer, so they can finish school. And then we'll see.'

'Because I'm not sure Italy is the best place to be at the moment. I'm not even sure Europe's the best place, just this afternoon they announced that Hungary—'

'—please Leonard, not now.'

'But it's important. They're saying there could be war if all this Schuschnigg business gets out of hand and I'm willing to bet Mussolini will come down on Germany's side if it does.'

'Leonard, please.' She put her hands to her ears.

'I'm only saying what Isaac would have said.'

They stood in silence, neither moving, and then Laura

realised she was clutching her head and she slowly lowered her hands.

Leonard felt ashamed. 'I'm sorry.'

They stood side by side looking out over the city. The sky had darkened and one by one lights began to flicker on up and down the street. A dog barked somewhere, setting off a volley of others and elsewhere a car horn sounded. Leonard thought of something: 'What about Marco? Have you spoken to him about staying on?'

Laura shook her head. 'Not yet,' she lied.

Leonard nodded, resting a hand on his sister's narrow shoulder. She leaned against him, the wool of his sweater scratchy through her dress.

'You've done so well,' said Leonard, 'all of you, the children too.'

'Thank you.' She did not say that every morning she woke up convinced Isaac was asleep next to her and that sometimes she could even hear him breathing, so that she had to turn on the light to prove to herself he was not there. That every morning the empty pillow was a shock. Instead, she squeezed his hand and smiled and looked out over the fading rooftops like someone who cared what she saw.

'You cannot imagine how sick I am of wearing black,' she said.

A week later Leonard, Miriam and his mother left for England. In fact Estella had taken the news of Laura staying on surprisingly well and their last days at Casa Grandolini passed off without drama. At the station, of course, she was inconsolable, but by the time the train was on the outskirts of Milan, she had calmed and was looking forward to getting home. The months away had been a strain and it would be good to be back in her own bed, her own kitchen, her own world. While Miriam dozed, she and Leonard ate the supper the maid had prepared for them and made plans for the following week. Friday was Purim and she wanted to have a special dinner and thoughts of what they would eat and who they would invite absorbed them as they crossed the border into Switzerland and headed north towards France. And then Estella dozed too, her head bobbing on her chest like a brightly painted buoy on a rocking sea.

It was at Boulogne the next day, while Leonard was waiting in the sheds for their luggage, that they heard the news. An elderly woman wearing a peacock feather hat was refusing to take her suitcase from the customs table, causing much impatience amongst the other travellers. Her watery eyes and blue cheeks (which, along with the peacock feathers, suggested a lifetime riding open top cars) were set firm and she met each push of the suitcase with an equally determined shove of her own. The *douanier*, a small man with a fine widow's peak, was clearly unused to such irreverence and he began to cite the various laws and statutes of which he was a custodian. But the woman, who spoke no French, merely shook her head, pointed at the suitcase and refused to move.

Leonard, fearing they would miss their boat, stepped forward. Placing a hand on her arm, he asked in English if he might help and as if kindness were the only language she understood, she nodded and began to weep. Pointing to the chalk cross the officer had drawn on her luggage, she tried to speak, but when the words did not come she opened her handbag and handed Leonard a folded newspaper. It was in German, but the date was today's and beneath the headline a photograph of National Socialist troops marching through cheering, flower-throwing crowds. Leonard stared, disbelieving. 'Austria?' he asked. She nodded again and afterwards, when he wondered what it was to be afraid, it was this moment in the customs shed that he would think of.

'She thought it was because she's Jewish,' he said, when at last he joined the others outside. 'She thought he had chalked her suitcase because she's Jewish, that's why she wouldn't move.' He gave a hollow laugh. 'What kind of a country has she come from if she thinks like that?'

'I'm glad she made such a fuss,' said Miriam, 'even if it was about the wrong thing. At least she put up a fight. I was watching her from the door and I don't think she would ever have moved if you hadn't gone to speak to her. I'm so proud of you, we both are.' She looked at her mother-in-law.

'Dreadful hat,' said Estella.

BY THE TIME THE TRAIN ARRIVED at London Victoria late that afternoon, 'Anschluss' was the headline on every evening edition. Leonard was grey with exhaustion, having spent the journey from Dover pacing the corridor, and Miriam was not much better, for hers was a permeable nature and she could not be cheerful when Leonard was not. Only Estella showed any spirit, but that was largely because her beloved youngest son was meeting them at the station, rather than due to any greater faith in the future of Europe.

Leonard's brother Bobby was a tall, imposing man, with thick dark hair and long limbs and a face that would not have been out of place on a mediæval saint. Towering above most people, his eyes had the faraway look of someone of whom little is asked and his expression was mostly benign. That he was Estella's favourite only encouraged this, for fault or failure were unimaginable, and even striding along a crowded station platform it was clear he led a blessed life.

'There he is,' said Miriam, as Leonard heaved their suitcases off the train.

'Where, where?' said Estella. 'Where is he? I can't see him.' Leaning on her stick, she took tiny steps from side to side, as if trying to relieve each foot of the weight it was carrying.

Suddenly she saw him and she gave a squeal of delight. 'My darling boy,' she cried and as he bent to embrace her she held tight to him, patting his back with her square hands. She kept on patting, even as he pulled away, so that he was obliged to mime his kisses for the others, because he could not reach them.

'You've lost weight,' said Estella, looking him over greedily, her fingers making dents in his coat sleeves. 'I can see it in your face. I knew you wouldn't eat properly if I wasn't there, you've always been the same. I'm sure you haven't been getting enough sleep either.'

Bobby smiled. 'I have a taxi to take us to Euston,' he said, 'we should just make the last train.'

He picked up two of the suitcases, but Estella told him to put them down and sent Leonard in search of a porter. Her kisses had left smudges of lipstick on Bobby's cheek and she wet her thumb and tried to wipe it away.

'Mamma,' protested Bobby, but she pulled him towards her and continued anyway.

'Have you heard?' asked Leonard, as the porter led them along the platform. 'Isn't it awful?'

Bobby nodded, peering down at Leonard from his great height. 'I did wonder whether you would get through, a fellow said they had closed the Brenner pass.'

'The Simplon goes via Lausanne,' said Leonard. 'It doesn't go anywhere near Austria.'

'He's been like this since we left,' said Estella, looking around for her handbag, which Miriam was carrying. 'Do cheer up Leonard, we're nearly home. Is that the taxi? Tell him we're in a hurry, the last thing we need is to miss the train and be stuck in the station all night. Leonard, don't let him take my vanity case. It has everything in it and I don't want it disappearing.' She turned, offering Bobby her elbow so that he might lever her onto the back seat. 'Ah, what a relief,' she said, 'my poor feet feel as though I walked all the way from Milan.'

'I brought you plums,' said Bobby, producing a paper bag from one of his pockets. 'I didn't know if you'd have eaten.'

'Oh, you are a treasure. Not a bite since breakfast. They had lobster on the Simplon, not that we could have eaten it of course. Do you suppose they take them on alive and boil them fresh? You wouldn't think they had room in those kitchens, they're nothing more than a corridor you know.'

'They mate for life, lobsters,' said Miriam, settling herself next to Estella. 'I read about it somewhere.'

'I don't think that's correct,' said Leonard.

Estella popped a whole plum into her mouth and chewed vigorously. 'You're thinking of swans,' she said.

◆　　◆　　◆　　◆　　◆

'LOOKS LIKE FRANCE IS GETTING a new government,' said Leonard. He had bought a newspaper at the station and stood reading it in the doorway of the compartment while Estella fussed about where to sit.

'I feel sick if I sit backwards,' she muttered, piling Leonard with her things and gesturing towards the overhead rack. 'Miriam, take off your coat, you'll be roasted if you keep it on. Bobby, you'd better sit in the middle so you can stretch your legs out. Do hurry, Leonard, people are trying to get past.'

'Chamberlain has asked for a meeting with Mussolini,' said Leonard, continuing to read. 'As if that will make any difference.' He pushed his mother's coat onto the rack above their heads.

'And Miriam's, put hers up too.'

Miriam passed him her coat, smiling apologetically, then squeezed in next to the window. Bobby, his hands folded peacefully in his lap, glanced at her rounded stomach.

'Not long now,' she said.

'I was twice her size with you three,' frowned Estella. 'I keep telling her, you don't eat.'

'I do eat.'

'Mamma's right,' said Leonard, looking up from his paper. 'You don't look after yourself.'

'I think you're perfect,' said Bobby, sitting back.

Miriam smiled weakly and turned to look out of the window.

'Are you still known as Darling Miriam?' asked Bobby, while his mother continued to give orders to Leonard. 'That's what Teddy calls you, isn't it? Darling Miriam?'

Miriam laughed and her reflection in the dark window laughed too. 'Yes!' she said. 'Golly, I shall miss being Darling Miriam now we're home. Do you remember the first time they called me that, Leonard?' He nodded. 'I was so nervous about meeting Laura and Leonard kept telling me to calm down, because when I'm nervous I get so red and he wanted me to look pretty. But the more he told me to calm down, the more nervous I was and the redder I got too—' She glanced at Estella who was straightening her rings and looking around.

'And then this little blonde boy came running out of the house and flung himself into my arms, saying, 'Are you Darling Miriam?' Because that's what Leonard always called me. 'Are you Darling Miriam?' And after that I wasn't nervous anymore—'

'Can we get a cup of tea on this train?' said Estella, leaning over and interrupting her. 'Leonard, do go and see.'

Leonard looked up from his paper. 'Jews are being forced to scrub the streets in Vienna,' he said. 'Doctors and professors, old people.'

Everyone glanced at him, and Miriam, placing a hand on his arm, said: 'Don't read it darling, it will only upset you.'

'Upset me?'

'I just meant—'

'—don't get excited, Leonard,' said Estella, frowning and peering at her daughter-in-law.

Leonard shook the newspaper. 'Don't you see what this means?' He looked from one to the other. 'Next it will be Czechoslovakia. Then Poland. Then what?' He shook the newspaper once again and stared at it, as if expecting the words to drop into his lap.

Miriam's eyes widened and she looked down. 'Leonard, I'm sorry,' she whispered, but he did not reply. For a long time nobody spoke, then Estella sat forwards.

'I thought you were going to get tea,' she said.

CHAPTER 12

It was after ten when the taxi pulled onto Moorfield Road and Estella was the only one awake, the plums having upset her stomach since Crewe. Peering out at the dark street, she instructed the driver to stop at the second lamppost on the right, then poked Leonard with her travelling stick and sat back, waiting for someone to open the door. When they didn't, for Leonard was gently waking Miriam and Bobby was still fast asleep, she rolled forwards and rapped on the window. 'I thought you were going to leave me in there all night,' she declared, leaning on the driver's arm as she climbed out, so that he took a step backwards to steady himself. She rearranged her handbag on her elbow and shuffled towards the gate, breathing heavily and concentrating upon each footstep as if making her way along a ravine. Just as she reached the step, a light came on in the porch and the front door was flung open.

'Did you forget us?' Estella said, seeing the familiar shape of her husband. Her tone was sharp but years of marriage had taught him not to take it personally.

'My dears, how I've missed you all,' the man declared, for he always spoke in plurals to his wife. He bent to embrace her but instead she clutched his arm and used him to get herself up the step. Then she turned, put a hand on either side of his face and kissed him with her damp, red mouth. 'They're all asleep. We'd have ended up in Stockport if I hadn't been watching.' And she peered into the hallway and sighed with contentment. Home.

Solomon Cansino hurried down the path to pay the taxi,

his kind voice booming greetings and provoking several lights to turn on and off in neighbouring houses. 'My dear child,' he said, as Miriam offered him her cheek, but he didn't stop to kiss her and instead turned to the driver, taking a gold money clip from his pocket and counting out the notes. 'That's fine,' he said, and Leonard, who had calculated the correct amount to tip, frowned and whispered that it was too much.

'Now let me look at you,' said Solomon, holding Miriam's shoulders. His eyebrows made two perfect arches and his eyes were dark and narrow. 'I hope you're looking after that grandchild of mine,' he said, his smile hidden beneath the droop of his moustache, 'because we're very much looking forward to his arrival. Hurry up inside, this is not a night to be standing on the street. Pick up those bags, Leonard. I've put the heating on in your room so it should be nice and warm for you. This house has been terribly quiet without you all, Bobby and I have been lost, just the two of us. Is this your mother's bag? Go ahead, Miriam, go ahead, you look dead on your feet. Mrs Perkins has left a tray for you all in the dining room, we didn't know if you would have eaten. Ah, that's better, Bobby.'

Bobby had turned on the lamps, the familiar sight of the green walls, the orange and brown tiled floor, the coat rack with its row of trilbies and raincoats, leaping into view.

'We're famished,' announced Estella. She paused to run her finger along the picture rail, peering at it.

'I think I might go straight up and start unpacking,' said Miriam, 'do you mind?' Tiredness had caused all her features to shrink and she looked pinched and disagreeable.

'Why don't you have a bite first, it will make you feel better,' said Leonard. He had imagined their return so many times and never once had it involved Miriam going straight to bed. 'Papa will be wanting to hear all our news, he's been waiting up for us.'

'Let the poor girl go up, Leonard,' said his father.

'Besides, I thought we could catch up on business, I had Marco Balestra on the telephone this morning, he said he might have someone for our cotton poplins. I didn't know you'd been talking to the Balestras, I was surprised to hear from him.'

'He called on Shabbat?' Estella said, clicking her tongue. 'Only Marco Balestra would call on Shabbat.'

'I wouldn't have picked up except I was worried it was you. Move aside there, Bobby, you're in everyone's way.'

'How odd,' said Leonard. 'I saw Marco in Milan but we didn't talk about the poplins. Perhaps Laura said something.'

'Well he's offering very generous terms and of course it's no bad thing to stay in with men like Marco Balestra, especially in times like these. We had quite a chat, I'd forgotten what an interesting fellow he is. Leonard, bring everything in here, I've lit a fire. I told him he was quite right to be closing that Milan office too, I can't see why anyone would stay in Italy these days. Sit down by the fire there, Miriam, you look chilled to the bone.'

'Have you been listening to the radio?' asked Leonard, watching as Miriam sat down.

'Terrible,' said Solomon. 'Just awful.'

'They're making old men scrub the streets,' said Leonard, because he couldn't help himself.

Solomon scratched his ears, which were small and rather delicate, then smoothed what was left of his thinning hair. 'Terrible,' he said again.

Bobby was standing in the doorway, his head bent so as not to bang it on the frame. 'Is Miriam not staying?' he joked, for she was still wearing her coat and hat. 'Leonard, take your poor wife's things.'

Miriam unbuttoned her coat.

'You look better already,' said Leonard, seeing the colour in her cheeks. He lifted the edge of the damp tea towel which was covering the tray of sandwiches, then lowered it again, without revealing what was underneath. 'Should we wait for Mamma? What is she doing?'

'I'll go see,' said Bobby.

Leonard picked up a book that was lying on the table and turned it over to read the title. It was a biography of Bismarck, not something he would have expected to find his father reading. 'Any good?' he asked.

Solomon nodded and began to talk about the book in such a way that it was clear that he had said the same thing many times over.

Leonard put it down. 'Sounds like propaganda to me,' he said, rolling the "r" of 'propaganda'.

And Solomon, who always deferred to his son in such matters — what else was the point of an expensive English education? — agreed that perhaps it was. 'Come on then,' he said, sitting down at the dining table and beckoning with his forefinger, darkened from the cigars he smoked, towards the briefcase Leonard was holding. 'Let's have a look at what you have been up to.'

'Oh Papa, surely it can wait until tomorrow,' said Bobby, who had come back in carrying a teapot. He looked around for somewhere to put it, eventually setting it on top of the Bismarck book. 'Poor Leonard is barely through the door.'

Leonard glanced at him with gratitude. 'I can go through it all with you tomorrow, Papa,' he said.

'Yes, yes,' said Solomon. 'But let me just have a quick look now. While we're waiting for your mother.' He watched as Leonard opened the briefcase. 'Give me the whole lot,' he muttered and he reached across and took the pile of papers from Leonard. He tapped them on the table, squared the corners and then began to go through each page, one by one. Leonard moved to stand by his shoulder, leaning in to offer explanations, pointing at details, but his father pushed him away. 'I can read for myself,' he said.

Leonard frowned. It reminded him of when his father would go through his school report with a red pen, underlining anything that was less than perfect. 'Is Mamma coming?' he asked Bobby, who shrugged and went out again.

'What's this?' asked Solomon, holding up a piece of paper.

'It's an option, Papa, with a new mill that's opened in Cairo. Uncle advised me to go and see them, he thought it might be useful.'

'You would do well not to listen to too much advice from the family, our interests are not always the same.'

Leonard nodded. He had never discovered the precise nature of the rift between Solomon and his only brother, but he knew better than to challenge it. He watched as his father continued to leaf through the papers, feeling aggrieved. He had worked so hard all those weeks in Egypt, it wasn't his fault nobody was buying fabric these days.

'She's on her way.' Bobby set down a jug of milk next to the teapot. 'Mrs Briggs was at the fence and they've been catching up. According to Mr Briggs — he works at the Town Hall, do you remember him Leonard? — if Hitler bombed Britain tomorrow there would be six hundred thousand people dead and as many injured.' Miriam gave a gasp. 'Not that they think he's going to,' he added cheerfully, sitting down opposite her and crossing his ankles. 'But if he did apparently you can expect fifty casualties for every ton of bombs dropped. Is a ton a lot?' He glanced at his father, but Solomon was still reading and paid him no attention. 'Oh, and the water heater's been on all afternoon, the daily forgot about it, so if anyone wants a bath they should have one now, because Mamma's turning it off.'

Leonard had moved to stand behind Miriam, his hands resting protectively on the back of her chair. She looked up at him, her face flushed. 'Go on,' he said, 'while the water's still hot.'

'Do you mind?'

He shook his head. And then, as is often the case, because her anxieties echoed his own, he became irritated and when he helped her to her feet, there was something rough and unkind in the gesture.

'Well, at least there's nothing binding,' said Solomon, sitting back and pushing the pile of papers across the table. He stretched out his arms, lacing his fingers and turning his hands so that the joints cracked. 'I think we should book your crossing sooner,' he said, turning to Bobby, 'we can't leave things like this.'

Leonard was silent, but a pained expression had come over his face and he seemed to be struggling with something. His father looked at him.

'There's no need to get upset about it, you did your best.'

Leonard nodded and stared at a spot on the fireplace that seemed to require his full attention. His chest felt tight with injustice and he wanted to explain to his father how difficult things had been, and how hard he had worked for even these smallest of victories. 'The general elections there have everyone unsettled,' he murmured, 'nobody dares make any kind of commitment, even the small shirt-makers are holding off.'

Bobby grinned. 'Who was it who thought when you said 'small shirt-makers' that it meant they were dwarfs? Was it Coco?'

'And there was the Bairam festival too, that didn't help matters. I wrote to you about how difficult things were, Papa, even the agents didn't think there was much point going around, but I went anyway.'

'It was Coco, I'm certain,' said Bobby, turning as his mother shuffled in with another teapot, hot water splashing out of the spout as she sat down. 'Do you remember that Mamma, when Coco thought the small shirt makers were all dwarfs?'

'I don't remember,' said Estella. She looked around. 'Did she go up?'

'Miriam? Yes.'

'She needs to eat more, she's skin and bone.' She pulled the cloth from the sandwiches and helped herself.

'I'll get some plates,' said Leonard, watching his mother push one of the sandwiches into her mouth, her thick fingers with their heavy rings suddenly revolting to him. He picked up the papers and pushed them back into his briefcase, frowning. Why was it he never remembered any of this? All those weeks struggling around Cairo in tight shoes, it had been the thought of coming home that had sustained him, had enabled him to go out again in the blistering sun and knock at yet another door. And for what? To be told it wasn't enough, that Bobby would need to be dispatched to sort things out. His resentment was in direct proportion to his earlier enthusiasm and it overwhelmed him, so that even walking out of the room looked like an act of violence.

'What's the matter with him?' he heard Estella ask, as he went down the hall. He slammed the kitchen door behind him and stood glowering on the red and white linoleum. Laura was right to stay away, he saw that now, and the weight of this revelation overwhelmed him so that he had to lean on the countertop to steady himself. He remembered how she had clutched at her head that afternoon in the dining room and how irritated he had been with her, because it seemed so dramatic and unnecessary. And yet here he was clinging to the kitchen cupboards like a man on a sinking ship.

The door to the kitchen opened slowly. It was Bobby.

'I can take them,' he said. 'The plates.' And he nodded to the shelf.

Leonard straightened up. 'I was just coming.' He stood back to let him past.

'Don't mind Papa,' said Bobby, 'you know how he is about the business, he's always been the same.'

'The business is our responsibility too. I don't think he realises how hard things are right now.'

Bobby nodded, and for a moment neither of them spoke.

'Don't you ever wonder what the point of it all is?' asked Leonard at last, moving towards the window and gazing out at the garden. 'Every day is a struggle and for what?' His eyes ranged over the knick-knacks and dusty cactus plants that cluttered the sill. Bobby stared at him blankly.

'I thought about it a lot while I was away. I watched all those men like Marco Balestra and I realised that in order to succeed in this life, you have to be a certain type. I saw them driving around in their big cars, or sitting in their clubs, and I realised that they were all the same, these men. There's a coarseness about them — perhaps "coarse" is the wrong word — a lack of refinement. They don't care about the things other people care about: a beautiful sunrise, a kind word. That sort of thing means nothing to them.'

He turned and looked expectantly at his brother.

'I thought you liked Marco Balestra,' said Bobby.

'I do.' Leonard searched his brother's face for something to suggest that he understood, but although it was a pleasant face and one he loved, he did not find what he was looking for. Above their heads, the boiler began to clank and Leonard raised his eyes, listening to the rush of water through the pipes as Miriam ran her bath. He sighed. 'Ignore me, I'm tired.'

'It's been a long day,' agreed Bobby.

'It has.' Leonard looked at his younger brother. 'You should take those plates.'

'Yes,' said Bobby, surprised to find he was still holding them. 'Will you take Miriam something up? She looked worn out.'

Leonard nodded.

In the dining room Solomon was explaining about propaganda in the Bismarck book.

CHAPTER 13

Upstairs, Miriam shivered. The daily had left the window open to air the room and the curtains billowed and sucked like a mainsail in a high wind. She quickly closed it and drew the cold, damp curtains, bending to touch the radiator which was hot. She switched on the light and then switched it off again and turned on the bedside lamps. Gradually the room became familiar: the chenille bedspread her parents had given them, the armchair with the tear in the seat that she hid with a cushion, the piles of Leonard's books, the dressing table that had been her grandmother's, with its bevelled mirrors and rose-papered drawers, the cast-iron fireplace surrounded by pink and yellow tiles. She sat down at the small stool she used to do her makeup and considered it all. It seemed impossible that she should have been away six months, for nothing had changed. It was all just as it had been before.

Miriam put her handbag on the dressing table and opened it. She took out her cosmetic purse and emptied it into one of the drawers; then she took her travelling scent, which she sprayed two or three times, and added it to the drawer. At the bottom of her bag were the keys for the suitcases, which she left there so that Leonard would know where to find them when he brought everything upstairs. She removed the pins and combs from her hair and shook it out, and then unbuttoned her dress and laid it on the edge of the bed. She took her favourite red flannel dressing gown from the back of the door, where it had hung all these months (she could never have worn red flannel in Milan) and put it on. It barely fitted her, but she knotted the belt anyway and then sat down on the bed to wait for the bath to fill.

As usual there was a pile of books on Leonard's bedside table, and she leaned forward to read the titles. There was his school edition of *The Iliad*, that he liked to read aloud to her sometimes; a collection of short stories by Somerset Maugham; several titles in French; a battered edition of *The Seven Pillars of Wisdom* that probably belonged to Bobby; and a Russian novel, *On the Eve*, whose pages had not yet been cut. Miriam smiled to herself, she liked that she had married a man who was so well read.

Downstairs she heard Estella shouting and she tried to listen, but the roar of the water tank in the roof and the hiss of the taps and the banging of a door somewhere prevented her. It would take a while to relearn the noises of this house: no cars constantly speeding past, no gramophone blasting out at all hours, nor the Chopin that Laura played when she was feeling sad, which was often. She wondered what they were doing right at this moment, Laura and the children, and she sat for a moment, gazing at the chintz curtains. Then she stood up and went to turn off the taps.

'AM I LIKE THEM?' ASKED Leonard, sitting on the bed facing Miriam. She was pink from her bath and he thought he had never seen her look so pretty.

'What do you mean?'

'Am I like my family?' asked Leonard again. 'Sometimes I feel as though I've nothing in common with any of them. And then other times, and this is worse, I feel I'm just the same.'

'Everyone feels like that,' said Miriam, bending her knees and pushing her legs under the covers. She tugged at the bedspread with her free hand, but it had been tucked in too tightly and would not move.

'Do they?'

She nodded. 'I find it reassuring. How dreadful would it be if you couldn't recognise yourself in the people you love, if you didn't catch little glimpses every so often of where you were going, or what you had been. I read something in one of my magazines the other day about how women think that the worse insult in the world is to be compared to their mother. Don't you find that sad? I do. I should be happy if someone told me I was like Mother.'

Leonard thought about this. Or rather, he thought about his mother-in-law, a cold, distant woman who, because she worried that the Cansinos thought Miriam wasn't good enough, had treated Leonard with disdain from the moment they met. That his wife was the happy, affectionate, uncomplicated creature that she was remained a wonder to him.

'Besides, how disappointed will you be if you can't see any of yourself in our baby? I know I will. I have it all thought out, you know. He'll have your eyes and mouth, and my hair.' She played with the fringe of the bedspread, twisting it around her fingers. 'And my skin too, because when we take him on all those wonderful trips, I don't want him to burn like you do and always have to stay inside or worry about wearing hats.' Leonard put his hand on hers to stop her twiddling. Miriam continued: 'And he'll have your intelligence and your kindness, mixed with just a little of my determination, because that way nothing will feel impossible. And he'll be sensitive, but not too sensitive (she did not need to say to whom this quality belonged) because he'll need to be robust in this world we've chosen for him. It won't do to take things too much to heart.'

She looked steadily at Leonard, but he avoided her gaze and began slowly to unlace his shoes. 'As I do,' he murmured, taking first one shoe, then the other, and placing them side by side on the rug.

'It's not a fault,' she said. 'In fact it's the thing I love most about you, I always have. But it's hard for you to feel things so deeply all the time and I wish life felt easier on occasion. For your own sake.' He sighed and she pressed his hand. 'Pass me my knitting, will you. I might as well do a bit to get me sleepy.'

Leonard looked around for her bag. He liked it when she knitted, for there was something very calming about the clack of the needles and she had a stillness that she didn't have at other times. Of course, now she was making things for the baby, there was a kind of magic about it too, as if she were knitting the fabric of their own small family. He had said this once, comparing her to the girl in Rumpelstiltskin, who spins straw into gold, but Miriam had laughed and said it was just a wool angora mix.

'I promised Mamma I'd lock up, do you want anything while I'm down there?'

She shook her head. 'Did you see how big that room looks without the piano? Baby will be perfect in there now, there's plenty of space for a crib and a little chest of drawers. I thought I'd put the rocking chair my parents gave us in there too, so I can feed him at night and won't wake you up.'

'I want you to wake me up. We're going to do this together, Miriam, I've told you.' He paused. 'I have no memories of Papa, you know, from when I was small, only of Mamma and the nannies.' The Cansino family albums were full of photographs of the three children and a variety of uniformed, miserable-looking young women. 'We knew that he loved us, but he just wasn't there very much. Not like Isaac was.' He thought for a moment, reflecting upon this. 'They'll be all right, you know, those kiddies. They couldn't have had a better start, I want it to be like that for our baby too.'

Miriam nodded, remembering something Laura had said to her in Milan. It had been one of her bad days and she had said how nothing we do really matters because sooner or later life shows its claws. That's what she had said. Life shows its claws.

When Miriam repeated it to Leonard, he said it was a quote from some Russian writer, she forgot whom. But the point was, it was true. Life *had* shown its claws: Isaac had died.

'What are you thinking about?' asked Leonard, for she had that faraway look she sometimes got now.

'I keep expecting to hear that record playing,' she said. She began to hum it quietly.

'That's the trouble with gramophones,' said Leonard, 'the same thing gets played over and over.'

'It was Teddy who liked it most,' said Miriam. 'Did you know it's about waiting for someone.'

'Of course. *Tornerai*, "Come back".'

'Oh. Well I didn't, it was Mamma who told me. After that, I always wanted to cry when I heard it, it was as if it had been written for those poor children, waiting for their father to come back.' She blinked and dabbed at her eyes with the belt of her dressing gown. 'Sorry,' she said, for she knew he hated it when she got upset.

Leonard leaned forwards and kissed her cheek. Then he stood up and went downstairs to lock the doors.

CHAPTER 14

By the end of the next day, which was Sunday, Austria had been neatly absorbed into the German Reich. Hitler was headed for Vienna to give his victory speech and Europe, most were saying, was headed for war. All eyes were on Czechoslovakia, generally agreed to be the next victim, and there was the usual polite debate as to who should do what and when. In France, Leon Blum was Prime Minister again and in Russia, Stalin enjoyed the last of his show trials and then sanctioned a Commissariat speech demanding greater cooperation in Europe. In England, the Archbishop of Canterbury gave thanks for peace.

And on Moorfield Road they read the weekend papers and listened to the wireless and agreed that there was nothing for it but that Laura and the children should come home. Estella railed at her daughter's stubbornness while Leonard sent telegrams and checked train times and Bobby and Miriam were dispatched to Palatine Road to see about that house. Only Solomon showed any kind of dissent, but he had always had a soft spot where his daughter was concerned, and telling her what to do did not come easily. 'Just leave it a few days, see if things settle down,' he suggested, before returning his attentions to the contents of Leonard's briefcase. 'I'm sure Laura will have her own thoughts about it all.'

But Laura's thoughts, as it turned out, were not required, for barely had it begun than the war scare was over. No one thought it was worth fighting for Austria. And with the exception of a few far-sighted individuals, Europe went back to doing what it did best: that is, sucking teeth and furrowing brows and putting extra guards on those much fought-for frontiers.

At the end of spring, Laura finally made up her mind to go to Brussels and she wrote to Solomon at his office to tell him this. She mentioned the business and the cousins and the familiarity of this city that she loved and made much of the new KLM flight routes and how easy it would be for her and the children to visit. She told him she was applying for a Belgian visa and how she had written to the Ministero dell'Interno, who in turn had written to the Consulat de Grèce (she had taken her husband's nationality when she married), who forwarded it to the Consulat Général de Belgique, who passed it on to the Ministère des Affaires Etrangères, who wrote back to the Consulat de Grèce, who then sent everything to the Ministero dell'Interno. She told him she was sure that moving back to Brussels was the right thing to do and how excited she was about the apartment on the Avenue des Nations, which was just the kind of place Isaac would have chosen. And she promised that if ever the international situation looked worrying again, she would come straight to Moorfield Road, because she knew how Mamma worried. All this she wanted her father to explain to the others, as it would be better in his words, and she asked that he tear up her letter and throw it away. But Solomon could never throw away anything Laura gave him, so he put it in a drawer instead.

◆　　◆　　◆　　◆　　◆

LEONARD HAD SET UP SOME chairs at the end of the garden, and he and Miriam were sitting out in their thickest coats drinking tea and flicking through a French rose catalogue he had sent for. Now things had calmed down, he had decided to stop worrying about Laura and the business and all the other matters he could do nothing about, and instead concentrate on enjoying a summer of peace and quiet in their own backyard. He had never much cared for gardening and certainly had no knowledge about it, but the catalogue had colour illustrations and it was difficult not to get carried away.

'Listen to these names,' he said to Miriam, sitting huddled beside him, '*Gloire de Chédanne Guinoisseau, Ville de Paris, Reveil Dijonnais, Marie-Louise Poucet,* aren't they wonderful? Only the French would give plants such romantic names, it makes you want to buy every single one. Look at the colour of this one,' and he held out the catalogue, 'what would you say it was?'

'It says '*orange-rouge*',' said Miriam, pointing at the text. 'Even I can understand that. Look, that one's called President Hoover.'

'*Président 'Oover,*' Leonard corrected and they both laughed.

'Why don't you order some?' said Miriam. 'It would be nice to have a bit of colour and we'll spend much more time out here once the baby arrives. That one maybe,' and she pointed at the photograph of *Ville de Paris.* 'I love yellow in a garden, it's so cheery.'

'It says they're *racines nues,*' said Leonard, reading the print at the bottom of the page, 'and that they're best planted during winter.'

Miriam nodded. 'I was thinking we might have a go at planting some vegetables too. What do you think? I've always wanted a kitchen garden, do you think anyone would mind if we put in a few potatoes? I know Dad would help us if we needed.'

'But isn't it just as easy to buy them?'

'Yes, but it's not the same.'

'So long as you don't expect me to do all the digging.'

Miriam indulged him. 'I'll dig, you just have to eat them. Although I might wait until this little man makes his appearance before I start. I'm getting to the point where even walking up the stairs feels like a day's work. He'd better appreciate all this trouble he's put me to when he arrives.'

She bent to pick up the rose catalogue Leonard had dropped and began flicking through it.

'Why do you always say 'he'? It might be a girl, you know. I don't want you to be disappointed if you have set your heart on a boy. You know that I don't mind what we have, don't you?'

Miriam thought about this. 'I don't know. I suppose I just have this feeling that it's a boy. But I don't mind if I'm wrong. Ten fingers and ten toes, that's what Mother always says.' She held out her own small hands as if in proof of this.

'You are clever,' said Leonard.

'I know you're teasing, but actually, it is clever when you think about it. Just one tiny mistake, one less toe, say, and straight away life is hard. There was a girl at school with an extra finger and that's all anyone ever knew about her.'

'Fewer,' said Leonard, 'one fewer toe.' He thought about this. 'One toe fewer. And actually I wasn't teasing, you are clever, you're growing life.'

'Potatoes are life too,' remarked Miriam. She rested her cup and saucer on her stomach. 'Roses not so much. But they are pretty. Do you remember that one we saw in Ullswater?' She meant on their honeymoon, which they had spent in the Lake District. 'It went all the way up the front of the house and onto the roof. And the smell, it was like when those women in Kendals catch you with their perfume sprays.'

Leonard preferred 'scent' but restrained himself from saying so.

'With their scent sprays,' said Miriam, as if she had read his mind. She leaned her head on the back of the chair and gazed upwards. She loved this time of day, when the shadows were lengthening and the chimneypots began to merge with the sky. She watched as a bird flicked and swooped in the eaves, its underside flashing white as it turned. 'The swallows are back,' she said, 'it's officially spring, look how beautiful he is,' and she followed it with her finger, drawing circles in the chilly air.

'Are you frozen?' asked Leonard, leaning over and tugging at her coat. She shook her head, but he took off his scarf anyway and arranged it around her neck. It wouldn't do for her to catch cold. She smiled and sunk her chin into her collar to show she appreciated it.

'We could grow carrots too, and perhaps some beetroots. Now is the time to start sowing seed. Dad always says by the time the swallows are back you should have your first rows in. There's nothing like a carrot eaten straight from the ground, it doesn't taste anything like a shop one. Do you really think they wouldn't mind?' and she glanced at the blank windows of the house. 'We could just do a strip along the fence, you'd barely see it.'

'I thought you weren't going to be digging until after the baby arrived.'

'Seed is different. I've watched Dad do it lots of times, all I'll need to do is pull up a few of the weeds and work it over with a trowel. It will give me something to do, I was so busy in Milan I'm going to be bored now my time's my own.'

Leonard smiled. 'It would do you good to be bored,' he said, picking up the rose catalogue and flicking through it again. 'No *Ville de Paris* then?'

'We could have both,' said Miriam. 'Like the French do. What's that chateau that Laura visited a few years ago? Rita was showing me her photographs from the trip and it had the most beautiful gardens you've ever seen. They had everything mixed looking tidy. I was surprised that Rita had taken pictures of the gardens at all, but she said it was because Teddy wanted a photograph of a particular butterfly. Anything with wings, that boy.'

'Chenonceau,' said Leonard.

'That's it.'

'We'll go there one day, I've always wanted to take you to France. There are boats that go along the river and you stop at all the different chateaux, imagine how romantic that must be. Perhaps next summer, when the baby's old enough to travel. We'll start in Paris and then drive south towards the Loire. And we won't hurry, we'll take our time, I don't want people to think we're cheap tourists.'

'Well, get you,' said Miriam, smiling. 'I should be happy to be considered any type of tourist.' And she leaned across and kissed his forehead, to show she was joking.

'We have so much to look forward to,' said Leonard after a moment.

Miriam agreed. 'I do feel bad about Bobby though,' she said.

'Bobby?'

'Going off to Egypt. It's because of us, isn't it, because of the baby?' She curved her arms protectively around her stomach. 'Mamma's so upset about him going, I heard her arguing with Papa this morning, she's worried the climate will be bad for his health. She said he gets attacks of asthma in hot weather, I didn't know he had asthma.'

Leonard frowned and she saw that he had lost his dreamy expression and was annoyed. 'Why shouldn't he go just this once? It's about time Bobby did something for the business, he's been tied to Mamma's apron strings long enough.'

'I should hate it if it made him ill though.'

'Of course it won't make him ill. That's just an excuse Mamma makes so Papa will keep him at home. She's always pretended he's the fragile, sickly one, which is ridiculous when you look at the size of him. No, it's about time someone else took some responsibility, Papa understands that, it's why he's sending him.' He shrugged. 'It's not as if he doesn't benefit from the business too. Or will do if things ever improve.'

Miriam nodded. 'In any case, I'm happy you're not

going, even if it means Bobby must. I don't think I could have borne it if you had to go away again, I miss you so terribly.' She shrugged. 'It's silly really.'

'No it isn't,' said Leonard. He sat up and took both Miriam's hands in his. Even in her gloves they were icy cold and he cupped them inside his own and blew on them. 'Let's go inside,' he said, starting to get up.

'You go ahead,' said Miriam, for the sky was a deep navy blue now and she wanted to watch the last bits of light disappear. Leonard sat down again, still holding her hands. 'I don't think I ever saw a single star in Milan, you know. Why is that? There was always the moon and Teddy said he could see Venus and Jupiter too. But no stars.'

'It's because of the street lamps, they make the sky glow. It's always the same in big cities.'

'I thought maybe they had disappeared everywhere.' She looked at him, her eyes pink-rimmed with cold. 'I'm glad they haven't.' And she shuffled her hips and edged lower in the wicker chair so that she might look up at the sky without cricking her neck. Leonard moved his chair so that it was alongside hers and did the same.

'You are sweet,' he said, turning up his collar and glancing at her still, watchful face.

Miriam continued to watch the silent sky until the garden was in darkness.

CHAPTER 15

At the end of April, Bobby left for Egypt. After the inevitable scene on the docks at Liverpool, with Estella weeping loudly and his father repeatedly listing the offices he required him to visit, his cabin below the main deck had been a welcome reprieve. The first leg of the crossing was rough, with a gale off the coast of Ireland spreading misery amongst the passengers, and it was not until they rounded Cape St Vincent that the weather improved and the usual idle pleasures could be enjoyed. It had been almost ten years since Bobby last visited the family in Alexandria, his trip coinciding with the stock market crash of '29, and that he was somehow responsible for the loss of the family fortune was a feeling he had never quite overcome.

The sea was flat and the sun high in the sky as the steamer moved slowly past the breakwater at the entrance to the Western Harbour. Bobby leaned over the railings, his chin on his hands, and gazed across the water towards the promontory of Ras-el-Tin, where Menelaus had enchained Phaetos and demanded to know the future. Kicking his foot against the painted railing, he narrowed his eyes and watched as sailing boats fluttered like cabbage whites along the yellow coast, their careless patterns interrupted by two hulking British warships, testament to the protective nature of Anglo-Egyptian relations. Fig trees ranged along the steep cliffs and in their midst, a vast stucco palace that spread a little further each year, like a wedding cake slowly melting in the sun. Beside him on the deck, a young couple with a shared Baedeker read loudly to one another, their eyes shaded against the brilliant sun. Listening to them, he discovered that the harbour's original name was *Eunostos*, or Harbour of Safe Return, and he liked this idea and smiled. (He also learned that, after cotton, Egypt's chief exports were grain, cotton-seed, beans, rice, sugar, onions and tomatoes.)

Bobby sank a little lower over the railing and closed his eyes, remembering the last time he had sailed into this harbour. How different he was then, with his schoolboy edition of Homer and his conviction, like Alexander, that he was about to conquer the world. Instead, he had spent his days babysitting his younger cousins and his nights, alone, at the open air cinema. And when he tried to seek out all those places he had read about: the Mouseion, the Library, the Soma, he found they existed only in history books. In their stead were tea salons and gentlemen's clubs and showrooms for the latest models of Fiat or Rolls Royce (the only cars thought suitable for desert roads). Once, he had begged his aunties to take him to Lake Mariout to see where Cleopatra had sailed her barge, but they said it was only worth going when the date caravans were there, and they took him for tea at Claridge's instead. There, over cream cakes and lemonade, he listened to the men talk cotton prices and the women gossip, and it seemed clear that the spirit of antiquity was well and truly lost.

The couple with the Baedeker were trying to remember the name of the King, and Bobby twisted his long neck and told them, 'Farouk. It's Farouk.'

'Not Fuad?' said the man, who was wearing white linen and a straw panama, as was his wife. He glanced at the front of his Baedeker and frowned, since it was dated 1929.

'Fuad was the father,' said Bobby. 'He died last year. Or perhaps it was the year before.'

'Oh yes, of course!' said the wife, with surprising enthusiasm. 'I remember now. And the Queen gave all his clothes to the rag-and-bone man, to pay him back for keeping her shut up in the palace all those years. I love that story.'

Bobby grinned and turned back to the view. Now they were closer to the port, the horizon danced with the thin, slanted silhouettes of feluccas. One or two came close to the sides of the steamer and Bobby could peer down at the rounded bales of cotton, tightly bound in brown hessian. But just as lazily as they drifted in, they seemed to slip away again and the men who sailed them, their faces hidden from view, never even looked up.

'We're staying at the Cecil,' said the woman, not ready to relinquish this first Egyptian acquaintance. 'We're doing the whole tour, Cairo, Luxor, then down to Khartoum. It's our honeymoon, that's why we're a little later than they recommend.' She gestured to the Baedeker. 'In the end we plumped for better weather in Wiltshire. It was Easter weekend, just perfect, and said we'd take our chances here.' She glanced up at the perfect blue sky. 'I think we did the right thing. Are you at the Cecil too? We could share a cab if you like?'

Bobby shook his head. 'I'm staying with family,' he said.

'With family? How nice,' she said, 'I always prefer to stay with people if possible. Hotel life is such a bore. But we don't know a soul in Africa, so we have no choice and must make do with our dear friend Karl.' She glanced at her husband and they both laughed. 'The other man in my marriage,' she said with a wink.

'Mr Baedeker,' said the husband.

'Oh,' said Bobby.

The docks of the Western Harbour were crowded with people and Bobby searched for a familiar face amongst the waving, shouting masses. Barefoot porters wove in and out, while officials in blazers and English ties stood motionless and important. Young boys with hairless chests, glossy like seals, appeared in the strip of water between the ship and the dockside, and immediately coins began to rain down and the boys, hands outstretched, disappeared beneath the surface. Over the Tannoy, an imperious voice asked that passengers not encourage the locals.

Seeing no-one he recognised, Bobby walked slowly towards the steps, where people were beginning to disembark. In amongst all that pale linen, his navy pinstripe suit seemed strangely formal, but he was used to being conspicuous and paid no attention to the curious looks. Leaning backwards as he walked down the long ramp with its flat rungs, he smiled serenely, happy to be in this warm, brightly coloured place. He no longer searched the crowd for his uncle but instead enjoyed how the light shone through the canvas sides of the gangway, and how his heels clinked on the smooth wood, and the way the woman in front of him held onto the side of her straw hat as if she expected a sudden wind to cast it from her head, when in fact the air was still. To his left, a man in a fez sat sideways on a chair, twisting slightly as if hiding something, and Bobby saw that it was a tiny monkey, its pink face dull and unresponsive. An official appeared and flapped his hands, and the man, his skin like oiled leather, picked up his chair and moved away, immediately setting it down on the other side of the ramp and assuming the same twisted position. Several other men, their heads wrapped and their feet dusty, followed him, for it seemed they had nothing else to do.

At the end of the ramp, Bobby paused. The crowd had already thinned out and the long line of cars and gharries were rapidly disappearing. He saw the couple from the deck hurrying away after a boy in a braided yellow uniform, the orange guidebook still held aloft, and he felt a twinge of dismay as he watched them go. But before he could wonder whether he should follow, he heard his name and he turned to see an elegant, fair-skinned European woman striding towards him, wearing a wide brimmed hat with a red ribbon, which she tipped to one side as she embraced him.

'There you are!' she said and her smile, for which she was renowned, lit up her face. 'We were wondering where you'd got to.'

'We', it turned out, was Estella's four sisters and their families, who were lined up in front of three open top cars on the far side of the dock. Bobby grinned submissively as they surged forwards, taking turns to cup his face in their hands and pat his long arms and say, with little variation, how handsome he had become and how very tall. They laughed as he confused their names and patted him some more, and then someone remembered his luggage and he was bundled into the back of one of the cars and driven around to collect it from the customs officer, whom it seemed was a friend as he let them straight through. And then the family, as magically as they had appeared, disappeared again, leaving only the auntie with the famous smile and a young girl in tennis whites. Bobby, who had been expecting his father's brother Saul, looked around the empty dockside.

'I can't think why you're staying with that dreadful man,' said the aunt whose name was Violette, 'I have heaps of room at my house, you'd be much more comfortable if you stayed with us.'

'Papa thought it would be best as I'm going to be working with Uncle,' said Bobby.

'Well, I think it's very foolish of you. If Leonard hadn't been staying with Virginie when he got ill, I don't know what would've happened to him. Saul Cansino certainly wouldn't have looked after him the way she did.'

Bobby shrugged. It was such attentions that had been blamed for Leonard getting so little done during his visit. 'I never get ill.'

'That's what Leonard said. And the next thing we know he can't lift his head from the pillow and the doctor was imagining all sorts of terrible diseases. Virginie was beside herself with worry.'

'It was just a touch of flu, *Leonard exagère*.' Bobby smiled. '*Leonard exagère*' was a family maxim.

Violette sighed, for she didn't have time to debate such matters. 'In any case, we intend to see lots of you while you're here, don't we Josie? We have all sorts of plans to entertain you. Did Leonard tell you there's the most wonderful cinema just opened? We went on the opening night and it's quite astonishing, General Motors have a stand in the front lobby and there's a magnificent luxury car just parked there by the bar.' She glanced at her watch. 'He's clearly not coming, you'd better tag along with us. Jump in the back Josie, Bobby, put your things in the dickie. Dreadful man, I could have told you this would happen.'

They left the port, weaving through the gold and silver bazaar and turning right by Napoleon's Fort Cafarelli, which was now a signal station. Bobby gazed in wonder at the white mosques, the shops signs in Arabic and French, the tall buildings with their wrought iron balconies, the palm trees and the parrots and the black-veiled women with babies on their backs, and it was as if he was seeing it for the first time.

Violette glanced at him, drumming her perfectly manicured nails on the steering wheel.

'I'm just longing to have you visit, you haven't seen the Rue Rolo house, have you? Did Leonard tell you we have views of the sea from both the north and the south sides. Of course, it's far too big for the four of us, we rattle around. But it's just the thing for entertaining. Do you remember Josette?' she said as an afterthought. 'She was rather a mousey little thing the last time you were here. Weren't you, darling?'

Josette nodded obediently.

'Of course I remember Josette,' said Bobby and he smiled his wide, friendly smile, turning to look again at his young cousin.

'You took me to see *Lucky Star*,' she said, still looking out of the window, her fingertips pressed against the edge of the seat so that the crescents of her nails flushed white.

'I remember,' said Bobby, although he didn't. 'I was terribly in love with Janet Gaynor.' He glanced at his aunt. 'I still am a little.'

'People say Josie looks a little like Janet Gaynor,' said Violette. 'Peroxide is a wonderful thing!' She glanced at her daughter in the rear-view mirror. 'Janet Gaynor is petite too. All good things come in small packages, that's what I tell Josie.'

'I was told it was 'tall' packages,' said Bobby, turning and winking at Josette. 'Do you mean I've had it wrong all these years?'

Josette giggled and leaned forwards to rest her chin on the back of her mother's seat. Violette glanced at her daughter, her hat casting a shadow over her eyes and then turned to look at Bobby.

'Darling, what a scream you are, how is it no one has snapped you up?'

'Do you know, it's a mystery to me too,' said Bobby with a grin.

'French Gardens, the Bourse, the Anglican Church,' said Violette, gesturing dismissively as they drove past. Bobby turned to look, the afternoon sun causing him to blink and close his eyes. When he opened them again the car had stopped outside the Café Baudrot on the corner of the Rue Cherif Pasha. 'You're not in any rush? Good, then you can join us for tea,' said his aunt. 'Clemmie said he might stop by too, you won't recognise him, he's quite the young man these days.' She smiled her dazzling smile and Bobby noticed that when she talked of her son her eyes had the same shine he was used to seeing in Estella's.

She leaned across Bobby and waved to an elderly Egyptian man who was standing beneath the yellow and white awning, handing him the keys to the car and treating him to the special attention she reserved for small children and natives. Then she stepped out of the car with a poise and elegance only taught in the best Swiss finishing schools, frowning tightly when her daughter did not. 'I think we might have changed your dress,' she murmured, considering Josette's tennis clothes, then she hooked her arm in Bobby's and led him through the door.

Inside, the café purred with the sound of satisfied appetites and Violette at once assumed a vivacious and purposeful expression which carried her like a wave from one side of the room to the other. Wherever she looked she was greeted by smiles and admiring glances, and she returned these with an ease that only the most sought-after society women achieve. This was, Bobby saw, his aunt's natural habitat, and he smiled and unbent a little, feeling he shared some of her success. Josette, her hands clasped to her chest as if ready at any moment to catch something, followed behind.

'I shan't stay long, I just want to say hello to Ariane, and then I'll leave you young ones to enjoy yourselves,' said Violette, considering her reflection in the mirror behind the bar and adjusting her hat accordingly. 'Isn't this heavenly?' she added to Bobby, and he nodded, understanding she meant the ruffled curtains, the high vaulted ceilings, the tiny cakes that sailed past on silver trays.

Josette's face fell. 'Oh don't go, Mummy,' she cried, 'we only just got here.'

'Josie, don't fuss,' said her mother. 'Oh look, there she is,' and she smiled and turned a little so that her fine features, her long neck, her full breasts, were shown to their best advantage. 'Bobby, darling, this is Mam'zelle Baudrot, our little bit of Paris right here in Alex,' and Violette leaned over to kiss the other woman, their cheekbones knocking pleasingly.

'*Ma petite Violette*,' said the woman, and they regarded one another carefully, like cats across a fence. She glanced with disinterest at Josette, then turned her attention to Bobby, resting her elbows on the edge of the bar and considering him. Then, pressing a thin cigarette to her red lips, she reached across and laid a wilting hand in his, by way of a greeting. '*Un grand garçon,*' she said.

Clemmie, it turned out, had not yet arrived and they spent several minutes discussing his likely whereabouts and whether they should wait for him here or go on home. Violette was persuaded to stay and order tea, although it was clearly the chance of seeing her son which convinced her, and Mam'zelle Baudrot called a waiter and told him to show them to the best table. The best table was, of course, the one most visible to all the others, and they were soon happily settled on what felt like a stage, while the waiter, a boy with ears like curled parsley, rearranged the cutlery.

'Do you remember coming here on your last day?' asked Josette, shaking out her napkin and then laying it carefully across her knees, which she thought bony.

'Me?' said Bobby, tugging at his eyebrow as he considered the menu.

'You don't remember?'

He shook his head, glancing up as a tray went past piled with tiny coloured meringues and following it with his eyes. 'I love macaroons,' he said, his thumb and finger still pinching his eyebrow.

'You don't remember how you promised to show me where Alexander the Great was buried?'

'Oh dear,' he said, 'was I very dull?'

'Of course not,' said Josette. 'Was he, Mummy?'

Violette, who was only half-listening, laced her fingers and stretched, admiring for a moment her slender upper arms, which had none of the sagging skin or blemishes of most women her age. That was the good thing about having children young, it took less of a toll on your body. 'You were perfect,' she assured him, 'you still are, no wonder you're Estella's favourite.' She gazed at Bobby.

'You are,' she said, although he had not protested. 'Every mother has one, they just don't like to admit it.' She glanced at her daughter. 'Josie's mine, aren't you darling?' she added, after a pause that was slightly too long.

Josette beamed, glancing around in the hope that others had heard this. Bobby saw another tray of cakes going past, and he craned his neck to see what they were, then called the waiter to ask. While he was there Violette ordered her usual *canarino*, which Bobby assumed to be a cocktail but which turned out to be hot water with a slice of lemon rind, and then a selection of different gateaux for the table. 'I see you have my sister's sweet tooth,' she observed, as he met each choice with an enthusiastic nod. 'How lucky you have so many places to put it all.'

'I used to be terribly fat,' said Josette unexpectedly.

'Oh darling!' said her mother, laughing, but there was something disagreeable in it, and Bobby understood that his aunt was a woman who liked pretty things around her. Josette, who understood this too, pushed away her plate in anticipation of the cakes she would not be eating, and wondered aloud where Clemmie had got to.

'He's probably caught up in some card game,' said Violette. 'He's quite the devil — that's Philippe's side of the family. I can't even look at a card table without losing a fortune. Although I do love to watch Clemmie play, he's quite mesmerising. There's a little Stefan Zweig story,' she smiled, delighting in her own erudition, 'I forget what it's called, about a woman obsessed with watching a poker player: well that's me. Josie's the same, aren't you darling? Clemmie gets terribly cross sometimes and insists we leave. He says we put him off.'

'I play bridge,' said Bobby.

'Really? You must tell Clemmie, he's always looking to make up a four.' She glanced at her watch, tiny diamonds glittering where the numbers should be. 'I should really go, I need to make sure your uncle has a nap or he'll be impossible later.'

She stood up just as the waiter arrived with their order, and made a great fuss about how she had to dash, and how sorry she was. But Alexandrian women rarely ate what was put in front of them, so the waiter only nodded and pulled out her chair.

'I didn't finish my story,' said Josette, 'about Alexander's tomb.'

'Oh, yes, you must,' said Violette, looking around for her handbag. 'I'll have your suitcase dropped off, Bobby dear, Rue Sinan Pasha isn't it? And don't be late back, Josie, I want you to look your prettiest tonight, and you know how long it takes to get your hair into any kind of shape.' She turned and wove her way towards the door, Josette watching her like an understudy trying to learn a part.

'So, tell me the story,' said Bobby, digging his fork into a millefeuille.

'Oh yes!' she said. 'You don't remember at all?' He shook his head, a large flake of pastry escaping his mouth and sticking to his chin. Josette pointed at it with a half-raised finger, causing Bobby to swat at his face with such vigour he might have been fending off a swarm of bees. 'Sorry,' he murmured.

Josette picked up her teacup, her eyes fixed on the tablecloth.

'Go on,' he said.

'Well,' she cradled the cup with the fingertips of both hands and delicately sipped at her tea, as she had watched her mother do, 'it's nothing really.' She paused, blinking, and Bobby leaned forwards.

'Go on,' he repeated, laughing.

Involuntarily, Josette laughed too, and the tea in her cup sloshed against the sides, so that she had to set it down on the saucer. 'We were here,' she said at last, 'well, not here, it was the old Baudrot-Groppi, further up Cherif Pasha.' She pointed with her freckled nose in the direction of the front door, then corrected herself and gestured towards the window instead.

'All the family had come to see you off from the dockside, but I had a piano lesson, and Mummy was insisting I go to it. Even though I hated piano and was awful at it.' She looked at him and in her eyes he saw the still-remembered injustice. 'I've given up now,' she added.

'Me too,' said Bobby, but he splayed his large hands along the edge of the tablecloth as though about to play a few chords. 'An octave and a half,' he said, 'like Rachmaninoff.'

'Does Rachmaninoff have big hands?'

'Famously.'

'Oh.' She held up her own small hands, blistered where she had gripped her tennis racket, then continued, 'Anyway, I was furious, especially as Clemmie was being allowed to go, and so Mummy sent me outside to sit in the car and calm down. Of course I didn't calm down, I just got more upset.' She smiled at this memory of her old, less tamed self.

'I wish I'd known,' said Bobby.

'You did,' said Josette. 'At least, you came out while I was in the car and said you needed me to help you with something. You said you'd worked out where Alexander's tomb was and you wanted to look for it before you left.'

'The Soma,' said Bobby, 'I'd forgotten about that.'

'You had this map of ancient Alexandria, and you decided that he had been buried in the middle of the Rue Fuad, right where the policeman stands on his box directing the traffic. And you took me by the hand and we walked straight up to the policeman. You were so tall, you were nose to nose with him, even though he was standing on a box. And you said, "Excuse me monsieur, but is this the site of Alexander's tomb?" And he got very angry and started waving his hands and telling us to get out of the road. But you wouldn't move because you were convinced that if you could just look underneath, we would find it, like in some Charlie Chaplin film, where you move a box and step into another world!' This was the most animated Bobby had seen his cousin, and he grinned, thinking how sweet she was suddenly. 'I thought you were going to be arrested,' she said, her eyes wide and her pale eyelashes batting like a doll's.

'What an idiot I was,' said Bobby, and he laughed his low, rumbling laugh.

'Luckily Mummy came after us to see what was happening, and she calmed the policeman down and made you go back to the café. And I had to go to my piano lesson.' She picked up her teacup again.

'How terrible of me causing such a ruction,' said Bobby, grinning and straightening his long legs, so that they stuck out on the other side of the table. 'I'm sorry if I scared you.'

'You didn't,' she said.

◆　　　◆　　　◆　　　◆　　　◆

LOUD VOICES WERE HEARD AND the café door swung open to allow a group of young people, all noise and straw Panamas, to burst through. Leading them was Josette's brother Clemmie, his tanned face creased in laughter at some amusing joke he had just told, his blue eyes coolly scoping the room. All heads turned to admire the newcomers, and Clemmie, his blonde hair falling over his beautiful features, soaked up their attention as bread soaks up a sauce. His hands pushed into the pockets of his immaculately tailored slacks, his English brogues clattering on the mosaic floor, he glowed with lambent complacency, like a colt that has never lost a race.

Josette waved and Clemmie glanced over, but his gaze rested upon his sister for only a second, then he turned and strode towards the bar. Here, he made a great fuss of embracing Ariane and then leaned across the countertop and proceeded to dictate to the barman, in a loud, ringing voice, the ingredients of a new cocktail he wanted to try. The others clustered around him shouting their own suggestions, the girls draping themselves over barstools or men, depending which was nearer.

Josette, who was used to being ignored by her brother, chattered happily to Bobby, pointing out who was who and where they lived and what their fathers did, so that Bobby, should he be introduced, would have no trouble making conversation. And then she gazed in the direction of the bar and hummed the tune of a song that was playing, while Bobby tasted all the cakes, because it was a shame to let them go to waste.

At last Clemmie turned around, glass in hand, and sauntered across the room.

'I'm exhausted,' he said, dropping onto a chair. 'You won't believe the day I've had,' and he picked up a fork and speared what remained of a lemon tart. Josette looked at him with expectation. 'What?' he asked. Then, barely missing a beat, he turned his gaze upon Bobby and declared, 'Of course, you've just arrived, how wonderful,' and he reached across the table and shook his hand enthusiastically. 'I see Josie's already introducing you to the delights of Alex,' and he glanced over his shoulder towards the bar, as though the only delights he could imagine were those he had brought with him. Bobby nodded and said what a nice time they were having.

'I don't suppose you can lend me a few *piastres*?' Clemmie's attention was back to his sister. 'Mummy will give it to you later, I'm a bit short.'

Josette looked down at her tennis whites. 'I don't have anything on me, I came straight from the club.'

'Damn.'

'I can lend you some, if you need it,' said Bobby, pulling out his wallet.

'Just put it on Daddy's bill,' said Josette, 'he won't mind.'

'Not for here,' said Clemmie with irritation. 'We're going on somewhere.'

'But Mummy wants you home. She has her thing tonight, remember?'

'Oh yes. I'd forgotten. Well, I'll be there, just tell Mummy I might be a little late.' He glanced at Bobby's open wallet. 'I feel awful, you've only just arrived and I'm borrowing money! You sure you don't mind?' and he took a five pound note and put it quickly into his back pocket.'

A girl with dark eyes and thick black hair pulled into a swinging ponytail sidled up behind Clemmie and slipped her arm through his. She was wearing a loose-fitting dress of the palest pink, and so lightly did it cover her fluid golden body that it seemed at any moment she might just step out of it. Josette pulled at the waistband of her tennis skirt uncomfortably.

'But Mummy's expecting you to drive me,' said Josette, her forehead wrinkling with concern and making her look much older than her eighteen years.

'Be a darling and take the tram, would you? I promised everyone I'd go on with them, you know how it is. Do you mind terribly?' He didn't wait for an answer but leaned across the table and kissed her firmly on the forehead. 'You're an angel. Shall we go then?' he asked the girl, whose dark eyes were quite empty of expression. 'Wonderful to see you,' he added to Bobby, 'thanks so much,' and he patted his pocket to show how grateful he was.

As if bound by magnets, the beautiful young people snapped back together and disappeared out of the door in a solid, ringing mass. Bobby watched them go, smiling, then turned back to Josette.

'I can come with you, if you like. I'm going to my uncle's office, but I can see you home first.'

She glanced at him, but there was something furious in it, and when she spoke her tone was sharp. 'I'm not a baby, I've taken the tram on my own before,' she said, and pushed away her teacup and stood up.

'Well I'll walk you out then,' he said, standing up too.

She shrugged, as though it was of no consequence to her what he did. 'Daddy has an account,' she added, for Bobby had taken out his wallet again.

Outside, the late afternoon sun sliced the pavement into shards of black and white, and the air was thick.

'If you liked,' said Bobby, following her down the steps, 'we could have another go at looking for the Soma while I'm here. One afternoon when you're free.'

'We mostly go to the beach,' she said.

'Of course.' Bobby glanced up the street, trying to get his bearings. His wool suit made his legs itch and he bent to scratch his shins.

'You shouldn't have lent him that money,' Josette said suddenly. 'I mean, you'll get it back, it's not that. But now he'll spend all night playing cards and Mummy will blame me, because I was the one supposed to bring him home.'

Bobby straightened up, and for a brief second their eyes were at the same level and something was exchanged, although he could not have said what. He stared at her and his legs itched more than ever, but this time he resisted scratching them. 'I'm so sorry,' he said, 'it didn't occur to me.'

'It doesn't matter.'

'I could go after him,' he said.

'It doesn't matter,' she said again, although softer this time.

'I hope I haven't spoiled everything.'

She thought for a moment, as if weighing up the significance of his blunder, and Bobby found he was holding his breath, waiting for her to speak. This must have shown on his face, because when she looked up at him she gave a sudden laugh.

'Of course you haven't, there's nothing to spoil.' Her eyes shone, and whatever he had briefly glimpsed was gone now. Josette held out her hand. 'Thank you for tea,' she said.

'Thank you for inviting me,' he replied.

A tram nearing the junction rang its bell and she turned around, staring at it without moving. Then, just when it seemed she would miss it, she set off running towards the road, jumping on as it pulled away and waving from the step as Bobby watched after.

CHAPTER 17

The various layers of cosmopolitan Alexandrian society were as follows: at the top, the British cotton brokers, with their grand houses and educated wives; then, just beneath them, the French bankers and Greek businessmen, whose tireless commerce kept Egypt's financial wheels turning; below these, the Italians, the Jews, the Germans, to whom the upper strata looked for their architecture, their cafés and their schools; and lower still, those born in Egypt but possessing European connections, such that they might occasionally slip in and out of the upper levels, like a coloured thread drawn through a piece of knitting. It was to this last group that Estella and Solomon's families largely belonged, and to which Bobby was automatically assigned upon his arrival in Alexandria.

By 1938 the Cansino family was something of a lost dynasty, that is, their better days were behind them. Careless investments in the late twenties had seen their wealth dispersed and their villas sold off, and if part of the Rue Nebi Daniel had once been referred to as Cansino City, no one remembered it now. Solomon blamed himself, of course, although the recklessness had been his brother's, and it was to rectify this failure that he repeatedly cast Leonard into the fray, hoping, like a fisherman on the banks of a river, that persistence would be rewarded. When it wasn't, he turned to Bobby.

As a businessman, Bobby was an unknown quantity. At school he had been average, the only subjects for which he showed any enthusiasm being Classics and Ancient Greek, a passion which soon dissipated upon receipt of his

Higher Certificate. Later, working with his father in the Manchester office, he was popular but not especially respected, (respect, believed Solomon, was akin to fear, something Bobby could never inspire) and he would sooner chat about football or the weather than negotiate the price of a spindle of raw cotton. His arrival in Alexandria, therefore, caused only the smallest ripples in the family pond, and Bobby discovered that if he were not to sink without trace altogether, he would have to learn how to play the game.

And the game in Alexandria was a different game from elsewhere. While the really wealthy men had got where they were through hard work and clever dealings, those lower down the scale had mostly profited from being in the right place at the right time. The challenge, in this case, was remaining in that place. An unpopular wife or a social faux pas were often all that was needed to oust an individual from favour, and as much business was done in the drawing rooms of the society ladies as it was around the boardroom table. Charm, a light touch, and the ability to mix a good gin cocktail were the skills needed to cut a swathe through this elegant, empty world. And the white gold which had built this modern city, a magical fairy dust that poisoned the lungs of its factory workers, was forgotten.

ON LEAVING THE CAFÉ THAT FIRST afternoon, Bobby walked slowly up the Rue Cherif Pasha towards the French Gardens, to where his uncle Saul had an office overlooking the Bourse. It was just after six when he knocked on the frosted glass door, his father's name etched beneath that of his uncle, provoking a series of deep barks on the other side. The door opened a crack and his uncle's red, puffy face peered through the gap, his right leg raised as he endeavoured to keep back the dog.

'Bed!' he insisted, not bothering to greet his nephew, 'Bed, Caesar!' and the dog, an enormous, long-eared, white-muzzled creature, retreated to lie in the middle of the room. 'You arrived,' said his uncle, turning away and wandering, barefoot, back to his desk, where he sat in a large armchair turned towards the window. 'Welcome.'

Bobby looked around at the musty, cramped little office, every surface piled with papers and files, and made a gracious bow, immediately regretting the gesture and pretending to study something on the floor.

His uncle nodded towards a chair, one of the few objects free of clutter, and continued to gaze out of the window. Bobby sat down and crossed his legs, his ankles in his red wool socks the only bit of colour in the dim, dull room. He began to chat about the crossing and how it had been rough around the Bay of Biscay, then calm as soon as they passed Cape St. Vincent and entered the Straits. He told him how the aunties had met him at the port, and that he had spent the afternoon in Baudrot, and how his suitcase would be dropped around later, just in case his uncle thought he was travelling especially light. And then he smoothed his hair, crossed his legs the other way and grinned. 'The family send their love,' he added.

'Good, good,' said his uncle, dragging his eyes away from the window. He sat back, his fingertips pressed together and considered Solomon's youngest son as he might a piece of fruit. He thought for a moment. 'I hope you're ready to work hard,' he said. 'There's none of your fifteen-hour weeks here.' The dog, already asleep on a rug, made smacking noises with its lips.

'I'm ready,' said Bobby.

Saul Cansino was a man who wore his life loosely, like an old jacket, and everything about him, from the sag of his chin to the swell of his round belly to the plumpness of his soft feet, suggested that this suited him. Even the loss of the family fortune did not trouble him, for his wife had money of her own and spent it easily. His world was a simple one, and he moved happily between the comforts of home and the comforts of his office with the sole ambition of being able to do exactly the same thing tomorrow and the day after and the day after that. If his children took advantage, if his brother had lost faith, if his wife thought him a fool, so long as it didn't interrupt his daily routine, what did he care?

And now here was Bobby Cansino, hot on the heels of his older brother, come to take up space and disturb his peace by asking questions about things that really didn't concern him and demanding answers he was not always inclined to give. At least Leonard he had been able to send off to Cairo and Tanta to check on suppliers and try to drum up business, but this one, like a tree that has grown too large for its pot, threatened to take up more room. He sighed, and the dog rearranged itself on the dirty rug and sighed too.

Over the next few weeks, Bobby accompanied his uncle wherever he went. He was, Saul's wife Louise liked to joke, not dissimilar to that revolting dog, except that he didn't try to sleep on their bed. The only time they were apart was travelling to and from the office, for Bobby soon opted to take the tram rather than sit in the back of his uncle's car while Caesar glared at him from the front seat, and it was these moments that Bobby came to cherish. Despite the heat and the crush, despite the tightness of his collar and the itchiness of his skin, this was the one time he had his thoughts to himself. Holding to the rail, he would gaze out at this fresh world of minarets and flawless blue skies, of gaudy yellow mimosa trees that left powdery trails along the windows, of trotting donkey-carts laden with cotton or sugar cane that stopped the traffic and caused the bus driver to hang out of the window and scream abuse. And rather than feeling lonely, as he had been told to expect, he felt strangely at home.

CHAPTER 18

For the third year in a row Violette had taken a cabin at the much sought-after Sidi Bishr 2 beach, a testament both to her tenacity and to her husband's wealth. From the beginning of June onwards, the family could be found there every afternoon, drinking lemonade in the shade of the green curtains and pitying those less fortunate as they trudged past with rugs and Thermos flasks. On the day they invited Bobby the annual summer migration of Cairene *haute société* was in full flood, and Violette had taken up her favourite position at the top of the cabin's wooden steps so that she might better spy upon the new arrivals. Quickly picking out several of interest, she sent Clemmie to invite them up for tea, and then set about arranging chairs and plumping cushions in anticipation of a few hours of pleasurable gossip. When Bobby arrived sometime later, his trousers rolled and his bare feet white against the sand, the terrace was aflutter with chirping women catching up on a winter of news.

One of the guests, a second wife in her sixties with a habit of pushing her lower jaw forward, like a drawer left open, was bemoaning the contents of her late husband's will. Glittering with the riches of a long marriage to a wealthy man, she dabbed at her tearless eyes and considered her audience.

'I'd have got more if I'd divorced him,' she declared, and the women, mostly second wives too, gushed with malicious sympathy.

Violette, catching sight of her oversized nephew hovering on the steps, waved to him to join them, pressing Josette to move up a little so that he might sit on the bench.

Offering a hasty introduction, she quickly returned the conversation to the subject of Mrs Gardiner's destitution, which was far more interesting. Clemmie, lazing in an armchair to his mother's right and in his element amongst so many women, pushed a glass of lemonade across the table.

'I begged him not to leave me in this position!' Mrs Gardiner was incapable of expressing herself in anything less than a shriek. 'But he did it anyway. Twenty-seven years and I'm left with nothing. Not even my girls got a penny, and they were like daughters to him.' She looked from one to another, clearly offering this as a salutary tale. 'In the end,' she said, 'the only thing that matters is blood, those ghastly grandchildren were all he cared about. While I'm left renting out rooms just to keep the wolf from the door.'

There was a gasp of horror from the table.

'Renting out rooms?' asked a woman in an elegant black turban.

'Bed and board,' said Mrs Gardiner triumphantly. 'Thank heavens for the Royal Navy is all I can say.' She rearranged the cushion behind her, sitting back with a loud sigh. 'Actually, it's not as terrible as you might think, everyone's awfully nice and I've always loved meeting new people, they can be fascinating, don't you think?'

Everyone agreed that new people really could be fascinating.

'You poor darling,' murmured Clemmie, tipping forward and taking her hand, so that sparks of light from her rings flashed on the wooden walls.

Mrs. Gardiner smiled valiantly, and stretched her lower lip over her teeth. The woman in the turban shook her head, and Violette, worrying that the mood had become a little morose, whispered to Josette to fetch the cakes. Several ribboned boxes were immediately produced, and the sight of all that sugar and pastry immediately led the conversation towards brighter topics.

Clemmie had heard a delicious bit of scandal about the wife of someone high up at the British Embassy, and he began a long and convoluted story, mentioning no names, which had the women around the table hanging on his every word. Sitting forwards, his ankle crossed over his knee to reveal a tanned, hairless shin, he dropped just enough hints that by the time he had finished, several reputations were in ruins. His mother, meanwhile, who knew the story to be quite untrue, poured tea and passed plates.

'And what about you, Mr Cansino?' asked someone. 'What skeletons might we find in your cupboard if we were to root around?'

'Me?' said Bobby in surprise. 'Oh, none I don't think.'

'Oh come, come,' said Clemmie. 'A bachelor can't reach the grand old age of — what are you, thirty? — without a few unsavoury stories to his name. Bet there's some spurned young lady back in Lancashire or Yorkshire or wherever it is. Or perhaps a whole string of them, I've always said Cousin Bobby's a bit of a dark horse.'

'No, I don't think so,' said Bobby, reddening.

'Stop it, Clemmie,' said Josette.

'Oh do look, I knew it! Bobby Cansino, you've turned quite pink!'

'I can't remember the last time I saw a man blush,' said the woman in the turban. 'The men in Egypt are so jaded, don't you find? Even the servants don't shock these days, and heaven knows I give them reason.' And she smiled and leaned across the table to pat Bobby's thigh, causing him to blush further.

A square-faced woman named Mrs Porter agreed enthusiastically. She glanced at her daughter, Mathilde, whose unmarried state was clearly of concern. 'A young man with a conscience, how refreshing. We were just saying the other day what a shame it is young men have become so aimless — not you, Clemmie darling, you're the life and soul,' she added quickly, 'but young men in general.' She leaned forward, as though by doing so her daughter might not hear. 'What's a mother to do? I've even considered going back to England, a season in London might be just the thing, but my sister tells me it's the same there. She has three girls at home, and not one of them showing any prospect of marriage. Mind you, she does live in Bedfordshire.'

'It's the decline in birth rates,' said Mrs Gardiner, repeating something she had read in her newspaper.

'Well, they'll decline still further if it carries on like this.'

Everyone laughed, and even Mrs Porter allowed herself a smile.

'We should all move to Germany,' said Mrs Gardiner. 'Germany's full of vigorous young men, apparently they breed like rabbits!'

'*Les arabes sont pareils*,' said another woman, speaking in French so that the houseboy, who was pouring out lemonade, would not understand.

Everyone shook their heads and agreed that they were. Mrs Porter sighed and sat back in her chair, brushing imaginary crumbs from her large breasts.

'Thank you, Amin,' said Violette, waving away the houseboy.

'Clemmie's German tutor was one of ten,' said Josette. 'What was his name, Clemmie?'

'He was Austrian,' said Clemmie, slumping down in his chair so that his head lolled and his golden hair fell over his face.

'Was it Hans?' asked Josette, but Clemmie had closed his eyes and was ignoring her.

'It's the same thing these days,' said Bobby, meaning Germany and Austria. Josette smiled.

'Is he the one we got from the Hess family?' Violette wondered. 'It's hard to keep track of Clemmie's tutors, they never stayed very long, did they darling?' and she leaned over to kiss his forehead.

Clemmie, eyes closed, shrugged.

'I never liked those Hesses,' said Mrs Porter. 'I've always said you can't trust a man whose eyebrows meet in the middle.' She glanced at Bobby to check she had not made a faux pas. 'And German really is a dreadful language, so unromantic. I was at drinks with the headmaster of Victoria College just last week, and I said, what kind of a foreign policy do we have if we're still learning the languages of our supposed enemies. I mean, I know we're not officially enemies, but I don't think anyone's in any doubt about the way things are going. And do you know what he said?' She paused, outraged. 'He said, "Madame—" (and I have to tell you, that rather put me out too, 'Madame' always makes me feel ancient), "Madame, that is why we learn them." ' She narrowed her eyes. 'I mean, what sort of reply is that?'

'Hear, hear, Mam'zelle,' said Clemmie, eyes still closed.

'If it were left to me, I'd ban the lot of them,' she continued, getting up a head of steam now. 'German, Spanish, Italian — no one learns Hungarian, but if they did, I'd get rid of that too. Any belligerent nation, I'd remove them from the syllabus. It's no different from raising children, you have to be firm.' She glanced at her daughter, quietly jabbing the tablecloth with the tines of her cake fork. 'Firm but fair,' she added, taking the cake fork and placing it out of reach.

'What about Japanese?' said Bobby. 'Would Japanese be allowed?'

Violette looked at her nephew in dismay. And then Clemmie roused himself and said something about a new Deanna Durbin film, and the conversation moved effortlessly into a discussion of the latest releases.

'POOR MRS GARDINER,' SAID JOSETTE, when everyone except Bobby had left. 'She seemed terribly upset.'

'I shouldn't worry too much about her,' said Violette,

running her finger along the rim of a cake plate. 'Is it pistachio I can taste? They put it in everything these days, it must be the new thing.'

'I don't think pistachios are new, Mummy,' said Clemmie, standing up and stretching, oblivious to the attempts of the houseboy to get past him to clear the table.

'But she's renting out rooms,' said Josette.

Violette looked at her daughter, as if marvelling that she should be so naive. 'She's just building a case, it's what they all do. In a month or two there'll be a petition to challenge his will and then all hell will break loose.' She removed the barrette holding her hair and let it fall to her shoulders, using her sunglasses as a mirror. Josette watched her, hypnotised. 'It's rather sad, actually, they think they've closed the deal by seeing him through his last days, but then they discover he had other ideas.'

'Mummy's an expert on these things,' said Clemmie, who had removed his shoes and was tipping sand over the railing.

Violette smiled and reached for Clemmie's arm, which she bit gently as she used to do when he was a baby. 'I'm nothing of the sort,' she purred, and she glanced at Bobby, who was handing plates to the houseboy, and stifled a yawn. Bobby quickly stood up.

'I should go,' he said.

'Oh darling, don't rush off, you're family,' said Violette, but she got up anyway and made much of kissing him and thanking him for coming all that way.

'Could he join us at the Sporting next weekend?' Josette asked suddenly. There was to be racing at the Club and everyone was going. 'Do you like horse racing, Bobby?'

'Of course he likes racing, he's English,' said Clemmie, pushing a pile of sweaters onto the floor so that he might lie down on the bench. 'They're all horse mad.'

'I don't know about horse mad,' grinned Bobby, 'but I do enjoy a flutter. When I was younger I used to be quite lucky.'

'No such thing as luck,' said Clemmie. 'Did you win pots of money? How delicious, everyone we know always loses. Why do you think that is, Mummy? Do we know the wrong people?' He shuffled along the bench, extending his legs so that his feet hung off the end.

'I think we probably do,' said Violette. 'Dreadful rotten lot.' And they giggled, as if sharing some private joke.

'Actually, I think in my case it really was luck,' said Bobby.

'I'm afraid I don't believe you,' said Clemmie. 'Nor does Mummy.' And he leaned back, resting his head in his mother's lap. 'Arm, Mummy,'

Violette moved her arm. 'At last!' she said, as a clattering on the steps announced the arrival of Philippe. 'There you are, we thought you were never coming. Really darling, you should have said you were going to be so late, we're being bitten to death sitting here and you know the welts Josie comes up in.'

'Sorry chérie, something came up.' He strode across the deck to kiss Violette, a handsome man with silver-grey hair and a generous mouth. He was older than his wife by some fifteen years but his self-assurance and physical ease more than made up for this. He took hold of her hand, pushing the gold bracelets to her elbow and kissing the underside of her wrist.

'Hello Daddy,' said Clemmie, gazing up at his father.

His father leaned down and ruffled his hair.

'Bobby's here, darling,' said Violette.

'Hello Uncle Philippe,' said Bobby, stepping forwards.

'Bobby Cansino,' said Philippe, thrusting a hand in Bobby's direction, 'I was just talking about you. Marco Balestra's in town, he was asking after you.' He turned back to his wife, who was smoothing Clemmie's hair. 'I invited him to join us on Friday, do you mind?'

'Bobby's coming too,' said Josette, offering her father a cheek.

Violette glanced at her watch, then at Bobby.

'I must go,' said Bobby, taking the hint, 'I'm driving to Tanta with my uncle tomorrow. I had a lovely afternoon, Auntie Violette.'

'Just Violette is fine,' said his aunt.

They watched him go, his large feet sinking into the sand. The beach was almost empty now, the voices of those who remained carrying eerily on the lifting breeze. At the edge of the water a nanny in full uniform chastised a small boy, each wave causing her to jig from side to side, as if tap-dancing. Josette came to stand beside her father, holding lightly to his arm.

'Did she have her Cecil lot again?' He called them this because they invariably stayed at the Cecil Hotel.

'Yes.' She glanced behind, to where her mother and Clemmie were playing one of their games. Clemmie was writing words on his mother's palm with his finger, the two of them giggling as she guessed each one. Josette turned back to her father.

'Mrs Gardiner is taking in lodgers,' she said, curious to see what her father would make of this, but Philippe had no interest in the Mrs Gardiners of the world and he only shrugged.

'He seems a nice chap, that Cansino boy,' he said instead. He glanced down at his daughter's small closed-off face and pale eyelashes, expecting to feel the same sadness he always felt, for he knew Violette did not love her. But there was something different about her today, something lighter.

'He's very nice,' she said.

'Perhaps I'll have a word, see if I can't help him with a

few new contracts. Can't be easy right now.' He glanced at her again, and she blushed and felt that he understood everything.

'Thank you Daddy.'

And Philippe, who had in fact understood nothing, squeezed her thin shoulders and said they should make tracks, he didn't want her coming out in welts, or whatever it was her mother had said.

CHAPTER 19

The road out of Alex was good and Bobby dozed under a thick blanket, for it was early and the dog liked the roof down. Fields of cotton rose up either side, the white seed heads like so many tiny clouds, and when they neared Tanta and looked down over the spreading landscape, Bobby said that this must be what heaven looks like.

'I hope not,' said Saul.

Although there were the usual vestiges of European civilisation here — a Sporting club, Barclay's Bank, Claridge's, the British Consul — the desert town had nothing of the sophistication such things might imply: it was, essentially, a cotton market. It was also extraordinarily hot. After lying down that first afternoon, his uncle reappeared only to hand Bobby a list of addresses, instructing his nephew to make the visits by himself, and then retiring with Caesar to his mosquito net. Bobby did as he was told, going from one place to another with his briefcase and his basic Arabic (*Sa'eeda, Inshallah, Baksheesh*), to find invariably that the man he needed to speak to was in Alexandria for the summer. '*Maahlesh,*' he would be told, 'never mind,' and this tall, strange, light-skinned man was given a chair to sit on and a glass of mint tea. And Bobby would sip the scalding sweet tea and imagine he was on a bench in the French Gardens, the leaves of the palm trees rustling and the flags above the Bourse blown straight. He would imagine the gentle wind that blew along the Corniche, lifting the white galabiyahs of the street-sweepers and causing the young girls strolling in swimsuits to rub their arms and shiver. He would imagine his aunt's beach cabin, with its bleached, cool deck and curtains pulled to just the right place, so that there was shade from the sun but a breeze too. And he would imagine Josette looking up at him, her bright expectant smile making him especially welcome, so that even now, sitting alone in a dirty backstreet in Tanta, the world seemed a warm, inviting place.

◆　　　◆　　　◆　　　◆　　　◆

THE TRAMLINE RAN DIRECTLY PAST the Sporting Club, so that when Bobby arrived he walked straight through the arched stone entrance, carved with the names *Katarincek, Dentamaro & Cartareggia*, and stood for a moment gazing out across the racetrack to the golf course and tennis courts beyond. People pushed past him, chattering and waving excitedly to acquaintances on the grandstand — for it seemed everyone knew one another — and Bobby apologised and did his best to get out of their way. He couldn't remember where Josette had said they would be, so he wandered towards the track and watched as the horses for the first race were cantered down to the starting line. Their sleek, sinewy forms gleamed in the evening sun, and even the jockeys, crouched low and weightless in the saddle, seemed to hold themselves apart, for fear of disturbing the perfect harmony nature had achieved. Instinctively Bobby looked around for a racecard, the old excitement quickly revealing itself, and a young Egyptian boy in European trousers and a mismatched jacket appeared out of nowhere and pressed one into his hands. Bobby thanked him and moved away, but when the boy followed him, hopping from one bare foot to the other, he realised he was waiting for him to make a bet. He shook his head, but the boy remained there, his small fingers opening and closing like sea anemones, so that Bobby searched his pockets for a coin just to make him go away.

But before he could give him anything, someone touched his arm and he turned to find Josette, flushed and breathless, hovering beside him. She was wearing a pink dress and heeled sandals and carried a parasol, which she swung about her feet causing little clouds of dust.

'Hello,' she said.

'Oh hello,' said Bobby.

'I saw you from the box,' said Josette, gesturing behind them to the stands. Bobby gazed at where she was pointing but it was a blur of hats and pale faces and so he nodded and said he hoped he wasn't late.

'Actually you're early, no one ever arrives before the second or third race. Have you picked any winners?' She glanced towards the track. 'Mummy's told everyone you're an expert, she's so pleased you could come.'

'I'm really not,' said Bobby, glancing at the boy still standing next to him. 'No,' he insisted, and then, guiltily, '*Imshi, imshi*', as he had heard his uncle say.

'You probably didn't see it before they built the new stand,' said Josette, taking his arm and pulling him up the grass. 'It's much smarter now.' She paused so that he might admire it, then ran ahead up the concrete steps, her fingers trailing on the curved metal rails. 'It was built by the same contractors who did the Corniche,' she added, suspecting that he liked such details. 'Italians.'

It was dark going up the steps, in contrast to the sunshine outside, and Bobby felt disoriented, so that when Josette threw open the wooden gate to her mother's box and pushed him inside, he was blinking and confused. He was also out of breath, and he stood for a moment, dabbing at his forehead with his cuff, gazing around the painted concrete room, with its slatted railings and bare floor and narrow trestles draped in damask cloths. His aunt was alone, except for the English governess, who was knitting, and three suffragis in white jackets with brass buttons, who stood pressed against the walls like telamons.

'Mummy, Cousin Bobby's here,' said Josette, and Violette turned and blew him a kiss, then carried on her conversation with several smartly dressed women in the neighbouring box. She was leaning on the wooden partition that divided the two boxes and twirling a pair of opera glasses that dangled from her neck, every so often lifting them to her eyes and scanning the crowd, like a game-hunter searching for prey. Josette smiled happily and the English governess, whose name was Patchett, yawned and said she wished these things didn't start so late.

'Patch likes to be in bed by nine,' said Josette, 'don't you Patch?'

The governess was concentrating on turning a heel and did not respond.

Josette stood for a moment, restlessly opening and closing her parasol and Bobby, stooping for the ceiling was low, said it would be too hot for the horses if it was earlier.

'No doubt that's correct,' said Patchett benignly. She finished her row and looked up at Bobby. 'So this is the young man I've heard about,' she said, tugging at her wool and sending the ball scuttling across the floor. 'You remind me of someone. Who does he remind me of?' She bent forwards to pick up her wool, groaning, then sat back again, her face red with the effort.

'Perhaps you met my brother,' said Bobby, although he and Leonard didn't look a bit alike.

'Come see,' said Josette, who was leaning against the front wall, her elbows resting on the wooden rail. She gestured with pride at the view, as if she had had it laid out just for him.

Bobby followed her, relieved to find the roof angled upwards and that he could stand up straight. There, beneath an empty Alexandrian sky, he saw the whole of Grand Sporting spread out before him, with its racetrack and tennis courts and golf course and swimming pools; he saw the rows of motor cars lined up along the main road, each with its uniformed driver leaning against the shiny bonnet and a back seat heaped with blankets for when it got chilly on the drive home; he saw the new apartment blocks which lined the tramway, and then beyond, the private villas with their wrought-iron gates and green lawns; and he saw the sea, blue and sparkling and extending towards infinity. Or towards Cyprus, depending where you looked. Bobby sighed, and Josette, who was watching him, smiled and said didn't it look like a picture in a magazine?

'Everywhere I go here I think that,' said Bobby. He rubbed at the back of his neck, which was sunburnt and prickled uncomfortably. And then he told her about the fields of cotton near Tanta and how they looked like tiny clouds and she laughed and said she had never thought of them like that, but it was true, they did. For the next ten minutes they exchanged their favourite views: she told him about New Year picnics near Lake Mariout when the desert was a carpet of wild orchids and narcissi as far as the eye could see, and he told her of climbing the clock tower of Manchester Town Hall and looking down over the rooftops; she responded with the view from the Great Pyramid at Giza and he gave her Edgeley Viaduct from the London train; Josette said the Lighthouse by the Royal Yacht Club coming home from a holiday in Europe, and Bobby thought about it and said that was one of his too.

'I'm already dreading leaving,' he said.

Josette was about to reply but then changed her mind and for a moment they stood in silence, watching the horses being turned in tight circles at the starting point.

'I've got it!' said Patchett suddenly, sitting forward and pointing one of her needles at Bobby. 'A young Lord Killearn, that's who he reminds me of.'

Josette turned around. 'The British Ambassador?' She raised an eyebrow.

'The very same,' said Patchett, pleased with herself, 'especially here,' and she covered the lower part of her face to show it was around the nose and eyes she saw the resemblance. 'It's uncanny.'

'It's because you're both tall,' whispered Josette, and Bobby nodded, because he got that a lot.

There was a gunshot, and they turned around to see the horses moving in a pounding mass along the straight, the crowd cheering and pushing forward to get a better view. '*Enfin!*' said Violette, at last breaking off her conversation and standing up. She held out her arms toward Bobby, kissing him rapidly on both cheeks and saying how well he looked, then flicked her eyes about the room to check that everything was in place.

'Mrs Patchett, perhaps you might move your chair into the hallway once everyone arrives,' she said, her gaze lingering on the governess's thick legs. 'Or at least back a little.'

'Yes dear,' said the older woman, lifting her ample bottom and scraping the chair backwards until it hit the wall. Violette flinched and put a fingertip to each temple, lowering them once the governess was settled again.

'I was just saying he reminds me of a young Lord Killearn,' said Patchett after a while, her needles clacking away. 'Mr Cansino, I mean.'

'Miles?' said Violette, with the vague, uninterested tone she always used for important men. And she took out her compact and carefully, moving the mirror from side to side, made some minor adjustments to her face.

WITH THE END OF THE FIRST race the guests began to arrive. Violette was waiting, cheekbones sharpened, as they came up the dark stairs and through the gate into the cool, light-filled room. The evening sun shone through the open walls, illuminating the engraved silver trays, the twinkling glasses, the tassels on the suffragis' red fezzes that swung forwards as they bowed their heads. Everything glowed.

Violette leaned against one of the tables, her hands fluttering with practised elegance as she greeted her guests. Like a florist putting together a bouquet, she gathered them up, placing this one here and that one there, so that all the disparate parts became a single, beautiful whole. She had selected her party wisely, for the space was small, and now she bound them one to the other, for vanity likes company. Exquisite in navy blue silk (everyone said so), she smiled and charmed and nobody could imagine a more cultivated hostess nor a more glittering collection of guests. Mostly they discussed one another.

'Don't tell me, another of the little frocks you bought in Paris? Darling, you are quite divine,' declared the wife of the Greek consul, who had arrived that afternoon from Cairo and was dressed head to foot in Chanel. 'I can't think how you do it.' She had a long, oval face and sad eyes, and a gloominess of soul founded upon millennia of cultural decline. 'Such style.'

'You are sweet, though I'm sure you must have seen me in it a million times!' Violette smoothed her silky haunches, her bracelets jingling. 'How marvellously you've done your hair. I can't do a thing with mine once the weather turns humid. Oh to be eighteen again and not to care,' she added, glancing at her daughter, and Josette, who had spent the afternoon at the hairdresser, managed a smile.

'I adore Paris!' said another woman, whose husband was something in the Civil Service. 'I won't shop anywhere else these days. There's a little *couturière* I've discovered on the Rue Bonaparte. She sews for all the big *maisons* and is an angel. If you promise not to tell a soul I'll give you her card.'

'Ah, how delightful,' gushed Violette. 'I'm always on the lookout for new addresses. And in return I shall give you my silk lady. She has a tiny shop in the dixième and will only see people by appointment. Philippe buys all his ties there now, his tailor says he has never seen the like of them.'

'Only the French understand quality,' someone said.

'How true, how true!' said someone else.

'Where is that wonderful son of yours? I'm not really a fan of young people, but I always make an exception for Clement.' This was Sukie Miller, a thin, sharp-featured American, with yellow blonde hair and puffy eyes. Recently separated from her third husband, she had the combative cheeriness often found in bored, rich women. 'I do hope he'll be joining us. I get all my best gossip from your son, he's the main reason I came tonight, the racing is such a bore.'

Violette beamed with delight. 'Clemmie? Oh, he'll be here any moment. He's at Ras el-Tine,' (she pronounced it *Tine* and not *Tin* because that was how it was written on the invitation), 'they always go on late. The King is quite desperate for company of his own age, and can you blame him? It's a terrible life for a young boy, sitting around while his uncles argue what's best for Egypt. No wonder he drives so fast.' She twirled her opera glasses, and Sukie Miller said, 'Simply awful.'

'And now there's poor Safinaz to think about too,' said the Greek Consul's wife with her usual weary shrug. She made a point of using the Queen's birth name to show how well she knew the family. 'A mere child, she's barely sixteen you know. Her poor father begged them to wait a few years, but you know what these young people today are like, there's no telling them.'

'Oh darling, sixteen isn't so young, think what we were like at that age,' said Violette, who like many selfish parents confused disinterest with liberalism. 'I wouldn't dream of telling Josette what to do, and I'm quite sure she wouldn't listen if I did, *tant mieux*. Would you darling?' Josette looked enquiringly at her mother, for she had not heard the question. 'Clemmie, on the other hand won't do a thing without my approval – I suppose it's a boy thing.'

'I suppose it is,' sighed Sukie Miller, whose lack of sons was more than made up for in husbands.

'But it's so difficult to strike the right balance these days,' lamented the Consul's wife, 'especially with girls. There are so many pressures on them to be independent, to make their own choices. Yousef—' she hesitated, correcting herself, 'Judge Zulficar, that is, worries terribly about whether they did the right thing, letting Safinaz marry so young. Of course, they would hardly have stopped her, any father would be delighted with such a brilliant match, but it hasn't been easy.' She glanced towards the front of the box where Josette was chattering softly to Bobby. 'I don't know how you remain so calm. Dear Safinaz is one thing,' she said, resting her jewelled hand on Violette's forearm, 'but not all girls are going to marry the King of Egypt.' And she shuddered, as if the thought of anything less were too much to bear.

'And a good thing it is too,' said Sukie Miller breezily, who held a more pragmatic view of marriage. 'From what I've heard, Queen Nazli is a positive tyrant and not at all the adoring mother-in-law she affects to be. My manicurist knows someone at the palace,' she explained, in case they should think she was gossiping. 'He says the two queens are at each other's throats from morning till night, Nazli got more than she bargained for in that one. Is that Porto? How very European! She took a glass, sniffing it as if to suggest a particular connoisseurship. 'One's always in safe hands with the d'Araquys.'

'I'm a creature of simple tastes,' confirmed Violette.

'Oh darling, it's such a relief.' said the civil servant's wife. 'You wouldn't believe what people serve these days. Just last week we were invited to dinner at a certain English cotton brokers, I mention no names, and we were given something the sommelier called 'Wine of the Pharoahs.' It's all the fashion amongst the Heliopolis set — vinegar would be a better description.' She paused, breathless with outrage. 'There's a reason nobody's made wine in Egypt for two thousand years.'

Everyone laughed and exchanged stories of similar affronts, of which it turned out there were many.

'Seriously, though,' said Violette, glancing again at her daughter, 'I do wonder whether we haven't done these girls a disservice, filling them with education and telling them they can be anything they choose to be. It hardly prepares them for real life, now, does it?' and she gazed in sorrow at her glittering party, as if therein she found the chains of her own confinement. 'I don't think Josette gives marriage a second thought,' she murmured, 'and why would she? She has everything she could want at home.'

'My girls couldn't begin to run a household of their own,' said the Consul's wife, thinking how just that morning, she had spent two hours with the cook planning lunch menus and longer still debating laundry bills, for the housekeeper was convinced they were being overcharged. 'They don't understand the first thing about managing servants, all they care about is whether their dress will be pressed for the next party.'

'We've been too easy on them,' said Violette.

'We've protected them too much,' agreed the Consul's wife.

They were interrupted by the arrival of a new guest, a man of around fifty in a tweed jacket and brogues, who stopped in the open doorway and raised his arms, like a maestro preparing for his favourite aria.

'The most beautiful woman in Alexandria,' he declared, and he seized Violette's hand and proceeded to shower it with kisses.

'Just Alexandria?' flirted Violette, and she smiled and left her hand in his, for admirers were to be encouraged. 'We were discussing the fates of our daughters, we've decided all is lost,' and she waved to Josette and said 'Josie darling, come say hello to Uncle Robin.'

'How delightful. Ah Josie, as pretty as ever, what a family, what a family. Whenever I want to remind myself that there is beauty in the world, I just look at the Demoiselles d'Araquy and my faith is restored. Let me see you. Like a gazelle, you are, quite charming, quite charming. Here, a kiss, just here,' and he pointed to a spot on his cheek, so that Josette had to stand on her tip toes to reach it. 'And who is that charming gentleman you're hiding there? Is there something I should know? Josie, my love, have you thrown me over for a younger man?' and he threw back his head and guffawed.

'You are impossible,' scolded Violette. 'Oh Josie, don't frown so! Why must young girls take everything so seriously? Robin, this is my nephew, Mr Cansino. Bobby this is our dear friend Mr Robin Barrows, he's a lecturer at the American university and terribly important.' (Everyone laughed and stood up a little straighter). 'Bobby is visiting Alex for a few weeks, we're showing him about.'

'So I see,' said the older man, and he winked and clapped Bobby on the shoulder vigorously. 'And what do you make of our glorious city?' He paused for effect:

'The radiant blue of the morning sea,
the cloudless sky and the yellow beach;
all beautiful and flooded with light.'

'Cavafy—?' said Bobby, but Violette interrupted him.

'Robin writes wonderful poetry,' she said, and Robin, who had not intended to claim ownership of the lines, smiled and bowed his head.

'Ah, a poet!' cried Sukie Miller, as though she had been looking for one all evening. She narrowed her puffy eyes and leaned closer. 'Tell me, where will I have seen your work? I read simply everything, I adore the arts.'

'Where would we be without culture?' said Violette.

There followed a lively consideration of recent productions at the Alhambra and everyone agreed it had been a marvellous programme this year. Someone mentioned a play they had seen on tour from the Ohel, (in Hebrew unfortunately, but awfully well done), and this drew them seamlessly into a discussion about the state of Palestine. A woman who knew someone at the High Commission said it was dreadful what was happening there, and the Consul's wife asked what kind of a world it was when diplomats had to fix broom heads to their front wheels to stop their tyres being punctured? That democracy was not what it used to be was lamented by all.

'Is it all right if we go and look at the horses, Mummy?' asked Josette, when at last there was a pause in the conversation. She had picked up her parasol again and was leaning on it, one leg lifted and at right angles to the other.

'You look like a flamingo!' shrieked Sukie Miller, and she smiled fondly, as women often do when they have said something cruel.

Josette blushed and straightened up.

'I thought we might look out for Clemmie at the same time. He should be here by now.' She peered into the distance, two deep lines appearing between her eyes.

'Don't frown, darling,' said Violette, adding 'Clemmie has been at Ras el-Tine,' for the benefit of those who had arrived late. She glanced at Bobby. 'Are you sure you don't mind?' she asked, and he shook his head and said 'Course not.'

'Cousins, you say?' said the poet, peering after them. He raised a thick eyebrow and grinned.

'You are brave,' said the Consul's wife as they disappeared down the steps, and the conversation, like a carefully thrown ball, rolled back to her favourite subject.

CHAPTER 20

There was clatter of footsteps and Clemmie burst in, flush with the success of his afternoon and the additional effort of running up three flights of steps. He was met with great excitement, a warrior returning from the field of battle, and for a moment everyone talked at once. Flicking his golden hair and pushing at the tails of his shirt, which had come untucked in the rush for the stairs, he beamed. And the sun, which had disappeared behind the stands, seemed to have come back out again.

'I saw Edward and Mrs Simpson downstairs,' he declared, when at last his afternoon was all told out.

'They're *here*?' asked the Consul's wife in surprise, for she was generally the first to know such things.

'He means Josette and my nephew,' explained Violette, who knew her son too well. 'They went to look at the horses,' she told Clemmie.

Clemmie rolled his eyes. 'You should keep an eye on those two, Mummy, Josie has the same look about her as when she convinced Daddy to buy her that horrid puppy. And remember how that turned out.'

'Oh do tell,' said the poet, 'I love a tragic puppy story.'

'There's nothing to tell,' said Violette, frowning at Clemmie, who was clearly in one of his teasing moods. 'It was a dreadful little thing, wasn't it Mrs Patchett?' This was the first time she had addressed the governess since the guests had arrived and Mrs Patchett looked up in surprise. 'It was a great relief to everyone when it ran off.'

'She says it ran off, but in fact she gave it to someone at

Daddy's club,' said Clemmie. 'Josie and I saw it one day, in the back of a car. Mummy still insists it was a different dog, but I'd know that vicious creature anywhere. Josie was beside herself.' He laughed and stroked Violette's wrist. 'Don't worry Mummy, I shan't tell.'

Violette sighed and turned around to help Hassan unload a tray. It was laden with little dishes of caramelised dates and cheese tartlets, and those delicious olives you could only buy from a certain Greek grocer near the Corniche. She picked up a plate of warm salted almonds and passed them around. 'My mother's recipe,' she said, and everyone gasped, because such homely provenance was rare in sophisticated Alexandria.

'Well I thought he was rather sweet,' said the poet, 'the cousin, I mean. And she could do a lot worse, especially if the British Army set up camp, which they're saying is only a matter of time. The last thing you want is her running off with some orderly in baggy shorts and desert boots.'

The Consul's wife gave a shriek and covered her face.

'I went to a rather good talk at the Amitiés Françaises recently,' said Sukie Miller, 'about the Ptolemies.' She paused and smiled confidentially. 'You know how mad I am about history.' The poet, who did not know, nodded encouragement. 'Well apparently the Pharoahs married each other all the time, brothers, sisters, mothers, sons, it was all the same to them. How did he put it — oh we rolled about laughing — "Keep the business in the family, and the family in the business!" How about it, Violette darling? ' and she laughed shrilly.

'Well I'm glad you're all amused,' said Violette, and she moved away and stood by the front railing, for the subject threatened to spoil her mood. From there she saw Philippe slowly making his way through the stands, shaking hands and swinging his gold tipped cane, purchased on the Faubourg St Honoré last summer. She leaned over and waved at him to hurry up.

At his side, in immaculate cream linen and an Optimo panama hat, was Marco Balestra. The two men raised their hands and saluted her, so that all around, people glanced up and thought how delightful she was, floating above their heads like some distant deity.

Bobby, leaning against the white painted fence which edged the racetrack, shaded his eyes with his hand and watched this too. It was like looking up at a stage, except that they were real people, with real lives, and he wondered what it must be to move through the world so unhindered. Bobby felt a pang of envy, but as quickly as it struck him, it disappeared again and he turned back to Josette with his usual, untroubled grin.

'Mr Balestra is with Daddy, do you want to go back up?' she said, since he had told her he was supposed to talk to him about a contract.

Bobby shrugged. 'Not unless you do.'

'I'm happy here,' said Josette. She wanted to say something, but she wasn't sure quite what, and so she poked the grass with her parasol, making holes in the dry ground. 'What's she like?' she said at last, for her train of thought had wandered.

'Who?'

'Your sister. Laura. Everyone says Marco Balestra is in love with her, is it true?' She had overheard her mother gossiping about this at the beach that first day Bobby had visited them. 'Not in a bad way,' she added.

'Golly,' said Bobby, who had never heard this. He thought about it for a moment. 'I don't think that can be right,' he said.

'Oh,' said Josette, and then, 'Sorry.'

'Really, I'm sure it isn't,' he insisted, because once an idea got into his head it went round and round like a buzzing insect until he had swatted it enough times that it gave up.

'He's just been helping her, that's all. Isaac's death was very sudden, there were a lot of things to sort out. And she does rather rely upon him, I think she feels he understands her better than the rest of us do.' This was the first time he had articulated this thought, but in saying it, he felt it was probably the truth. 'Our lives are very different.'

'People here make up stories all the time,' said Josette.

'Laura would hate to think people were saying that,' said Bobby, although he wondered if she really would. 'Careful, you'll break it.' He put his hand on the parasol so that she stopped jabbing at the grass. They stood in silence for a moment.

'Have you never met her?' asked Bobby after a while. 'I felt sure you had.'

'No, no, I have. It was just a long time ago and I was young, so I don't remember much. Except that she had beautiful hair and that she brought me a Lenci doll with real leather shoes and a satin dress.'

'Lenci?'

'It's Italian. There's a photograph somewhere of her with it, she's sitting in the dining room with the doll on the table in front of her. Mummy was so cross with me that day because I was shy and didn't say thank-you properly, but Laura said it didn't matter and that her girls were just the same when they got presents.' She hesitated. 'She said she had chosen the pretty one because it reminded her of me.'

'It must be lovely then,' said Bobby, but there was a strangeness in those words, and immediately he wished he could take them back.

Josette seemed to wish it too, for she blushed and stared at her shoes, her stockings dusty from the dry ground. Her heart was beating fast and the earth trembled beneath her, as if in sympathy, but then she realised it was the pounding of the horses' hooves she could feel and she turned around just as they flew past. The jockeys sat high above the leather saddles, like brightly coloured grasshoppers, and the air was briefly charged with heat which seemed to linger there, even after they were past the finish post. It was as if something awful had just happened, except that rather than feeling afraid, she was filled with a quiet elation.

All around them people were moving and over the Tannoy system a voice announced the winners in several different languages and the crowd cheered. A man in a white galabiyah was balancing on a ladder, chalking up names on a blackboard, and below him, people craned their necks and said what a close finish it was and what a shame they hadn't got better odds. The horses, who had turned around and were trotting back down the straight, lifted their heads and made small jerking movements, to keep off the flies that landed on their eyes, their flanks, their flicking tails. In the stands, the women lowered their opera glasses and went back to their chattering.

'Do you still have it?' said Bobby, after a while, meaning the doll.

'Oh. No,' said Josette, 'I'm too old to play with dolls now.' She looked up and saw her father waving from the box, beckoning them to come up. 'We should go back, they'll be wondering where we got to,' she said, and it seemed that what had happened between them had passed, for Josette had her usual bright smile.

Bobby felt a sense of relief and, with it, a desire to confess something.

'I read all the newspapers before I came this evening,' he said, stooping as they walked towards the stand, his head bent so that their eyes were on the same level. 'I wanted to be able to keep up, everyone here is so worldly and well-informed. Don't you find?'

Josette had never given it much thought, and she said so.

'That's because you're used to it,' said Bobby.

She shrugged. 'Perhaps.'

And they made their way slowly back up the concrete steps, pushing past the waiters with their trays of lemonade and the young boys waving racecards, and stopping occasionally so that Josette could say hello to all the people she knew.

II

PART TWO

CHAPTER 1

Lucia Arditti was not herself. At the beginning of September she had read a small notice in the newspaper (one of Il Duce's *Informazione*, announcing that Jewish children could no longer attend public schools) and since then she had not stopped crying. At the time the family was at the coast, where they went every year for the summer months, but almost immediately they returned to Milan, for Lucia was distraught and it was frightening the children. Dr Ferri was called, prescribing pills and chastising her for getting so worked up, but when she remained inconsolable, her thin face glassy and unresponsive, it was decided to send for the rabbi, and it was into his capacious hands that Lucia was now delivered.

The rabbi was a gentle man, with wiry grey hair and a long beard that he wound around his forefinger when he spoke. He had known Lucia since she was a young bride, and liked her, for she was a kind woman and always quick to lend a hand if someone was in difficulty. Now, he observed, closing the dining room door behind him, it was Signora Arditti herself who was in need, and he smiled and twisted his beard, only too happy to be of help.

She was not the only one, of course, who had been unsettled by the publication of the new laws. His telephone rang without cease those first few days, and his wife no longer took messages but instead told people they could find him in synagogue, for he spent all his time there. Parents, teachers, community leaders, they gathered around the rabbi as a kind of working committee, offering one another reassurance and talking about the Jewish schools that were being set up in other cities across Italy. What mattered most, they agreed, was that they remain calm, for Il Duce was merely testing their fortitude, he meant no real harm. '*Tra il dire e il fare c'e' di mezzo il mare*' they reminded one another, between the saying and the doing there is the sea.

It was to just such logical reasoning that the rabbi now treated Lucia. He was not insensitive, he understood that people respond differently in these situations but because he knew her well, he allowed himself to be firm. He explained how all this was not really a surprise to him, that it had been building for some time, that this latest exclusion was part of a natural progression. First there had been that Orano book which stirred things up, then the various articles setting Zionism against Fascist Italy, for it seemed the two were implacably opposed. Then the phrase '*problema ebraico*' started appearing in editorials, and distinctions were made between Italians and Italian Jews, where before they had been the same thing, so that people began saying things like 'We mourned Julius Caesar too, you know,' as proof of their loyalty. And then just a month ago it had all come to a head in the discovery of a pure Italian race, to which, it was said, the Jews did not belong.

The rabbi shook his head, his forefinger worked so tight inside his beard that it seemed to be growing there. 'My dear girl, you haven't made a murmur at all these other inconveniences.' He chose his words carefully, *inconvenienti* being the noun he felt best expressed the Jewish position. 'Why now, why this?'

'My children must go to school.' Lucia glanced at the old man and shook her head, the gesture causing her eyes to spill with tears, as though the movement had squeezed a valve somewhere.

'Now, now, enough of that.' He felt in his jacket for something to dry her face, but his wife could not launder his handkerchiefs fast enough these days, and his pockets were empty. 'Of course your children will go to school, that's never been in question.' Again he shook his head, as though he could not understand how such an intelligent person as she could be so mistaken. 'We'll make our own school, your husband's explained all this to you. We'll make our own school, an excellent school with only the very best teachers and none of this marching nonsense. No skiing either, I've never understood how throwing yourself down a mountain on bits of wood could be seen as anything other than foolish.' His blue eyes twinkled, and he leaned forward so that Lucia should look at him, for no one could ever resist his twinkling blue eyes. 'There, that's better, that's the Lucia Arditti I know.'

The door opened a crack and Raphael, not liking to intrude, asked if he might bring the rabbi a glass of water.

'Come in, dear boy, come in. We're feeling much better.'

Raphael glanced at his wife. She looked away, dabbing at her face with the hem of her dress.

'We're just talking about the new school,' the rabbi continued. 'Our children will have the best of the best, I have university professors offering to teach *primo grado* — oh, what an education we'll give them. And no more marching!' He glanced at Lucia, as if this was a joke they shared.

'Have you found a building yet?' asked Raphael, following the rabbi's lead and keeping to practicalities.

'Paolo Varinetti has offered the lease on one of their old sewing machine factories, I went down there this morning. A bit of cleaning up, it'll be a wonderful space for the children.'

'I know that building,' said Raphael with enthusiasm, 'Off the Premuda? But it'll be perfect, all those skylights and windows! Think how bright it'll be, Lucia, you've always said that children need sunlight to learn, the Ruffini is a gloomy old place. And the rent?'

'A little high, but Signore Varinetti's assured me there's room for negotiation. Besides, people are being very generous, we'll not lack funds.' He paused just long enough for Raphael to remember where he had left his wallet. 'You should come see for yourself, Lucia.' He had untangled his finger from his beard, and now touched it to Lucia's two hands, lying motionless in her lap. 'It'll cheer you up to see how positive everyone is.'

'Perhaps,' said Lucia with effort, for the two men were gazing at her and clearly expected a response.

'Then that's settled.' The rabbi stood up. He had other visits to make this afternoon and he checked his pocket watch, attached to his belt by a gold chain, frowning when he saw he was late. 'I don't suppose you're acquainted with the Guerinis? He's asked me to call by. Apparently his wife's got it into her head they should move to Switzerland.'

'I know her sister, Sofia,' murmured Lucia.

'But Filippo Guerini is Italian,' said Raphael, then blushed, for this is how it happened, you started talking the way they did. 'I mean he's not a Jew.'

'The wife is, apparently.' The rabbi snapped shut the pocket watch. 'Russian, I believe he said, they have persecution in their blood. I'll do what I can. Don't get up, dear, your husband will see me out. I'll expect you at synagogue then.' He paused, smiling down at Lucia's bent head. 'Good girl.'

In the hall, the younger children had made a speedway for their tricycles, and were racing one another up and down the narrow passage while Netta watched. She was holding the rabbi's hat.

'How like her mother she is,' said the rabbi, smiling. The girl flushed with pleasure, for she could think of no greater compliment. The rabbi took his hat and spent a moment adjusting it in the mirror.

'Would you like Luca to drive you?' said Raphael. 'The Guerinis are off San Damiano, he can easily drop you.'

'Luca is out, Papa. He said to tell you.' In fact Luca had been out since they got back from the beach, taking full advantage of his mother's indisposition.

'Oh.'

'No, no, the walk will do me good, don't trouble yourselves.' There was little chance of him walking, for someone always stopped to offer a lift. 'Besides it'll give me time to consider my best approach. The wife is a follower of that Weiss fellow, I'll take Fascism over his psychoanalysis nonsense any day of the week. You know where you are with Fascism.' The blue eyes were twinkling again, and Raphael grinned and said, yes, they had that to be thankful for.

'Is she going to be all right?' This was Netta, the question seeming to fall from her lips involuntarily, for straight away she covered her mouth and looked down.

'Mammina? Of course,' said her father, but he had been saying this ever since the beach, and Netta turned to the rabbi, preferring his opinion.

'Mammina's going to be fine. A little time and rest and she'll be back to her usual self. Dr Ferri prescribed something, you said?' He looked to Raphael for confirmation. 'Good. A day or two and she'll be back on her feet. These are difficult times.' He sighed, cupping the girl's face in his hands and pressing it as he might a ripe melon. 'We must have strength of spirit.' He pressed again, repeating '*forza d'animo, forza d'animo,*' for it seemed to him that this was the key to everything. Then he swung through the door and charged down the steep stairs with the vigour of a man half his age.

CHAPTER 2

Some time later, Raphael's father arrived. He was supposed to be in Asti for his annual game shoot, but had delayed his departure when he heard about Lucia, and now he strode into the dim hall, throwing down his hunting hat, with the feathers sticking out of the rim, and looked around in expectation.

'Where's is she? Where's my favourite daughter-in-law?' He wore tweed breeches and the shooting socks Lucia had knitted him, with their coloured bands and tassels, and he clapped his hands as he spoke. 'Children, come, take me to your mother, I want to hear about this new school of yours!'

The children gathered around their grandfather, chattering and tugging on his coat, but it turned out that they knew very little about anything, except that their mother was still not to be disturbed. Raphael, who had disappeared into his study the moment the rabbi left, heard them and came out.

'Papa.'

Gabriel Arditti kissed his son firmly on both cheeks, his eyes locking with the younger man's and thus avoiding the abandoned tricycles, the unpacked suitcases, the piles of shoes and beach paraphernalia which covered the floor. The main cog had stopped turning, and the engine that was this family had ground to a halt.

'A week in the hills, how I wish I were coming with you!' said his son.

'And yet every year I invite you and you say no. I shall bring you back a brace or two of grey partridge, how would that be? They say the partridge are plentiful this year, something to do with fewer crows stealing the eggs. I have a good feeling about this week, I think I shall beat my record.'

'You say that every year, Papi,' said Netta, sidling up to her grandfather and slipping her hand into his.

'It's true, you do,' said Raphael.

'Yes, but this year's different, you'll see.' He bent to kiss the top of Netta's hair, glancing at the dining room door. 'Can I put my head in?'

'Of course. She'll be happy to see you.'

'I won't stay long.'

Netta let go of her grandfather's hand, moving to the other side of the hall and perching on the arm of a chair there. From this position, she saw her mother only from behind, her hair loose over the shoulders of her beach dress, her elbows pressed to her sides. It was just enough to know she was still there, to reassure herself that it was not because her mother had vanished that they were kept from the dining room. That her mother might up and leave her was a possibility with which Netta, like many nervous children, did battle every day.

'Did you park on the street?'

'The car, I almost forgot! I'm blocking the road, would you have one of the boys move it for me.' He gave his son the keys, with the rabbit-foot pendant, and Raphael in turn passed them to Netta. 'Be sure you tell them to lock it, I have all my luggage inside.'

'I can do it for you, Papi, I know how to drive.' Netta stroked the soft fur. 'Mammina says I park better than she does.'

'Ah, these girls know how to do everything these days. Soon there will be no need for us men, eh? You'll be sure to lock it? Twice now I've had my maps stolen, they'll take anything they can find.' It was understood by 'they' that Gabriel meant the refugees. 'Any trouble, remember my Browning is in the trunk. No doubt you're a bull's eye shot too!' His fingers rested on the brass door handle.

'I don't like shooting,' said Netta.

'No, no, quite right too.'

'Besides, Mammina says that we should feel sorry for the poor refugees, that it isn't their fault they're in this position.'

'I must remember that,' said her grandfather, 'the next time I'm picking glass out of the upholstery.' He let go of the door handle and took a step back. 'You're young, my dear,' he peered at Netta across the dim hallway, 'when you're older you'll see things differently. The world's a hard place, it's no good being too soft, soft people are crushed.'

Netta looked away. He meant her mother, she was sure of it. And yet there was nothing soft about Lucia, even when she wept there was a sharpness to her. Soft was Auntie Allegra, with her pillowy breasts and plump, dimpled arms. Netta stood up, her fist balled around the rabbit's foot. 'I shall never think like that,' she said, tears pricking her eyelids. 'No matter how old I am, I'll never think like that,' and she jumped from the chair and ran out onto the stairs.

'Don't mind her,' said Raphael, crossing the hall and closing the front door, which Netta had left open.

Gabriel frowned. He was listening for his car, relieved when at last the familiar rumble of the Lancia's engine reached him.

'I don't know what's wrong with her,' continued Raphael. 'One minute she's sweet, the next minute she's fighting with everyone and storming out.'

'You're not firm enough.'

'I've tried but it only makes things worse.' Raphael sighed. 'Girls are different, you had four sons, Papa, you never had a daughter.'

'I know you need to be firm. And not just with children, with your wife too. Yes, I mean with Lucia too. You are lax, Raphael, you don't assert your authority and this is the result. I'm not saying you should raise your hand, of course not, only cowards and brutes resort to violence. But your wife must respect you. Your mother, God bless her memory, would never have behaved like this, not ever. She'd turn in her grave to think of you calling in the rabbi.'

Gabriel had not intended to say so much, and he stopped. for Raphael's head was bowed and he was nodding.

'Never mind, never mind all that.' He put a hand to his son's shoulder and pulled him into his chest, and to Raphael it was as if he was a small boy again, huddled under his father's prayer shawl with his brothers. How simple it had all been then, leaning into his father, breathing in his smoky, sweet smell as he repeated the prayers, his mother watching over them from the balcony. 'It's hard on you too.'

'It's because it's the schools. If it'd been anything else she wouldn't have reacted like this.'

'She's a mother, it's normal that she worries about their education.'

'It's not that — she thinks he's going after the children, that he wants to hurt her children. She says she won't obey a man who hurts her children.'

'She said that?'

'Over and over. That's why I sent the servants home, I was worried they'd hear her.'

Gabriel could hardly bear it. 'Il Duce loves the children, how could you let her think such a thing?'

'I can't control how she thinks, Papa. I did what I could, I sent the servants away and I called Dr Ferri and the rabbi. If in her heart she still thinks Il Duce has betrayed her, what can I do about it?'

Gabriel shook his head sadly. 'I'll talk to her, I'll make her see sense.'

'Good luck to you.'

CHAPTER 3

Although it was the middle of the day, the dining room where Lucia sat was dark, for the windows were small and faced north. She was at the table, a pile of newspapers spread before her, and when Gabriel came in she narrowed her eyes and frowned, as though she couldn't make out who it was. He was shocked to see how old she looked, how pinched and frail-looking, but he came straight up to her, kissing her cheeks and sitting down beside her.

'I'm on my way to Asti, I wanted to see you before I left. I'm wearing your socks, do you see?' He lifted his leg and turned it this way and that, so that the tassels jiggled. 'Finest socks I've ever owned.'

'I'm glad,' said Lucia.

'I've promised Raphael I'll bring back some of those little grey partridge you like, perhaps you can ask Maria to make a special sauce?' The Ardittis' cook was Sicilian and known for her sauces. 'It will be our celebratory meal.'

Lucia glanced up. 'What are we celebrating?'

'You feeling better. Because you will, you'll feel better by then, I promise.'

Lucia held his gaze. 'Nothing's wrong with me.'

'My dearest Lucia.' He smiled and reached for one of her hands, which was resting on the pile of newspapers. She withdrew it to her lap. 'Come now, this is me you're talking to. You forget how well I know you.'

She looked away, fiddling with the belt of her beach-dress, arranging it so that the pattern of the belt matched up perfectly with the fabric of the dress. He watched her in silence, then sat back, folding his arms across his tweed chest.

'Do you know, I'm surprised at you, Lucia Arditti, I thought better of you. Out of all my sons' wives, I thought you were the one I could count on. And then one small "hiccup",' he used the English word to emphasise the foreignness of it all, 'and you fall apart. Did you know Cecilia registered all three children for the Turin school without so much as a murmur?'

'Cecilia's a fool.'

'Cecilia's a good Fascist.' He spoke sternly, for this was at the heart of what he wished to say to her. 'Cecilia understands that we have nothing to fear, that Il Duce is our friend.'

'Ah, if one more person tells me he's our friend!' cried Lucia, throwing up her hands and in doing so knocking over a cup that was on the edge of the table. Her cheeks glittered with tears but there was a colour in them suddenly, and her eyes, which before had been empty and dull, looked straight at Gabriel. He reached across and righted the cup, moving it to the other side of the table.

'You shouldn't talk that way, you don't know what you're saying.' He spoke sternly, thinking how right his son had been to send the servants home.

'Oh really?' Lucia continued to stare at him. 'Why? Might I be thought "disproportionate"? The word was *sproporzionata* and she articulated each syllable, spitting them at him like cherry stones.

Gabriel shook his head. 'That's not what was meant, you're deliberately misconstruing it.'

'One Jew for every thousand Italians, that's what he'll allow. Read it, read it for yourself!' She pushed the pile of newspapers towards Gabriel. 'It's all there in black and white.'

Gabriel sighed. He had read it already, he had read all those articles and *Informazione*, but they only made him more determined to prove his loyalty. And not just to Il Duce, but to

Italy herself, for Jews like him were a part of Italy, they had been there from the start. He thought of his grandfather, who had marched straight out of the ghetto to liberate Milan from the Austrians and who spoke of his *Italia bimbe*, his young Italy, in the same way he spoke of his children; of his cousin who had taken Hebrew classes with Luigi Luzzati, prime-minister of Italy before the Great War and a Venetian Jew; of his son, Raphael's brother, who had once courted that Sarfatti woman, now Il Duce's mistress and proof if anyone needed it that Fascism loves the Jews. 'Please, calm yourself,' he said. 'I hate to see you upset like this.'

'Why do you defend him?' Tears trickled down her thin cheeks but her voice was quite steady.

'There is nothing to defend.'

'Then all this,' she brushed her hand over the pile of newspapers, sending several of them scattering across the table. 'All this is nothing?'

'Please, you're making yourself ill — I thought the rabbi had reassured you, I thought you were feeling better.'

'Better?' She slumped forward, her breath coming in small, quick gasps.

'You're overreacting — Il Duce just wants to be sure of us, to know we'll not abandon him the moment things become difficult. Remember Caporetto.'

At the mention of Caporetto, Lucia's body jerked upright and then she was on her feet, the chair flung from beneath her and clattering across the parquet like a skittle. 'Caporetto? You compare this to Caporetto? Caporetto was a massacre! If men deserted it's because they knew they were being ordered towards certain death, they were no match for the German guns. How can you speak of Caporetto? Is death what it takes to be a loyal Italian? Is that the price you're ready to pay? Well not me! I should be ashamed to sell myself so cheap, and my children too. You may choose to sacrifice your family to the Fascist dream, so may the rabbi and Cecilia and all the others. But not me, I never will!'

She turned away, swaying slightly, her hand reaching for the edge of the table to steady herself. Gabriel gazed at her thin back, which shuddered as she tried to collect herself. He was hurt that she could speak to him this way: theirs had always been such a happy relationship, she was like a daughter to him. He leaned forward, his elbows resting on the table, and covered his eyes with his hands. He heard the scrape of Lucia's chair as she set it upright and then a creak as she sat down next to him.

'Papi, I'm sorry,' she murmured, calling him by the name the children used.

Gabriel took a handkerchief from his pocket and blew his nose. He coughed a little, clearing his throat. 'I'm sorry too.'

Lucia took his hand in hers. With her thumbs she stroked the black hairs that escaped his cuff and which he sometimes trimmed with moustache scissors. 'This isn't pride,' she said, her voice a whisper, 'I've no pride for myself, please understand that. I didn't mind the propaganda, the forced resignations, even all this talk of Jews being "recent guests" — I understand that sometimes we must sacrifice our immediate comforts for the greater good of Italy. "To discriminate is not to persecute," they said, and I believed them. Why wouldn't I? But when they go after the children, when they announce laws for the protection of schools, and what they are protecting them against is my babies, then I have to act.'

'But of course,' said Gabriel, 'it's only normal you should feel like that. But this will pass, I promise. You must just hold steady.'

Lucia shook her head. She had let go of Gabriel's hand and she looked past him and out of the window, beyond the tracks of the railway towards the trees and open spaces of the Sempione Park. 'I cannot tell my children to march where Il Duce chooses (she said *"marceremo come Duce vuole"* as in the song) when he's marching them back into the ghetto.'

'There is no ghetto.'

'Not yet, no. But ever since I read that announcement I've had the most terrible presentiment that my life is unravelling, that something dreadful is about to happen to us. I can't sleep, I have these dreams that wake me up all the time, and so I get out of bed and I sit here, and then the same pictures fill my mind, I feel like I'm going mad. I've tried to tell myself that this is nonsense, that I'm just being hysterical and that there's no foundation for such anxiety, that I must get a hold of myself. But every time I come back to the same thing, that my children must go to school, and if they cannot go to their school, the one on the Via Ruffini where they've always gone, then everything is finished for us.'

She hesitated. She wanted to say that it was finished for him too, for all of them, but she knew that he would not understand, and so she talked only of herself and her children.

'All I can think about is leaving. From morning until night, it's the only thing on my mind, you cannot imagine how it torments me. I feel sick to my stomach, everything seems rotten now, that's why I can't bear to go out, to speak to people, to see everyone going about their day as if nothing were wrong. I know, I know, it's the shock of everything, "nervous exhaustion" Dr Ferri called it. That's why he gave me those pills to help me sleep, but I'm afraid to take them. I'm afraid they'll dull my brain so that I'll not be ready. My children are Italians, they should go to Italian schools. If they cannot then we must go away. Just until things get better. If I'm away from here I'll feel calm again and be able to sleep— I'll be able to think clearly.'

'But you can't leave Milan, this is your home, you have property here.'

'My children have to go to school—' Lucia ran her nail along the edge of the dining table, leaving a faint line on the heavily waxed surface. 'That Balestra woman was right, leaving when she did. I saw her, you know, just before we left for the beach, I was with Netta at the Galleria and we saw them coming out of Rina. They were spending the summer in Cortina and then leaving straight for Brussels. 'Leaving for a better home,' she called it. Can you imagine? How rude, I said to Netta afterwards, how rude to say such a thing, this is our home. But now I see she was right.'

'That was different, her husband had died. Yours is still here and he's worried about you. I don't think I've ever seen Raphael so worried.'

'He hides himself away in his study, he won't even look at me.'

'He's afraid.'

'He thinks I've lost my mind. And perhaps I have, I can't tell any more. All I know is that I cannot bear this life — he says he'll send the children to the Jewish school whether I like it or not.'

'But surely you—'

'—no! I will never allow it. If they can't go to their own school, to the school on the Via Ruffini—'

'But you know they can't—'

'—if they cannot go there, we must leave. It's the only answer, we must go away. If my husband won't agree, then I shall leave on my own with the children. I'll take them to Switzerland, like Signora Guerini wants. Anywhere but here.'

Gabriel gazed at his daughter-in-law, and he saw that she meant it, that she would leave her marriage, her home, her life, rather than submit. For a long time he did not speak, and Lucia too was silent, her breathing steady and slow, and when eventually he looked at her, he saw that she was weeping again. Gabriel put his hand on hers, pressing it firmly.

'I'll speak to my son. I'll delay my trip and I'll speak to Raphael, I'm sure we can find a solution.'

'You'll speak to him about our leaving Milan?'

'There might be another way. Let me think about it — I won't let you down.'

Gabriel kept his word and directly he left Lucia, he went to Raphael's study and spoke with his son. He told him that something must be done, that Lucia was unwell and that for the moment it would be unwise to cause her further stress or anxiety. He knew of a boarding school in Bern, just over the border, and suggested that perhaps the children should spend a term there, until things settled down. That way, Lucia could have the time she needed to recuperate, to get her strength back, and after Christmas the children could return to Milan and life could go back to normal. Raphael accepted the idea without argument and a week later, Gabriel set off at last for his game-shoot and the children left for Switzerland.

CHAPTER 4

It was quite by chance that the Balestras left Milan when they did. There had been a problem with Laura's Belgian visa (she had been promised a *carte blanche* but had so far only been given a *carte jaune*) and three times she had been obliged to delay their move. Afterwards, when the newspapers were full of Il Duce's new racial laws, and people everywhere were lamenting the precipitous state of Europe, it seemed their timing was especially fortuitous. Fate, Laura liked to think, had been on their side.

This giving of herself up to a dominant force was a habit with Laura. An overprotected childhood had yielded to a comfortable, affluent marriage, and it seemed quite natural to let others take charge. Despite being articulate and well-informed, she was quite without moral energy, mostly because she had never had need of it. There had always been someone else to judge the world for her, to assess its dangers and to react accordingly, and even now, alone for the first time, she took solace in this fact.

And so it seemed quite out of character when she refused all offers of help in packing up the apartment. The reason she gave was that it was easier that way, that with all these visa problems she had no fixed date and could be waiting around for weeks. But mostly it was to avoid the need to be cheerful, to reassure everyone that she was doing fine, when quite possibly she wouldn't be. This feeling of being constantly observed, of having her every move and mood analysed and reported back, bothered her. There was a kind of ownership in such solicitude, as though she and the children were being projected onto a large screen to which everyone had access, and about which everyone had an opinion. With an almost superstitious faith, Laura thought that if she could do this part well and unobserved, then her life would be her own again.

It was just over a year since Isaac's death and, with quiet ceremony, Laura unpicked the black cloth patches from the children's coat sleeves and burned them in the hall stove. Then she filled a large bag with her own sombre wardrobe and gave it to the maid, along with several boxes of Isaac's clothes, for she could not bear to bring it all with her. Only his best things were kept: his silk top hat, his cashmere evening coat, the tweed suits and handmade shirts he ordered from his English tailor, his polished leather shoes. These the children refused to part with, and they were packed into a large trunk with his paperweights and his other precious things. The trunk was then carried down the wide, dark stairs and carefully placed inside the removal van, with the furniture and Laura's piano, which would be driven to Brussels by road.

There was a melancholy to the apartment now that it was empty, and even Teddy, who had at first delighted in the lack of furniture by riding his scooter in and out of the rooms, wandered around without aim. It was strange how fresh the wallpaper was where it had been hidden by cupboards or pictures, how the parquet retained the shapes of the rugs, how you could walk into a room expecting to see a table or a chest and for a moment it was still there, like the shadows left by a flashbulb. There were so many memories within these walls, not just of their father, but of the countless tiny details that constitute family life, and the leaving of them was hard. But children are made of permeable stuff, and as long as Laura was sunny and forward-looking, so too were they. Happiness, it turns out, is mostly imitation.

On their last afternoon in Milan the sky was the colour of a Bianchi bicycle and the air still. The children had been sent outside while Laura and the maid saw to the last of the packing, and they lay draped across the two ironwork benches that, summer and winter, made up the sole furnishings of the large, square courtyard. Rita had been reading but it was too hot and now she was stretched out on her back, her feet hanging over the end, gazing up at the rows of windows above. The shutters were all closed, the building's one defence against the stifling heat, and only those on the Balestras' floor showed signs of life, for the hinged lower sections had been wedged open. Through the narrow gap Rita could see flashes of her mother's green dress as she moved from room to room, and there was something reassuring about this, as if she were bound to them by an invisible string and could never be further than this distance. Rita sighed contentedly, and turned to look at her siblings, who had moved away from the benches and were peering at something near the brick path.

'What are you doing?'

Although the children were fluent in several languages, between themselves they spoke English.

'Teddy found a butterfly, come see.' Coco was crouched beside her brother, their fair heads pressed together.

Rita slowly rolled over and sat up, her feet, in their short socks and brown and white leather shoes, swinging listlessly. 'Poor butterfly,' she murmured. She gazed across the cobbled courtyard, wondering if it was worth getting up. 'Do you remember that?' she demanded, humming the tune, 'Auntie Miriam used to play the record all the time. "Poor Butterfly" — how did it go?'

'I think it's a moth,' said Teddy, 'it has feathery antennae.'

'Something about blossoms.'

'It's so pretty,' said Coco, peering at its black and white wings. 'Look, it has a red petticoat. Come see, Rita.'

Rita sighed and sat back, her head resting on the top of the bench. 'Can't you bring it here? It's too hot.' Her hair was sticking to her face and she shook it out, the dark curls springy in the heat.

'All right.' Teddy cupped his hands around the motionless insect and stood up, glancing at Coco. 'Do you remember the little crabs in Le Zoute, how they nipped when you picked them up? They were so small but they really hurt.'

'*N'importe quoi*, Teddy,' Coco giggled, because that is what everyone had said.

'*N'importe quoi*, Teddy,' repeated Teddy. He sat down on the bench next to Rita and slowly lifted his thumbs so that she might see the moth.

'Did you know that the colour comes off if you touch their wings?' said Rita. She looked at him to see if he believed her and he nodded, opening his hands a little wider. She stroked the top of one wing and then held up her finger to reveal a fine, greyish powder. 'See.'

'Can I try?' asked Coco, leaning forward. She too dabbed a finger at the moth. 'Do you think it's dead?' she wondered, lowering her voice.

Teddy looked closer.

'Which are the insects that only live one day?' said Rita. 'Is it dragonflies?'

'I don't think it's dragonflies,' said Coco.

'Mayflies,' said Teddy, because he always knew this kind of thing.

'Oh yes.'

They all peered at the moth, reflecting upon this.

'Poor mayfly,' murmured Rita. And for some reason this was terribly funny, and all three burst out laughing and whenever they looked at one another they laughed more, so that it was several minutes before they were quiet again.

Upstairs, Laura stopped what she was doing and smiled.

At last Teddy stood up. 'I'm going to ask Mammy if I can keep it,' he said with purpose.

'She'll never let you,' said Rita.

Teddy shrugged. 'She might.' His mother often told him he couldn't do something and then changed her mind. He closed his fingers around the moth and set off across the courtyard, but as he did so its wings suddenly began to thrash against his damp palms. He grinned and turned back to the girls. 'It's alive,' he said, and he began to run towards the ornate glass doors which led into the hallway, his hands clutched to his chest as if in prayer.

'Bring something to drink!' called Rita, as he leaned his elbow on the brass handle.

'Lemonade!' added Coco. The door clanged shut.

Rita lay back on the bench and closed her eyes, and her sister did the same. Through the open shutters they could hear their mother calling instructions to the maid, and they listened as a series of sharp bangs suggested another packing box being hammered closed. Rita stretched her arms above her head and yawned. She felt strangely at peace, lying here in the hot sun, and she thought she should like to stay like this forever. She let one of her arms drop to the ground and languidly swirled her fingers in the dust, imagining she were lying on a boat and that the cobbles were a shallow lake. 'I wonder what it will be like,' she said.

Coco turned onto her side, tugging at her dress which was caught between the slats, and squinting at her sister. 'What will what be like?'

'Brussels. I can't seem to remember anything from when we lived there before. Do you think it will be the same?'

'If you can't remember, then it doesn't matter,' said Coco. 'I don't remember anything either.'

'You and Teddy were babies, it's normal,' said Rita. She thought for a moment. 'Do you think we'll forget Milan too? If, years from now, we'll say the same thing about here? Perhaps that's what happens when you get older.'

'I'll never forget,' said Coco. She was irritated by the remark about babies but this was their last day and she had promised herself not to get into any fights. 'No matter how old I am, I'll always remember here. I might be ninety and I'll still remember what this feels like, right now, right this minute.' She lay back and stared up at the sky, making a mental list of everything she felt: the damp heat of the afternoon, the slatted wood pressing on the top of her spine, the distant chime of the tram bell on the Via Washington, the way her dress stuck to her bare skin.

Rita sighed. 'I shall remember only that it was too hot,' she said, draping an arm across her face, blowing warm air into the crack of her elbow, where it tickled. 'Dratted Uncle Marco, this is his fault.'

'How is the heat Uncle Marco's fault?'

Rita ignored this, continuing to blow on her skin. After a moment she turned her head and gazed at her sister. She was in a mood for reminiscing.

'Do you remember those bathing-suits Granny knitted for us when we were small? And how itchy they were and how Mammy still made us wear them, because she said Granny had worked so hard and we should be grateful?'

'Mine was purple,' said Coco.

'Yes,' said Rita, 'and then it turned out that Granny didn't even knit them, she got someone else to do it, and Mammy still made us wear them. She said it would hurt Granny's feelings if we didn't. I never understood that. There's a photograph of us wearing them, I think it was in Riccione, and we all look so cross, even Teddy. The cousins were there too, do you remember?'

'Yes,' said Coco, 'Auntie Allegra said we looked like little gypsy children, and when I told Mammy they got into a huge argument.'

'I don't remember that.'

'Well, maybe not an argument, but Mammy said Auntie Allegra was a snob and that it served her right if people thought she went on holiday with gypsies. "*On dirait de petits tziganes.*" ' She rolled the words around her mouth, liking how they sounded. 'That was the year Teddy cut his hair.'

'With Daddy's nail scissors — I'd forgotten about that! He cut it right at the roots.' Rita mimed the scissors with her fingers, drawing up a chunk of her fringe and snipping enthusiastically. 'He said it was getting in his eyes. Mammy took him straight downstairs to the hotel barber, but there was nothing he could do, it was too short. How funny he looked, what was it Uncle Leonard called him when he saw the photograph?'

'A proper thug!' said Coco with delight.

'A proper thug,' repeated Rita. She smiled. 'How sweet was Teddy when he was little? Those long blonde curls. We were so mean to him too, always dressing him up in our old clothes, putting ribbons in his hair. He made such a pretty girl.'

Coco thought about this, overwhelmed with a sudden melancholy. 'I wish we never had to grow up. I loved being little, didn't you? I should have liked to stay little forever.'

'I prefer being older,' said Rita matter-of-factly. 'You can do more.'

'Yes, but nobody pays you much attention, not like when you're small. I was the perfect baby, you know. Mammy said so, you can ask her. I never cried, I just smiled and looked around me.' She shot a glance at her sister. 'You were a screamer. Teddy too.'

'Yes, yes,' said Rita, stretching out her legs so that her feet pressed against the arm of the bench. She had heard this all before. She closed her eyes, her mind wandering back to the bathing suits. 'I so wanted one like Sylvie's, do you remember it? It was yellow with tiny blue flowers and it tied around her neck with a big bow. I begged and begged.'

Coco did not remember, but she nodded anyway. 'The cousins always have pretty things,' she said.

'That's because Uncle Marco spoils them,' said Rita, repeating something she had heard the adults say.

'Uncle Leonard thinks we're spoilt too, I heard him tell Granny.' Coco fanned her face with the side of her hand, contemplating this idea. 'I don't think we are, do you? I can think of lots of things I'd like that I don't have. A puppy, for instance.'

Their musings were interrupted by a loud scraping noise, and they looked up to see their mother leaning out of her bedroom window, pushing back the louvred shutters. Teddy was at her side, his hands held out in front of him.

Laura waved to the two girls and then turned to her son. 'Go on,' she urged.

'I knew she wouldn't let him keep it,' said Rita.

Teddy opened his hands and for a moment the moth did not move, its wings folded at its sides. Then it lifted into the air, a speck of red and black, and was gone. Teddy gazed at his palms, which were covered with a fine dust, then rubbed them on his shorts and glanced up at Laura. She smiled and tousled his blonde hair, then leaned out to close the shutters again.

'Lemonade!' shouted Coco, just as they banged closed.

'He didn't hear you,' said Rita.

They lay there in silence, the heat of the afternoon making them fidgety. Something had bitten Coco and she kept scratching at her ankle, her leg bent and pulled across her body, until Rita turned over and flung a book at her to make her stop.

'Ow!' protested Coco, although it hadn't hurt. She continued scratching her foot, frowning. The sense of melancholy was still with her, and she had that thick feeling in the back of her throat she got when she was about to cry. 'Aren't you scared?' she asked suddenly, although as soon as she had said it she remembered that Rita was never scared, not about anything.

'Scared? Why?'

'What if we don't like it?' She meant Brussels, speaking in French, making new friends, but when Rita said, 'School, you mean?' she nodded.

'School is school,' said Rita. She picked at a bit of lint on her dress, dropping it over the back of the bench and watching as a breeze caught it and carried it off.

'Uncle Marco says it's full of Jews and Freemasons,' said Coco. She leaned forwards to inspect her leg, continuing to scratch.

'What is?'

'Our new school.'

'He said that to you?'

Coco shrugged. 'Not to me, to Mammy. The last time he was here. He said, "Isaac would approve, it's full of Jews and Freemasons." Those were his exact words. Do you think it's infected?' She twisted her leg, pointing to the red welts that streaked her ankle.

Rita did not reply.

'Uncle Marco is a Freemason,' continued Coco. 'I asked Mammy and she said it wasn't illegal in Belgium, that it's only Il Duce who doesn't like it. Do you think Daddy was one too?'

'Of course not.'

'What even *is* a Freemason?' asked Coco, and Rita shrugged and said how was she supposed to know.

They sat in silence for a moment, then Rita stood up.

'I'm bored, I'm going inside,' she said.

'But Mammy wants us to stay here. She says we'll be in the way inside.'

'She meant you two little ones. The only reason I had to come was to keep an eye on you. Bring my book, please, when you come. I don't want to forget it.'

'Bring it yourself, I'm not your servant.'

Rita looked at her for a long moment, and then walked towards her and stooped to pick up the book from beneath the bench, tucking it inside the waistband of her dress. She dragged her hands through the thick curls of her hair, pulling them away from her face. She felt cross and did not know why, all she knew was that she wanted to be by herself. She often felt like this now, as though she were pulled so taut she could snap, like the time her mother was playing the piano and three strings broke one after another, making a sound like pistol shots. The man who came to repair it said it often happened in these damp old apartments and that other strings could go at any time, even when it wasn't being played. He said it was best not to think about it.

'I'm coming too then.'

'Can't I ever go anywhere by myself? Stay here and wait for Teddy!'

'But I don't want to, I want to come with you.' Coco stood up, tiny beads of sweat glistening on her top lip.

'Oh, for God's sake,' said Rita, 'why do you always have to be such a baby?'

'You're not allowed to say "for God's sake—" ' Coco started walking across the courtyard, looking up at their mother's window.

'Tell then,' said Rita coldly, 'and I'll tell what a baby you are. Coco Balestra, scared of her own shadow, can't go to sleep without a light on.' Rita warmed to her theme.

'Can't go to sleep without checking under the bed and inside the wardrobe, and even then, still asks Mammy to lie with her. Coco Balestra, afraid of—'

'—Stop!' cried Coco, her eyes brimming with tears. 'Why do you have to be so mean?'

'It's not mean if it's the truth.'

Coco trembled, her fingers pulling fretfully at the front of her dress. 'You're such a—' she searched for something sufficiently wounding, 'you're such an Estella!'

Rita gave a sharp laugh. 'A what?'

'An Estella,' said Coco, with less conviction.

Rita smiled, her lips thin. 'Wait until Mammy hears you called me that,' she said evenly. 'She'll probably spank you.'

'She was the one who said it first,' said Coco, then immediately regretted it. Rita stared at her.

'When?'

'Doesn't matter.'

'When, when did she say it?'

'I can't remember.'

'So it's not true then?'

Coco said nothing. She was torn between the desire to prove herself right and a certain shame about the circumstances in which she had heard this. For it was in a private conversation with Marco that her mother had expressed this, and she would know immediately that Coco had been listening at the door, just as she always knew such things. She remembered the sadness in her mother's voice that evening. She had been asking Uncle Marco what she should do about the Carasso apartment, and sharing with him how difficult Rita was being, who at that point was barely speaking to her. 'She has a lot of Estella in her,' Laura had said, and she must have begun to cry, for Coco heard the sofa creaking and then Uncle Marco speaking more softly, as if he were comforting her.

'So it's *not* true then?' Rita demanded.

And Coco shook her head.

The glass doors to the courtyard swung open and Teddy appeared, followed by the concierge carrying a large tray, with glasses and an enamel jug. 'It was too heavy,' said Teddy, holding the door. He grinned, and the concierge, a stern-faced woman with black eyebrows, muttered and said she had enough to do today without running up and down the stairs.

'Thank you so much,' said Rita, hurriedly sitting down and making room for the tray.

'Yes, thank you,' said Coco, for they were rather afraid of the concierge, who never hesitated to complain to their mother when they had been too noisy on the stairs, or left their bicycles in the wrong place.

'Say it again,' said Teddy, tugging at the woman's arm as she turned to leave, 'say what you just said.'

The concierge rolled her eyes.

'*In bocca al lupo!*' said Teddy, unable to wait. He grinned at the two girls, still holding the concierge's arm.

'It means "good luck",' said Rita.

'It means "good luck",' said her brother, affecting not to hear. '*In bocca al lupo! In bocca al lupo!*' he repeated, following the concierge across the courtyard. At the door, he darted ahead, heaving it open and making a low bow as the old woman walked through. 'It's going to be my new saying,' he said.

In the bedroom, Laura was packing the last of her best things, neatly folding her furs into fat, silky squares, arranging her jewellery boxes in the spaces between, slipping her silver brushes and mirrors, engraved with LB, into the pockets of the suede lining. She felt strangely serene, not at all as she would have expected to feel on their last day in the apartment, and this troubled her, as if it should not be so easy to leave a life behind. It was curious how hard it could be to make even the smallest of decisions (should Rita be allowed to stop Latin, was Teddy old enough to take the tram alone) and then here she was moving them halfway across Europe with barely a moment's hesitation. She closed the lid of the trunk and pressed the catches so that they clicked shut, then quickly stood up, her briskness of movement a habit now. She picked up the trunk and half lifted, half dragged it into the hallway, where she set it down with the other luggage.

The maid, Nina, was in the kitchen, putting the last of the food into a wooden crate. Laura leaned against the doorjamb, taking in the empty cupboards and bare surfaces.

'Is everything finished? Is that the last of it?'

Nina nodded, twisting the corners of a bag of rice into tight screws.

'Good, perfect. I can't believe we're almost done. And there was me saying I should have booked us on a later train, that we'd never be ready to leave tonight!' She noticed a cobweb in one of the cupboards and caught it with her fingers, shaking her hand when it remained stuck to her.

'Although how we'll manage with all that luggage on the train,
I can't begin to imagine. We really ought to have gone by car,
that would have been the sensible thing to do, but I don't
know that I could have managed it on my own.'

'No, Signora.'

'Even the four hours from Cortina exhausted me, it
was always Signore Isaac who drove before.' She picked
distractedly at the tips of her fingers. She was thinking about
that last drive through France after Isaac had died, his body
in the car in front. She had been sedated for most of it, and
it was only later that the grotesqueness of the situation had
hit her and she had become hysterical. She shook her head,
as if physically to banish these thoughts. 'No, most definitely
the train is best. And the children love the Simplon, for
them it's a treat. What time did Paolo say he'd be here?'
Paolo was Nina's brother and was driving them to the
station.

'He'll be here at six o'clock, Signora.'

'He knows not to be late? The traffic is so
unpredictable at that time of day, and we have a lot of
luggage, does he know we have a lot of luggage?'

'Yes, Signora.' This was the third or fourth time Laura
had asked her. 'He knows.'

'Good. Perfect.' Laura said again. She turned away,
wandering into the dining room, empty except for a broom
and a small pile of dust in one corner, then back into the hall,
looking for something to do.

'Did the children have something to drink?' she asked,
raising her voice, and Nina called back saying, yes, she had
given them some lemonade. Laura stood gazing at the stack
of suitcases by the front door. She suspected that most of this
could have gone in the removal lorry, but there was always
the risk of things being mislaid and so she had agreed that
the children could each pack a suitcase with their most

precious things. The result was now filling the width of the hallway, and she had no idea how they would get across Paris when they had to change trains. She sighed, wondering if it had been a mistake to insist upon doing this alone.

Rita's handbag sat open on top of her suitcase and Laura reached inside and took out the autograph book Leonard had bought to replace the one lost in Vittel. She held it in her hands, gently running her fingers over the calfskin cover, remembering how the waiter had rushed to clean up that terrible afternoon, looking around helplessly when he found Rita's book, spattered with poor Isaac's blood, and then hiding it beneath a pile of napkins. Those first few days Rita had talked more about the lost book than she had her father, pestering everyone to call the hotel and see if it had been found, until Marco finally shouted at her to stop being so ridiculous. There were more important things to think about. That was when Leonard had bought the new one. He had gone to WH Smith and chosen the nicest one they had, and he and Bobby had straight away written little messages on the first pages. She read Bobby's now, smiling at his sloping, rather feminine handwriting and careful words. 'Hoping that you will always take life as it comes and make the best of it.' A strange sentiment, given the circumstances. Leonard's was not much better, written in French and something about not wasting time for you didn't get it back. Perhaps everything had unfortunate connotations at such times.

Laura continued flicking through the pages, smiling at the page of endearments from her mother in Hebrew, Ladino, French and English, reading the notes from the new friends they had made just weeks ago in Cortina. Even now, a year later, nobody knew what to say, herself included. And the one person who would have known, who had always been able to find the right words, especially when it concerned his eldest daughter, was gone. Laura felt suddenly weary, and all the vigour seemed to drop out of her, so that she sat down on one of the packing cases and closed her eyes. It occurred to her that 'feeling low,' as everyone termed it, was as much a physical state as it was an emotional one. She frowned and closed the book, dropping it back into Rita's bag. This was exactly why she was leaving Milan, she reminded herself, and she stood up, flexing her back, dropping her shoulders. She ran her hands over the skirt of her green dress, smoothing it flat. So that she wasn't constantly tormented by the past, by these memories that spooled around and around her mind. So that she might be able to think about something else.

She wandered back into her bedroom, crossing to the window and pushing open the shutters. 'No, not yet,' she said, when the children looked up expectantly. She watched them for a moment, feeling that particular rapture mothers feel when admiring their own creation, and the children, sensing this, became more exuberant, more expansive in their performance. Teddy had been remembering some game they used to play, and now he galloped around the courtyard, leaping imaginary fences, refusing others and having to turn and approach again. The girls giggled and shouted encouragement, their voices shrill, and when at last he came back to them, they collapsed in a heap together, panting. Laura smiled, and despite the fact that Coco's hair was a mess, and Rita's dress crumpled, and Teddy had his shirt untucked and no belt, she allowed herself a moment of pride. Whatever humiliations she had suffered in the last year (because pity, for Laura, was a kind of humiliation) her children had not shared them, and this was gratifying to her. If she had achieved nothing else, she had achieved that, and she leaned against the window, admiring them.

'Signora?'

'Oh Nina, good, is he here?' she asked, meaning Paolo.

'Not yet, no.'

Laura glanced at her watch, 'No, of course, we said six, didn't we.' She gazed at the maid, tapping her fingers on the wide sill. 'Is everything all right?'

'Everything is fine, Signora.'

'Oh good.' There were scratches in the parquet where the furniture had been moved and Laura traced them with the toe of her shoe. 'I should have had this floor waxed,' she said.

'I can do it when you've gone,' said Nina.

'Oh, would you? That would be wonderful. Although I don't want you to be too tired for starting with your new family. Six children, isn't it? They'll certainly keep you busy.'

Nina bent to pick up a button that had wedged itself between two boards, considering it for a moment and then dropping it into the pocket of her apron. 'I didn't take the position, I wasn't sure what your plans would be. I kept thinking they might change.'

'But— why would they have changed?'

'I don't know, Signora.' She did not say that she knew about the problems with the visas and that both the lawyer and Signore Cansino had advised not leaving before it was sorted out. Nor that, had Laura asked, she would have packed up her bags and gone with them, wherever they went, for she could not imagine working for another family than theirs. 'Anyway, it doesn't matter now. It was about the children I came to speak to you. I thought I might put some fresh clothes aside for the journey. You know how dusty they get when they play outside.'

Laura nodded. 'What do you mean, things might have changed? How could they?' She frowned, trying to make sense of this.

'I just hoped—' began Nina, but just then there was

the sound of a car horn on the street outside, and they heard a man's voice shouting to the concierge to open up the main doors.

'Watch the back, I don't want to hit anything!' and there was a grinding of gears as the car reversed over the kerb, followed by another volley from the horn.

Laura continued to stare at the younger woman, her cheeks flushed with concern.

'I'm so sorry, Nina, if I gave you a false impression. It was never my intention. Even without everything that's happened—' She lifted her hands and then dropped them again, for she generally avoided direct references to Isaac's death. 'Even without everything that has happened, things would be difficult for us.' In truth Laura had paid little attention to the recent developments, Marco having assured her that it was the Jews from the East that they were aimed at, but now she shrugged and said, 'We could never have stayed.'

'It was silly of me.' Nina's eyes reddened, and she looked at the floor, embarrassed.

'No it wasn't,' said Laura, and she cupped her hands around the younger woman's face and tilted it upwards. 'You have been like family to us Nina. I'll never forget that. Never.'

Nina raised her eyes, meeting Laura's, and in that brief glance something passed between them and they were in complete sympathy. After a moment Laura let her hands fall to her side. Nina cleared her throat.

'I thought perhaps their new blue cottons, what do you think? They must look their best on such a journey, so that everyone can admire them and think what a beautiful family you are.'

'Oh yes, the blue cottons are just right,' said Laura with relief. 'I love Teddy in that colour, it brings out his eyes, especially now that he's tanned from our holidays. And the girls too, they're becoming so pretty, don't you think?'

'Oh, yes.'

'I've told you what a stir they caused in Cortina, you can't imagine how many compliments I received.' She laughed, as if such success was an embarrassment to her, although she continued to talk of it anyway. 'They were constantly being invited out, to parties or to play tennis or golf, they were very popular. Teddy too, although mostly he stayed with me, you know how he is. He's not as confident as the girls.'

'It will come.'

'Oh, there's no hurry. I was just the same at his age. The girls take more after their father, or certainly Rita does. I look at her sometimes and I can't believe she's mine, she's so self-possessed and grown up, nobody would think she's just fourteen.' She glanced towards the window, inclining her head a little, the way you might tip a bottle to stop the contents spilling. 'Look at them. They have so much to look forward to.'

The two women stood in silence, gazing down upon the heads of the children.

'Signore Isaac would be so proud of them. How much he's missed in this one short year, it goes so fast.' Laura pressed her hair, all ten fingers kneading it into place.

A loud knocking caused them to turn around and Nina hurried out into the hallway to open the door. Paolo was standing at the top of the stairs, his hat in his hands.

'Perfect, you're here,' said Laura, who had followed her out. She gestured towards the luggage. 'I'm sorry there's such a lot, it's terrible how much one accumulates.' She watched as he picked up two of the bigger suitcases, swinging them into the air, then turned back to Nina. 'Will you call the children then? Can I leave them to you?'

'Of course. Wait until you see how smart I shall have them, you'll be the talk of the train.'

Laura laughed with delight, stepping out of Paolo's way and then following him out onto the landing. She leaned over the banisters, watching as he disappeared down the dark stairs.

'And their hair too,' she said, coming back to the open door, 'Teddy will fuss, but be sure to brush their hair.'

CHAPTER 6

The next day they arrived in Brussels.

'Do you know where we are yet?' asked Teddy. They were in the taxi, rattling through the cobbled streets to the south of the station, heading towards Ixelles.

'Of course,' said Laura. She leaned forward to close the window, but the children all protested and so she left it open. 'Nothing has changed much. Not here, anyway.'

'Everything looks so grey,' said Rita, gazing at the endless rows of blank-faced, terraced houses, 'and there's no trees.'

'Of course there are trees, darling. The driver hasn't brought us a very nice way, that's all. Anyway, there's lots of trees where we are, the apartment looks out over the park, we'll just be able to cross the road and feel like we're in the country.'

Rita did not reply.

'Why do all the houses have those lacy curtains? And where is everybody?' asked Coco, picking up on her sister's bad mood.

'It's midday, everyone's having their lunch. All Belgians eat at the same time. And much earlier than we're used to, most families have their evening meal around five o'clock. Can you imagine?' She sat back against the leather seat and arranged her travelling coat around her legs. It was a dim, overcast day and the air was cool. 'Put your sweater on Teddy, you'll catch a chill. You too Coco.'

'We had lunch at that time in Milan,' said Teddy, taking the pullover she handed him and holding it in his lap.

'Well, not quite.'

'Actually we did,' said Rita, 'if Nina wasn't there, or Auntie Miriam. We're not complaining,' she added.

'Is Uncle Marco meeting us there?' asked Teddy. In his last letter Marco had sent a photograph of his new Simca and Teddy was longing to ride in it. 'And the cousins, will they be there too? It's been ages since we saw them, who do you think will be taller, me or Sylvie?'

'Girls are always taller at your age,' said Rita, stretching out her legs and resting them on Coco's seat. 'Do these shoes make my feet look big? I can't decide if they do. In any case, you'll soon catch her up, Uncle Marco's family are all short.'

'Papa wasn't short, he was Uncle Marco's family,' said Coco, pushing Rita's feet away.

'Yes he was,' said Rita. 'You don't remember.'

'Yes I do. I remember perfectly, don't I, Mammy?'

'Well, he wasn't especially tall,' said Laura carefully, for she knew how these kinds of conversation escalated. 'Uncle Marco is still in France, I believe.' She had received a postcard from Allegra just the day before. 'They won't be back for another week or so, apparently the weather's lovely this year.' She picked up her handbag and opened it, taking out random objects — her address book, a compact, a pair of sunglasses — and setting them on her lap. 'Coco, did you put my change purse back? It doesn't seem to be here.' She continued emptying her bag.

'I definitely put it back. Perhaps you dropped it.'

'Well, it isn't here. And I shall need it to pay the driver — really, Coco — Ah, no, here it is.' She held up a small purse, smiling in relief. 'Right at the bottom.'

'I told you I put it back.'

'Uncle Marco thinks there's going to be a war,' said Rita, with the same indifference as she had regarded her shoes.

'That's why he's staying in France. I heard you talking to him on the telephone,' she added, when Laura began to object.

'Isn't there already a war?' asked Teddy, twisting in his seat to look at something.

'In Spain, yes, but not here,' said Rita. 'Don't you know anything, Teddy?'

'I do wish you wouldn't speak like that,' said her mother, 'there's really no need for it.' She opened her handbag again and took out her compact, dabbing at her face while the three children watched. Looking up, she smiled, the same bright smile she had worn since they left Milan. 'Uncle Marco is just being cautious, that's all.'

'He's worried about Seppy,' said Rita. 'He thinks if they stay in France then Seppy won't have to be a soldier.' Seppy was the eldest of the cousins and everyone's favourite. 'But it won't work, they send you a letter and it finds you wherever you are, I've read about it.'

Laura frowned. 'Coco, do stop pulling at me, what is it?'

'Seppy has to be a soldier?' Coco had seen the newsreels at the cinema, she was in no doubt as to what war meant.

'Of course not,' said her mother, 'he's just a boy.'

'Actually, he's eighteen,' said Rita. Then: 'If there is war, will we go to France too?'

'No, we'll go to Manchester, as I've told you before. And please don't make that face, I promised Granny and Uncle Leonard and I intend to keep my word. But I'm quite sure it's not going to come to that.' She checked her face one last time in the compact, then snapped it shut. 'A lot more has to happen before we need to worry about war. And if it does, well, we'll do what's necessary, just as everyone else will. The most important thing is that we're all together.' She pressed Coco's hand, and Coco, reassured, wriggled closer.

'If Uncle Marco is in France,' said Teddy, after a while, his hands clamped between his knees as he peered out of the window, 'then who's going to meet us? Are the people it belongs to going to be there?'

'I believe the Carassos are in France too.' Allegra's letter had been full of chatter about how she had bumped into this person at the market, and that person on the terrace of some hotel, and Sofia Carasso's name had come up several times. 'Their housekeeper is expecting us though, so we won't be sleeping on the street, if that's what you're worried about. I have to say I'm rather relieved. I'm not sure I have the energy to be sociable today.'

'I hope there's a lift,' said Coco. 'I don't think I can carry my suitcase another inch.'

'There's a lift.'

'A shared lift or just for us?' asked Teddy. In Marco's building each large apartment had its own private lift, something the cousins often boasted about.

'Shared,' replied Laura. 'And please don't say things like that in front of Uncle Leonard or I'll never hear the end of it.' She smiled at Rita, who, at fourteen, might understand such things, but Rita gazed at her blankly and went back to staring out of the window.

'Or Granny,' said Coco, 'Granny's even worse about things like that. Like when you wore your new coat and she said she felt like a poor relation!'

Laura nodded, not listening. She was looking at Rita, thinking how unreachable she could be sometimes. What was the word one of her teachers had used? *Distaccata*? Aloof. She had been so cross at the time, but now she saw it was not an unfair observation. Laura sighed. She had promised herself that the children would always remember this as a happy day, and she looked around for something to give them. 'There's the tram!' She pointed at a small, single carriage tram as it rattled past the window. 'That's called the 'O', it's the line Daddy used to take when we lived here.

We're nearly there.'

'Daddy took the tram?' Coco could not imagine her father in anything but his beloved motorcars.

Laura laughed. 'When we were first married, yes. Rita remembers, don't you darling? He took you with him sometimes, when you were very small.'

'I don't remember,' said Rita, but her tone was less fierce, and she pivoted a little in her seat so that they could see her face.

'Well he did. And you were terribly spoiled by the ladies in the office, they'd dress you up in all the silk samples and push you about on a mail trolley. They called you *l'Imperatrice du Japon*, you were so sweet.'

'The Empress of Japan?' Despite herself, Rita smiled, and Laura did not tell her that the Empress they had meant was an ocean liner.

'*L'Imperatrice du Japon*,' said Coco enviously. 'I wish I could have been an Empress.'

'You were other things,' said Laura, smiling. 'Ah, here we are, the Avenue des Nations. I told you there would be trees. Isn't it pretty?'

They were on a wide, leafy boulevard, and where before they had looked out upon office buildings and apartment blocks, they now saw elegant red brick villas, with turrets and vast iron gates and landscaped gardens that led onto the park. '*La perle de la capitale*, that's what they call this part of Brussels,' she said. 'Just look Rita, that's the Carassos' old house, isn't it lovely, I think it's an embassy now. Oh, and there's Uncle Marco's, on the corner there. Wait and see how close we are, you'll be able to walk between the two. Isn't this exciting?'

'*La perle de la capitale*,' repeated Coco.

'How fancy,' said Teddy, bouncing up and down so that the springs in the seat made a grating sound.

The taxi pulled across the avenue, with its strip of neatly mown grass dividing the two lanes of traffic, and stopped in front of an imposing brick and stone mansion block. Long bays of mullioned windows divided the building into horizontal layers, an arched entrance and pediment the only decoration on an otherwise sober facade.

'It's like a palace! Which one are we, the third floor?' Coco counted the layers of windows.

'Wait until you see the views. Sofia showed me photographs, you can see for miles.'

The driver began to unload their luggage and Laura and the children stood for a moment gazing up at their new home. Freshly painted pillars strung with shiny chains ran the length of the property. And beyond, either side of the main doors, were narrow unplanted flowerbeds separated from one another by raked gravel. Laura took an envelope from her bag: Sofia had sent her a list of instructions.

Before she could read it, however, one of the windows on the top floor swung open and a young man in an open-necked shirt, the sleeves rolled past his elbows, stuck his head out. He stared down at them, shading his eyes (although the sun was hardly out) and seemingly debating whether or not he should greet them.

'Madame Balestra?' he said at last, in the same accented French that their cousins spoke.

Laura was not in the habit of shouting up at windows, but she called, 'Yes, good afternoon.'

'Who's that?' asked Coco, peering upwards.

'Excellent! I'm coming down, don't move.' The head disappeared.

'Who is that?' repeated Coco, who hated not to know such things.

'Shhh, Coco, don't be rude.' Laura felt suddenly flustered and so distracted herself by counting suitcases and sending Teddy back into the car to make sure they had not left anything. Then she quickly paid the driver and waved him away just as the front doors opened and the man from the window strode towards them. He wore loose grey flannels and leather moccasins, and his hair was wet.

'I was expecting someone older!' he declared, shaking Laura's hand. 'It took me a moment to realise who you were. You must think me very rude.' He grinned, clearly untroubled by such a possibility. 'Emmanuel Carasso, Sofia's son.'

'Mr Carasso, how nice.' Laura looked at the children, straightening Coco's plaits, smoothing Teddy's jacket. 'What a sight we must all look, I do apologise. We've been travelling since yesterday evening.'

'Not at all, not at all,' said the young man. 'And call me Manu. If you call me Mr Carasso I shall think you mean my father.' He leaned forwards, grinning. 'I'm not really supposed to be here, but the water was off in my house and I wanted to take a bath. When Kasha said you were arriving today, I thought I might as well make myself useful, that's why I looked out.' He ran a hand through his damp hair. 'Is that from Sofia?' He pointed to the letter in Laura's hand and she nodded. 'Those things are like military dispatches, please don't tell her I interfered, she'll have me shot.' He winked at the children to show he was joking, but they stared back impassively. 'My father likes to say that if only Denikin had known about Sofia Carasso, we'd still be in Moscow. He's probably right.'

Laura smiled, folding the letter and putting it in her bag. The young man watched her, his hands thrust deep into his pockets. 'How funny that I was expecting someone older,' he said again, and Laura said, yes, wasn't it.

'Right then,' he said, 'shall we get you inside? No, no, leave all that, Kasha will bring it.' To Laura's horror, he put two fingers to his mouth and gave a loud, piercing whistle.

'It's a useful skill in a house like this! Come on, I'll take you up. Your furniture arrived this morning, by the way, I bumped into the removal men just as they were leaving. Charming fellows, turns out most of their work is for Comasebit, you know, the refugee committee. Two of the *camionisti* were German Jews.' He raised his eyebrows.

'We're not refugees,' said Laura with a small laugh.

She waited for him to say something but instead he bent down and removed one of his slippers, shaking out a piece of gravel. Just then an elderly man wearing a full-length leather apron came hurrying out of the main doors. 'Ah, Kasha, good. *Eto sem'ya Balestra*, I beat you to them.'

The old man bowed his head and began to move the luggage inside the building.

'Really, I'm sure we'll manage, if you have things to do,' said Laura. 'I don't want to take up your day, the children and I can easily sort ourselves out.'

'It's my pleasure.' He stood back to allow the manservant past. 'Besides, you must all be exhausted, that night train from Italy is the worst. I took it myself last month, from Lausanne, and barely slept a wink. Some poor fellow threw himself onto the tracks just south of Vallorbe and we stopped for over three hours. Apparently we got off lightly, when it happens in Italy it takes twice that long to get going again.' He grinned and looked at the children. 'So, have you picked your bedrooms yet? That's always the most important, don't you agree?'

'We drew lots, Teddy gets first choice,' said Coco. She looked at her mother.

'We'll see,' said Laura.

'I'd choose the corner one if I were you,' said Manu, putting his hand on the boy's shoulder. 'If you lean out you can just see the edge of the Uccle golf course. Do you play? I don't have much time for it myself, but it's a good course.

I can take you over there some time if you like?'

'Oh, we wouldn't dream of imposing on you,' said Laura quickly. 'I'm sure their uncle will take them. Do you know my brother-in-law, Marco Balestra?'

'Marco? Of course. He's your brother-in-law, I hadn't made the connection. Are they still in La Baule? Half of Brussels seems to be there this summer.' He waved them through the front door, which Kasha had wedged open with one of their suitcases.

'Apparently the weather's lovely this year,' said Laura.

Inside it was cool and dark, with a grey marble floor and white walls. Laura glanced at the children, trying to read their thoughts, but they were following her as though in a dream and their faces were without expression. She remembered all the pomp and colour of the Casa Grandolini, and for a brief instant her resolve wavered. Had she made a terrible mistake? She hesitated, resting a hand on the edge of a Chinoiserie table and staring with unseeing eyes at the pattern of finely etched dragons and peacocks. Manu, thinking she was feeling faint, touched a hand to her arm, and she turned, startled.

'You look like you need a cup of tea. Sofia left instructions for the maid to lay up a tray and bring it down as soon as you arrived. It's the one benefit of living downstairs from my mother, you'll never go short of anything.' He ushered the children into the lift. 'Did you know she sends Kasha over with our breakfast every morning? I thought she'd stop when they moved to this house, my apartment is a good ten minutes away, but no, whatever the weather, there are fresh croissants and hot coffee on the doorstep at eight every morning. It drives Lise mad. Lise's my wife.'

Whether it was the prospect of tea, or the news that this exuberant young man was married, Laura could not have said. But something in her relaxed, and she followed them into the lift with renewed vigour.

'I think that's adorable,' she said, her arms draping around the children as the doors closed. 'I should love to have my breakfast delivered to me.'

'You don't even eat breakfast,' said Rita, speaking for the first time.

'Nor do I, really,' said Manu, laughing. He was feeling in his pocket for something, and as they stepped out of the lift he produced a bunch of keys, holding them up in the air. 'Who would like to open the door?' he demanded.

'Rita?' said Laura, and Rita took the keys.

'Turn it hard to the left, it's a little tricky at first. You have the Bolsheviks to thank for this door,' he said, glancing at Laura and grinning. 'It's the same as they use for bank vaults, my mother won't have anything else.'

'She's probably right.'

'Oh, I don't know,' said Manu. 'I keep telling her, come the next revolution, it will be the authorities that come knocking, not the rebels, and no door on earth will keep them out. Give it a shove,' he said, turning to Rita, and he pushed with his hand on the door so that it swung wide open.

For a moment the children did not move, gazing at the airy, light-filled room as they might at a bonfire or a starry sky. And then, with a sudden rush, they launched themselves inside.

'Welcome home,' said the young man.

CHAPTER 7

Violette had one of her heads and was lying down in the drawing room, a damp washcloth across her eyes, and her feet in Mrs Patchett's lap. She had spent the afternoon on the telephone with Estella, fielding questions about Bobby's imminent return and listening to the hardship of having one's children flung to the four corners of the earth. 'I should hardly call Brussels the four corners,' Violette had muttered, before throwing herself down on the sofa and demanding that Mrs Patchett massage her pressure points. Conversations with her sister always upset her. There was something crude in them, something false and provincial that hung in the air for hours afterwards, like when the houseboys fried herring. She would be glad when Bobby finally sailed and she was rid of it all, and she sighed, a long, noisy exhalation through her nose that lifted the washcloth and caused Mrs Patchett to glance over. 'That's the one,' said the older woman, and she pushed her thumbs harder into the soft, powdered soles of Violette's feet.

Alexandria in September is at her most beguiling. As the beaches empty and the fickle summer hoards retreat into the desert, she merely rolls over and turns her attention back to herself. Stretching her bronzed limbs, lifting her face to feel the first cool breezes of autumn, she waits patiently on the wharf at the Inner Harbour, on the platform of the Gare du Caire, in the newly built Imperial Airways hangar at Dikheila, to welcome back her own. This year, however, was different. With all the troubles in Europe, the inhabitants of cosmopolitan

Alexandria had largely stayed put, forgoing the usual trips to Switzerland and the Austrian Alps for fear of getting caught up in some Fascist coup or worse. And so *la rentrée* had none of the usual stopping and starting, and was merely a seamless continuation of all that had come before: of the lunch parties and cocktail evenings and intimate little costume balls for three hundred guests. Violette didn't think she could remember her dance card so full, and even Clemmie, whose social appetite was rarely sated, admitted he was beginning to flag. It was, they agreed, quite a time.

For Bobby, then, the imminence of his departure trailed him like an unwelcome stranger. He had grown used to this varied, sociable world, with lunch one day at the Sporting Club, the next at the Cercle Suisse, the next with friends of the d'Araquys on a boat in the harbour. What's more, it had grown used to him too, his awkwardness increasingly charming, so that where before people had looked askance, now they said, 'Ah, what a breath of fresh air you are!' When he thought of returning to Manchester, of his old life moving between house and office, office and house, his heart shrunk until it was as small and hard as a marble, rolling around his leaden chest.

❖   ❖   ❖   ❖   ❖

'SHE THINKS HE'S GOING TO be torpedoed crossing the Bay of Biscay.' Violette's words were somewhat muffled, due to the washcloth.

'Who does?' Philippe was making himself a drink, pouring Scotch over perfectly square ice cubes. 'Who will be torpedoed?'

'My dreadful sister thinks Bobby will. She said I was holding onto him just long enough for war to break out, that I take pleasure in her suffering.' Violette lifted the cloth and sat up on her elbows. 'As if I care what he does. Make me one of those, darling. Lots of ice, my head is pounding.'

She slid herself along the sofa and sat up, smoothing her hair which had been set and dried that morning and which shimmered in the dim light. She took her glass and patted the cushion next to her. 'Sit with me, I've had a horrid day.'

Philippe smiled and sat down, resting his elbows either side of himself on the back of the sofa. 'How was your bridge? I called by the Club on my way to lunch, but Ahmed said you'd left.' He stroked her bare neck, then leaned over and kissed his favourite part, just below the ear. 'Clemmie was there, sunning himself on the terrace. I thought you were going to speak to him about that.'

'Bridge was dull,' she said, ignoring this last, 'I was playing with that Miller woman, the American, do you remember? She spent the entire game pumping me for information about Robin Barrows, it quite put me off. Poor Robin, I feel awfully responsible.'

'I should think he'd be delighted.'

She glanced at him with irritation, for he had a particular tone he used for men like Robin. 'Anyway, I decided I couldn't face being interrogated throughout lunch so I made my excuses and came home.' She sighed. 'Only to spend all afternoon being interrogated by my sister instead. Really, I don't know what I do to deserve it.'

'Poor darling.' He continued to stroke her neck, sipping at his Scotch. He was thinking about his own day, which had been rather a pleasant one, then remembered something. 'I stopped into Sednaoui, I bought you a little present. I had some business to discuss and somehow I ended up in the silks department, they've just received a new shipment.' He reached for his briefcase, taking out two ribboned packages and handing one of them to his wife. She smiled.

'You spoil me,' she said. She had been hinting for weeks about the new Hermès squares everyone was wearing.

'I got one for Josie too,' he added, seeing her eye the second package, 'I thought it was time she had a few nice pieces. She so admires the way you dress, I thought you wouldn't mind.'

'She's a little young, darling.' The pleasure had somewhat gone out of the gift now and she put it down, leaving it for the moment unopened. 'I do wish you'd checked with me first.' Her headache seemed to have returned, for she pinched the bridge of her nose and sighed wearily.

He changed the subject. 'I have to go to Cairo this weekend, there's a problem at one of the mills. How about we make a weekend of it? It would do you good to get out of Alex, you never get a minute's peace when we're here.'

'It's sweet of you,' she smiled. She had no intention of traipsing around the cotton mills of Cairo. 'But you know I'm no company when you're working, I get dreadfully bored.'

'Oh, the business won't take more than a morning, I just need to show my face, that's all. In fact, you wouldn't even need to come to Cairo, we could stay at Mena House, you always love it there. After the day you've had, you don't feel like doing anything, I know, but you'll love it once we're there. They always look after you so wonderfully.'

'I suppose it might be nice to get away for a few days. Oh,' she shook her head, remembering Estella, 'it's Bobby's last weekend, Estella is insisting he leaves by Monday.' She picked up the package again, turning it over and straightening the ribbons. 'According to Estella, Hitler is going to declare war on Monday. I don't know where she gets these ideas.'

'Unfortunately she gets them from the newspapers,' said her husband, 'they're all saying the same thing. Well, then Bobby can come with us, he can sail from Port Said instead. He'll be better off on one of the big mail-boats.'

'Oh darling, I don't think Bobby will want to spend his

last weekend with us! He'll want to spend it with the young people.' She laughed and patted her husband's knee, and Philippe frowned, for there was something condescending in the gesture.

'Obviously I meant the children too. Of course if you don't think they'll want to, I'll keep to my plan and go alone.'

He was peevish now. He knew this tendency for younger wives (and in Alex they were all younger) to regard their husbands as fools, and he was wary of it. Violette shook her head.

'I wouldn't dream of you going alone!' Now that the invitation included Clemmie, there was more potential in it. 'No, we'll all come, it's a wonderful idea. Bobby will love to see the pyramids, he has only ever seen them from the train. Perhaps you should take your clubs and you and Bobby can have an early morning round. Poor Clemmie, he feels terrible that he doesn't play, he knows how much you love it.'

'What I loved was playing with Josie.'

'Now don't be like that.' She looked at him sternly, hugging her slender shoulders. 'It's not good for girls to do too much sport, they get so—' she sought the right word, 'so mannish.'

Philippe stood up and held out a hand for her glass. 'Top up?'

Violette shook her head. 'I must start getting ready. You haven't forgotten it's the Petersons' tonight?' He had. 'I'd call and cry off, blame my head — and it would be true too — but you know how sensitive Kiki is, she'd never let me forget it. Do you think you can get our usual rooms? We simply must have a view of the pyramids, it's hardly worth going otherwise.' She remembered the scarf and now she opened it, dropping the ribbon and paper to the floor and shaking out the blue and gold square. 'Oh darling, I love it! How clever you are to choose just my colours.' She stood up and went to stand beside Philippe, looking past him at the mirrored doors of the sideboard and arranging it into a loose bow. 'What do you think?'

'Beautiful.'

'The scarf or your wife?' She was flirting now, pleased with the gift and how it suited her.

'Both,' he said. He lowered his head so that she could tidy his hair, combing it behind his ear with her fingernails. He liked it when she fussed over him.

'There,' she nodded at the mirror, 'what a handsome couple.'

'Indeed.' He gazed at his wife's reflection, thinking how lucky he was, and she, who intended that he should always feel like that, looked back at him with new severity.

'I'm really not sure about your giving Josie the same thing, darling.' She pursed her lips as though it pained her to say it. 'She idolises you as it is, I don't think it helps to shower her with expensive gifts. That's for a husband to do. And how can we hope for her to find a husband when she's still so attached to her Daddy?' She narrowed her eyes. 'I'm right, darling. You know I am.'

'I wasn't really thinking of it like that. I just wanted to give her something pretty.'

'I know darling, but young girls are complicated. And Josie more than most. You'll take it back? I can ask Mrs Patchett to do it while we're away, if you prefer.'

'In fact, I wanted to speak to you about Mrs Patchett,' Philippe began, and the conversation turned to whether or not they really needed a nanny, as it often did these days. Violette, satisfied that she had made her point, said she thought they probably did.

◆　　◆　　◆　　◆　　◆

'TORPEDOED, CAN YOU IMAGINE?' They were finally leaving the house, Violette tapping her heels as she waited for the chauffeur to open the door, then dropping onto the back seat with a sigh. 'Sometimes I wonder how Estella and I are in the same family, we're not in the least alike.' She reached between the seats and twisted the mirror so that she might check her face, for Philippe had been hurrying her. 'Oh darling, look at the state of me,' she said, baring her teeth and rubbing at smudges of lipstick she found there, 'I'm enough to frighten the natives. Poor Hassan, what must he think.'

The driver, hearing his name, looked round.

'*Mush mush*, Hassan,' said Philippe, waving him on.

'Promise me we won't stay long, darling.' Violette leaned back against his arm, her head tilted forward so as not to flatten her hair. 'I'm really not in the mood.'

Her husband smiled, for this is what she always said. 'We'll just show our faces and then leave.'

CHAPTER 8

The hotel, with its golf course and swimming pool, its billiard room and its celebrated French chef, was situated on the very edge of the desert. From every window, from the gardens and from the terrace where the guests gathered before dinner, the pyramids rose up like angular yellow mountains, and it was not unusual for people to compare it with some little Pyrenean ski lodge they had once stayed at. Ignoring the clanging of the nearby tram, the gentle braying of donkeys with names like Teapot and Plimsoll, they would order *Asperges de Paris* and *Turbot d'Ostende* from the tasselled menu and imagine themselves in Europe. And they took their tea with milk, for the hotel had its own cows.

The d'Araquys arrived by car. Bobby had said his goodbyes to Uncle Saul and the various aunties that morning, and his suitcases were strapped to the roof as the trunk was full. The drive was spent reading aloud from Forster's Guide (Josette had given him the new edition as a leaving present) and when they turned at Giza and the pyramids leapt into view ahead of them, Bobby was overcome with joy. Not so Clemmie who, upon arrival, fled the car as from a burning building. 'What kind of guide book has poems in it? One more 'brave man,' and I think I might have killed him,' he hissed to his mother, striding ahead of her up the wooden steps.

'You're such a heathen, darling,' smiled Violette.

The interior of the hotel, with its mosaic floors and mashrabiya windows, its brass doors and carved mahogany woodwork, was everything an Edwardian traveller once imagined of Egypt. Rattan chairs and tables inlaid with mother of pearl immediately beckoned, and Clemmie cast himself onto a tapestried cushion and announced he would wait for them there. By some usual miracle, he bore no trace of the long desert drive, and was as fresh and fragrant as if he had just emerged from a cool bath. Insisting there was 'no rush, no rush,' he gave his mother a long look, and she smiled and said it would only take her five minutes to change and come back down. The others were encouraged to take a nap.

Dinner was a triumph and the head waiter, an Italian with whom they all spoke French, fussed around the table with a solicitude that flicked on and off like a light switch. Violette responded with her best attention, using his first name and hushing the table every time he spoke. Afterwards they took their coffee on the terrace, the pyramids looming black and dull, and it was as if someone had cut huge, clumsy triangles from the moonlit sky. Bobby, giddy from the wine they had drunk with their meal, had picked up another guidebook from the front desk.

'According to Herodotus,' he declared, 'the main diet of the workers who built the pyramids was radishes. Imagine hauling lumps of stone over thirty foot long with just a few radishes to keep you going.'

'I hate radishes,' said Clemmie.

'Then it's lucky you weren't an Egyptian slave,' said Philippe. 'Chérie, would you like a nightcap?' he said, turning to Violette. She would.

'I can't imagine Clemmie as anyone's slave,' said Josette with a giggle. 'He's awful at being told what to do.'

Everyone laughed, and Violette said, 'It's quite true darling, you would have been no good as a slave.'

'I'm not sure there were many other career choices,'

said Philippe, leaning back in his chair and allowing a waiter to light his cigar.

'Oh, Clemmie would have found something,' said Violette, and she smiled at her beautiful son, as if imagining all the glories to which he might have aspired. Thin wisps of cigar smoke drifted across the table and she batted at them with her hand. 'Darling, must you? You know I hate it getting in my hair.'

Philippe picked a shred of tobacco from his upper lip, then turned his head to exhale in the opposite direction. 'Sorry, my sweet,' he said.

'Perhaps you'd have been a robber,' said Bobby, taking an olive from a bowl on the table and popping it in his mouth. 'There were tomb raiders as early as the Twelfth Dynasty,' he added.

'Highly likely,' said Philippe.

'No it isn't,' said Violette.

The waiter arrived with Violette's drink, and they sat in silence, watching as he rearranged the table, flicking at crumbs with a folded napkin, laying out fresh coasters. He picked up the half-eaten bowl of olives and Bobby thrust out a hand, saying no, they were not finished, but the waiter merely nodded, lowering his tray and replacing it with a new, full bowl in the exact same place. Bobby blushed and Josette saw her mother gaze without expression at Clemmie, in that way they did when they shared a secret that no one else knew. Josette looked away.

'Isn't that one of your Cecil lot?' said Philippe, leaning towards his wife and gesturing with the rim of his glass towards the other side of the terrace.

Violette blinked, then turned a little in her seat and glanced in the direction he had pointed. 'I can't see,' she said, turning back.

'The blonde with all the diamonds.' Philippe sucked on

his cigar, and then peered at it to see if it was still lit. 'Although that doesn't narrow it down much,' he added, winking at Josette.

'Abigail Gardiner, Mummy,' murmured Clemmie, who had also turned to look. He smoothed the edge of the tablecloth and then glanced at his mother through thick, golden lashes. 'We should invite her to join us, I'm longing to hear what's happening with her case.'

'Her case?' said Philippe, 'What case?'

'You know this,' said Violette.

'I don't know anything about a case,' said Philippe.

'Darling, you do, I told you about it,' said Violette. 'You just pretend you don't, to make me look like I'm gossiping.' She smiled, reaching a hand to his leg and pressing it affectionately. 'Bobby will go back to Manchester thinking me quite awful.'

'Oh no,' cried Bobby, 'not at all!'

'Did you sort out your ticket?' asked Josette, for her mother and Clemmie were exchanging glances again. 'Why don't you ask at the desk, they can call up and arrange everything.'

'It's taken care of,' said Philippe, 'sorry, I thought I'd said. There's a fellow at Bibby Line who owes me a favour, he was happy to oblige.'

'The little Greek one?' asked Violette, who kept a tally of these things.

'Turkish, with the moustache. You have a berth on the *Staffordshire* leaving Sunday evening. I telegrammed your mother the details.'

'Sunday?' said Bobby, and then as an afterthought, 'Thank you, that's perfect.'

'So soon,' said Josette.

Clemmie stood up, flicking his head as usual, so that his hair momentarily cleared his eyes, only to slide back seconds later. 'Can you let me out, Mummy?' he said, and Violette stood up so that he could get past.

Bobby stood up too, the sides of the wicker chair rasping as he heaved himself upright, and Josette glanced at Violette, for she knew how his English manners grated. 'Why is he constantly getting up and down every time someone moves?' she had demanded that first day at the beach, 'he's like an enormous jack-in-the-box.'

'Sit, sit,' said Violette, her eyes on Clemmie as he wove his way through the closely packed tables. But Bobby remained standing.

'Would anyone mind if I went for a walk?' he said. He gestured beyond the palm trees and elaborate fretwork of the terrace. All evening a steady train of camels and donkeys had picked their way up and down the sandy road leading to the hotel, but now everyone had gone. 'I could do with stretching my legs before bed.'

'Is it safe?' asked Josette, turning to her father.

Philippe said he thought it probably was.

'Look at the size of him,' said Violette, reaching out a hand and batting her nephew's stomach. 'Nobody's going to give him any trouble. Go, go! You can tell us all about it tomorrow, how exciting to be so young and intrepid. Oh look, Clemmie couldn't resist.'

On the other side of the terrace Clemmie was leaning over Mrs Gardiner's table, and as they watched he turned and pointed towards his mother. The two women waved at one another.

'I think I might go to bed,' said Josette, watching as Bobby backed away through the maze of tables. She bent down to find her sandals, which she had kicked off earlier.

'All right, darling,' said her mother, her eyes still fixed on the other side of the terrace. 'Tomorrow we'll go to Cicurel, just the two of us,' she added, seized with a sudden generosity. 'How would that be?' Josette mumbled something in reply, but her mother wasn't listening. 'Philippe dear, they're coming over. Please don't say anything to upset anyone. And put that out, would you?' She pushed an ashtray at him across the table.

'I think I'll go up too,' said Philippe, holding out a hand to Josette so that she might help him up. 'You don't mind do you, chérie?'

'Go, go,' said Violette, waving them away. Then she threw out her arms, like a trapeze act reaching for the next bar, 'Abigail, darling!' she cried, 'how simply wonderful to run into you! Sit, sit, Clemmie and I want to hear all your news!'

CHAPTER 9

The road beyond the hotel was in darkness, with a single lamp burning in the window of the post office to the left. Bobby walked briskly, striding out along the sandy track, eager to leave the noise and clamour of the terrace behind. At the curve in the road he slowed his pace, for the air was warm and he stopped to remove his jacket. Behind him the lights of Mena House flickered and danced, but already he felt excluded from them, for he was leaving this place, he was being cast out. This must have been how Alexander felt, walking away from the city he loved, obliged to return to his old life of war and pillaging. Bobby sighed and started off again, his melancholy easier to bear now that it was heroic.

'Wait for me!' A noise on the track behind him made Bobby turn. In the distance he could just make out a slight figure running toward him and he stared. 'Wait for me!' It was Josette.

He started back down the road towards her, kicking up clouds of dust in his haste. When she saw this she stood quite still, holding something out to him.

'You forgot your book,' she said, handing him the guidebook he had left on the table. 'Here, I brought it.'

Bobby stared at her. He could think of nothing to say, and so he stared at the cover of the guidebook, as if to make sure it was indeed his. 'I'll walk you back,' he said at last.

'Actually, I thought I'd come with you. They make an "ineffaceable impression" at night. That's what the book says.'

'What?'

'An ineffaceable impression,' she repeated solemnly. She held out her hand and he looked at it for a moment before taking it, just as he had the book. 'Come on,' she said.

They walked in silence. The track was steeper here, and they had to keep stopping to catch their breath. Walls of rock rose up at either side, and thin scrubby trees bristled darkly, casting long shadows across their path. The sky was wide and navy blue.

And then suddenly there they were, standing on the edge of the desert, the impossible bulk of the Great Pyramid soaring above them. Bobby stopped, his head craned upwards, his shoulders slumping as if in defeat. Josette, still holding his hand, looked up at him.

'Well?'

He turned to her and smiled, his big, gentle smile that had none of the complexity of other peoples' smiles (even her father's had a certain knowingness) and then pointed towards the top of the pyramid.

'My father slept up there once,' he said, 'when he was a student at the university, there was a whole group of them. When the sun rose in the morning he said it looked like the sand was on fire, and that whatever colour the sky was, the desert was a brighter version, as if it were made of water, not sand. Can you imagine that? The desert looking like a big lake?' He kicked at a small stone with the toe of his shoe, sending it skittering off to the side. 'You should hear him talk about it, he said it was then that he really understood there's divinity in the world.'

Josette looked puzzled.

'God,' said Bobby. 'It was then that he understood God.'

Josette considered this. 'He was probably here during the flood season,' she said.

'The flood season?'

'The water from the Nile used to come right up here, before they built the dam at Aswan. Instead of camels they had little rowing boats, I've seen a photograph.' Something altered in Bobby's expression, and she stopped. 'Of course, it was probably God too,' she said.

Bobby glanced beyond her towards the road. The hotel was no longer visible, but he felt its presence nonetheless. 'We should go back, they'll be waiting for you.'

Josette shrugged. 'They think I'm in bed.' She released his fingers and walked towards the entrance of the Great Pyramid, now closed, gesturing to him to follow. 'Don't fuss,' she added, smiling at him over her shoulder.

Bobby hesitated, but something in her smile emboldened him, as it had been intended to, and in a few strides he was at her side. Just then a young man in a galabiyah appeared, stepping silently out of the shadows and causing Josette to squeal and jump backwards. He was holding an oil lamp high above his head and the yellow light gave an unnaturalness to his features.

'*Imshi!*' she cried, '*Imshi!* Go away!'

The man stared at them for a moment, lowering the lamp and letting it swing at his side. Then he nodded and began to walk away.

'No, wait,' said Bobby, feeling in his pocket for some change, 'here.' He went after him, pressing a handful of coins into the young man's hand. '*Leiltak sa'ïda,*' he said, which he had read in the guidebook and which meant "May thy night be happy". In the darkness the man laughed.

'You're so nice,' said Josette, 'I don't think I know anyone who's as nice to people as you are.'

'Is that a bad thing?'

Josette shook her head. 'Of course not.'

They looked up at the silent mass of stone rising high above their heads, obscuring the moon, and causing a kind of dryness in the back of their throats, as though the rock was drawing all the moisture from the air. A bat swooped and cartwheeled to their left, and it was joined by another and then another, their taut, black wings making a clicking sound in the empty night. Back towards the road someone was shouting, but it was too far away to make out what they were saying, and anyway, someone was always shouting in Egypt, it was how it was. Josette felt a rush of affection, although whether it was for Egypt, or the pyramids, or for something else altogether, she could not have said, and she glanced at Bobby, wondering if he felt it too. But Bobby was looking straight ahead, his two hands reaching in front of him, palms pressed against the stone, and was taking long slow breaths that caused his chest to rise and fall.

'Do you feel unwell?'

'Not at all,' he said, surprised.

'I thought perhaps you were dizzy.'

He shook his head, dropping his arms and turning towards her. After a moment, Josette stepped back, bending down and pulling off her sandals.

'Come on,' she said, and suddenly she had hauled herself up the first of the enormous steps and was standing above him. She hovered there, looking down at him.

'Be careful,' said Bobby, reaching towards her. 'You could fall.'

But Josette only laughed and turned around, her thin, bare legs kicking away from him, rising up through the murky night as he pulled off his shoes and followed.

IT TOOK BOBBY ALMOST THIRTY minutes to reach the top, and when at last he hauled himself across the final ledge, his limbs burned with exhaustion and his breath came in short, noisy rasps. Josette was lying on her back, but at the sound of his arrival she sat up, smiling triumphantly, and patted the stone next to her. Bobby remained where he was, kneeling and looking around at the bleached, colourless landscape. The moon was tilted on its side, a tiny sliver of white in the black night, and any light it gave off was quickly swallowed up by the endless expanse of desert. To the right were two more pyramids, and just ahead, the softer outlines of the Sphinx, crouched in its pit. Josette pointed behind him and he turned around, and there was the river, glittering and shifting, bound on either side by fields. Narrow canals ran at right angles to the river, and they too glittered, as did the straight, newly surfaced road towards Cairo, dotted here and there with the distant specks of headlamps, and reminding Bobby of his imminent departure.

He moved towards Josette and sat down heavily, leaning forwards to inspect his long feet, which were grazed and sore from the climb.

'I should have kept my shoes on,' he said. 'The book says you should dress for mountaineering, it was mad to climb barefoot.'

'You don't always have to do what the book says,' said Josette, on her back again and staring, wide-eyed, at the empty sky.

'No, but in this case it would have been sensible.'

'You don't always have to be sensible either.'

He nodded but said nothing. After a while he lay back on the warm stone, shuffling down a little so that his shoulders were level with hers, and turned his head to look at her, while she continued to gaze straight ahead.

'Perhaps you'll come to England some time, and I'll be able to show you around,' he said, so that she would understand how grateful he was for the welcome he had received. 'We don't have pyramids, but I could come to London and show you St Paul's Cathedral and the Tower of

London and Buckingham Palace. We could watch them Changing the Guard,' he added, and he grinned, because she had told him how Mrs Patchett knew all the Christopher Robin poems by heart and would recite them at bedtime instead of prayers.

'I shall probably go to Switzerland,' said Josette, 'so long as there's no war. And if there is a war, then I suppose I shall just stay here and get a job. Or marry. Mummy was married at my age, she thinks it's what nice girls do.'

She spoke without expression and Bobby was not sure how she felt about this so he just said, 'Oh.' And then, after some thought, 'I don't think there will be war.'

'Switzerland it is then.'

They continued to lie there. Bobby remembered the guidebook and he took it out and held it close to his nose so that he could read it in the moonlight.

'Tell me something,' said Josette, and he glanced at her and saw that her eyes were closed and that she had twisted her hair beneath her head so that it was as if she was resting on a small yellow cushion. He turned to the guidebook, flicking through a few pages and then starting to read. He told her how once there would have been a capstone where they were lying now, made of pure gold, but that these were always the first things to be looted. He told her about how, beneath them, the interior of the pyramid was divided into chambers, and how the limestone walls were so skilfully jointed that it was impossible to see where one stone ended and another began. He told her how the dead king's sarcophagus was made of thick slabs of granite and that, if you struck the sides with something hard, they rang like a bell. And all the time her eyes were closed and she said not a word.

At last Bobby closed the book and set it down on his chest, so that it rose and fell with each breath. He sighed, squinting up at the narrow moon. '*Leiltak sa'ïda,*' he murmured, remembering how nice the words had felt in his mouth. He scratched his head and neck pleasantly.

'We should go back.' Her eyes were open now.

'A bit longer,' said Bobby, but she appeared not to hear him for she stood up and turned away. He watched as, without a word, she walked to the other side of the platform and swung herself over the steep ledge.

As with the climb up, Josette went ahead of Bobby, dropping from block to massive block, as if it were something she did every day of the week. Behind her Bobby puffed and wheezed, but she didn't slow down, and when he called after her to make sure she was all right, she said yes and continued. When at last she reached the ground, she stood for a moment looking around herself, and then concentrated upon finding her sandals and strapping them on, so that when Bobby arrived, she was standing there waiting for him, his shoes and socks neatly laid out on the cool sand. She smiled, but there was a fury in it, and when he crouched to fasten his laces he had the sense that she would like to strike him.

And perhaps it was that which caused him to act as he did. Or perhaps he had always known it would eventually come to this, it was just a matter of time. Later, when people would ask him, he would talk of pyramids and war and the full moon (in his memory it was always full) and everyone would sigh and forget that they were cousins and think only how romantic it must have been. Which it was.

'Must you go to Switzerland?' he said suddenly.

She looked at him, and it was that same frenzied smile.

'*Must* you go to Switzerland?'

'What do you mean?' she said, her eyes boring into his, so that it took all his courage not to look away.

But he couldn't tell her what he meant, and so instead he bent his head and kissed her lightly on the lips. It was a kiss for Egypt, a kiss for this magical world he was now obliged to leave behind, a kiss goodbye. But when he raised his head and looked at her, her face was suffused with such joy that instead of grinning and explaining that leaving places always made him do silly things, he kissed her again.

'We should go back,' he said, pulling away and looking for his jacket, which he had dropped somewhere.

'Not yet,' said Josette, and then her arms were around his neck and her face was pressed against his chest, so that he could feel her warm breath through the cotton of his shirt. And suddenly Bobby was filled with a kind of exhilaration, and he was reminded of the time he had broken his leg and been given morphine. The feeling of abandonment as the drug coursed through his veins, the gentle, expanding release as each part of his body gave itself up to its power, that was how he felt now.

'You're cold,' he murmured, for she was trembling. 'Here, let me find my jacket, you can put it on.'

But when he tried to move, she only clung to him tighter, and so he stayed where he was, clasping her thin body in his arms. And then together, holding tight to one another, they walked back down the narrow sandy track towards the hotel, wondrous at what they had done.

CHAPTER 10

Towards the middle of September, Allegra Balestra left La Baule and returned to Brussels. Marco had been back since the beginning of the month, for he had work to do, but they had agreed to keep the children out of the city until this Czechoslovakia business blew over. Now, tired from the long train journey and hurt that Marco had sent his driver to meet her rather than come himself, she had arrived home to find the house locked and nobody in. At the very least the maid should have been there, and she returned to the car, sitting down heavily on the back seat and wondering what to do. The chauffeur, who had worked for the family for years and was used to their ways, suggested he drive to Marco's office and pick up the keys.

'Oh yes, of course, that's the thing to do,' Allegra said, fanning her hot face with her fingers. She glanced at him in the mirror, smiling gratefully. 'Perhaps I'll just find myself a nice bit of shade and wait until you get back.' She began fastening her skirt, which she had loosened during the journey. 'I don't think I can bear any more driving, I feel quite done in. Over there,' she pointed to a bench on the other side of the road, 'I'll sit myself there.' The driver nodded, and hurried around to help her out again. 'Take your time, I shall be quite happy,' she assured him.

Beneath the arching branches of a linden tree, Allegra sighed and closed her eyes. She had not wanted to come back to Brussels. She had seen the photographs of Madrid and she felt sure that this would be the fate of all cities if Hitler had his way. When a number of friends announced they were keeping away until the situation improved, she decided that she would too, and arrangements were made in La Baule to hold onto their rooms after the season ended. And although Marco at first resisted, when he heard that both the Hallemans and the Carassos were staying on too, he relented. 'At least this way we won't need to worry about Seppy,' he agreed, for their son was at that age when boys got ideas in their heads and ran off to join the Reserves. The only sticking point was Laura.

Allegra had felt terrible that she was not there to welcome her sister-in-law when she arrived in Brussels. She said so all the time to Odette when they were having lunch, to Sofia Carasso when she saw her at the market, to Marco when he telephoned from the office and gave her updates on the family's progress. At last, around the time the newspapers announced a temporary reprieve, her conscience got the better of her and she agreed to leave Seppy in charge and make a short trip to visit Laura in her new home. At the same time she could collect a few things they would need in La Baule if the weather changed.

It was strange to think of her sister-in-law in Brussels, especially here on the avenue. For years this had been Allegra's domain, 'le nid de maman' as the children called it. And it was true that she felt like a bird sometimes, perched there in her beautiful apartment, surrounded by her family and the things she loved. She had a favourite window where she liked to sit and watch the world go by, and when people who knew her went past, or the children returned from school, they looked for her there and waved. That was where she sat each evening waiting for Marco, watching for his yellow Simca to come hurtling around the bend, jumping up when she saw it and quickly turning on the wireless or picking up a book, so that he wouldn't think she did nothing all day. Just remembering it now made her smile.

How hot it was, even here in the shade! She wafted the front of her blouse, wishing she hadn't worn a corset, and pulling at the stays to allow a little air to reach her damp, heavy breasts. She had lost three kilos this summer (La Baule was famous for its cures) but when she put her travelling suit on this morning it felt just as tight as it always did. Nora, her eldest daughter, thought she should stop torturing herself and buy clothes she was comfortable in, but it was easy to think like that when you were seventeen. Besides, ever since Lucia Arditti had told her she was letting herself go — '*Ti sei lasciata andare!*' her cousin had said, in that high-handed way she had — Allegra had felt so self-conscious. Of course, Marco assured her that he loved her just the same however she was, but it was true that age had not been kind to Allegra. She frowned and sat up straighter, her handbag pulled into her stomach, her fingers laced protectively around both.

At the sound of a man's voice she glanced up, thinking it might be the chauffeur back again, but instead she saw a young man on a bicycle, shouting over his shoulder as he pedalled. His hands were raised from the handlebars and now he put them in his pockets, laughing, while behind him a young boy shrieked delightedly and tried to imitate him. Behind the boy a woman, cycling more slowly and with a look of great concentration, urged them both to be careful. The woman, Allegra saw with surprise, was her sister-in-law.

'Laura!'

Hearing her name, Laura turned her head, the movement causing the bicycle to weave from side to side, so that she went some distance before she could stop. When at last she had climbed off and was hurrying back towards Allegra, she was laughing.

'Allegra! I'm so happy to see you!' She waved to the others, who had continued. 'Teddy, Manu, come back! Allegra is here!'

At the sight of her so fresh and full of life, Allegra was seized with a sudden envy, and as Laura came towards her, she could hardly look at her. But Laura seemed not to notice, catching at Allegra's hands and kissing her warmly.

'What luck you saw us! Marco said you were coming today but for some reason I thought it was this evening – dear Allegra! To think we almost cycled straight past!' She held onto Allegra's hands, squeezing them as she spoke. 'Teddy, come and say hello. He pretends to be shy, but he really isn't – Look Teddy, it's Auntie Allegra!'

She released Allegra's hands so that she might steer Teddy forward. Allegra, recovering herself, gazed at him with affection. 'Teddy Balestra, I never would have recognised you. You have got so big, has someone been stretching you?'

'I'm almost as tall as Mammy.' At nine his body was beginning to lose its babyishness, his limbs taking on a new angularity. 'Aren't I, Mammy?'

'I can believe it.' Allegra glanced at Laura. 'The girls are the same. I feel I blink and they've grown two inches.'

'How well you look,' said Laura, struck by that sadness a woman's face takes on as she ages, 'France clearly suits you. Do you know Emmanuel Carasso?' She turned to Manu, who was leaning over his handlebars. 'Manu, this is my sister-in-law, Allegra Balestra.'

'We've met,' he said, holding out his hand and adding, 'Sofia's son', for that was how most people knew him.

'Of course!' said Allegra quickly.

'Manu's been giving me a golf lesson,' said Teddy. 'He says I'm a natural, I have a perfect swing.'

'We were just on our way back,' said Laura. 'Manu insisted we take the scenic route around the park, he thinks I need practice with my cycling.' She removed her sunglasses, setting them on her head. Allegra noticed a sprinkling of freckles along the top of her cheeks.

'You look about sixteen,' Allegra said.

'It's this dress,' said Laura, pleased. She smoothed the front of her blue dress, and Allegra saw it was patterned with tiny white and yellow daisies. 'It's my *marguerite* dress, that was what they called it in the shop, Rita made me buy it.'

'I want her to buy a 'teddy' bear dress next,' said Teddy, and Laura pulled a face, for this was a joke he had made many times.

'Doesn't he need to be back?' asked Manu, glancing at his watch, 'I thought they all had a tutorial?'

Laura frowned. 'He does, yes. Teddy, jump on your bicycle, the girls will be waiting for us.' She turned to Allegra. 'They have a Flemish lesson, Manu found a teacher for us on the next street. Double Dutch Rita calls it!'

'Flemish lessons?'

'I thought it would make it easier once school started.'

'Oh, no one worries about Flemish these days,' said Allegra, 'not in the private schools anyway.'

'No, I know, it's just Manu has been telling us about the Lyzeum, and it's true it's so much nearer.' She blushed, and Allegra felt a flicker of irritation, for no doubt this young man disapproved of private education.

'Oh, well you must do what you think best.'

'I haven't decided anything yet— yes, yes, I'm coming!'

Teddy was spinning his pedal.

'I'll go ahead with him,' said Manu, 'Lise will be wondering where I've got to. You can leave the bicycle in the hall, I'll come by for it later.'

'Oh would you? Yes, thank you!'

They watched the two race away up the avenue.

'Lise is Manu's wife,' said Laura, and Allegra said she knew. 'They're a lovely family, this is Lise's bicycle. Did you ever imagine you would see me riding a bicycle?

At first I was petrified, but the secret is to concentrate on pedalling.' She wrinkled her brow to show how hard she thought about it. 'I just think about my feet, I don't think about anything else.'

Allegra nodded and looked at her own feet, squashed inside her travelling shoes. The patent leather was dull from the dusty path and her stockings were twisted. She frowned and bent to adjust them.

Laura watched her in silence, seeing her crumpled jacket with the damp patches beneath the arms, her thin, short hair parting to reveal a white scalp, her thick neck. 'What we put ourselves through,' she said, meaning the stockings.

Allegra straightened up. 'I must look a sight.'

'Oh no, you look lovely!'

'And I brought such a pretty dress to change into. Really, I don't know where the maid has got to.' She sighed and gazed up at the windows of the apartment. 'I suppose it's my own fault for not carrying a key.'

'Marie? Marie is with me.'

Allegra looked at her in surprise. 'With *you*?'

'In the apartment. Did Marco not tell you? I needed someone to help with the boxes and Marco said Marie would do it, I thought you knew. Oh Allegra, how awful, I'd never have said yes — Is that why you were sitting here?' She looked at her sister-in-law with wide, anxious eyes. 'I feel dreadful.'

'Perhaps he did mention it, it must have slipped my mind.' Allegra smiled and shrugged her shoulders, but Laura continued to gaze at her.

'And locked out? After such a long journey! It's all my fault. Wait here and I'll go and fetch her.'

Allegra shook her head. 'Really, it doesn't matter. The driver has gone for the keys, he'll be back soon.'

'But the traffic's always terrible at this time of day. At least come with me to the apartment and wait there. We can send Marie to meet the driver. Will you? Will you come back with me now? I'm so longing for you to see everything. It takes two minutes, you can't believe how close we are.'

Allegra looked down at her travelling suit, at the grimy creases around the elbows and waist, at the stain on the skirt from breakfast. 'I suppose you've seen me now,' she said, and she tucked her arm through Laura's. 'Lead the way.'

CHAPTER 11

Over the last year or so Allegra had watched with curiosity the building of the Carasso apartments, wondering at the simplicity of the design, the plainness of the brick and stone facade and the shallow, almost flat roof. When Marco first mentioned Laura's plans, she had been surprised, for she didn't think it was her sister-in-law's style, the Milan house was so much grander, with its frescoed entrance and wide, curving staircase. She was sure that once Laura visited, she would change her mind and look for somewhere more obviously imposing, somewhere more like Allegra's own house, and she comforted herself that any stay on the Avenue des Nations would be brief.

Nothing could have prepared her, then, for the impression the apartment made upon her that morning. Coming out of the lift she was reminded of any good hotel, with its long narrow corridor and expensive carpets, and she smiled at the framed prints of Old Brussels, straightening their edges as she passed. She watched as Laura struggled with the lock, surprised to hear that the doors were all imported from Sweden, for she did not associate the Swedes with security. And then she followed her inside, smoothing her skirt and looking around for Marie, a few stock phrases ready to be handed out when appropriate.

'It's not in the least finished,' said Laura, leading her into the drawing room, with its cream carpet and plain walls, the afternoon sun streaming through the wide curtain-less windows and causing everything it fell upon to shimmer. Two yellow silk sofas took up the centre of the room, facing one another across a low table, and all around, in piles, books were stacked like many small towers. By the hearth, an enormous vase of camellia branches took the place of a fire, the waxen flowers and glossy leaves almost too perfect to be real. And at the opposite end of the room, Laura's piano, its curved side gleaming bluish-black, its lid raised like a mussel shell in deep water.

Allegra gazed around in silence. It was not at all what she had been expecting.

'Of course, it's all your fault,' said Laura, leaning on the back of one of the yellow sofas.

'My fault?'

'That I got myself into such a state that first day. Didn't Marco tell you?' She twisted her rings, remembering how she had sobbed down the telephone. 'It was that rule of yours, about how all a nice home needs is fresh flowers and good curtains, I couldn't get it out of my head. Poor Marco, he thought I'd lost my mind.'

'It's Lucia Arditti's rule really,' said Allegra defensively. She glanced at the bare windows. 'But you had beautiful curtains in Milan, why didn't you bring them?'

'I did, I even arranged for the removal men to hang them. But here they didn't look at all like they did in Italy, they were so drab and heavy.' She shrugged. 'Fortunately Kasha was here so I had him take them straight down, I think Kasha thought I'd lost my mind too.'

'I'm so sorry.'

'I'm teasing, it's not your fault really! Well, only a little. In any case, it turned out for the best, because once the curtains came down, I saw that everything else was wrong too, all that dark furniture I brought from Italy, you remember the carved mahogany that Isaac liked? In Milan I never gave it much thought, but perhaps it's something to do with the light here. I hated it all.' She moved around the sofa and sat down, gazing at her sister-in-law through half-closed eyes. 'Is that terrible of me?'

'But where is it? The furniture.'

'I got rid of it.' Still the same narrow-eyed gaze. 'I had Kasha borrow a van and take it all to the Centre for Refugees, the Carassos know the director there. Of course, it was horribly wasteful of me, think how much I spent having it brought here. But the moment everything was gone I felt better, I felt like I could breathe.' She took a deep, exaggerated breath to prove this was the case. 'Marco was wonderful about it, he didn't bat an eye. I was worried he might go dashing off to the Place Roupe to get it back!' She laughed, her fingers tracing circles on the cushion as she spoke, clearly proud of her impetuosity. 'But instead he had his driver take me to Vanderborght, he said the business had an account there, that we could sort out what I owed later. And so I bought the two sofas. Don't you think they're lovely? I adore yellow. I thought perhaps I'd have curtains made in the same fabric, what do you think? Too much?'

Allegra looked around. She was thinking about her own apartment, crammed full with antique rugs and paintings and bits of furniture that nobody ever used but which required constant dusting and polishing. She thought of the cupboards filled with silver and the chairs she was forever having reupholstered and she wondered how much of it she would keep if she had a choice. 'It's lovely,' she said.

'Do you really think so?'

Allegra nodded. She was standing by the fireplace and now she bent to smell the strangely scentless blossoms of the camellias. 'Isn't it early for these, I don't think I've seen them in September before.'

'I suppose I just needed to make a fresh start.' Laura still had her sunglasses on her head and now she took them off, opening and closing the metal arms as she spoke.

'I didn't realise until I arrived, until the children and I were standing here that first day. Of course, the children weren't happy about me getting rid of everything, Rita in particular kicked up a fuss. But as Coco said — they do say the funniest things — "Daddy isn't in the sideboard!" ' Laura gave a small laugh, leaning forwards and bending the glasses almost flat. 'You can tell me if you hate it, I shan't mind.'

'I wouldn't change a thing,' said Allegra softly. She moved towards Laura, sitting down and taking her hands, putting the sunglasses on the table. 'Do you know what it is?' she said, looking around the glowing room. 'It feels like you. Everywhere else you have lived has felt like Isaac, but here feels like you.'

Laura gazed at her. 'I love that you say that.'

'It's true.'

'No, really, it means so much, I've been in a dreadful muddle about everything.'

'Well it doesn't show.' Allegra smiled. 'Truly it doesn't, you're a lesson to us all.' She pressed Laura's hand then looked around decisively. 'I really should find Marie, the driver will be wondering where I've disappeared to.'

'Marie? Oh yes, of course, she's in the dining room. Come on, I'll show you.' Laura jumped up, taking Allegra's arm and helping her to her feet. 'You have to admit they're comfortable. Goose-down, the man at Vanderborght said, I'm forever falling asleep on them.' She led Allegra back into the hall and through another door on the opposite side. 'Mind the boxes there. Marie, look who's here! Between us we left poor Madame Balestra stranded on the street.'

The maid, a stout woman of around forty, who had worked for Allegra since the children were babies, looked up from a pile of dinner plates she was unwrapping. She immediately put down what she was doing, wiping her hands on her apron.

'Is that the last box?' asked Laura. 'What a wonderful job you've done, I can't believe you found room for everything.'

Marie held open the doors of a narrow marquetry sideboard to show the stacks of porcelain, all different sizes, with their monograms and gold rims.

'The refugees nearly got this too,' said Laura, glancing at Allegra. 'I shan't have any use for it now. But the children prevailed, they want to divide it between them when they have their own homes. Certainly there's enough of it. Twenty-four of everything, isn't it Marie?'

'Twenty-four,' agreed the maid, carefully closing the doors and giving the wood a quick rub with her apron.

'Quite double the size of ours!' said Allegra, looking at Marie. She saw that the maid admired her sister-in-law, that she was impressed by Laura's obvious disregard for the very things Allegra clung to. 'Is that newspaper they were packed in? What a job to wash them all, you must be worn out, Marie.'

'I said she should just put them away as they were but she insisted on soaping and rinsing each one. I really am so grateful.'

'I couldn't have left them as they were,' said Marie, evidently pleased by such praise, 'in this light you catch every speck.' As in the drawing room, the sun blazed through the wide, curtainless windows. 'Some of them I had to do three times before I was happy.'

'Well, it's lucky that you had the time,' said Allegra, making an effort to sound light-hearted. 'But I'm afraid I shall have to steal you back now.' She quickly explained about the driver and gave various instructions regarding her luggage and some bits of washing she needed doing. 'I'm taking the sleeper train from Paris tomorrow night, so I shall need you at home.'

'Tomorrow?' Laura had been moving towards the door to see Marie out, but now she stopped. 'But that's so soon!'

'I must get back to the children.'

'But I thought you'd stay until the weekend at least.' There was a petulance to Laura's tone.

Allegra, glancing at the maid, shook her head. 'Surely you've been following the news, it doesn't look at all good. In fact I was surprised when Marco said you were still here, I assumed you'd have left for Manchester by now. That is what you're planning, isn't it?'

Laura's shoulders slumped and she wrinkled her brow as she had done earlier when talking about pedalling the bicycle. 'I know, I keep putting it off. I can't seem to make up my mind what to do.' She leaned against the doorframe, and for a moment she seemed to forget the other women.

'Perhaps we should let Marie go,' said Allegra gently. Laura stirred.

'Of course, yes!' She wrenched open the door, reaching around the frame for the light switch so that the narrow corridor was suddenly illuminated. 'Do you have your bag? Oh yes, there it is. Thank you, Marie, you've been a treasure.' She pressed the maid's arm, watching until she reached the lift then closing the door and leaning back against it. She gazed at her sister-in-law for a moment. 'Do you really think there will be war?' she asked abruptly.

Allegra shrugged, pulling at her corset which was pinching again. 'Marco says not, he thinks Chamberlain will sort it out, he says diplomacy's what the English do best.'

Laura nodded. He had said this to her too. 'Then why go back?'

'Because I don't want to take any chances. Odette Hallemans — you'll meet her, she's one of my dearest friends — she has the most awful stories about what it was like here during the last war. She says she could never go through that again, that's why they bought the villa in La Baule, so that they'd have somewhere to go.'

'I suppose you're right.' Laura continued to gaze at Allegra, thinking how much older she looked these days, how there was no trace of the beauty she had been when they first met. She remembered how she had been in awe of her then, with her thick auburn hair pulled into a loose knot at her neck, her oval face and naturally fine brows, so unlike her own. How far it was from the overweight, sallow creature she was now. As if fearing Allegra might be able to read her thoughts, Laura suddenly moved away. 'I haven't even offered you something to drink!' she said, gesturing to Allegra to follow, 'Come into the kitchen, I have some of Kasha's iced tea, he makes it to a secret recipe. Really, Allegra, you cannot imagine how kind everyone has been, I've hardly lifted a finger since we arrived.' She looked searchingly at the other woman. 'We've been quite spoilt.'

Allegra smiled. 'I can see.' She gazed around the kitchen, taking in the smart fitted cupboards with their glass shelves, the marble countertop, the new gas oven with its door still papered shut, the American refrigerator. 'What's that?' she asked, pointing to a metal hatch on one wall.

'Oh, you won't believe it,' said Laura, reaching across and sliding open the door. Inside was an empty shelf and pulley ropes. 'It's connected to the Carassos' kitchen above. This apartment was intended for Manu, Sofia had it put in so that she could send their meals down!' She was opening cupboards, looking for glasses. 'Don't you think that's adorable? Poor Sofia, she was devastated when they changed their minds, she dotes on Manu. Of course, when I took the apartment I said she should have it blocked up, but now she has Kasha send things down to us instead! Ah, here we are.' She held up two cut glass tumblers. 'Do you recognise them? You gave them to us for our first wedding anniversary.

There were twelve originally, but I'm afraid these are all that's left, you remember how clumsy Isaac was.'

'How nice you still use them.' In amongst all this modern luxury, the two old glasses seemed especially poignant. 'I remember them, we bought them in Liège. Perhaps I can find you more, they can be your house-warming present.'

Laura beamed and kissed Allegra's cheek. She busied herself pouring their tea, taking small cubes of ice from a box at the top of the refrigerator. 'Can you smell the cinnamon? Here, try it. There's more sugar if you like it sweeter.'

'It's perfect,' said Allegra.

They stood looking out of the window onto the garden below, sipping their tea. 'Do you really have to leave tomorrow?' said Laura. 'It would be so nice to have some proper time together, we could go shopping, you could show me all the new places. I took the children to the English Tea Rooms yesterday, do you remember how we always used to go there when the children were babies?'

Allegra nodded, the memory of that time bringing first joy, then a kind of melancholy, as always happened when she thought of those early years. 'The English Tea Rooms, I haven't been there in ages. Do they still have those little toasts we used to order, what were they called?'

'Pikelets. Yes they do!'

'Pikelets, of course. What was it the children called them? *Pickalets?*'

'*Pickalets.*' Laura smiled, she had forgotten this detail.

'Rita was quite insistent, do you remember? She refused to pronounce it any other way.'

'That's Rita.'

'How delicious they were.' Allegra's mouth was watering just at the thought of them, and she took another sip of tea.

Laura gazed at her. 'Do say you'll stay, Allegra, there are

so many things I'm longing to do now I'm back. It'll be like old times.'

Allegra sighed, removing her spectacles. There were dents either side of her soft nose, and she rubbed at them distractedly. 'I can't, I promised the children.'

'But when do you ever do something for yourself?' persisted Laura, forgetting that it was not for Allegra's sake she was asking her to stay, but her own. 'No one is as devoted a mother as you, I'm sure they won't mind. My three adore it if I have to be away, I often travelled with Isaac.' She was leaning against the countertop, as though it were an obstacle she was trying to push away. 'And it would be nice for Marco too if you stayed, I bet you never spend time alone. It's important in a marriage, you know.'

Allegra did not answer.

'We women are all the same,' continued Laura, refilling Allegra's glass, 'always putting ourselves last — and to what end? If the last year has taught me one thing, it's to seize every opportunity for happiness in this life, you never know what might be around the corner.' She glanced significantly at Allegra, and Allegra, to whom people were always saying things like this, looked away.

'I really would love to,' she said. 'Believe me, I can't think of anything nicer. But I promised the children, and it will only worry them if I change my plans now. I'm sure you understand.'

After a silence Laura said that she did. Allegra set down her glass.

'Well, at least let's make the most of the time we have,' she said. 'What would you like to do? Would you like me to come with you to Vanderborght and see about ordering those curtains you mentioned? I think the same yellow would be wonderful, not too much at all. And then we could take the children for tea somewhere. Have you been to Wittamer yet?

They'll have their mirabelle tarts by now, I adore mirabelles, don't you?'

'But you have things to do.'

'Nothing that can't wait,' said Allegra. 'And perhaps Marco will join us if we go to Wittamer, he loves an excuse to get out of the office. I think he's rather bored, in fact he says hardly anybody is around.'

'It's true that everywhere is very quiet.' Laura smiled, but her smile had none of the vigour and cheer of before. Allegra felt suddenly sad, and this bright, elegant apartment no longer impressed her with its simplicity, but seemed instead to be empty and lifeless.

'So shall we do that? Shall we go to Vanderborght? Only you must keep me in line, I'm not allowed to look at a single thing for myself.' She clasped her hands together, looking at Laura expectantly. 'What do you say?'

Laura turned on the tap to rinse the glasses. 'Well, if you think you have time — only we'll need to wait until the children finish their lesson. Shall we take my car?'

'Car, taxi, tram — anything but a bicycle!' said Allegra. She shook her head, gazing at Laura affectionately. 'What was it you said? You just think about your feet, you don't think about anything else.' She laughed, and there was a kind of relief in it.

'But it's true,' said Laura.

CHAPTER 12

When Leonard first returned from Milan, he was determined to be cheerful. The memory of how things had been with Laura troubled him, and in his heart he felt he had failed her and the children. She had needed him to be calm and reassuring, and instead he had fretted and upset everyone, so that it was a relief to be back in Manchester and no longer responsible. From now on, he promised himself, he would concentrate his attentions upon his own family; that is, upon Miriam and this coming baby. His days henceforth revolved around the many preparations that attend a birth: when he wasn't at the office he was painting the spare room, or calling about a pram or cot he had seen advertised, or digging the garden in anticipation of those roses they were going to order. At weekends they would take a picnic and watch the cricket, or visit Miriam's parents in St Anne's, the bracing sea air pinking their cheeks and curling Miriam's hair, so that Leonard said it wasn't possible she was about to have a baby, she looked too young.

But of course it was possible. And when the baby came, it did what all babies do and took over. Even with four adults in the house there seemed not to be enough hands, and Leonard was constantly running here and there, fetching special powders from the chemist, searching for that particular blanket without which the baby could not sleep, entertaining the endless stream of visitors that a new arrival provokes. The birth had been difficult and Miriam spent the first few weeks in bed, her small face grey with exhaustion and the knowledge that her body was not this agile, loyal thing, but could turn on her in her moment of greatest need. Yet as her strength returned, she seemed to forget this betrayal and there was a new authority to her movements that was lacking before, so that Leonard was sometimes afraid of her. It was as if she had glimpsed some truth that was visible to her alone, and now everything she did, everything she believed, was coloured by this. She could not have said what this truth was, any more than someone waking from a deep sleep can give a clear account of their dreams, but its confirmation was in this baby. This tiny, red, angry baby, that cried all night and for which she felt a love more intense than any she had known possible. It was this love which made Leonard afraid.

Meanwhile, the seasons were changing and the short summer nights were replaced by longer dusks and crisp, sharp mornings. Leonard had taken to sleeping in Bobby's room, for the only way to settle the baby was to take him into bed, and Miriam worried Leonard would roll on him, a possibility he protested. As the first light of day pushed through the curtains, Leonard would lie quite still, his knees pulled up, listening to the familiar sounds of his father moving around upstairs, shaving and getting dressed. In these moments Leonard could forget his wife and son sleeping in the next room and think himself a young boy again, full of hope for the life that lay before him. He would remember the old house on Lancaster Road, with its formal gardens and tennis court, where he and Bobby had learned to play, and where Estella, happier then, would watch them from beneath an ancient catalpa tree. He would remember his plans of going to university and his conviction, like most adolescent boys, that so long as he worked hard and led a virtuous life, he would be rewarded. And although this was not how things had turned out, the memory of this former self fortified him.

Leonard had responded to the worsening news in

Europe by joining the ARP, his evenings now spent at the Warden Post on Christchurch Road, assembling gas masks and organising working parties to dig trenches and fill sandbags. He was an immediate success, his natural love of order quickly seized upon and deferred to, and for the first time in years he felt he was being truly useful. When it turned out that the government had failed to issue gas masks for infants, it was Leonard who was sent to reassure the anxious parents, advising them to wrap their babies in blankets and carry them to the nearest shelter. His calmness, all the more surprising because he had a baby himself, was a revelation to them all, and especially to Leonard. Emboldened, he began to keep a notebook in which he wrote ideas for increasingly elaborate safe-rooms and underground refuges, taking as his guide the deep shelters he had read about in Spain. Inspired by the thought that the people themselves had built them, not the government, he concluded that fear was not in fact a weakness, but on the contrary a source of unity and resistance. It was with this in mind that he wrote again to Laura, long rousing letters scribbled during lunch or while on a break at the Warden Post, pleading with her to leave Brussels before it was too late. Into these letters he poured all his new theories of collective strength and human resilience, confident that, as his sister, she would understand him and come home. Home, it seemed to Leonard, was safety.

Autumn had come quickly that year, the trees seeming to change overnight from green to orange to yellow, and the grass heavy with dew. The mornings were foggy, and the sun was glimpsed only a moment or two as it rose behind the houses before it was hidden in thick clouds. In the gutters, spiky split husks of horse chestnuts lay beneath mounds of leaves, smashed open by young boys who pocketed the shiny fruit to soak in vinegar or bake, ready for competition. Bushes glittered with iridescent webs, large amber-coloured spiders unmoving at their centre, as if they had woven themselves a frame rather than a trap; when it rained, drops of water clung to the fine threads like varnish. Walking through the park to the tram, the paths crunched with acorns, falling in record numbers and leading the park keeper to predict a cold winter. Squirrels and jays rushed to bury them, while on the ponds, geese beat their wings and flexed their long necks, readying themselves for departure. Silky mushrooms appeared overnight in the dim woods, to be trampled by blackberry pickers wearing wellington boots and thick gloves; and the air swirled with dancing, spinning sycamore seeds, caught on the slightest of breezes and carried away. And over by the bowling green, working day and night, men with pickaxes and shovels cut trenches through the cool, dark earth, in preparation for a war that seemed inevitable.

◆　　◆　　◆　　◆　　◆

LEONARD SAT ON THE BOTTOM stair, lacing his shoes. In his bag he had his Duty Respirator, his steel helmet with its painted 'W', and a sandwich, since he went straight to the Warden Post from work. Sometimes, if the baby settled and could be left with Estella, Miriam would walk over with a flask of soup, for she liked him to have something warm in the evenings, but mostly he made do with cups of tea. Indeed, in the last week he seemed to have barely been home, working into the early hours to make sure they were as ready as possible for what was coming. Just yesterday, gathered around the wireless at Christchurch Road, they heard the news that Czechoslovakia had mobilised, and someone said, 'Well that's that then.' meaning bombs could start raining down any moment.

Leonard sighed and stood up, taking his hat from the hall table and pausing in front of the mirror to put it on. As he did, he heard footsteps on the landing above, and he turned to see Estella slowly descending the stairs. Her face was swollen and her eyes rimmed black, and she was twisting the belt of her dressing gown round and round.

'You're up early, Mamma,' he said, 'is everything all right?'

'I didn't hear you come in last night. I was worried.'

'I was at the Post, you knew I was.'

She made a vague gesture with her hands.

'Papa will be back tomorrow.' Solomon was in London for a meeting of one of his committees. 'You'll feel better when he's home.'

She sighed, her eyes welling with tears.

'Poor Mamma,' he said, reaching for her arm and helping her down the last of the stairs. For days he had been urging her to go and stay with Miriam's parents on the coast, and now he repeated the suggestion. He told her she would feel safer there, that it was silly staying in the city for no reason, and that perhaps if she went, Miriam would relent and go too. But as always Estella shook her head and refused, saying she needed to be here when Laura and Bobby arrived.

'Did you speak to Laura yesterday? Her trunk box should be working by now, did you call her and tell her how worried you are?'

'I tried, but the line was busy. I didn't like to bother her later in case I woke the children.'

'You wouldn't have woken the children.'

'I might, she's been putting them to bed earlier.'

'What about Bobby? Did you telephone Uncle Saul? It's disgraceful that we've had no news, we need to know when he's arriving.'

'I thought you were going to call him. You know I can't bear Saul, just the thought of talking to him makes me anxious.'

'I can't do everything, Mamma!' exclaimed Leonard, 'why does it always have to be left to me?' He stopped, biting his lip, and forced himself to speak more gently. 'Will you send a telegram then?'

'Saul won't answer a telegram.'

'Then call one of the aunties, call Violette again. I don't know why you're so funny about asking her, especially when they've been so good to Bobby. If anyone knows what he's up to it will be Violette.'

'Oh, Leonard, won't you? I feel so embarrassed, calling again, as if I don't know the slightest thing about my own son. You know Violette, she'll try to make something of it, she'll think he doesn't talk to me.'

'Well, does he?'

Once again her eyes became glassy and unfocused. 'Won't you call, Leonard? If you call from the office they'll think it's because of the business.'

Leonard sighed and looked away, and for a moment neither of them spoke.

'I'll see what I can do,' he said at last. He picked up his bag, putting his head through the long strap and arranging it crosswise over his jacket. 'But it won't be today, I've already got too much to do today.'

Estella nodded. 'You're a good son.'

He smiled. 'Go back to bed, Mamma,' he said, and he kissed her soft cheek, watching as she turned and shuffled back up the stairs.

The house was quiet as Leonard let himself out of the front door, and he took care not to trip over the empty milk bottles or slam the gate. The postman was just wheeling his bicycle into the road and Leonard hurried to meet him, waiting as he looked through his mail bag and exchanging pleasantries about how cold it was getting and the gales they had been having further north.

'You've heard he's off again?' said the man. 'He' was Chamberlain. 'Waste of time, if you ask me. Only thing those thugs understand is brute force. Nothing for number Sixteen, I'm afraid.' He blew on his hands, then rubbed them against one another. 'Short and sharp, that's how to do it.'

'Short and sharp,' repeated Leonard, glancing back at the house and feeling that same tightening around his heart he always felt when he imagined what lay ahead.

'Should have had done with him back in April,' the man continued. 'Be over with by now.' and Leonard said, yes, April, as though between them they could trick time and somehow be on the other side of this.

Leonard carried on towards the station. It had rained in the night and the leaves on the pavement were slippery and stuck to his shoes, so that he had to keep stopping to knock them off. Every so often he saw a tree trunk which had not yet been whitewashed, and he made a note of it in his book so that he could send someone round later. He observed which houses had put up blackout blinds, and which had just painted the glass, and which had as yet done nothing at all, because those he would need to keep an eye on. When he passed a man digging in his front garden, he stopped and asked how many it was for, and gave him advice on depth and which roof to choose. And everywhere he saw a kind of steely calm, as though people were resigned to what was coming, and wished simply to get on with it.

The dawn sky was a deep violet blue, with that bright sheen which often comes after wet weather, and the air was cool. Despite the earliness of the hour, the streets were busy and lorries piled high with sandbags or planks of wood obstructed junctions and blocked entrances, causing drivers to lean on their horns and shout angry tirades from their windows. Leonard hurried along Lapwing Road and into the station, boarding the train and remaining by the doors, leaning against one of the upright poles and giving himself up to its swaying, rattling progress. He felt invigorated, his mind full of plans for the day, and he gazed around the carriage, new ideas constantly suggesting themselves to him. There should be volunteers at all the main meeting places, at the city art gallery and the libraries, outside Lewis' and Kendal's, reminding people to go and get their gas masks fitted; maps of distribution centres should be posted on every street corner; they should ask the ladies of the Guild and W.I. to provide refreshments; there should be jigsaws and board games for children.

He continued to make lists as they neared the city, moving further down the carriage as more passengers joined. As they crossed the viaduct at Cornbrook, the sun was just rising and the sky beyond the wharf was streaked orange and red, casting a warm glow on the faces of the passengers. Below them on the canal, the portholes of the boats blazed as if on fire, and the water was black. How beautiful it all was, how full of life. An old man bending to sit down, his hand feeling for the seat beneath him, a woman with her headscarf pulled so tight her eyes were stretched, schoolchildren pushing one another every time the doors opened, so that occasionally one of them fell off and had to jump on again. Leonard saw all this, and then he imagined the bombs falling, buildings crumbling all around them, the train filling with poison gas and the faces of these same people as they climbed over one another to escape. He had seen the pictures of Shanghai and Nanking, he knew how thin the veneer of civilisation could be. He closed his eyes, and when he opened them again he saw they were pulling into Manchester Central and, along with everyone else, he elbowed his way towards the doors and climbed off.

On the way out of the station he saw two men he recognised as Full-Timers standing by the ticket office. The taller of the two had a loudspeaker, but he was not using it, only swinging it at his side, and in the hands of the other was a large placard, upon which he leaned as they chatted. Leonard felt a rush of annoyance. 'Three-quid-a-week-army-dodgers', that's what some people called the ARP, and it was no surprise when you saw them standing around like that. Feeling in his pocket for his badge, with its silver crown and bold letters, he pinned it to his lapel and strode towards them.

'Leonard Cansino,' he said, holding out his hand. 'Christchurch Road.'

'Oh hello,' said the taller man. 'Arthur Cooper. And this here is Mr Hopkins.' He gestured towards his colleague, who grinned and shook hands.

'Stirrup pump,' said the latter, 'did I see you at stirrup pump training?'

'Quite possibly,' said Leonard, looking past him and pointing to the upside down placard. 'Shouldn't you be walking around with that? No one can read it when it's like that.'

'It's too crowded for walking around, it was getting in the way.'

'But surely that's the point, Mr Hopkins, to get in the way,' said Leonard. 'Come along now, every minute counts you know.'

'Righty-ho,' sighed Mr Hopkins. He glanced at the other man then lifted the placard and moved away, the words 'Be Fitted and Be Safe,' bobbing above his head.

'But Precautions generally, Mr Cansino, seem to be progressing well,' said Mr Cooper, one expert to another. 'Civilian morale is the hardest part, I find. You can get very worn down.'

'And why aren't you using the station Tannoy?' asked Leonard. 'If you used the Tannoy you'd be heard everywhere.'

'Oh, but this is just as effective,' said Mr Cooper, holding up the megaphone. 'More personal too.'

Leonard shook his head. What was wrong with everyone, why were they so resistant to trying new ways? He wanted to take the man by the shoulders and give him a good shake, but instead he glanced at his watch and said, 'Come on, I'll go with you. Where's the signal box, do you know?'

Mr Cooper gestured with his chin beyond the central concourse. 'They'll never let us though, they need it to announce the trains.'

Leonard smiled, catching at the man's elbow and steering him through across the busy hall, 'We'll see, shall we?'

The signal box was beyond the main platform and Leonard bounded up the steps, excited at the prospect of getting something done. This was what Miriam called his 'slaying dragons' mood. Nodding to Mr Cooper, he rapped on the door, holding up his newly issued Card of Appointment and gesturing to Mr Cooper to do the same. The man who opened the door seemed startled.

'Gas masks? Nobody said anything to me about any gas masks!'

'And nor will they!' said Leonard, pressing past him into the small wooden office. A glassed off cabin in the corner held the PA system, a young woman sitting painfully still in front of an open microphone. 'That's why Mr Cooper needs to get the word out. She can keep going with her announcements, of course, we don't want people missing their trains. But in between, Mr Cooper can do his bit. How does that sound?'

The man shrugged and returned to his place on the switch panel. Leonard gestured to Mr Cooper to go ahead, but when he looked uncertain, Leonard opened the cabin door himself and slipped inside. The woman, busy announcing the 9.03 to Cheadle Heath, glanced up in surprise.

'All right if I jump in?' he mouthed, when she had finished speaking. She nodded and moved aside.

Leonard cleared his throat and leaned over the microphone. 'Go and fit your gas masks.' He paused. 'Go and fit your gas masks NOW.' He rested his knee on the desk, straining forward to see out of the window of the signal box. People were looking up and he nodded, continuing to repeat the same words, over and over, until the woman gestured to her watch and he was obliged to stand back. He turned and grinned at Mr Cooper.

'You didn't say anything about distribution centres,' said Mr Cooper, when Leonard joined him in the office.

'They'll work it out.'

'People will think there's somewhere in the station. This'll just have confused them.'

Leonard smiled, for there was a kind of exhilaration in simply being heard, and he looked back towards the window, the sun gleaming on his upturned face.

'What a beautiful day,' he said. 'Look at that sky, Mr Cooper, did you ever see such a sky?'

'There was a solar halo last night,' said the other man, 'and the night before. Means there's a cold winter coming, or so my wife's dad says.'

'I heard that too. Perhaps a good snow fall is what we need, we'll see how Hitler likes his Blitzkrieg under ten foot of snow.' Leonard moved towards the door. 'You'll keep going then? It's important work, you know, people are going to need these gas masks.'

The man sighed. 'Thirty-five million they've produced. That's what I read.'

'You'd better get on with it then,' said Leonard.

He hurried down the steps and out of the station, filled with fresh determination for the day ahead. Automatically following his usual route across the bridge towards the office on Lloyd Street, he suddenly changed his mind and decided to head for the Control Post instead. Who knew how many of these days were left to them? He should listen to his own advice and make every minute count. He adjusted his hat, rubbed his badge with the sleeve of his jacket, and set off at a brisk stride in the opposite direction. Taking deep, invigorating breaths, the sharp autumnal air filled his lungs and swelled his chest, and he felt he might achieve anything to which he set his mind. All around him, people rushed past, their faces closed to him, their eyes straight ahead, but each one of these people Leonard felt he loved. Just as he loved this city, with its anonymous brick buildings and its grey streets, its smoking chimneys and its dank waterways. He loved all of it, and he believed it loved him back.

CHAPTER 13

It was after midnight when Leonard, his heart still full, got back to Moorfield Road. Searching for his key, he heard a car turn into the street, and he looked around just as a taxi came to a stop by the front gate. Thinking it must be Solomon back from London, he faltered, for his father was sure to ask about the office, and Leonard would have to admit he had not been. He frowned, remembering all the good work he had done today and resolving to defend himself. What did cotton poplin matter when war was coming? What did anything matter? He found his key and opened the door, setting his bag on the mat inside, and then turning around to greet his father. But as he did, the gate swung open and a young boy, his blonde hair falling in his eyes, came running through, his arms outstretched towards Leonard.

'Teddy!' gasped Leonard, staring at him for a brief second and then opening his arms. 'Teddy, what are you doing here? Where are the others?' He glanced at the upstairs window, remembering the baby. 'I'm so happy to see you,' he whispered, hugging him.

'I called the office,' said Laura, climbing out of the car. 'Did you not get my message?' Her face was pale and there were dark shadows beneath her eyes, which the streetlamp exaggerated.

'I didn't go in today,' said Leonard, hurrying towards her and stooping to kiss her cheek. 'Hello Rita dear, hello Coco. What a wonderful surprise, I feel like I'm dreaming!'

'Oh dear, how awful. I thought you'd be expecting us.'

Laura turned towards the driver, as though it was his fault for bringing them, 'Perhaps we should go to an hotel.'

'An hotel? Of course not!' exclaimed Leonard. 'Come on, get everything inside. Mamma will be so pleased to see you, she's been fretting terribly. And wait until you meet the baby!' He beamed proudly. 'He really is a fine baby, even if I do say so myself. Is this all there is? You don't seem to have brought very much.'

'We came by air, Marco got us the last tickets. The French have called up the Reservists, did you hear?'

'I'd heard something. Well, better they do. It's about time everyone started taking this seriously. Is that everything? Good.' He rearranged the doormat with the toe of his shoe, then quietly closed the door. 'Keep your voices down, kiddies. Here, come into the drawing room. I'll just nip upstairs and see what Miriam thinks about beds.'

'Oh don't wake her, Leonard, we'll be fine here for tonight.' Laura was taking off her coat and checking her reflection in the mirror above the fireplace. 'Have you decorated in here? Something looks different. Girls, sit down, you too Teddy. What a relief to be finally here, you can't imagine what a state I've been in. I looked out the window this morning and it was as if all of Brussels was on the roads, I'm afraid I panicked.' She smiled apologetically. 'I had visions of just the children and me being left there. Luckily Marco pulled some strings and got us a flight out — I don't know what I'd have done otherwise.'

Teddy grinned at his uncle. 'A Junkers,' he said. 'They have special basins under the seats, for being sick.'

'Do they really?' said Leonard, ruffling the boy's hair. 'Do you suppose Mr Chamberlain had one when he went to Berchtesgarten? Perhaps with a special crest? Coco, is it possible you've got even prettier? Come here and let me look at you properly. I think you have.'

'Mammy says I can have a perm.' She flicked her long, straight hair, tied back in two braids.

'I said I'd think about it,' clarified her mother, glancing at Leonard. 'They all have them these days,' she added, for she knew he disapproved of such things.

Leonard sighed, taking off his hat and dropping it on the low table. 'How fast they grow up,' he said, and Laura, thinking how parenthood had softened him, smiled and said: 'How lucky you are, having it all ahead.'

'Rita held her basin the whole way, Mammy said she looked green,' said Teddy, grinning. He looked at Rita for confirmation.

'Shut up, Teddy,' said Rita.

'Perhaps I should make us a hot drink,' said Laura. 'Then we can all get some sleep. I, for one, am exhausted. Is Bobby's bed made up, do you know? The girls can go in there, Teddy and I will make do on the sofas. I feel terrible turning up like this, what a shame you didn't get my message.'

'I don't know why you didn't call here. Here makes much more sense.'

Laura was gathering up their coats, piling them on the back of an armchair. 'Are you sure this room hasn't been painted? I always remember it as rather gloomy, but it isn't, not at all.' She glanced at Leonard. 'Miriam's influence, no doubt. It's good for Mamma to have her around, even the walls seem brighter.'

'Unless there was a problem with the line? Mamma says it goes off sometimes. Was there a problem with the line?'

Laura shook her head. 'There was no problem with the line.'

She had picked up the coats again and was carrying them into the hall. 'Help me with these, would you?' she said, turning back and looking at him significantly. Leonard followed her out.

In the hall they had to whisper, for any sound carried straight upstairs. Draping the coats over the banister, Laura murmured, 'There's something I need to talk to you about. Before I see Mamma. I've had a letter from Bobby.'

'From Bobby?' Leonard led her into the kitchen where they could speak more freely. 'Has he left finally? It's typical of him, not letting anyone know, Mamma has been so worried about him.' He did not say she had been worried about Laura too, because Laura was here now and there was no need. 'When is he arriving?'

Laura turned away, looking out of the dark window into the garden beyond. 'He isn't.'

'What do you mean "He isn't"?'

'He's staying in Alex.'

'But Papa wants him back, he's told him to come back. Oh really, this is too much!' All the injustice of his position as the one who was always here, the one who was expected to pick up messages and fetch home absent siblings, rose up in him, and he frowned at Laura.

'I knew this would happen,' said Laura, for she was tired and quick to feel aggrieved too. 'I knew I'd end up getting the blame. I can't think why Bobby thought it would be better coming from me, I'm the last person he should have asked.' She leaned forward and ran her finger along the condensation which had gathered at the bottom of the window pane. 'He knows how it always gets with me and Mamma.'

'What do you mean "better coming from you"?'

Laura exhaled and slowly turned around. 'He's in love with cousin Josette.' In fact, in his letter he said they were getting married, but Laura had decided it was best to approach the matter in stages. 'I got the letter last week, I've been in such a fix about what to do.'

Leonard was astonished. 'Cousin Josette? But she's Rita's age.'

'Actually, she's eighteen.'

'And Bobby is—'

'—it's the same gap as with Isaac and me.' Perhaps that was why he had asked her to tell everyone. 'Anyway, you have to help me with Mamma. He's worried she's going to hear it from someone else first.' She turned back to the window. 'You should turn the heating down, that's why you're getting condensation. It's terribly warm, this house.'

'I can't believe it, I had no idea they were even friends. A week, you say? You've had the letter a week? Then she'll almost certainly find out! Why didn't you call?'

'Because it's not an easy thing to tell someone on the telephone,' said Laura. 'If it were, then perhaps Bobby would have called himself!' Again, the sense that she would be blamed for this. 'Anyway, they're keeping it quiet for now. I called Violette, she said that only close family know anything about it.'

'There's no such thing as close family in Alex,' said Leonard gloomily. 'How was Violette? What did she say?'

'I think it's caused quite an upset.' She smiled. 'You know what Violette is like, she'll have had her sights set on some cotton baron.' Despite all the anxiety of the last few days, how shocked she had been to see soldiers on the streets of Ixelles, how she had dreaded telling everyone about Bobby, Laura felt suddenly amused. 'Poor Violette, I can't imagine what she must be telling all her smart friends. Bobby's hardly the catch she was hoping for.'

Leonard, who could not help but see himself in the same terms, grimaced. It had been like that with Miriam at first. Her mother had wanted her to have nothing to do with him, believing her pretty daughter could do so much better. He sighed and folded his arms. 'In love? What does that even mean?'

'It means he's happy.' She put a hand on Leonard's shoulders, as she did with the children when she wanted their full attention. 'And that's the main thing, don't you think, Leonard, that Bobby's happy? I'm sure that's all Mamma will care about, that's all she wants for any of us.'

Leonard, remembering that Estella must be told, looked even more miserable. From the hallway came the sound of voices.

'I need to get them into bed,' said Laura, sliding a finger under Leonard's cuff so that she could read the time on his wristwatch. 'Is that correct? The poor things, it's so late. And you should go to bed too, you must be exhausted.' The kitchen door opened and Coco put her head around. 'I'm coming darling, I'm just making tea. Go back into the drawing room and I'll bring a tray.'

Coco remained where she was, watching as her mother began running taps and opening drawers.

'Please don't worry about anything, Leonard,' continued Laura, filled with a sudden desire to take charge. 'I'll speak to Mamma tomorrow and it will be fine. She may even think it's a good thing, Marco says Philippe d'Araquy is one of the few men doing well in Egypt right now.'

'You told Marco?' He moved so that she could get to the cups, hanging on hooks beneath the shelf.

'He was there when I got the letter.' She glanced at Coco, so that Leonard should understand to speak carefully. 'In any case, Marco won't say anything, he doesn't gossip.' This was not strictly true. 'Coco, are you hungry? Would you like something to eat? Do you have anything I can give the children, Leonard?'

'Try the top shelf,' said Leonard, pointing towards the pantry. 'If Miriam has made anything, she usually puts it up there. Towards the back.' Laura smiled, understanding that this was a hiding place from Estella.

'I'll have a look. Here, take this and I'll follow you through with the rest.' She handed him the tray she had filled.

'While you're waiting, get Teddy to show you his sketchbook, you won't believe how good he is.' She opened the door for them to go out, watching as Coco ran along the dark hallway back to the others, followed by the hunched silhouette of Leonard.

WHEN SHE JOINED THEM A LITTLE later, bearing Estella's silver teapot and a plate of biscuits, Leonard was kneeling on the floor looking at Teddy's sketchbook.

'These are terribly good,' said Leonard. 'Such detail, I didn't know we had an artist in the family. Did you find something?'

Laura nodded. 'Have you told Uncle Leonard what you want to be?' she said, even though she knew it irritated Teddy when she boasted. 'An aviation designer,' she continued, before he could answer. 'Imagine that, instead of Junkers and Faireys we might have Balestras? Oh dear, look at Rita, she's flat out.'

Everyone looked at Rita, who had fallen asleep on the sofa, her head tilted to one side, her mouth open. Laura took a rug from the back of one of the chairs and laid it over her legs.

'Dead to the world,' said Leonard, sitting back on his heels.

Laura smiled. 'Dead to the world' was one of Miriam's expressions.

'I've so missed Miriam and her funny way of putting things. Is that her, do you think?' she said, because it sounded as though someone was moving around upstairs. 'I do hope we haven't woken the baby.'

She had left the door to the hallway open, and Leonard stood up and closed it.

'It's just the pipes,' he said, surprised that she should have forgotten the sounds of this house. He sat down again, clasping his hands between his knees. 'So how is Marco?' he said, because it seemed polite to ask.

'He's well,' said Laura, and as she said it she thought how few people there were about whom she could give that answer. Certainly no one in her own family could be described so cheerily, there always being something or other that was troubling them. 'He should have arrived in La Baule by now, he left around the same time as us.'

'In the Simca,' said Teddy, who took note of such things.

Leonard raised an eyebrow. 'Is France so much safer? Surely the same planes that can bomb Belgium can bomb France too?'

'La Baule is on the coast,' said Laura, pouring more tea and refusing to engage with the subject. 'Apparently it has the longest beach in Europe.' She glanced at Teddy. 'How long did Uncle Marco say it was? Ten kilometres?'

'I don't know that I'd like to be in France right now,' continued Leonard. 'They're predicting another Commune if Daladier goes to war, the country's completely divided. At least here there's some kind of political stability, we're not about to start a revolution.'

At the word 'revolution' Coco looked up, her eyes wide. 'I wish we'd gone to France,' she said to her mother.

Leonard frowned. 'Revolutions are bloody, terrible things,' he said sternly. 'They are not at all what they might seem in your story books. Look at Spain.'

'Oh Leonard,' said Laura, smiling and setting her cup down on its saucer with a sharp clink, 'you'll give us all nightmares. Coco and Teddy, if you have finished go and brush your teeth, you can use the sink in the kitchen. Go quietly though, remember the baby. No, no, leave Rita, let her sleep.'

'I don't mean to give you nightmares,' said Leonard.

'Of course you don't. And I'm quite sure we'll all sleep like babies. Actually, better than babies, if what I hear about your little man is anything to go by.' She laughed to show there was no ill feeling. 'I know what I wanted to ask you,' she went on, leaning forward and tapping her finger on the low table. 'Do you remember that Tennyson line they were always drumming into us at school, the one he wrote on the train to Manchester? Something about the "grooves of change"? I was trying to remember it for the children today, it came to me for some reason on the plane but I've quite forgotten how it goes.'

Leonard knew the line she meant. *'Let the great world spin forever,'* he said. 'That one?'

'Yes! *Let the great world spin forever,'* she repeated, sitting back, her head tilted to the side, *'down the ringing grooves of change.* I love that line.'

'He thought trains ran in grooves,' said Leonard, 'like trams.'

'I suppose ringing rails isn't as good.' She looked around as Teddy came back in. 'Uncle Leonard remembered the poem,' she said, but Teddy, pale with exhaustion, only looked at her blankly. 'Pyjamas,' she declared, pulling him towards her and beginning to undo his shirt buttons. He was sleepy enough that he allowed her to do it.

Leonard stood up. 'I'll go and make up Bobby's bed.' He didn't mention that he slept there himself these days. 'I just need to change the sheets.'

'No, don't Leonard, it's late. We'll be fine here, I'll put the cushions on the floor. It'll be like camping. We can sort things out properly tomorrow.'

'Are you sure? I don't like to think of you sleeping on the floor.'

'Oh, I think we'll survive,' she said, smiling. 'You mustn't fuss so much, Leonard.' She stood up, looking about resolutely.

'Surely that's what they teach you in that ARP of yours, to keep calm in the face of adversity. Well, consider this adversity, just for one night.'

'ARP — All Right Presently,' murmured Leonard, picking up Teddy's sketchbook and handing it to her.

'Oh, that's clever! Did you hear that, Coco?' Coco was back, wide-eyed and clutching her nightdress, for the dark hallway frightened her. 'ARP, Uncle Leonard's new job, it stands for All Right Presently.'

'Actually, that's just—' began Leonard, but Laura was ushering him out, her hand firm on his arm. At the bottom of the stairs, whispering now, she again referred to Bobby's letter and promised that she would sort everything out the next day. 'Go up,' she said, pressing him onto the first step, 'go up to that little family of yours.'

Leonard hesitated, feeling that there was still so much to say to one another, and knowing that tomorrow, when everyone was there, it would be impossible. 'Don't you wonder what it's all for?' he asked suddenly. He gazed intently at his sister, feeling in that moment that she was the only person with whom he could share this fear. 'One bomb and it's all finished, and it won't matter if Mamma minds about Josette, or if I boiled Baby's milk for long enough this morning, or if we repainted the drawing room because —' The words trailed off, and Leonard continued to stare at Laura. Upstairs, beneath a chenille bedspread, his wife and baby slept peacefully. But for how long? He blinked, imagining the planes flying overhead, the bombed-out buildings, people huddled inside damp, airless shelters.

'You mustn't think like that,' said Laura, the fingers which still held his arm tightening involuntarily. 'Really you mustn't.'

Leonard nodded. For a moment neither of them spoke, and then Laura said, still whispering: 'Wait until you see the presents we brought for Baby, I'm afraid you'll say we've spoiled him, but I couldn't resist. The most divine little fur jacket, I do hope it fits.'

'You shouldn't have,' murmured Leonard. He looked past her towards the drawing room where the children were still moving around. 'I'll fetch some blankets,' he said.

When Estella came down the next morning, Laura and the children were eating breakfast with Miriam. The baby was propped upright on his mother's lap, and when the door opened, Teddy was holding a teacup to his tiny pink foot and declaring it the smallest thing he had ever seen. The sun, which had not long risen, shone through the square panes of the kitchen window, bleaching their upturned faces and causing the air to shimmer dustily, as though it were made of fine lace. On the stove, a pan of water bubbled.

'Ah, there you are, Mamma,' said Laura. She had been up to her mother first thing, waking her up and sitting with her while she did her face. 'Make room for Granny, everyone. Teddy, put down that cup, give Granny a kiss!' She turned to Rita, who had caught her dressing gown between two chair legs and was trying to untangle it. 'Darling, jump up, jump up!' she insisted, and she flapped her hands to make her go faster.

Estella, her small feet shuffling in their slippers, offered her powdered, sweet-smelling cheek to each of the children, then looked past them at Laura. She had wept when she saw her that morning, and she still had the hollow feeling she got after crying, as if something had been depleted. 'Happy?' Leonard had asked when he put his head in before leaving, and she had been irritable with him, because of course she was happy. But there was a kind of melancholy too, and Laura, sensing this, smiled and reached for her mother's hand.

'Sit down, Mamma,' she said.

Estella nodded, but for a moment she did not move, her gaze drifting around the room, now on Laura, now on the children, now on the bubbling pan into which Miriam was lowering an egg, now on the baby who had been laid, protesting, in his pram by the back door. Droplets of steam glittered above the stove, and the wall was glossy and streaked with thin rivulets that later would be brown and dull. On the table, empty eggshells and jammy knives sat atop a pile of dirty plates, and Rita added to them with bits of toast that lay scattered on the blue and white cloth.

'I hope we weren't too noisy,' said Laura. 'There was a lot of excitement over Baby, what a darling he is! Teddy had him talking, I've never seen anything like it.'

'Talking?' Estella sat down heavily in her usual chair, watching as Miriam poured her a cup of tea.

'It was babble really,' said Miriam, 'but you know how he concentrates sometimes, and seems to be having a conversation.' She blushed and reached for the pile of plates Estella was pushing across the table. 'We were making room for Baby,' she explained, for she knew how Estella hated stacking.

'Do you remember Teddy at that age?' said Laura, looking first at her mother, then at the two girls. 'He was just the same, arms and legs going at all times. I couldn't put him down, do you remember?' She stood up and walked over to the pram, smiling and rocking it with her foot. Miriam, her face shiny from the hot pan, counted the minutes on her wristwatch trying to remember when she had put the egg in.

'Does it make you want another one?' asked Coco suddenly, looking at her pretty mother and thinking how nice it would be to have a baby of their own.

'Heavens, what a question!' laughed Laura.

'How can she have another baby without Daddy?' demanded Rita, who, at fourteen, knew something of what was involved. She looked crossly at her sister, then at her mother too, for it seemed to her that everyone was stupid this morning. She had not wanted to come here, she had pleaded for them to go with Uncle Marco to France. And now, sitting in this hot, cramped kitchen, she felt entirely justified. She remembered the last time they had sat here, on the morning of Leonard's wedding, and how Daddy had been cross then too, saying what a miserable country this was and how he didn't see how anyone could live in it. Well, she also felt like that, and now her mother had made them come, promising it would only be for a little while when everyone knew that wars went on for years.

'I don't see why she shouldn't,' said Estella, buttering a slice of toast with particular determination. 'Your mother is a young woman, please God, she has her life ahead of her.' She glanced at Miriam for confirmation.

Miriam, deciding the egg was surely cooked by now, bent over the pan and did not answer.

'Oh Mamma!' exclaimed Laura, laughing again, although this time less naturally.

'Thank you for my nice breakfast, please may I get down from the table?' said Rita, waiting until her mother nodded, then roughly pushing back her chair. Miriam, passing Estella her egg, put a hand on the girl's shoulder and squeezed sympathetically. Of the three, Rita was her favourite, although she would not admit it, not even to Leonard. She saw how hard it was for her being the eldest, how much she took upon those narrow shoulders and — Miriam's heart ached at the thought of it — how much was in turn put upon them. She had tried to tell Leonard, to explain to him that what Rita needed first and foremost was love; but he had this idea that it was in the children's success that Laura would find happiness again, and so this was the thing he focused upon.

'Make sure you put on something warm,' Miriam said to Rita, 'we could take Baby along the high street later, if you liked.

He'll fall asleep and then you and I can look in the shop windows.' She remembered how Rita had liked wandering through the Galleria in Milan. '*Guardare le vetrine*' they had called it. Again she squeezed Rita's shoulder and this time the girl turned, lifting her face to her aunt and forcing a smile. Miriam kissed her lightly on the cheek.

'I think we might have to do our gas masks first,' said Laura, glancing at the kitchen clock, 'Leonard said they're running a bit low, particularly in the smaller sizes. He said he would call when he was leaving the office and that we should meet him at the Town Hall. Aren't we lucky, getting such special treatment?'

'Oh, well perhaps we can go afterwards,' said Miriam, but Rita only shrugged, slipping from her aunt's grasp and disappearing out of the door.

'I've got mine already,' said Estella, tapping the top of her egg with a spoon. 'Your father has too. Although I've told Leonard, a mustard bomb will have to drop down this chimney before you'll see me in it. Dreadful, ugly things.'

'They're not so bad,' said Laura reasonably. She glanced at Coco, who had burst into tears when Leonard showed them his mask that morning — she had a horror of things covering her face. 'Besides, better to be safe than sorry, wouldn't you say?'

It seemed she wouldn't, for Estella did not reply.

'Please may I get down from the table too?' asked Teddy, who had been getting increasingly restless.

'Let Rita have the bathroom first,' said his mother.

'We don't have as many as you do,' said his grandmother, picking the shell from the top of her egg as though it were some precious relic she were uncovering. 'How many bathrooms did Leonard tell me that flat has?'

'Just two.'

'Just two,' repeated Estella.

Teddy, puzzled by such an exchange, looked pleadingly at his mother. He had spied a rubber ball in the garden and he longed to be released to play outside, all this sitting down and talking making him fidget. Laura shook her head again, and continued to describe the layout of the apartment, the one they didn't know if they would be going back to. Teddy sighed and swivelled around so that he was facing the baby in his pram. He reached out a hand and pressed on the front of it, so that the pram tilted forward and he could see the baby's face. The baby stopped kicking and stared at him, his eyes wide. 'He likes you,' said Miriam. Teddy shrugged and let go, so that the pram lurched back again.

'I had a Coco-egg,' said Coco. This was when her mother scooped an overcooked egg into a cup and mashed it with butter.

'Did you now?' said Estella, lifting her finely drawn eyebrows.

'We were listening to the wireless, I was distracted,' said Laura. 'Daladier is flying to London again, he's suggesting an international commission. Teddy, stop doing that, Auntie Miriam wants Baby to sleep. Oh all right, go outside if you must.'

Teddy grinned and leapt from his chair, disappearing out of the door before she could change her mind.

'Of course the French are all communists,' said Estella, her spoon raised. 'I hear they board the trains singing the Internationale.'

'I think they sing the Marseillaise too,' said Laura. 'Oh look at that yolk, perfectly cooked. Well done Miriam, how clever you are. No need for a Coco-egg when Auntie Miriam is in charge!'

THE DAY PASSED UNEVENTFULLY. Breakfast was cleared away, to be followed almost immediately by lunch, which in turn gave way to tea and cake and discussions about what they should eat that evening. Solomon got back from London and went straight out again, and Leonard called to postpone fitting their masks, because he had remembered that it was Sunday and the Town hall would be closed. 'It doesn't feel like a Sunday,' said Coco, and everyone agreed that it really didn't. The sun began its slow descent. On the evening news they heard how Hitler's memorandum had been rejected by Benês, and how Gamelin had been invited to Downing Street to give a briefing; they heard how Poland and the Czechs had agreed to discuss their differences, and how everything hung on Hitler's Sportspalast speech the next day, when war would or wouldn't be declared. Outside, the street lamps gave off a shiny haze, and in the darkening sky stars flickered and grew sharp, so that Teddy, sitting at the window after his bath, could trace the seven points of the Plough, the distinctive 'W' of Cassiopeia, the pole star. Bats circled and swooped around the brick chimney stacks of the neighbouring houses, and the moon, just visible through the still-leafy branches of a horse chestnut tree, was a sliver of lemon.

Downstairs, Laura filled rubber hot water bottles for the children, wrapping them in old towels so that they wouldn't scald. All day she had been looking for the right moment to broach Bobby's letter, and now she came and stood next to her mother, who was playing Patience at the kitchen table.

Estella glanced up. 'Bedtime then?' She yawned and began to gather up her playing cards.

'Wouldn't it come out?'

Estella shook her head. 'I need sevens— are you sure they're going to be all right through there?' Mattresses had been laid out on the drawing room floor for the children. 'I don't like to think of them not in a proper bed.'

'It's an adventure for them,' said Laura, putting a hand on her mother's arm to stop her getting up. 'Mamma, there's something I need to talk to you about. No, don't look like that, it's nothing terrible, but I do need you to listen for a moment. It's about Bobby.'

'Bobby? Oh look, there they all are. Three sevens in the same pile, that's the children playing their Pelmanism.' She turned the cards face up. 'No wonder it didn't come out.'

Laura leaned forward a little, her hand still resting on her mother's arm. 'The thing is, Mamma,' she said, 'I've had a letter from him, from Bobby — I've got it with me if you'd like to read it.' She looked around for her bag but it was in the other room. 'In it he writes — well — he writes that he's very happy, that everyone has been awfully kind.' Laura laughed, a small, sharp laugh that caused her mother to glance at her and frown. Estella had picked up all the cards now and was tapping them on the table, pressing the corners together. Laura sighed: this was ridiculous, she was behaving like a nervous schoolgirl. She took a deep breath. 'He writes that he's fallen in love — that he's fallen in love with Cousin Josette and that they intend to be married.'

The words were out and she felt a kind of recklessness. Laura braced herself for what was coming, wondering if it might have been better if she'd waited until her father was home too. Estella turned her head a fraction.

'Yes, I know.'

Laura stared at her. 'You know?'

'Yes. I called Violette yesterday morning. I was tired of waiting for Leonard to do it, so I called her myself.' She cut the cards then ran her thumbs along the near sides, so that the two halves fanned together. 'I needed to find out about his boat.'

'Oh Mamma—'

'—of course she was delighted to be the one to tell me, there was lots of nonsense about how she thought I knew and how dreadful she felt for spoiling their surprise. Knowing my sister she plotted the whole thing, she's always loved to get one up on me.' She glanced at Laura. 'I knew something like this would happen if he went over there, I begged your father not to send him.'

Laura was confused. 'But why didn't you say anything? All day we've been together and you haven't said a word. If I'd known —' She gazed uncomprehendingly at her mother. 'I've been so worried about telling you.'

Estella shrugged. It was not for her to make other people feel better about this. One of the playing cards had a tear in it, and she licked her fingers and pressed the edges together again. 'Well you didn't need to be.'

Laura nodded, sitting down next to her mother and spreading her fingers along the edge of the table, as though it were the keyboard of a piano. She was thinking about the letter, searching for some detail she could offer her mother. 'She plays tennis. Apparently she's very good. That's nice, isn't it, that Bobby should have someone who has an interest.'

'Virginie says she's mousy.'

'You called Auntie Virginie too?'

'I needed to talk to someone.'

'Of course you did.' Laura smiled. 'You're being awfully good about it. Though I still think Bobby should have told you himself. You should never have had to hear it from Violette, it's bad enough that he asked me—'

'Oh, I don't blame him. Boys hate to tell their mother this kind of thing.'

Again Laura smiled, for her mother always had excuses for her youngest son. She thought of something Estella had said earlier, about Bobby walking through the door.

'You know that this means he's staying in Alex though, don't you? You're not still expecting him home?' Perhaps Violette had not been clear.

Estella shrugged. 'I didn't expect you but you came.' She stopped shuffling the cards, and placed them on the table in front of her, her small grey eyes with their painted lashes looking directly at her daughter. She smiled, and there was a kind of triumph in it that surprised Laura.

'But I'd always said we would, I promised.' She returned her mother's gaze with what she hoped was equanimity. 'It's not at all the same thing.'

'Perhaps not.' Estella turned to look at the kitchen clock. 'This is what I mean about your father, he's never home. I could sit here all night waiting for him.' She began to get up, leaning heavily on the table. Laura watched her.

'Poor Mamma,' she said, 'what, with everything else that's going on at the moment —'

She stopped as Coco, her hair loose about her shoulders, padded into kitchen. She handed her mother a hairbrush then turned her back, waiting.

Laura seemed to reflect for a moment, then began brushing Coco's long, straight hair, so that it lay flat and smooth on the back of her nightdress. Methodically, using her forefinger and thumb, she divided it into three parts and worked it into a plait, holding out her hand for a ribbon to secure the end.

'There,' she said. 'Bed now, it's late.' She pulled Coco towards her and kissed her cheek, then glanced at Estella, 'Give Granny a kiss too.'

Coco bowed her head to her grandmother, her hand immediately rising to her face to wipe away the traces of lipstick. 'Are you coming soon?' she asked Laura, for she could never sleep unless her mother tucked her in.

'Soon, yes,' said Laura, looking at Estella. She knew,

she thought. She knew and she was quite calm. Wait until I tell Leonard, how silly we were to fret.

'Take these for me, Coco,' she said, picking up the swaddled rubber bottles, 'one each, they'll warm the sheets.' She checked the stoppers, then turned them upside down to be sure they didn't leak. 'I won't be long,' she said.

As she put away the last of the supper things, leaving a cold plate for Leonard and her father, Laura asked about the conversation with Violette, marvelling at her mother's composure, and astonished by how easily she spoke of it. She was astonished that the news had been so well received, even more so having come from Violette d'Araquy. But when Estella began to talk of the wedding, of where it would be held and how many people they would invite, Laura had to stop her.

'I'm quite sure it'll be a small affair, given the political situation. Even Violette won't be throwing parties if there's a war on.'

Estella shrugged. 'Then they'll simply have to wait. She's young enough, I can't see why there should be any hurry.' If she had to give up Bobby, then it was going to be on her terms. Laura couldn't help but smile.

'And Papa, is he pleased? He has always rather liked the d'Araquys, hasn't he?'

'Has he? In any case, I haven't told him yet.'

'You haven't *told* him?'

'How can I, he's hardly here.' This is what Estella had warned would happen if he took on all those extra responsibilities: he would miss out on what was happening in his own family.

'Oh but Mamma, you must!'

'And I will, just as soon as he's home long enough for

us to have a proper conversation. The same goes for Leonard.'
She stood up, still holding the playing cards, and Laura
understood that she was taking them upstairs with her so that
the children should not use them. 'I don't know what it is
about the men in this family, they seem to think certain
matters don't concern them.' 'The men' seemed not to
include Bobby, for she continued: 'Poor Bobby, he'll be
married before anyone here thinks to take notice.'

'Oh, Mamma, I really don't think that's fair.'

'I suppose you've already told Leonard.' This had not
occurred to Estella until now and, even in saying it she was
doubtful, but the expression on Laura's face revealed it to be
true. She gazed at her daughter for a long moment, feeling
aggrieved, for intimacy between her children was never
something she had welcomed. As a mother, she ruled by
division: complaining to one child about the others,
encouraging grudges by her favouritism, regarding loyalty
between themselves as an act of treachery. 'You two have
always liked your little secrets,' she said.

'Well, as it turns out, it wasn't one,' said Laura
sharply. She stopped. She had promised herself they would
not do this. 'I'm sorry Mamma,' she said quickly, stepping
towards the door and catching her mother just as she was
going out. 'Don't let's fight, I hate it when we fight.'

Estella did not look at her, but she nodded.

'Would you like me to help you upstairs?' continued
Laura, solicitude being the easiest means of reparation.

'I thought the children wanted you.' Estella glanced
towards the drawing room.

'They'll wait, I'll get you settled first. Mind Rita's bag
there, let me move it — do you want your shawl? Why don't
I bring it anyway, then you'll know where it is.' Thus they
made their way upstairs, stopping at the middle landing for
Estella to catch her breath, stopping again at the top,

although this time with the excuse of listening for the baby. 'It's wonderful how you've taken it,' she said at last, when Estella was perched on the edge of her bed and Laura was saying goodnight. 'All day I've been trying to imagine how I'd feel if it were Teddy— I suppose it will be, one day, and I don't think I shall be nearly as good about it as you.'

Estella thought about this and agreed that no, she probably wouldn't.

Leonard let himself in with his key and was about to go straight upstairs when he saw that the lights were on in the dining room. Reaching around the door for the switch, he was surprised to find Laura still sitting at the table, her dark head resting upon her folded arms, her eyes closed. He smiled, remembering when they were younger and she would get up early to practise the piano before school, only to fall asleep again before she even lifted the lid. Their mother had said she lacked commitment, that it was another sign of her contrariness, but Laura had always insisted she was in fact practising. She was dreaming the notes, even if she wasn't playing them. Leonard wondered what she was dreaming now.

Sensing his presence, Laura opened her eyes, sitting up quickly and pressing at her hair. 'You're back.' She pushed out her chair and stood up. 'There's a plate for you in the kitchen, I'll get it.'

'Thank you, I'm famished. Spam sandwiches was all there was on offer at the depot. I kept explaining that I don't eat pork and every time they said, 'but it's spam,' as though I was some kind of simpleton.' He laughed, taking off his coat and following her into the hall.

'Well, this is chicken.'

'How is everyone? Did you have a nice day?' He bent to unlace his shoes, looking around for his slippers. 'I hope Baby behaved himself and didn't give you any gyp. You heard about Daladier, I suppose?' His slippers were where they always were, by the stairs, and he put them on. Laura came out of the kitchen holding his plate.

'Baby was a sweetie,' she said. She went back into the dining room, where earlier she had laid a place for him at the table and set down his plate. She pulled out a chair and sat down alongside.

'I thought you'd be in bed.'

'I wasn't tired,' said Laura, though this was clearly untrue. 'What a long day it is for you, you must be worn out.'

'I am a bit.' He sat down, grinning at her and rubbing his head where his hat band had been. 'How was Mamma? Did you have a chance to talk to her? I've been terribly distracted thinking about it today, I almost rang you up.'

Laura nodded. Since her conversation with Estella earlier, she had been going over and over it in her head. Now she looked at Leonard, her expression oddly watchful. 'She already knew. She called Violette yesterday, apparently you suggested it.'

'She knew?'

'And she's fine about it. Actually, maybe even more than fine, she seems pleased.'

Leonard had picked up his fork and started eating, but now he stopped, a bit of chicken suspended in mid-air. 'She was pleased? Well I never. I suppose it just goes to show, you never know how someone's going to respond. She understands it's serious?'

'She's already planning what she's going to wear to the wedding.' Estella had called down to her, just as Laura was settling the children: 'Green voile,' Laura told him now.

Leonard grinned. 'Well I never,' he said again. He picked up his knife and fork and continued eating. After a while he said: 'Well, at least that's one less thing to worry about. It's really not looking good, the French are adamant that they'll stand by their agreement. What a mess everything is.'

And Laura said, 'Isn't it,' because what else was there to say?

The fire had long since burned down and the last of the embers glowed in the grate. Silvery ash covered the hearth and every so often a gust of air came down the chimney and blew puffs of it into the room. The yellow tiles with their pattern of leaves and flowers were dull and hot to the touch, and on the chimneypiece the photographs Laura had brought of the new apartment curled at the corners. A vase of dried papery seed-cases cast oval shadows on the chimney breast, and the hump-shaped clock ticked. Earlier, the children had draped their nightclothes over the fireguard when they went upstairs for their bath, as they used to do over the hall stove in Milan, but when they had come to get them they were streaked with soot. As a result, they had all gone to bed wearing Leonard's shirts.

'The clothes off my back,' he joked, when Laura told him this now. He picked up his plate and carried it through to the kitchen and she heard him rinse it and set it on the draining board with a clink. When he came back into the dining room, she was flicking through the newspaper he had brought with him, and he stood watching her from the doorway. She looked up.

'Go to bed, Leonard, I'll lock up.'

'You don't mind?'

She shook her head. 'Of course not.' She turned back to the newspaper, her eyes skimming a story about a new production of Troilus and Cressida. Leonard stood for a moment, reading over her shoulder.

'Ulysses as a Balkan statesman,' he said. 'Whatever next?'

Laura did not reply. She finished reading and then she closed the newspaper and folded it into four, just as Leonard always did. She held it out to him and he put it on the table, then changed his mind and dropped it into the fire instead. 'I've been thinking,' he said, turning back to Laura, 'whether it might be an idea for you all to go to St Anne's tomorrow. Miriam's parents are there, it'll be safer. If you all went, then perhaps Mamma might be persuaded to go too.'

'But I hardly know Miriam's parents.'

'It would only be for a few days. Until you could find an hotel or a house to rent.'

'In St Anne's?'

'There's talk of evacuating the major cities.' Leonard was gathering up his belongings, leaving them ready for the morning.

Laura considered this. She had been to St Anne's years before and remembered it mostly for being windy. 'I don't think I could move the children again,' she said. The thought of it made her feel indescribably weary. 'I think it's best if we just stay here, at least until we have definite news.' There was something in the way she spoke that made Leonard feel equally weary, and so he sighed and said, 'If you're sure.'

'Besides, Marco is quite certain it'll all blow over. He says the Germans want this war even less than we do.' She stood up and took one of her mother's magazines from the table, flicking through it just as she had flicked through the newspaper. 'He thinks they'll come to some sort of agreement. I had a long talk with him about it before we left, it's wonderful how calm he is about everything. He says that in the end, this isn't really about Czechoslovakia, it's about reminding Germany that there's a legal, civilised procedure.'

'Marco said that?'

'Yes.' Over the past few weeks they had talked a lot about such things, and she was surprised by how thoughtful Marco had become, how he always seemed to know what was going to happen and have a response to it. In particular they had talked about Italy, and she blushed to remember how reluctant she had been to leave, and the arguments she had put forward for keeping the office open. Now, when he had told her of Lucia Arditti's illness and how the children had been sent away to Switzerland, she saw how easily it might have been her and she felt grateful. 'It's a shame you didn't see more of him in Milan, you'd enjoy speaking with him,' she said.

Leonard had not forgotten the role he suspected Marco of playing in Laura's move to Brussels and so he did not reply. He picked up a knitted blue rabbit from a pile of toys on the floor. 'Is this from you?'

'Rita made it, isn't it sweet?' She watched as Leonard examined it, pulling at the long ears to make sure they were firmly attached. 'Marco has a point, don't you think? It's in nobody's interest, going to war.'

'I'm not sure if you were living in Czechoslovakia you'd say that.' There was a lot more he could offer on the subject, but it was late and she would just think he was being argumentative. He set the rabbit down on the sideboard, arranging it so that it was sitting upright. 'Clever old Rita.' He yawned, lifting his elbows to his shoulders and stretching, so that the seams of his shirt creaked and his fingertips reached almost to the ceiling. 'You'll turn off the lights then?'

Laura nodded, but as he turned away she said suddenly, 'It wasn't just to make us come here, was it Leonard? Bobby's letter, I mean. Because we'd have come anyway, I promised you that we would.'

'Bobby's letter?' Leonard yawned again, tucking his shirt tails back into his trousers. 'What do you mean?'

'It's just that it seems strange that Mamma already knew.' She held his gaze and in her eyes there was that same expression of watchfulness as when he had first come in. 'I'm not angry, I know how much you worry about me and the children. It's just I'd rather know, I'd hate to think of you all plotting what to do about me.'

'Plotting?' At first he couldn't make sense of anything she had said, but slowly it began to dawn on him. 'You think I told Bobby to write to you so that you would come here rather than stay in Brussels? But how could I? It was you who told me about Josette.' He smiled at the ridiculousness of it all, but Laura's expression remained the same. 'Or do you think I knew too? Is that it? You think we all knew but we pretended not to, so that you would come. This is too silly, Laura. Surely you don't think that? You might as well say I made the whole thing up, that there's nothing going on between Bobby and Josette, it was all just an elaborate ploy!' The amusement with which he had spoken at first had hardened to something like irritation. 'Is that really what you think?'

'Shhh, Leonard, you'll wake the children!' She looked down, trying to remember all the reasons that she had suspected him, but it was as if they had evaporated, for she couldn't think of a single one. She felt suddenly foolish. 'I'm sorry, Leonard, I don't know what came over me. Of course I don't think that.'

He continued to stare at her, hurt that she should accuse him like that and unable to let go of that hurt without further reassurance. She understood this, for he had been like that even as a boy, and she stood up and came to stand in front of him, taking his hands in hers.

'I was just so surprised when Mamma said she'd spoken to Violette. And when she said it was because you'd told her to.'

'But of course I told her to. All week I've had her fussing about his crossing, forever asking me to call up the port and check the arrival schedules, or to telephone Saul. You know how she gets about Bobby. And I haven't had a minute to do anything, not a minute.'

'I know you haven't, Leonard. I can see how busy you are.'

'And why shouldn't she call up Violette? It's hardly a conspiracy for sisters to talk on the telephone. Of course, I didn't think for a minute she'd call, she told me she wouldn't—'

'Leonard, you're right and I'm sorry. I don't know what it is about being here, I always get like this. I seem to revert to being a twelve-year-old again.' She shook her head. 'I'm so ashamed of myself, I don't know why I even said anything.'

'Well, I'm glad you did. Imagine if you'd gone on thinking that.'

'I wouldn't have.'

'Well I hope you wouldn't.' Leonard gazed at her, but although his eyes were stern, he was smiling. In the grate, the folded newspaper had caught fire and shreds of paper, like bright burning butterflies, fluttered up the chimney. Laura watched, her face lit up by the purple and orange flames.

'It's all this uncertainty,' said Leonard, after a while, 'it does something to you. One of the fellows in my unit has been hearing voices. I was on duty with him last night — 'dooty' he calls it — and he kept saying would I turn the wireless down, he couldn't hear himself think. But the wireless wasn't on. I spoke to the supervisor and we sent him home, he was fine today, he just needed a good night's sleep.'

'No doubt that's what I need too.'

'Everything feels better after a good night's sleep.' He remembered how peaceful she had looked when he had first come in. 'You'll see, you'll be yourself again in no time.'

She nodded.

'And you don't mind locking up?'

'Of course not.'

He grinned, bending to kiss the top of her head. 'Sleep well, then.'

'I really am sorry, Leonard. I don't know what came over me.' But she did know, it was what always happened to her when she came back here. And it was why, no matter what happened tomorrow or next week or next month, she knew she could not stay.

'We'll come and get our gas masks tomorrow,' she said, as he turned to go upstairs.

'Perfect. Come around midday, I'll get off for half an hour and we can take the kiddies for lunch. Does Rita still love ginger cake? I know just the place to take you all!'

When Daniel Sutton remembered his time in Milan, he blushed at how young he had been. In the six months since, he had passed his Higher Cert, travelled to North America on a cricket tour of the Empire, applied to read medicine at Cambridge and enrolled on a part-time economics course to keep him busy until he went up. He had tasted corn-on-the-cob in Lake Kagawong, gone to parties where there were girls (and even danced with them) and been the only passenger on the Queen Mary not to get seasick during the roughest crossing on record. The schoolboy he had been in Milan was just that, a boy, and he viewed him with disdain.

Older and wiser then, Daniel returned to Dundee, his future unfurling before him like one of those concertina postcards his mother liked to buy, showing the seafront at Torquay or castles along the Rhine. His was a comfortable home. When he pictured it, he saw his parents standing in the doorway of their white stucco villa, his mother clutching her handbag, his father with his hands hanging loosely at his sides, legs slightly apart, the way the army had taught all of that generation to stand. 'At ease,' he would say whenever anyone pointed a camera at them, and his mother's mouth would slacken and her shoulders drop, so that in every photograph she looked dumpy and morose. And his sister, she was there too, laughing and standing a little apart as though leaving a space for Daniel where he could neatly insert himself, an arm around his mother, an arm around Ruth. He liked to think of them like that, waiting patiently for his return. He liked that he left a gap.

In the first few weeks after he got home, Daniel made much of his newfound leisure. He borrowed his mother's car to visit friends, some of whom had been at school with him, and came home in the early hours, driving too fast and scattering gravel on the front lawn. He listened to the BBC and argued spiritedly for the chance to 'get at him' — 'him' being Hitler — while at the same time sleeping late and enjoying the best attention of his mother's cook. On occasion he called into his father's office, helping out with bits of paperwork or being dispatched to the shop floor, his importance as the boss' son making up for the dullness of the work. But mostly he spent his time getting used to being at home, so that home, in turn, might get used to him.

◆   ◆   ◆   ◆   ◆

DANIEL'S MOTHER WAS TYING up the dahlias beneath the drawing room window, their large, garish heads bobbing around her as she pushed them into place. The wind was getting up, whipping around the side of the house, and she was irritated because already she had broken several stems so that they stuck out at odd angles across the lawn. Daniel, who was sitting in a deckchair reading, watched her for a moment.

'Why don't you leave it for Mr Tennant? Isn't that the gardener's job?'

'Can you see my secateurs, Daniel?' his mother asked.

'By your foot.'

'Ah yes, thank you. Fiddlesticks, there's another one down. Oh dear, Daniel, call your sister, would you? I need another pair of hands, or the whole lot will be on the ground.'

Daniel put down his book and stood up, walking

around the house and shouting up at Ruth's bedroom. She appeared at the window, pushing her hair out of her face.

'Mother wants you to help her,' he said.

'Now?'

'Yes.'

'Can't you? I'm in the middle of something.'

He shook his head. 'She asked for you. Besides, I don't know the first thing about flowers.'

'And I do?' said Ruth, but she closed the window and moments later appeared at the back door, pulling on her boots and frowning at Daniel, who was waiting.

'Do you remember that postcard I sent from Italy,' he asked, 'the one with all the spears and dead bodies? Well, that's what the flowerbed looks like.'

Ruth grinned, buttoning her cardigan so that it went right up to her neck. 'The Uccello?' she said, to show she knew about such things, and Daniel nodded. 'Poor Mother,' she added.

Daniel's book was lying on the ground and he picked it up and sat down again on the striped seat, flicking through it to find his page. He sighed loudly, as if the walk around the side of the house had worn him out.

'Seriously?' asked Ruth over her shoulder, crouching down next to her mother. 'You're just going to sit there and watch? Fine manners they taught you at that school of yours, letting the women work while you relax and read a book.'

'What have you been doing all day?' said Daniel good-naturedly, without looking up.

'Bamboo, Ruth,' said their mother from behind the dahlias. 'And mind the tuber, make sure you don't go in on top of it.' She leaned over, her tweed skirt riding up her thick waist, her fingers flicking at the soil. 'See,' and she pointed at the curve of woody root just below the surface.

'I know, Mother,' murmured Ruth.

Mrs Sutton straightened up, tugging on her hem so that her skirt righted itself and simultaneously popping two buttons on her blouse. 'Besides, Daniel will be working hard soon enough. He starts his economics course next week.'

''Tis true,' said Daniel, turning the page of his novel and taking care to avoid the gaping blouse.

'Not if there's a war he won't,' said Ruth. She glanced at her mother, who had discovered the popped buttons and was hastily doing them up. 'Belinda Dent's brother has joined the Territorials. She says he went into town to return a library book and came back an officer in the Fife and Forfars. He has a uniform and everything.' She turned to her brother, still reading. 'Doesn't your library book need returning, Daniel? I should have thought it was well overdue.'

'Ruth dear, must you be so provocative?' said Mrs Sutton, picking up the broken stems and arranging them into a bouquet. 'It's very unbecoming.'

'Unbecoming?' repeated Ruth but, quite unexpectedly, she laughed and then Daniel, looking up again from his book, laughed too, so that their mother, who saw nothing amusing in her comment, frowned and felt cross. This is what always happened when the two of them got together: they turned everything into a joke, a joke which invariably excluded others. All this past week, when everything had looked so wretched and all anyone talked of was bombs and the end of civilisation, she couldn't say a word without them sniggering or making fun. Even yesterday, when they heard that the British Fleet had been mobilised, Ruth had made some clever quip that had set the two of them off again. Mrs Sutton stepped carefully out of the flowerbed, her secateurs held aloft, and watched as Ruth pushed another bamboo into the unforgiving ground.

'He's been made a Second Lieutenant,' Ruth was saying, back to speaking of her friend's brother. She turned to Daniel. 'He'll probably be sent to France, Belinda says she's been polishing his boots for him. I hope you don't expect me to do that!'

Daniel made some reply but Mrs Sutton did not hear it, for her heart had clamped shut at the mention of France. She stood quite still, rearranging the stems of dahlias, listening to the sparrows bickering in the beech tree above her head. Everything had poignancy at times like this. She supposed it was a kind of nostalgia, but nostalgia for the future rather than the past; for what would not come again, rather than what had been. The last time sparrows would gather in that tree, the last time she would tie up the dahlias, the last time she would sit down with the cook and plan the week's menus. Because this time, if war came, it would come to this house too, to this town, to these peaceful hills. Everyone said so. And the devastation that had been wrought upon France last time — and which, when she suggested a motoring holiday through Picardy one summer, had made her husband's eyes fill with tears — would be wrought here too.

From the other side of the house she heard the crunch of tyres and she glanced at her watch, surprised to find that it was already lunchtime. She pulled off her gardening gloves and dropped them into the trug with the secateurs, then hurried away across the lawn.

'Your father's home. Wash your hands and come inside for lunch,' she said, and once again she heard them giggling, because once they started it was like this no matter what she said. She straightened her back, determined to ignore them, and touched a hand to her greying, wiry hair, smoothing it flat so that when she appeared through the rosebushes onto the driveway, she was her usual, bustling self.

'Ah, there you are, dear,' she said, as she did every day. She walked ahead to the front door and pushed it open, standing back to allow her husband to pass and taking his hat, which she placed on the hall table. She glanced towards the dining room, where she saw the maid was fussing with the cutlery and she called to her, handing her the flowers and suggesting the pewter jug would be nice. 'Mr Sutton needs five minutes and then we'll be in. Tell cook to hold off serving the soup, Mr Sutton likes it hot.'

She disappeared up the stairs to change her blouse, for the buttons were threatening to pop again, leaving her husband standing in the hallway. 'Wash your hands, dear,' she said, 'I won't be a tick.'

He nodded. He found lunch at home tiresome but his wife insisted upon it. She said otherwise they barely saw each other, what with his club and all the extra hours he was doing at the office, and that now Daniel was home it was important they spend time as a family. All this he understood, of course, but still he saw it as a chore. He glanced at his hands, which were perfectly clean, and walked into the dining room. He removed his jacket, draped it on the back of his chair and then sat down, taking care not to drag the rug which was new. He tapped his fingers on the table impatiently, then picked up his napkin, setting aside the ring engraved with his initials 'HS', shaking it out and laying it on his lap. Then again he tapped his fingers on the edge of the table. After a moment he leaned forward and vigorously shook the polished silver bell that stood alongside his placemat

Harold Sutton had done well for himself in life. He had started out as a sales boy and worked his way up to running one of the biggest department stores in Dundee. Of course, it hadn't hurt that he married the boss's daughter, but that didn't balance the books every day, that didn't influence how many bolts of cotton were ordered, how many silk petticoats the ladies in haberdashery sold. He was proud of his ability to get the best out of his staff, to negotiate prices with suppliers that he knew even his father-in-law could not have bettered, and he enjoyed the respect this earned him.

He had a good head on his shoulders, Harold Sutton, and he liked that people knew this.

The door to the kitchen opened and the maid appeared, carrying a tureen which she deposited on the sideboard. In her wake followed Daniel and Ruth, who had come in through the back door, still laughing about whatever it was that had amused them earlier. Their father frowned and checked his watch.

'Where on earth is your mother?' he demanded, turning around in his chair and looking towards the hallway. 'Really, why can no one ever be on time for meals in this house? Thank you, and a bread roll please,' he said as the maid placed his bowl in front of him and turned back to the sideboard to fetch the others.

'It's in front of you, Daddy,' said Ruth, pointing to a basket, but her father continued to wait, so that the maid stopped what she was doing and hurriedly returned to the table, seizing the tongs and delivering a small white roll direct to his side plate.

'Thank you,' he said, picking it up and pushing his thumb into the soft dough inside. His preference was for the crust, so he would carefully hollow out the middle and discard it on his plate, leaving just the outer shell. This he would tear into two and spread with a thick layer of butter, explaining, should he be dining with someone other than his family, that the crust of the bread was one of his great pleasures in life.

'We started without you,' he said as his wife flustered through the door in a new blouse. 'Here,' and he pushed the remains of his bread roll across the table, 'have this.'

'No thank you dear,' said Mrs Sutton, but he ignored her and pushed it closer. 'Has there been any news?' she asked, for the children wouldn't dare make fun when their father was here.

He bent to take a spoonful of soup, his head lowered to the bowl so as to avoid getting any on his waistcoat.

'Well, he's gone again, waved off by all the usual gang, Halifax, Sir Simon, Kingsley Wood, very jolly they all were. Seems we might just have got away with it. Is this the new one?' (He meant the new cook, for the old one had recently left.) 'It's not too bad.'

'Do you think so?' asked his wife, adding, 'That we might have peace?' In case he thought she meant the soup.

'That's the feeling. 'Course, as you know I never doubted it. Mr Chamberlain is a businessman, negotiating deals is what he does. People would do well to have more faith in such men. The panicking I've seen this last week, just on the shop floor.' He rested his spoon on the edge of the bowl, looking around at his family. 'Frankly it's shameful.'

Mrs Sutton nodded.

'The *Courier* reckons it was the King of Italy saved the day,' said Ruth. 'If it *is* saved.'

'Don't say 'reckons', dear,' said her mother.

'Opines?' asked Ruth, glancing at Daniel. 'Posits?'

'Which reminds me,' said Mr Sutton, speaking to his wife, 'I had a letter from your friend Mrs Arditti this morning, she wants me to give her a reference, or some such thing.' He patted the pockets of his jacket, trying to remember where he had put it.

'A letter from Lucia Arditti? To the office?'

Her husband produced a lilac-coloured envelope and held it up. 'I can't imagine what they must have thought, look at the colour of the thing.' He glanced at Daniel, as though only another man would understand such horrors, then opened it and began to read, his eyes scanning the page. 'Hopes we're well, often thinks of Daniel, must be proud— Ah, here we are, she needs a "character reference" for a visa application – to come to England, I assume – and wondered whether she might put my name.' He looked at his wife. 'Did you know about this?' She shook her head, holding out her hand for the letter so that she might read it herself, but her husband held up a finger, for he had not finished. 'Also, do we know a certain Mr Leonard Cansino of Manchester? Do we? She says Daniel met him while he was there and would I mind getting in touch with him and asking him to be a referee too?' He folded the letter and pushed it back into its envelope, skimming it across the table towards his wife. 'I have to say, I think it's a bit much.'

'It's postmarked Switzerland,' said Mrs Sutton. 'What on earth is Lucia doing in Switzerland.'

'It's in the letter, something to do with schools. Perhaps your mother can help, isn't this what she does now?' He peered at his wife, raising his bushy eyebrows.

'Not really, dear, Mother works with the poor and needy.' She slipped the letter beneath her placemat, thinking it would be better if she read it later.

'I have his address,' said Daniel suddenly. 'Mr Cansino's. He gave it to me so that I might send him a photograph I took. I showed it to you, do you remember, the one with the children.'

'Oh yes, in front of the Leonardo.' Mrs Sutton put a hand to her upper arm, remembering the diamond-shaped black patches on the children's sleeves. 'Was he pleased with the photograph?'

Daniel did not answer. He had never got around to sending it, the envelope with the photograph was somewhere amongst his school things. Indeed, he had forgotten all about it until now.

'Well, then, perhaps I can leave it to Daniel to get in touch with him,' said his father, sitting back in his chair as the maid came in to clear. 'Very good,' he said, tapping the side of his empty bowl. 'Tell cook the soup was very good.'

'Shakespeare, I believe it is,' said Harold Sutton, straightening his cutlery and addressing himself to his son. '*Out of this nettle*', and so on.'

Daniel nodded.

'Hotspur,' said Ruth.

'Not many fellows would have that at their fingertips,' continued Mr Sutton. 'You have to admire the man.' Traces of the soup remained on his top lip and he wiped it with his napkin. 'Henry IV, actually,' he said, glancing at his daughter.

The door from the kitchen opened and the maid hurried in, holding a large platter. Ruth, who had been about to protest, changed her mind.

'*Sole meunière*,' said Mrs Sutton. 'I ordered plaice but when the boy delivered it, he said they were all out and Mr Briggs had sent sole.' She stretched her neck to see the contents of the platter and Daniel, watching her, was reminded of a turtle.

'Plaice is my favourite,' said Mr Sutton.

'I know, dear.'

'I thought I might go down to the airfield this afternoon,' said Daniel, 'if mother doesn't need her car. I wanted to get a look at that Mercury they're testing, the new mail-plane, you know. Come with me if you like, Ruth.'

'If you mean the piggy-back plane, it's been cancelled,' said his father, choosing himself a piece of fish. ' "In view of the international situation," is what they said. Now that's a company I should have invested in, their stock must be through the roof.'

'Who's that, dear?' said his wife. 'Thank you Mary, serve the others first.'

'Imperial Airlines. I never thought it would catch on myself, just shows.' He helped himself to boiled potatoes. 'I thought you might come by the shop, Daniel, if you've nothing else on, we could do with an extra pair of hands on the floor. Mr Evans in Haberdashery says it's worse even than the last time, the girls can't stock the shelves fast enough— salt please, Ruth— ten bolts of black wool serge in a single morning, you've never seen anything like it. I'd put one aside to bring home but even that went. Don't worry, dear, I'll order more.'

Mrs Sutton nodded, relieved. She had been avoiding starting on the black-out curtains. It seemed to make everything so much more likely. 'Perhaps we won't need them now,' she said hopefully.

'I can come too, if you like,' said Ruth, looking eagerly at her father, 'I don't have anything planned.'

'You stay and help your mother, there's a good girl.' He paused to work a fishbone to the front of his mouth and then removed it into his napkin.

'I don't think she needs my help.' Ruth turned to her mother. 'Do you? If it's just the dahlias, I can finish them this evening.'

'Actually, I thought we might make a start on that lavender I've been drying. Mary has set the machine up in the sunroom. If I run up the bags, you could fill them. We could listen to the afternoon concert at the same time.' She glanced at her husband and saw that he was pleased. The last few times he had taken Ruth to the shop with him she had got into rows with the customers, he said she didn't have the right manner for dealing with the public.

'Lavender from the garden?' he said now, to show his approval of the project.

'From outside your study window,' said Mrs Sutton proudly.

'Oh well in that case,' muttered Ruth. She knew there was no point insisting. Her mother would only think of increasingly mundane activities to distract her with. Lavender-bags? She thought with envy of her friend Gladys Logan. Gladys' mother was a teacher, and Gladys was to accompany the class to Aberdeen if it was decided to evacuate. She had cycled over to see her yesterday and found her writing out luggage labels and filling in billet forms with a self-importance Ruth could only dream of.

'Gladys Logan's brother has joined the Territorials too,' she said now, looking significantly at Daniel.

'Do stop with that, Ruth,' said her mother.

◆　　◆　　◆　　◆　　◆

'IT'S SO UNFAIR,' SAID RUTH, when lunch was finished and she and Daniel were alone again. In the kitchen their mother could be heard complimenting the cook on the soup.

'I'd just as rather stay here,' said Daniel, picking up the book he had brought in from the garden and shoving it into his jacket pocket.

'What, and sew lavender-bags with mother? I'm sure you would.'

'It'll be more fun than selling knicker-elastic to anxious housewives.'

'The knicker elastic is all sold out, didn't you hear?'

They continued like this as they wandered into the hall, batting the conversation back and forth as they climbed the stairs to Daniel's room. Ruth lay down on the bed, picking up his copy of the *New Statesman* and then making herself comfortable against the pillows to read it. Daniel stood in front of the mirror, knotting his tie.

'What a good-looking chap I am,' he said, turning his head from side to side. He was too, for in recent months there had been some kind of transformation, everything that had been angular and outsized now finding its proper place. 'A young Rhett Butler,' one of his mother's friends had said, and it wasn't far off the mark, with his full mouth and sharp, hazel eyes, often misremembered by people as blue. His hair was longer since he had left school and he combed it to one side so that it lay in neat waves above his forehead. 'Are all your friends hopelessly in love with me? Do say they are.'

'Oh most definitely,' said Ruth, without looking up. 'They burn with thwarted passion.' This was a phrase they had recently found in one of their mother's magazines, amusing themselves by dropping into the conversation whenever possible. 'Would you even know what to do if they were?' She turned the page, crossing and re-crossing her ankles as she read.

Daniel thought about this. In Montreal he had danced with the daughter of the Governor and in Alberta there were girls too, but holding hands was as far as it went. In fact, the only girl he had kissed who wasn't family was that friend of Netta Arditti's in Milan, and to say he had kissed her was stretching the point. He remembered that afternoon at the Duomo, the way the girl in the yellow dress had taken his hand and pulled him after her, laughing and flicking her hair, running faster when Netta tried to follow them. He remembered how she had led him out of the lift onto the sloping roof of the cathedral, the sun bouncing off the frilled ramparts, and how she had suddenly kissed him, full on the lips, with no warning, so that he stumbled backwards, knocking into a gentleman with an umbrella who glared furiously. She had looked at him for a moment, as if to see what he would do, and then she had turned away and gone to stand at the other end of the roof, so that when

Netta arrived, seconds later, he was on his own. Afterwards, it was as if it had never happened.

'Probably not,' he said, in answer to Ruth's question. He leaned into the mirror, touching the bridge of his nose, smoothing the dark hairs there, first one way and then the other.

'If there is war,' said Ruth from the bed, 'I shall join the Women's Legion, I've already looked up the address in London.'

'Don't you have to be eighteen?'

She shrugged, as if such details were of no consequence. 'They particularly want motor-transport drivers, the War Office says. I think I should be rather good, racing around the streets of London. I drive mother all the time.' She glanced at him. 'I can do those for you, if you like, I have tweezers in my room.' She rolled off the bed and ran out, returning with her manicure set. 'Sit down.'

Daniel sat down on the edge of his bed, looking up at his sister. She tilted his head back, frowning a little.

'In fact, most people think I'm older than eighteen,' she continued, which couldn't possibly be true as she was short like their mother and had the plump cheeks and malleable features of someone much younger. 'Don't move. There!' She considered the end of her tweezers with a kind of glee, ignoring his protestations. 'I haven't finished,' she said, pushing him back down.

'I feel like you're enjoying this,' said Daniel.

'Hold still, couple more. There, done. Have a look.'

Daniel walked over to the mirror and gazed at himself for a moment. 'Thanks.'

Ruth watched as he brushed off his lapels, flattened his hair, found his wallet and tucked it into the pocket of his jacket. 'Won't you be just the tiniest bit disappointed?' she asked, leaning forward, her voice lowered.

'Disappointed?'

She meant if there wasn't a war.

Daniel looked at her with curiosity. 'Will *you*?'

She shrugged.

Downstairs, his mother was calling from the hallway, in her arms his father's hat and coat, and his own school boater, and he shouted that he was coming.

CHAPTER 18

Lucia Arditti had written to everyone she could
think of. From the moment she had safely
deposited the children at boarding school in
Bern, she had turned her attentions to her own departure,
determined to follow after. An old school friend had a summer
house in Lugano, just over the border, and at first Lucia
wanted to move there, for that way Raphael could still get to
and from the office in Milan. But Raphael, who didn't like to
drive, was having none of it. Then she heard of a committee
helping Jewish families emigrate overseas, to countries such as
Cuba and Brazil and Papua New Guinea, and for a while she
set her mind upon that. But once again Raphael refused even
to consider it, claiming he was too old to start his life again,
and reminding her that she was too. To each of Lucia's
suggestions, Raphael gave a reason why it wasn't possible, and
for a while the resulting stalemate seemed to suffice. With
time, Raphael felt sure, Lucia would see things more clearly,
and life could get back to how it was before. '*I bei vecchi
tempi,*' he would promise, smiling at her from one end of the
empty dining table, and she would nod wistfully, gazing back
at him from the other.

Without the children, the apartment was a hollow
shell. Nobody banged doors or played the piano or had loud,
angry rows about clothes that had been borrowed or books
not returned. Beds remained made, and drawers remained
tidy, and when spaghetti was left over from supper, it was still
there the next night, untouched on the pantry shelf. There
were no shoes to trip over coming through the door, and the

hallway was just that, a hallway, not a velodrome or a roller-skating rink or the place where everyone seemed to congregate when they were supposed to be somewhere else. The telephone almost never rang, unless it was Raphael to tell her he was late, and there was no longer a search for the car keys every time she wanted to go out, for they were exactly where she had left them, in the bowl by the front door. The wireless was tuned to the news, there was no stack of sleeveless records by the gramophone, the cushions on the sofas remained plump and straight. Her favourite cup broke because she herself dropped it.

And yet not once did Lucia consider bringing the children back. When Netta wrote repeatedly, saying she was miserable and sick for home, she told her 'Coraggio!', 'Cheer up!' and sent her a pair of skis in the post. When the news was full of Czechoslovakia and war promised to break out at any moment, she made no mention of the crisis, and wrote only of films they ought to see and when it might snow. When the King threatened to abdicate if Il Duce didn't step in, and all of Europe proclaimed Italy the blessed peacemaker, she might have been listening to a dull play for all that it impressed her. And when, on every street corner and on every front page, the headlines promised peace for our time, and Raphael said, 'There, I told you things would work out,' she gave him that same wistful look of hers and said, 'Perhaps.'

When Lucia was a child, her grandmother used to sing her a song in Ladino about a little goat, *cavretiko*, that is eaten by a cat. She had forgotten the words, even much of the meaning, but the tune kept coming back to her, so that wherever she was, whatever she was doing, she found herself humming the same phrase over and over. When Raphael asked her what it was, she said she didn't know, and it was true, she didn't. Indeed, she would have been surprised to learn that a version of the same song was sung in Jewish homes everywhere, for she thought of it as her own.

But there was a comfort in it that went beyond the familiar, almost as if, through this little tune, generations of wise and worldly ancestors were offering her their allegiance.

In early November, Raphael left for Egypt. He had delayed his trip many times already, and business was beginning to suffer. Lucia drove him to Venice, waving him off on the *Marco Polo*, then turning the car around and driving back across the Ponte de Littorio to the mainland. She drove fast, with her usual disregard for other motorists, glad to have her thoughts to herself again. That morning there had been a letter from Leonard Cansino, offering to do anything he could to help, and she needed to sit down and decide what to do. When Raphael had discovered all the people she had written to he had been furious, had accused her of humiliating him and ruining the family name, and the only way she had been able to calm him down was to say that she had been ill when she wrote them and that she was better now. When the replies had come, from Harold Sutton, from a businessman Marco Balestra knew in London, now from Leonard Cansino, she had hidden them.

The roads were empty at this time of day, and she was quickly past the factories and petroleum tanks of the port and speeding towards Verona. Soon the dull volcanic grey of the Euganean hills gave way to sloping vines and mulberries, punctuated here and there with cypress trees, like exclamation marks. At Desenzano, on the banks of the Lake Garda, she stopped for an early dinner, parking the car near the castle and walking to the Hotel Due Colombe, where she and Raphael had eaten breakfast that same morning. The terrace was quieter now, and the view across the water less brilliant than it had been earlier, as though it had grown weary in the course of the day. Gulls bobbed listlessly, the evening light glancing off their white backs and every so often one would fly up, mewing, then drift back down again. Fishermen, their nets shiny with fish, rowed to shore.

Lucia sat down at the far end of the terrace. Someone had left a copy of that day's *Corriera della Sera*, and she picked it up and idly turned the pages. A young family was seated nearby, and she glanced over, noticing that they were English and enjoying the children's chatter. The mother, elegant in a beige wool coat with a fox collar, almost identical to the one the Queen of England wore in all those photographs, was also reading the newspaper, an English one, and talking animatedly with her husband. Every so often she would look over at Lucia, and then at last she leaned across: 'Isn't it simply awful?'

'Excuse me?'

'Simply awful.' She gestured to the newspaper, lowering her voice. 'What's happening in Germany. I shan't sleep tonight, they say it's still going on.'

Lucia was confused.

The woman's husband picked up the newspaper and held it out to her. He glanced at his wife, her habit of starting conversations with strangers clearly something he didn't appreciate. 'Pogrom,' he murmured, 'I don't know what it is in Italian.'

Lucia took the newspaper and looked at it. On the front page was a photograph of a burning building, a synagogue. 'It's the same word,' she said.

'Oh.'

Lucia continued to hold the newspaper, but she did not look at it. She was thinking about Raphael and their conversation that morning, sitting right here. 'Better times are coming,' Raphael had said, lifting and smoothing his tie, sipping his coffee. He was referring to the new French Ambassador in Rome, to the promised Anglo-Italian accords, to the apparent cooling of relations with Germany. 'Ciano sees straight through that brainless champagne salesman,' he said, 'there'll be no alliance with Ribbentrop as long as Ciano is around.'

He did this, Raphael; offered her logic and facts as a bulwark against what he saw as the tide of her emotions. And it worked, sometimes. What was it he had promised this morning, when she had asked when all this race business would be over? 'Before the winter fog sets in,' he had assured her, which in Milan meant any day.

'You can keep it if you like.' The woman began to gather up their things, waving to the children to come. She buttoned her coat, the fur collar lifting and settling around her pretty face. 'I don't think I can bear to read any more.'

'Thank you.' Lucia glanced again at the newspaper. That tune was in her head again, the one about the little goat, and she stood up suddenly, finding she was no longer hungry. She had that same pressure behind her eyes as she had that day at the beach, but this time she didn't cry. She smiled a small, precise smile, and then turned and walked away, leaving the newspaper folded on the table.

'I do wish you wouldn't,' said the husband, picking up his wife's gloves and handing them to her. 'You don't know what her politics might be.' Then they too walked away across the terrace, the warm yellow lights of the hotel beckoning them inside.

The next day, Lucia closed up the apartment on the Via Leopardi and drove to Switzerland.

CHAPTER 19

When Leonard said that he would do anything to help Lucia, he meant it. Like everyone, his relief at war being avoided was profound, but in the weeks that followed he became convinced that appeasement had been a terrible mistake. The events of Kristallnacht, as it came to be known, and the decidedly uneven reporting of it horrified him, and he no longer trusted things would work out. When he tried to tell his family this, they dismissed his fears as 'typically Leonard', for he had a habit of gloominess, and even Miriam urged him to cheer up. Only Lucia, in her long, rambling, desperate letters, seemed to share his foreboding, and her wellbeing soon became inextricably linked with his own. It was Leonard who suggested she focus all her efforts on coming to Manchester, who called the Foreign Office and pleaded the family's case, who went back to the house on Palatine Road and offered the Ardittis as future tenants. Somehow, in helping Lucia he spied his own salvation. Or at the very least, a lessening of his despair.

The news that Bobby and Josette were to be married by the end of the year landed like a rocket in amongst all this. Laura, now back in Brussels, was delighted, saying a party was just what everyone needed; Estella saw it as a deliberate attempt by Violette to sabotage her outfit, for no decent dressmaker could work that fast; Solomon was outwardly happy but displeased at having to travel over Hannukah; and Leonard, speaking for both himself and Miriam, went into an immediate panic, for this was no time to be going to North Africa. Hadn't Mussolini just set his cap at Tunisia? As they went back and forth on all this, Laura unsure if she should take the children, Solomon wondering if a train was less of an *aveirah* than a boat, Leonard now worrying Il Duce had his eye on Suez too, life intervened. The baby came down with chickenpox and could not possibly travel, and when Miriam said she would stay behind, Leonard insisted that he must too, for this was no time to be apart. This in turn resolved Solomon's dilemma, for if Leonard was at home then there was no need to worry about burning tea lights in the cabin or what time sun sets on board a ship, for there would be candles in the window of Moorfield Road just like always. Only Estella continued to fret: about her dress, which hadn't come out quite as she expected, about the journey, about seeing Violette. But because what really upset her was losing Bobby, there was not much anyone could say to help.

◆　　◆　　◆　　◆　　◆

ON THE DAY THE FAMILY WERE due to arrive, Bobby joined his uncle at his club on the Rue Rosette. 'A bit of calm before the storm,' Philippe had suggested, and it was true, for a wedding really did seem to make for squally weather, everyone rushing around and getting cross, and nothing Bobby said being right. Here though, tucked away in a quiet corner of the Muhammad Ali Club, he saw that it might all work out. After a lunch of roast pheasant — the steward said it was the last of the season and reserved especially for Monsieur d'Araquy — they took their coffee outside so that Philippe might smoke. At this hour the veranda was deserted, as the club's members had either returned to the office or were asleep in one of the button-backed leather armchairs inside, and Philippe gestured towards the empty tables, implying that Bobby should take his pick.

'But away from the balustrade,' he said, for too often he had been sitting here and seen his son parading in and out of Baudrot, or speeding along the Rue Cherif Pasha in some society hostess's expensive car. It was an entertainment he preferred to avoid.

They settled into rattan steamer-chairs at the far end, where a gap in the canopy allowed the last of the afternoon sun to warm their faces. Philippe was in a ruminative mood, and mostly they did not speak, as Bobby too was glad of an opportunity to collect his thoughts. Everything had happened so quickly, from that first kiss at the Great Pyramid to now, sitting here waiting for his family to arrive so that they might witness his marriage. He felt a rush of apprehension, for it seemed to him sometimes that he had not thought this through, that he had wandered into this new life in much the same way as a guest in a strange house wanders into a room where the lights are on and someone has lit the fire. He goes there not because it's where he's supposed to be, but simply because it's more welcoming than elsewhere. Bobby sighed, and his uncle, distracted from his own reveries, looked up.

'Do you need to go? What time do you need to be at the port?'

'Not for ages,' said Bobby, scratching his neck vigorously: he seemed to be starting one of his skin-attacks. 'Their boat is expected around six, Josie's going to meet me on the dock with all the aunties. We'll go straight to the Cecil so they can get settled in, then Laura arrives just before midnight. Poor thing, she'll be exhausted. I hope she still feels up to coming tomorrow.'

'Oh, this picnic business?' Clemmie had taken it upon himself to throw Bobby a 'bachelor party', an idea which had gone through various incarnations (each rejected by Josette) until it arrived at its present form, a picnic for everyone at Lake Mariout. 'What about your parents?'

'Violette wants them to spend the day with her and Josie. She says that with me out of the way they can get to know Josie properly.' He smiled. 'Mamma will love her no matter who's there, I just know it. Papa too.'

Philippe nodded. Clearly nothing was to be allowed to spoil Clemmie's outing. They lapsed into silence again, Philippe lighting another cigar and exhaling lazy smoke rings into the sky above their heads. A light wind rattled the flagstaffs on the buildings opposite, and every so often that yellow dust which is particular to Egypt turned in eddies across the veranda. Philippe remembered something Violette had wanted him to ask. 'Your brother Leonard, it's sure that he isn't coming?'

'Quite sure.' Until a few days ago he had been hoping Leonard might yet arrive, but a telegram sent when the boat docked at Malta confirmed that it was only his parents on board. It surprised him how upset he felt about this, for it didn't feel right to be marrying without Leonard at his side. 'The baby's been ill,' he said now.

'Such bad luck.' His uncle sent another round of smoke rings drifting into the air between them. 'He was to have been your best man, I suppose. Or whatever it is you call it.' Violette had used a particular word but he couldn't remember it right now.

'My *shomer*? Sort of, I suppose.' There was a whole world of differences between an Alexandrian idea of a wedding and a Manchester one. 'I hadn't really thought about it.' He was more concerned about Estella's reaction to the Christmas tree in the Cecil ballroom.

'Violette wondered whether you'd like to ask Clemmie?' Philippe tilted his handsome head, with the streaks of grey around his temples, looking past Bobby towards the street. He was clearly uncomfortable with his commission, sensing that Violette's main motivation was to make this Clemmie's day too.

'Clemmie?' He thought about it. 'As my best man? Of course, what a good idea.'

'Now don't feel you have to. No doubt you have a whole list of people you could ask.'

'But I don't. I don't at all. Do you think he'd like to? I should hate him to feel obliged, he's done so much for us already, organising the picnic and so on.'

Philippe thought it unlikely his son had ever done anything because he felt 'obliged,' but he did not say so. 'I should think he'd be honoured. But think about it first, talk to Josie. This is your day, remember.'

At this, Philippe stood up, leaning over the balustrade and gesturing to the traffic-policeman in the middle of the crossroads, which set off a chain of events that would result in Philippe's chauffeur waiting at the front door of the club when he stepped out moments later. Bobby stood up too.

'I'll ask him tomorrow,' he said, 'at the lake. I should have thought of it myself, I hope Violette isn't cross with me.'

'Violette? Violette adores you. She could never be cross.' He smiled and patted Bobby's arm. 'You should get some ointment for that,' he said, for Bobby was scratching his neck again.

Bobby blushed, immediately dropping his hand. 'I will. I think it might be because of the weather. I always seem to get it when the seasons change.'

'The seasons never change in Egypt,' said Philippe, bending to stub out his cigar. He straightened up and regarded the younger man with that same amusement with which everyone seemed to regard Bobby these days. Then he turned and walked inside.

CHAPTER 20

L aura was standing on the steps of the hotel
when Bobby drove up in his uncle's car, the
canvas roof rolled down and the back seat
laden with wicker picnic-baskets. She ran to meet him with
the small, quick steps of a young girl, laughing and teasing
him for being on time — the bells of the Coptic cathedral
were chiming the hour — and waving towards the doorman
who had been waiting with her. She wore a sleeveless white
tunic, belted at the waist and dividing into wide, billowy
trousers, her only jewellery a strand of pearls wound twice
around her neck.

'Did you sleep well?' asked Bobby, leaning across to
open the door.

'Like a log,' she said, smiling. She hesitated, for the
passenger-seat was covered with sand and what looked like
dog hairs.

'Oh sorry, that's Caesar,' he said. 'Saul lets him sit up
front.' He reached behind into one of the baskets and took
out a linen napkin, which he arranged over the offending
upholstery. 'Sorry,' he said again, keeping his hand on the
napkin as she sat down.

'No one's up yet,' said Laura, glancing up at the rows
of ornate Moorish-style balconies. 'I half expected Mamma to
be here, I think she's feeling a bit left out.'

'Clemmie wanted it only to be the young people,' said
Bobby, slipping the car into gear and turning back towards the
sea.

'Of course,' said Laura, so that it shouldn't seem like

she was being critical. 'Lucky me, being taken for a young person!'

'Oh, but you're the star guest.' He turned to smile at her. 'Everyone's so excited you're coming.'

Despite the earliness of the hour, the sun was warm on their faces, and Laura looked about herself contentedly, her hand trailing out of the open window. To their right the waters of the bay shone flat and calm, a single sailing-boat drifting on the horizon. 'It's snowing in Manchester,' she said, searching in her bag for her sunglasses. 'I spoke to Leonard before I left, he feels simply awful that he isn't here.' She glanced over, curious as to how Bobby felt about his brother's absence. He was scratching his neck and she reached across to catch his hand. 'I had to promise I'd take lots of photographs, you must remind me. Oh, do turn here! I love the French gardens!'

Bobby turned, slowing to allow a group of elegantly dressed women to cross the road, parasols bobbing above their heads like outsized hats. Just ahead of them was the old Hotel Majestic, with its two round cupolas, and on their left, a church and synagogue side by side.

'I go there sometimes,' said Bobby, pointing to the church, 'if the synagogue is particularly full. Do you think it matters?'

'You go to church?'

'Not for services, just to pray. I like that it's quieter.'

Laura gazed at the church. 'I shouldn't think it matters at all,' she said after a while. 'Although perhaps don't mention it to Papa. Or Leonard, for that matter.'

'Oh, I wouldn't.'

They pulled onto the Rue des Soeurs, the buildings shabbier now, the windows mostly shuttered. Tramlines ran on either side. And overhead, cables buzzed and swayed in anticipation of the carriages that rattled back, and forth, their striped blinds lowered. Women all in black, their faces covered, kept pace with the car, some carrying small children or balancing baskets on their heads, while beneath dusty awnings, men played backgammon and drank tea. Laura no longer trailed her hand in the breeze, but kept it on her lap. 'Do you know where we are?' she asked.

'Of course I do. We're near the Cotton Exchange. Look, do you see?'

Laura saw. A thin greasy film of white lay on every surface, on the pavements, on parked cars, on the backs of men crouched in doorways. Isaac had often talked of this place, of the strange silence that the cotton commanded, offering to take her there so she could see for herself the humble origins of the city's wealth. She had not been interested, just as now, listening to Bobby chatter about the pressing machines and the size of the bales, and the *cri* the cotton made when all the air was squeezed out, she was not interested either. She took a silk square from her bag and wrapped it around her hair, then sank a little lower in her seat.

They crossed the canal and continued to follow the tramline, the road slowly rising as they left behind the city. It was here that Augustus had built the suburb of Necropolis, with its racecourse and amphitheatre, but there was little trace of such imperial pastimes now, in their place a goods-yard belonging to the Egyptian Railways and a series of carefully laid out municipal gardens. Laura closed her eyes and when she opened them again, the road had narrowed and they were alongside a string of goats, roped nose to tail, being led along by a boy not much older than Teddy. They were so close she might have run her hand along their coarse ridged backs, and she turned to Bobby, smiling.

'How sweet they are, they look like they've been cut out of folded paper!'

Bobby kept his eyes on the road. 'Not for much longer,' he said, and he nodded towards a building on their right, clearly the slaughter house. Vultures, hunched like old men, were lined up along the edge of the roof. Laura, who had been reaching for her camera, shuddered and looked away.

Here and there, the desert was beginning to encroach, in places the road almost hidden beneath drifts of gritty limestone. At Meks, its fashionable hotels closed for the winter season, they stopped to consult the map, and Bobby pointed towards the sea, to a small island just visible on the horizon.

'That's where Napoleon landed on his way to conquer the pyramids. Three hundred ships in one night, can you imagine?'

Laura shook her head. She couldn't.

'I've been reading about it.' He leaned across her knees to take something out of the glove-compartment. It was the guidebook Josie had given him as his leaving present. 'Five thousand men, it says here. It took all night for them to disembark. Listen to this: "*In him, as in Mark Antony, Alexandria nourished imperial dreams.*" Who does that make you think of?'

Laura shrugged. 'Who?'

'Il Duce of course!'

Laura thought about this. 'How political you are these days,' she said, smiling and turning back to the map.

The road led past limestone quarries, then swung sharply left, leaving the sea behind and running directly south. Lake Mariout spread out before them, a cool expanse of grey and blue, traversed at its narrowest point by an embankment, onto which Bobby now drove. To their right, the hulking warehouses of the Egyptian Salt and Soda Company. To their left, reeds and grasses and flat glimmering water. Seagulls whooped and dived, while in the shallows, egrets picked their way about like young girls afraid to get their skirts wet. Laura tightened the knot of her headscarf and watched as a speedboat appeared on the far side of the lake and raced towards them. Bobby watched too.

'It's probably Clemmie. A bunch of them came up last night. Is he waving, I can't tell.'

'Keep your eyes on the road. Why last night?'

'They were shooting duck. He asked me to go along, but Josie thought it a bad idea for me to be around guns the day before my wedding.' The very mention of Josie's name made him smile. 'I'm sure it's him, I recognise the hat.'

The boat came closer and drew alongside the causeway. Two men lounged in the centre seats, rifles slung between their outstretched legs, while behind them, a local in a galabiyah and tweed cap steered the boat. On the ledge below the mounted propeller was a mound of dead birds, their white breasts and glossy green-black necks gleaming in the sun.

'That's him,' shouted Bobby above the roar of the boat's engine. He waved, and the younger of the two men lifted his hat in reply, his blonde hair falling over his eyes and causing him to flick his head repeatedly. Laura smiled and tilted her sunglasses, then watched as the boat turned and skimmed away across the lake.

'The fellow with the moustache is a Grenadier. Captain Webster. His regiment swapped out last month but for some reason he seems to have stayed around. He and Clemmie are thick as thieves, they're always together.'

'They've obviously had a successful morning,' said Laura.

'Apparently Webster's a dead shot. Is it straight on from here?' They were reaching the end of the causeway, ahead of them dark strips of cultivated land dotted with the first of the wildflowers for which this area was renowned. Beyond this, the desert.

'I think you just follow the railway line, it's another six or seven miles by the look of it.' She folded the map and pushed it into the pocket of the door. 'I'm having such a nice time,' she said. 'I can't remember the last time I did something like this.' She thought of the children and how much they would have enjoyed it, and felt a sudden remorse for having left them in Brussels.

As if he had read her mind, Bobby said: 'I wish you'd brought everyone. I understand why you didn't, but I still should have liked them to see me married. They were there for Leonard's, after all.'

Strands of hair had escaped from Laura's scarf, and she turned her head, tucking them back into place. 'I know,' she said, 'but there was less chance of them catching dysentery at the Midland Hotel.' She smiled, for he looked suddenly downcast. 'I'm teasing, Bobby. I'll bring them soon, I promise. They need to catch up with their schoolwork first, that's all, the Italian system is awfully behind.'

'You promise?'

'I promise.'

They were on the outskirts of a village, above them a small mosque silhouetted against the sky. Bobby said something about the view from the hill, and the wonderful colour effects in the evening, and Laura opened the guidebook and read exactly the same phrase, word for word. 'You are funny,' she said. He shrugged and glanced behind them, for a train was approaching, causing a flurry of men in long white robes to gather alongside the tracks, their wares draped over their arms ready to thrust through open windows. 'Not far now,' said Laura, reaching for the map, but Bobby was already accelerating away, clouds of dust rising in their wake.

CHAPTER 21

They drove in silence, the landscape monotonous now. Bobby was scratching again, and so Laura took off her silk scarf and draped it around his neck, as the sun was hot and she knew how he tended to burn. She had been shocked when he met her at the station at how tired he was, how inflamed his skin looked, but when she mentioned it to her mother later, Estella said it was just Egypt. She said all Europeans suffered like that at first, and when Laura said 'I don't,' she said it was because Laura had her father's thick skin. Now, listening to him cough and tug at his collar, noticing the angry welts that spread from his hairline down inside his shirt, she felt she should say something but she feared making him feel worse. And so instead she talked about herself.

'I know you were all against it,' she said, her hair blowing around her face, 'but I can't tell you how happy we are in Brussels, everything has worked out perfectly. You will visit us, won't you? For as long as you like, I have plenty of room and Josette will adore Brussels. There's so much to see and the people are terribly sophisticated. It's silly, because it was always me who resisted moving back there. Isaac often spoke of our returning, and I never wanted to, I was settled in Milan. But now I couldn't imagine being anywhere else.' She glanced at him and he reached across and patted her leg with his big hand.

'I'm glad.'

'And Marco is so kind to me, he really is. He spoils us, always popping in on his way somewhere, taking the children to the cinema or me to lunch. I don't know what I'd do without him, it would be much harder, people are always so suspicious of a woman on her own.'

'Surely not, they must know your position?'

'Oh, you know how women are – I should probably be the same.'

Bobby wanted to tell her this was ridiculous, but he remembered what Josie had said the night before, about how beautiful his sister was, and how she had hardly dared speak to her. He had teased Josie for this, and said how flattered Laura would be when he told her, but rather than mention it now, he changed the subject.

'The king has a villa here, do you think that's it? Over there, with the high walls, it looks rather grand, doesn't it? Clemmie says it isn't, particularly – he's been to parties there – that it isn't a patch on those Rue Rolo houses, everything's covered in sand. Do you see, with all those trees around it – you wonder how anything grows here, don't you?'

Laura turned to look, but as she did a car appeared on the road behind, sounding its horn as it raced towards them. It passed them with just inches to spare, and Laura gasped and closed her eyes, but when she opened them again she saw Bobby was laughing.

'It's Clemmie. I can't believe he caught up so quickly! He drives like a madman. Violette despairs of him, she's terrified he'll have an accident.' He turned to Laura, his eyes wide. 'We should hurry up, they'll be waiting for us.'

When they arrived at the station, the car that had overtaken them was blocking the entrance, but Clemmie and his passenger were nowhere to be seen. Bobby parked in the shade of an eucalyptus tree on the other side of the street, and climbed out, stretching his long limbs indulgently. Several mules were tied to a railing nearby, and locals with bare feet and dusty galabiyahs were busy strapping baskets onto the animals' backs. In the distance, a low rumbling announced the arrival of the train they had seen earlier, and just as before, Bedouins in long white robes and keffiyehs began to appear at the edges of the tracks. One, a young boy with the beginnings of a moustache, carried a large jute bag, open at the top, and as he passed the car, he stopped and held it out to Laura. Inside were hundreds of tiny snakes, and she recoiled, horrified. The boy laughed, scooping up a handful and letting them slide through his fingers, then turned and sauntered towards the station.

'Did you see that?' said Laura.

'See what?' Bobby was lifting the baskets from the back seat of the car.

'The bag was full of snakes, little black ones.' She shuddered. 'I thought they were dates,' she added.

'It's the right season,' said Bobby, tightening the buckle on a basket. 'For dates anyway.' He looked up and grinned. 'I don't know about snakes.'

The train was pulling into the station, its doors swinging open and releasing a flood of shrieking passengers that converged upon the narrow platform in a single, heaving mass. Laura wondered which of them were her brother's friends, and she watched his face for any clues, but Bobby was still unloading and paid no attention. Soon, a small circle had formed around Clemmie's car, and she tugged at Bobby's arm.

'There's Clemmie,' she said, as he appeared on the steps. 'Come on, we don't want to be the last ones.'

'*Mes chers cousins*!' Clemmie threw up his arms as they crossed the street, his handsome face radiant with good health. 'I hope we didn't startle you back there. I can't resist an open stretch of road, and Webster here was rather encouraging me. You must think us terribly rude.' He ran down the steps and seized Laura's hand, kissing it and turning her towards the waiting group. 'Everyone say hello to Madame Balestra!'

'Please, just Laura.' She smiled at such formality. 'I'm so excited to meet Bobby's friends, I wouldn't have missed it for the world.' One by one, the group stepped forwards to be introduced. With the exception of Webster, they were all extremely young, the girls thin and fragile-looking, the boys strikingly similar to Clemmie. It occurred to her that she was easily the oldest, and she felt suddenly self-conscious, her hand rising to her brow, where in the last year faint lines had appeared. 'What a lovely idea, a picnic. It was so clever of you to think of it.'

'Well, Josie had her *enterrement de vie de jeune fille*, I thought we should do something similar for dear Bobby.' He had moved around the back of the car, and was directing one of the mule-drivers to empty the boot. 'Even if he's not so *jeune* any more!'

Bobby laughed, scratching at his chest and neck and gazing about himself with wonder. Laura saw a flicker of disdain cross Clemmie's face, but then his usual easy smile returned. 'Are we all here then? I'm starving, Webster and I have been up since four, haven't we, Webster?'

'Twenty brace and no breakfast,' said Webster, who was leaning on the bonnet of the car, smoking a cigarette. Laura smiled.

'I saw, the boat looked rather laden down. You're obviously good shots.'

'Webster says even the ducks in Egypt are lazy,' said Clemmie, 'that they fly lower here than they do elsewhere. Suits me, that's what I say!'

Everyone laughed, and one of the girls tucked her arm through Clemmie's, resting her pretty head on his shoulder. Clemmie patted her, as he might a dog he was fond of. 'Come on, let's be off.'

He led them along a narrow path beside the station, through the communal gardens with their neat lawns and carefully planted flowerbeds, and away from the town. Laura kept an eye out for the boy with the snakes, but to her relief he was nowhere to be seen. She glanced at Webster, walking silently beside her.

'I saw the strangest thing just now,' she said. 'A boy carrying a sack filled with tiny snakes. I thought he was a date seller, that was why I looked. Why would anyone be carrying around a sack of snakes?'

Webster looked at her, his eyes pink and strangely incurious. 'To frighten beautiful women,' he said, in the tone of a man for whom flirting is a necessary bore. 'Fellow in my regiment kept a scorpion for much the same reason.'

'How original,' said Laura, playing along. 'And did it work?'

Webster shrugged. 'It frightened me,' he said, and laughed noisily, so that everyone turned around. When they turned away again, his expression reverted to its previous blankness.

'You're in the Grenadiers, my brother tells me,' Laura said, when it was clear he was not going to continue. 'How do you find Egypt?'

He thought for a moment. 'Vile country.' He looked at Laura, clearly expecting a response, but when none came, he continued: 'Too much sun, no discipline, sand that gets into everything, government that would rather be allied to the Boches or the Eye-ties than they would to us. If it were up to me,' he paused, offering his arm to help her, for the path was uneven here, 'I'd leave them to it, see how they managed then.'

'Then I'm glad it isn't,' said Laura, smiling, 'up to you, I mean.' She let go of Webster's arm. 'Oh look, daffodils!' she said, pointing to where the land sloped towards the lake, everything glowing with a kind of iridescent yellow.

'I think they're narcissi,' said Bobby, who had read it in the guide book.

'Aren't they the same thing?' asked Laura, but nobody seemed to know.

Ahead of them, Clemmie was deliberating where to set up the picnic. A cluster of trees near the water was deemed the best option, and slowly they picked their way towards it, the mules following behind, their hooves leaving evenly spaced circles in the soft earth. Webster was now walking with several of the girls, and it seemed he was telling some kind of joke, because they were laughing and fanning back and forth around him. Laura slipped her arm through Bobby's.

'Do you actually know any of these people?'

'Some, I do. Why?'

'They're not what I expected, that's all. They're all so — young.' This had seemed a reasonable observation in her head, but now she had spoken it she felt foolish.

'Everyone's young in Alex,' said Bobby. He was scratching his neck again, and Laura caught at his hand, frowning.

'Whatever you do, don't scratch during the wedding, people will think you have some terrible disease. Scabies or ringworm or one of those other things you can never get rid of.' She smiled to show she didn't mean it as harshly as it sounded. 'Sorry, what were we saying?'

'You were hinting I needed some older friends.'

'Oh yes.' She smiled. 'You know what I meant! I meant friends of your own.'

She watched as the group ahead of them spread out, calling to one another and arguing that here, this precise spot, was where they should have their picnic. Clemmie, whose mind was set upon a stretch of shady bank between two weeping willows, ignored them, waving to the mule drivers to follow him, which they did. Gradually, the others drifted over too.

Laura turned to her brother. 'It's just that I've been thinking about it a lot recently. Thinking about friendship, that is.' She hesitated. It was mostly Marco's friendship she meant, but she spoke in more general terms. 'I don't think I really understood it before, I confused friendship with sociability. But it's not at all the same thing.' She sighed, for she wasn't being clear. 'You need someone you can count on, that's what I'm saying.'

Bobby had bent down to tie his shoelace, and much of this was addressed to the top of his head. When he stood up again, he gazed at her for a moment, then smiled his usual, good-natured smile.

'Did Papa tell you what he has given us as a wedding present? Josie doesn't know yet, she's going to be so thrilled.' He took off his hat and wafted his face with it, which was red and shiny. Laura shook her head, surprised by the sudden change of subject.

'No, what?'

'The beach hut, the one he owns with Saul. They must have come to an arrangement, since he said it's to be ours outright. Saul has had the use of it till now, so I suppose it's only fair.' He put his hat back on, lowering his head so that Laura could adjust it for him. 'It's at Stanley Bay, which isn't exactly where Josie would choose, but where the d'Araquys have theirs is by ballot, and you really need to know the right people.' He shrugged, at peace with the fact that he did not. He paused for a moment. 'I love that you worry about me. And I know I can count on you, no matter what. On all of you, Leonard, Mamma and Papa too.'

This was not what she had meant, but still she said, 'Of course you can.' She looked past him, towards the lake where Clemmie was overseeing the unpacking of the various picnic baskets, directing everything to be laid exactly where he stood, so that soon he was surrounded by such a display of riches that he might have been a young god receiving sacrifices.

They walked down the hill to join him.

CHAPTER 22

'**D**o you know what I love about Cousin Bobby?' Clemmie asked, lifting his glass and gazing thoughtfully at Laura. They were sitting a little apart from the group, Clemmie having drawn her away on the pretext of picking flowers for the mothers. Handfuls of tiny narcissi lay on the rug beside them, and Laura was dividing them into two bundles and tying them with ribbon from the cake boxes.

'No, tell me,' she said, maintaining the same frivolous tone with which they had conversed all afternoon.

'I love his innocence,' he said, taking the bunch she held out and holding them to his nose. 'Mummy says innocence is underrated these days, that people are so jaded. I'm awfully jaded, aren't you?'

Laura laughed, as such a combination of youth and affectation was amusing to her. She looked over to where Bobby was sitting, just able to make out a story he was telling about Horace and Virgil and ancient Mareotic wine. 'I hope you'll be kind to him. He's very fond of you.'

'Fond' was not a word Clemmie thought much of, and he said so. Laura laughed again.

'What would you prefer? Admiring? Respectful? Reverent?'

'Any of the above,' said Clemmie, winking and picking up the champagne bottle. He reached across to fill her glass but she shook her head.

'I think I shall be needed to drive,' she said, glancing again at Bobby. 'He doesn't usually drink,' she added.

'It was sweet of him to make me best man,' said Clemmie, 'I'm sure it was Mummy's idea. She worries about me feeling left out, which of course I never would.' He picked up a cushion, shook it, and arranged it beneath his head. 'I don't think I shall ever marry, I don't see the point. I mean, I look at people sometimes and I wonder, what good has being married done you? Take Webster for example.' He pointed at the officer, who had rolled up his trouser legs and was wading in the shallows of the lake, poking the rushes with a long stick. He was followed along the bank by several of the girls, who giggled and shouted encouragement. 'He has a wife and two brats back in England, you know.'

A loud cheer went up as a bird, wings beating furiously, rose out of the reeds. Webster, gripping the stick like a rifle, mimicked shooting it, his whole body jolting violently as though from the ricochet. He grinned, then turned back and continued poking the rushes.

'That's how he gets so much leave,' continued Clemmie. 'Guardsmen with families get Christmas off.'

'Christmas that he's spending here.'

Clemmie shrugged, murmuring, 'As I say,' and closing his eyes.

Laura finished tying a bow on the second bunch of flowers, tugging at the two loops so that they were exactly equal and then laying them down on the rug next to her. This seemed an odd conversation to be having on the day before a wedding, and she said so, brushing specks of pollen from her front and making to stand up.

Clemmie, his eyes still closed, agreed that perhaps it was.

Laura moved away to join the others. She was tired and beginning to get a headache, and crouching down next to Bobby, she suggested they start to head back. 'Tomorrow is a big day,' she reminded him. 'You want to be feeling your best.

Besides, I think we ought to spend some time with Mamma, the others will have left by now.'

'Papa's there,' said Bobby, who was enjoying himself. One of the girls had made him a necklace of pink daisies, and now he took it off and draped it over Laura's hair. 'That's better. You look more festive now.'

Laura smiled and removed the daisy chain, laying it on the rug. 'Besides, I promised Josie I wouldn't let you overdo it. I can drive, if you don't feel like it.'

'Did you know,' said Bobby, leaning forwards and pointing towards the lake, 'that in the Middle Ages, all this was land? There were over one hundred and fifty villages here, just think about it. Fields of barley, vineyards, even orchards, it was like Kent only with more sand.' This was the third or fourth time he had made this observation, but it seemed no less pertinent for the repetition. 'No wonder they hate us. It's like someone flooded —' he tried to think of an appropriate comparison. '— it's like somebody flooded Romney Marsh!'

'No wonder *who* hates us?'

'The Egyptians. They say they don't but it's not true. You have to live here to really understand. September was terrible, all anyone talked about was Article Seven and you could see they were furious.'

'It was the same everywhere. You mustn't worry about it. Do you have your hat? Let me get it for you.'

'Of course I don't blame them for hating us, we cut through the dunes.' He shook his head, gazing towards the horizon as though the crime were happening now. 'Imagine, all this was once land.'

Laura found his hat and passed it to him, and then began to line up the empty bottles of champagne scattered around them. 'It was a long time ago,' she said, turning around as Webster, holding his shoes, wandered up behind her.

'We're heading back, my brother has a big day tomorrow. Will you make sure they clear all this up? All this rubbish must be taken back on the mules, will you make sure of that?'

'Actually,' said Webster, rubbing his face with his free hand, 'if you're going now, I wouldn't mind coming with you. Need to be back in Alex for something, it would help me a lot.'

'Fine with me,' she said, looking past him as she gathered up Bobby's belongings. 'But I'm leaving now, you need to be ready to go immediately.'

'I'm ready,' he said, grinning and making a mock salute. He gazed at Bobby. 'Want some help getting him up?'

'He's perfectly fine.' She held out her hand to her brother, who was scratching at his neck, chest, torso. 'Captain Webster needs to get back to Alex too,' she said. 'Do you mind if we give him a ride?'

Bobby turned to look at the other man. 'Of course not! In fact, perhaps you know — I've been trying to remember the name of the fellow who cut through the dunes. I can only remember Abercrombie, but it wasn't Abercrombie.'

'Hutchinson,' said Webster. 'Here, let me.'

'Hutchinson,' repeated Bobby, 'of course it was. How could I forget Hutchinson?'

'The French certainly haven't,' grinned Webster. 'Here we go.' He reached past Laura and took Bobby by the elbows, hauling him upright, holding on to him while he swayed slightly. 'Should have been a Grenadier, a big, tall chap like you. You got everything? Righty-ho, let's be off.'

Going back, the ground was softer than it had been earlier, and several times Bobby stumbled or sunk his foot into some mud, so that they ended up walking on either side of him. He was fascinated by everything, wanting to stop and look at the vetch growing in a crevasse, to smell the wild garlic, to take a photograph of the view back towards the lake, so that later he could work out where those villages were. Each time they persuaded him to keep moving, only once relenting and allowing him to sit down on a ledge above the quarry, where spiky red flowers grew directly out of the rock face and Africa seemed its most unforgiving, miraculous self.

At the station, the men selling rugs had gone and they crossed the street and climbed into the car. Laura insisted upon driving and there was a brief wait as she adjusted the seat and the mirrors and then the seat again, before at last pulling carefully out onto the road. Bobby, settled happily in the back, promptly fell asleep.

'Thank goodness I came,' said Laura after a while, 'who knows how long that lot will keep going. Poor Bobby would have turned up to his wedding in the most terrible state.'

'If he'd turned up at all,' said Webster, who could never resist an opportunity to sow discord. She glanced at him, and he gestured straight ahead. 'You can speed up here if you like, it's pretty much a straight road all the way.'

'Thank you, but I've seen how you and my cousin drive.'

'Fair enough.' He tugged at his trouser legs, the cuffs of which were still damp. 'He's a lucky man. Perhaps if I'd had a sister like you, I wouldn't be here now.' He was doing his best to charm her, but Laura was in no mood to play along.

'You would be home with your wife instead?'

Webster smiled, turning to look at her with narrowed eyes. 'More likely I wouldn't have a wife.'

'Oh really?'

'I'd have been bundled into the back of a car and whisked away to safety, just like dear Bobby here. Think what my life might have been.'

'You seem to enjoy yourself well enough.' She shifted gears. 'Besides, there isn't the slightest similarity between you and my brother. He adores Josette, the last thing in the world he would want to do is let her down.' Unwittingly she had speeded up, the tyres bouncing over the uneven surface of the desert road, the springs in the back seat groaning beneath Bobby's weight. She glanced in surprise at the speedometer, then immediately lifted her foot so that the car slowed and the wind that had been whipping at her hair became a breeze again.

'Shame, I was enjoying that,' said Webster.

She ignored him, slowing yet more, as ahead of them were the beginnings of a village, with the usual low built huts and stools set by the side of the road, where men would sit smoking or watching the horizon for the train. But now the stools were empty, and there was only a group of children playing in the shadow of an old mango tree, the ground stained black where fruits had fallen and been left to rot. The children had their backs to the road and were shouting and playing with something Laura could not see, and the scene so charmed her that she turned to Webster and smiled.

As she did, however, something darted in front of the car. She neither saw it nor felt it, but later she would remember a loud pop like the sound of a balloon being burst. She slammed her foot on the brake and the car skidded across the narrow road and came to a stop in a haze of yellow dust. The children were now on the other side of the road, and for a moment she wondered how they could have got there, but then she realised that the car had spun around. Webster's arm had shot out to stop her falling forwards and she gently pushed it away, turning around to make sure Bobby was not hurt. His eyes were open and he grinned at her, bemused.

'I was having the strangest dream,' he began, but Laura turned away, not listening. She was looking at the children, who were no longer playing but staring blankly at the car.

'Wait here,' said Webster, climbing out. Laura's foot was still pressed to floor, and she released it, then tugged with both hands on the handbrake. She watched as Webster walked around the front of the car and stood looking at something, his head tipped to one side. He glanced at her through the windscreen. 'I think we must have hit a dog.'

'A dog?' She felt suddenly faint, and she leaned forwards, her head resting on the steering wheel. She heard Webster call to the children, and then the word *kalb* repeated excitedly, over and over. After a moment, he got back into the car.

'Obviously some stray dog they were tormenting. It's run off. Do you want me to drive?' She had opened the door and was climbing out, walking around the front of the car to where Webster had been standing. 'Come on, get in, it's never a good idea to hang around these places,' he added, sliding across into the driving seat, feeling in his pocket for his cigarettes. 'Damn it, they're wet, how the hell did that happen?' He held up the packet. 'Y'don't smoke, do you?'

'Where could it go?' She bent down, touching at something dark and sticky on the headlight. She held up her hand, her fingertips traced coppery red. 'If it's injured, we should find it.' Through the grimy windscreen she saw Webster's expression register distaste.

'For Pete's sake, wipe your hands,' he groaned, 'you don't know what it's got.' He looked around for something to give her, but she was already bending down, rubbing her fingers on the sandy road. In the back of the car, Bobby started snoring. 'Christ Almighty,' he said, hurling the packet of wet cigarettes onto the roadside and then climbing out of the car.

Laura was still bent down, but she was looking towards the children. 'How do you say "where?"' she asked him, without turning around.

Webster looked at the group of children. They were transfixed by the sight of this elegant European woman crouched in the middle of the road, their dark eyes unblinking. It was that same watchfulness you saw with all these people, and he felt a surge of irritation. '*Ayna?*' he shouted, marching towards them, '*Ayna kalb?*'

There was a flurry of discussion between the children, then one of the boys pointed a stick towards a low building on the other side of the road. Webster stared for a moment, and then turned and walked back towards Laura.

'He says it went behind there.' He took hold of her elbow and helped her to her feet. 'Get in the car and don't move, the slightest bit of trouble, lean on the horn. And cover yourself up too.' He took off his jacket and handed it to her, waiting as she put it on then walking around the back of the car to the boot. When he re-emerged he was carrying a rifle, and he moved with a new deliberateness, as people do when they feel themselves to be more powerful. He gestured to the boy with the stick to come with him, and Laura watched as the boy nodded and ran across the road, pointing at something on the dry earth then darting ahead. Webster followed after, the rifle swinging at his side.

'We've stopped again.'

Laura turned around and saw Bobby looking about himself, his eyes bleary with sleep.

'I know, we'll be off in a moment. You were out cold, do you feel better?' She smiled, glancing towards the building where Webster and the boy had disappeared. 'Go back to sleep, I'll wake you when we get to Alex. You're staying with us at the Cecil tonight, aren't you?'

He said he was.

'Good. Mamma thought we could all have a quiet dinner up in the room, just family. Would you like that? I'm sure you'll not be wanting a late night—'

There was the sudden, unmistakeable sound of two gunshots, one after the other. Laura turned to see Webster striding around the side of the low building, a look of grim resolution on his face. Forgetting what he had said, she flung open the door of the car and ran towards him.

'It's fine,' he said, 'get back in the car.' He spoke harshly, walking past her.

'But I heard shooting?' She hesitated, looking past him to where the young boy with the stick had just emerged. 'What happened?'

People were beginning to appear out of houses further along the road, looking about nervously, calling to one another.

'Get back in the car,' repeated Webster, climbing into the driving seat, his rifle beside him. 'All right, old chap?' he added, nodding towards Bobby. Laura lingered where she was, her hands pressing nervously at her hair, and then slowly, stiffly, she walked around to the passenger side. Before she had even closed the door, Webster thrust the car into gear and sped away.

'You shot it?'

'What else was I going to do? She was injured.'

'She? It was a female?'

He nodded, his eyes hardening at the memory of the dog's swollen belly, the teats hanging full and pink.

'We should at least have buried it,' said Laura. She remembered the vultures they had seen that morning at the slaughterhouse, and now she looked up, searching the sky for the distinctive black-edged wings. Nothing. She turned back to Webster. 'We should at least have buried it,' she repeated. 'We should go back. It was my fault, I hit it.'

'Hit what?' It was Bobby, leaning forward, his head thrust between the seats and looking from one to the other.

'A dog. It ran across the road and I hit it. I wasn't even driving fast. I don't know how it happened.' She turned

344

back to Webster, frantically twisting her rings. 'Did you really have to shoot it? Couldn't we have taken it to a veterinary clinic? I'd have paid.'

'And where would you have found a veterinary clinic?' asked Webster. 'Better to just put it out of its misery.'

Laura shook her head, glancing at her brother and trying to keep her voice steady. 'Then the very least we should have done was bury it. I don't see why we had to drive off like that.'

'Don't you?' Webster looked at her grimly. 'Have you never heard of Denshawai? I shot the dog because it was the kindest thing to do, but I wasn't going to wait around to discuss it. These people are unpredictable.' He gestured towards Bobby, who had sat back again. 'He's getting married tomorrow. Last thing he needs is to be accused of taking potshots at the fellahin. They could have done that, you know. That boy could have said I fired at him and hit the dog instead, they'd be rioting from here to the other side of Christmas. I drove off because I didn't fancy being held responsible for the next uprising.' He paused and rubbed his forehead. 'There's a Mustafa Kamal in every one of these villages, believe me.'

Denshawai, Kamal — the words were sufficiently familiar to stop Laura arguing further, and instead she opened her bag and took out a bottle of scent, tipping it onto a handkerchief and using it to clean her hands. Then she tidied her hair, checking it in the mirror, and added a fresh coat of lipstick. After a while Captain Webster glanced at her.

'Feeling better?'

She nodded. 'It was the thought of the vultures —' she said quietly.

'Did you know,' said Bobby, leaning forwards again, 'That in Ancient Egypt, a vulture was the hieroglyph for mother.'

'I didn't know that,' said Webster.

'I didn't either,' said Laura. She glanced at Bobby, who nodded amiably, then turned back to Webster. 'I'm sorry if I was rude. I got myself rather worked up, I don't usually speak to strangers like that.'

'Don't give it another thought.' He turned to her and grinned. 'Anyway, now we're not strangers.'

'No, we're not.' She pulled his jacket a little tighter around her for she was chilly. She closed her eyes, trying not to think of anything — not the picnic, the dog, her brother in the back of the car, Captain Webster — and kept them closed until they were in front of the Cecil, and the same doorman from this morning was hurrying down the steps to greet them.

'Back safe and sound,' said Webster, leaning across her to open the door.

She thanked him, giving him back his jacket and climbing out. 'Wave to Mamma,' she said to Bobby, pointing above them to where Estella sat watching from the balcony, her distinctive black parasol wedged in place. Bobby waved.

'Well then,' said Captain Webster, his gun now safely stowed inside his bag, his trousers unrolled, 'if I can't be of any further service, I'll be off.' There were specks of dried blood on his shirt and he brushed at them with his hand then buttoned his jacket. 'Good luck tomorrow, old chap. Still time to change your mind, of course.'

'Come on,' said Laura, taking her brother's arm, 'we'd better go up, I simply must take a bath before dinner. Thank you again, Captain Webster. It was a pleasure meeting you — if we don't meet again before I leave, please know how grateful I am for your help today, I don't know what I should have done.' This was mere politeness. She had already decided that if Webster hadn't been there to distract her, she wouldn't have hit the dog in the first place.

'I need to take Saul his car,' said Bobby, looking around helplessly.

'I'll sort all that out, let's just get you upstairs.' She walked ahead of him into the lobby, with its palms and mirrors and tables arranged for intimate conversations. 'What a sight we must both look,' she said, although a glimpse at her reflection suggested no such thing. 'Do you think Mamma has been sitting there all day? You go ahead, I'll have a word at the desk, I'll get someone to wash it and drive it round this evening.'

'How you look after me,' said Bobby, smiling his big, gentle smile. He was still sleepy, and he swayed a little, standing there in a sea of marble and gilt. 'I'm a lucky man.'

'Even luckier tomorrow,' she said. 'Go on, I'll follow you up. I want to put a call in to the children.'

'Will you give them my love, tell them that if it were up to me, they would be here?' He was walking backwards towards the lift, his hand raised behind him like a sleepwalker searching for the walls of a room.

'I'll tell them. What is it?' He had stopped, halfway inside the lift, and was staring intently at her. 'Is something wrong?'

'Nothing. It's just I had such a wonderful time today. I'm so happy you came, you'll reassure Mamma won't you? She worries that I won't fit in, you'll tell her what a success it was today?'

'Of course I will.'

'And you enjoyed yourself?' She nodded. 'I think you made quite an impression on Captain Webster. No, really, I've never seen him so solicitous, he was definitely taken with you.'

Laura rolled her eyes. 'Go,' she said.

THE NEXT DAY, BOBBY and Josette were married.

III

PART THREE

CHAPTER 1

Miriam Cansino, wanting to do her bit to help, had been spending all her time at the house on Palatine Road. A telegram had arrived in May confirming the Ardittis' visas, and Leonard immediately called up the landlord to collect the keys. He was afraid the house would be damp after a winter left empty and wanted to open a few windows, set a fire in the grate. But when he and Miriam went round, they found the garden overgrown with weeds, walls yellow with mildew, a dead pigeon on the upstairs landing. Remembering that the house was to have been for Laura, Leonard began to rail against the owner, slamming doors and insisting they must find somewhere else. But Miriam, settling the baby in his pram, said that all it wanted was a good clean. Straight away she set about scrubbing surfaces and sweeping floors, washing windows and beating carpets. Leonard was sent off to borrow a lawnmower, then, upon his return, sent off again for a ladder and toys to entertain the baby. Her hair pulled back from her face, an old tea towel protecting her dress, Miriam glowed with activity, and it was all Leonard could do to make her leave that evening.

The next morning she was back, and the morning after that, bringing with her bits and pieces from Moorfield

Road to make it look more homely. For those few short weeks, she imagined the house was hers; she found herself hoping that, just as Laura had changed her mind, so might this family, but when she told Leonard he laughed and said she didn't know Lucia Arditti.

'Well nor do you, really.' They were standing outside the station, waiting for Leonard's train. In the bottom of the pram were freshly ironed pillowcases and a cake, for the Ardittis were arriving that afternoon.

'Don't be cross. I just meant I doubt Lucia will give up the house, I've never seen someone so determined.' He put his hand on Miriam's, squeezing it. 'We'll still be in and out of there, though. They'll be relying on us to show them around, to introduce them to people.'

'Well, if I have time.'

She glanced at him, and again he squeezed her fingers. 'That's my girl.'

'I wasn't saying I didn't want them to come. Just that it's been nice having somewhere of our own to go.' He nodded and said it had, and she brightened. 'Go on, you'd better run or you'll miss your train. I'll meet you at the house later. I thought I'd lay out tea in the garden, in Switzerland they must eat their meals outside all the time.'

'They won't know they've even left,' grinned Leonard. He waved to some acquaintances as they strode past, then turned back to Miriam. 'We'll have a place of our own soon, I promise. Now Bobby is settled, Papa thinks business is sure to pick up. And when it does, we'll find another Palatine Road, and we'll have tea in the garden every day if you like. Just the three of us. How does that sound?'

Miriam smiled. Now that she knew he felt the same way she had no need of further assurances. She pushed aside the baby's frilly sunshade so that Leonard could kiss his cheek. He was enormous now, wedged upright against a pile of pillows, and as Leonard approached he began to wail. Quickly Miriam put her finger in his mouth. 'It's his teeth,' she said.

Leonard tilted his hat. 'If you say so.' The baby was always crying when he came too close. 'I'll see you this afternoon. Stay out of trouble, the pair of you.'

He hurried away into the station, turning to wave as he disappeared through the gate. Miriam watched him go, feeling a surge of emotion such as only Leonard inspired in her. It was a mixture of contradictory impulses, of fierce love and of more measured admiration; of vulnerability and of protectiveness; of reverence and, though she hesitated to admit it, of pity too. She took her finger from the baby's mouth, rocking the pram and thinking about this last. It was the one part of her marriage for which she had been unprepared. In the early days, when they were getting to know one another, she had felt only awe for this man, so much better educated than herself, so clear about matters of conscience and how one should behave in the world. Then one day he had told her about a time in his youth when he had been sent to a sanatorium, and about a friend there who had died. When he spoke of this his eyes filled with tears, and she had been surprised, for the men in her family never cried; indeed, emotion provoked a kind of fury in her father, such as on her wedding day, when he had snapped and complained at everyone. And so when Leonard began to weep she had smiled and pretended not to see, and later he had said how good she was for him, how he had a tendency to brood. After that they had never spoken of it again, but recently — and perhaps it was because she was a mother now — she found herself returning to it, wondering what it must be like to be a little boy alone and have a friend die. So that in quiet moments like this, watching from a distance, it wasn't Leonard the man she saw, but Leonard the little boy, and her heart ached.

'Poor Daddy,' she murmured, rearranging the sunshade, fussing with the baby's hat. Then she turned the pram and crouched down, repeating 'choo choo' and pointing, until the train was out of sight.

◆　　◆　　◆　　◆　　◆

MIRIAM WAS UPSTAIRS WHEN the taxi arrived, and she watched from the window as the doors opened and a family climbed out. Leonard strode towards them, his arms outstretched, and, though the window was closed, she heard cries of greeting. In particular she heard those of a tall woman in a lambskin coat, much too warm for the season, who stopped at the gate and gazed up, a look of rapture on her tired, thin face.

'Home,' she heard the woman say. 'Now we are home.'

Miriam stepped away from the window and moved towards the landing, savouring these last few moments before the house must be given up. At the top of the stairs she listened again, the baby perched silently on her arm like a large owl, and she heard Leonard explaining about the heating system, which they wouldn't need just yet but which was worth getting the hang of. He pointed out the light that wasn't working, and the door handle the landlord had promised to replace, and then, less apologetically, the tulips that Miriam had picked that morning as tight buds but which were now papery and full. Still the only voice she heard reply was Lucia's, and when she peered over the banister she saw that the rest of the family must have remained outside, for the hall was empty and the front door wide open.

'Miriam!' Leonard was calling for her, first from the kitchen, then the garden, then the kitchen again. The baby danced on her arm, kicking her with his soft feet and throwing himself backwards, so that she was obliged to hold him with her other hand too. 'Ah, there you are!' Leonard was back in the hall again, peering up at her from the stairwell. 'I knew she was here somewhere. Miriam, come and meet Mrs Arditti.'

There was a shriek from Lucia, followed by a long tirade in Italian. 'All right, come and meet Lucia! Oh dear, how quickly you do away with our English formalities! Do hurry, Miriam. She loves everything, she wants to thank you.' He paused, waiting for her to respond, then added, 'I'll start making the tea,' because he knew that would hurry her up.

When she reached the hall, she saw a girl of about fifteen standing on the front step, her head tilted to one side and her gaze fixed on a spot above Miriam's left shoulder. It was Netta, grown taller and less childlike since Milan, and now wearing spectacles too.

'Hello,' said Miriam.

'Hello.' Netta's eyes momentarily rested on Miriam and then snapped back to their previous position. She was trying to make the upper edge of her glasses line up with the door lintel.

'We met at the Duomo, do you remember? You were a bluebird.' The girl's reluctance was comforting, as though she were mirroring Miriam's own.

The girl nodded, but remained where she was in the doorway.

Three small boys appeared behind Netta, nudging around her and then running, full tilt, past Miriam and out into the back garden. Seconds later came Luca, grimly polite, then Raphael, who shook Miriam's hand and then wandered off after his sons. In the garden, Leonard was talking about the swing the landlord had agreed to.

'Ah! There you are!' Lucia came back into the hall, beaming and looking from one to the other, so that it was unclear who she meant. (She meant Miriam.) 'I'm so happy at last to meet you, I hear so much about you. *Cara*,' she turned to Netta, 'you still have my bag? Do not lose it, it has everything we own.'

'Si, *mammina*,' said Netta, holding up a bulging leather purse.

'In English, *cara*! From now on we speak only English!' Lucia thrust her head into the vase of tulips, inhaling extravagantly. '*Bellisima*!'

'Yes, *mammina*.'

'And this is the darling baby.' Lucia, speckles of pollen decorating her nose and forehead, looked exultantly at Miriam. She held out her arms, ignoring the baby's protests as she took him from his mother and then turned and sailed back down the hall, waving to them to follow. 'I love babies!' she announced over her shoulder.

◆   ◆   ◆   ◆   ◆

WHEN MIRIAM JOINED THEM in the garden, they were discussing the occupation of Prague. Lucia had laid her coat on the grass and was sitting on it with the baby, while Leonard poured cups of tea and handed round the cake. Raphael Arditti, excusing himself, took his into the house, and after a while Luca followed him, and through the open windows Miriam watched their listless progress from floor to floor, at each landing stopping and gazing out at the group in the garden. The younger boys sat down next to their mother and Netta, having refused tea, continued to tilt her head and stare, this time at a length of guttering over the back door.

'And rather than resist,' said Leonard, referring to the Czech president, 'he fainted clean away. Lost consciousness and had to be revived by the Fuhrer's doctor!' He glanced at his wife, for she had heard him say this many times. 'You couldn't make it up.'

'You couldn't make it up,' echoed Lucia. She was holding one of the baby's feet, flexing it back and forth as she spoke. Since their arrival at Victoria that morning, the terror she had been feeling over the last ten months had simply evaporated, replaced by a kind of euphoria. She looked around joyfully, taking in the table laid for tea, the neatly trimmed grass, the climbing rose which began on the other side of the fence and spread to cover the back wall. Bees hovered around the open flowers, slipping one at a time inside the wide petals then launching themselves skywards, their legs dangling beneath them like the yellow gourds children wore when swimming. 'It is like a dream.'

'Nightmare, more like,' said Leonard, his mind still on Prague. He picked up his teacup and lowered himself into one of the deckchairs Miriam had found in the shed. The canvas had stretched, tipping him backwards, so that now all Lucia saw of him were his knees, black and shiny in his work suit. 'And Chamberlain hardly distinguished himself either, not at first anyway. He changed his tune when he saw how unpopular it was. What was the word he used?' He leaned forward to peer at Miriam.

'*Disintegrated*!' said Lucia, for it had been all anyone talked about. 'Oh the fuss it caused. My father-in-law drove all the way to Lake Como, just to show me the newspapers.' She smiled. 'He thought I would change my mind. I said to him, did you not see the guns along the Maloja road? Hundreds of guns, all aiming at the Italian border. This is when you know it's time to get out of Europe.' There was a gleefulness to her words, and the youngest boys, sensing this, grinned and began to shove each other. '*Basta, basta*, you will squash the baby.' She winked at Miriam to show she was only joking, then glanced again at her daughter. 'Come, *cara*, sit,' then, 'Netta loves babies too.'

'Si, *Mammina*,' murmured Netta.

Lucia nodded contentedly, closing her eyes and feeling the sun, warm upon her eyelids. Once again she had the sense of being in a dream, and she gave herself up to it, her thoughts loose and without direction, her jaw slack. Nobody spoke, and even the little boys were silent, lying on their stomachs on the edges of Lucia's coat, picking daisies and bits of grass and giving them to the baby. The bees still thrummed on the roses, the baby gurgled and cooed, the deckchair squeaked as Leonard crossed his legs one way and then the other. Inside the house, father and son continued to wander from room to room, their thin-soled shoes resonating dully on the painted boards and cheap rugs. A magpie dropped noiselessly into the longer grass at the end of the garden, its black and white head bobbing above the waving green, and Miriam watched it, murmuring 'Morning Mr Magpie' beneath her breath. Lucia opened her eyes and gazed about herself with such wonder, so like a little girl, that Leonard, setting down his cup, began to laugh.

'It does me good just to look at you,' he said. 'You're going to be happy in this house, I know it. And don't be surprised if the neighbours walk right in and introduce themselves. People here are friendly. And you'll come to our synagogue, if you don't mind a bit of a walk to get there. I want our families to spend time together. We must really get to know one another, don't you think?'

'Oh yes, of course,' said Lucia. 'But what a day this is, England is a glorious country!' She looked about herself triumphantly, her gaze once again falling upon her daughter. Netta was staring skywards, so that her eyes seemed to roll back in her head. 'Netta, stop that, you look *squilibrata*!'

'*Sta cercando Dio.*' This from the youngest of the three boys. His mother turned to him.

'What d'you mean, "looking for God"?'

Netta's eyes rolled higher. The eaves of the roof were

at a particularly pleasing angle, and from this distance exactly the same thickness as the rim of her spectacles.

'The nuns say God is all around,' continued the boy, enjoying having his mother's attention. Lucia sighed, for in her haste to remove the children from Italy, there had been certain compromises. A thought occurred to her.

'Which God?' She glanced at Leonard, who smiled and affected indifference. 'Which God you are looking for, Netta?'

With weary resignation, Netta lowered her gaze and turned towards her mother. She blinked, her eyes enormous behind the thick glass. It was one thing teasing her brothers, quite another to attempt it with her mother, for Lucia had a way of looking at her that made Netta feel quite transparent. She sighed, and began to explain about the horizontals, but just then Miriam squealed and lunged towards the baby. A fat purple earthworm was dangling from his clammy fist and he was gazing at it in delight, trying to bring it to his mouth. Gods of all denominations were forgotten in the rush to take it from him and later, when the baby had stopped screaming and the adults were pretending to laugh, the conversation had moved on.

'And your sister, Madame Balestra, will she come?' asked Lucia, smoothing the coat so that it lay flat. 'I hope she doesn't mind that we're stealing her house, I feel even more guilty now I see what a nice house it is.' She smiled at Miriam, who had put the baby in his pram and was pushing him around the lawn. 'She mustn't leave it too long. There was a woman from Zagreb on the train, she said the hotels are full of Czechoslovakian refugees, all of them desperate to get to London. It will be the Polish next. She must hurry.'

Leonard had written to Laura that morning saying much the same thing, but to Lucia Arditti he said, 'Oh, I don't know, I'm not sure it's as urgent as all that. It's only if there's to be a war that Laura will come, and that's not likely.'

'Not likely?' repeated Lucia, with surprising fervour. '*Dice chi?*'

From the lawn Miriam shot a glance at Leonard, for she knew how defensive he got on the subject of Laura and the children. He rolled his shoulders once or twice, like a boxer about to throw a punch, but when he spoke it was with his usual, even tone. 'There's a chap at the depot who works for one of the Beaverbrook papers, I forget which one – did I say the Express, Miriam?' She nodded and said she thought so. 'Anyway, according to him no one expects war for at least two years, and even then it's not certain.' He brushed cake-crumbs from the front of his shirt, gave his tie a shake. 'What is it they say? *C'est pas magnifique,*' he paused to pop one of the larger crumbs into his mouth, '*mais ce n'est pas la guerre.*'

'Nonsense.' Lucia stood up, bending to pick up her teacup and carrying it to the table, where she set it down with a clatter. As an afterthought she straightened the cup so that the tiny gold flowers on the rim matched up with those on the saucer. 'Besides, I am not talking about war, I'm talking about persecution.' She glanced towards the door, where Raphael had at that moment reappeared.

'I'm looking for Luca,' he murmured.

'*Persecuzione!*' said his wife, holding out her hand for his cup. She turned back to Leonard. 'Have we learnt nothing from history? From the Crusades, from the massacres at Granada or Fez or Strasbourg? Better one day as a lion, Il Duce says, but he doesn't mean us when he says this, we Jews are not lions. We Jews are sheep for them, herded from country to country across Europe.' She spoke matter-of-factly, collecting up the other tea things and stacking them on the table. 'But if to be a sheep means to survive, then for me I am glad.' And she began carrying everything inside.

Leonard watched her go, unsure how to respond. After a while he turned to Raphael. 'What do you think?' he asked. 'Not too bad, is it?'

He meant the house. He even gestured to the house as he said it, but Raphael Arditti was like a man woken from a deep sleep, for whom everything is confusion. He stared at Leonard blankly.

'You remember Daniel Sutton?' said Lucia, coming back onto the terrace. She was buttoning up her cardigan, her chin pressed to her chest. 'The boy who stayed with us last year?'

'Oh, he was lovely,' said Miriam, now standing next to Leonard. 'We liked Daniel.'

Lucia fixed the last button and looked up. 'I received a letter from his mother. He's joined the army.'

Miriam gasped and instinctively glanced towards the pram, as though the army might be about to take her son too. Lucia smiled, her mind wandering briefly as an image of herself as a new mother flickered before her eyes. Lucia was someone for whom envy was quite impossible, who in looking at a younger woman saw only the potential for shared experience, for friendship. She saw this now in Miriam. 'His poor mother, she's distraught. She begged him not to — but you know how these young boys are.' She glanced at Raphael. 'Remember Luca when he wanted to join the International Brigades? *Grazie a Dio* that's all finished.'

Raphael nodded wearily. The last few months had taken their toll on him, and now everything he said and did seemed slow and mechanical, like a clockwork toy whose spring has almost unwound.

'And now Daniel, he's in some training camp! Gas Attack I think it is, I have the letter here somewhere. Sounds *horribile*, no, 'Gas Attack'?'

They agreed it did, although Leonard said he was sure it was only Defensive.

'In any case, I have written to say they must come over as soon as he's back. You too, all our rescuers together. What do you say, will you come? I throw wonderful parties, in Milan I'm famous for them.'

'We'll come with pleasure,' said Leonard, 'though I think calling us rescuers is a bit strong.'

'You are our rescuers,' repeated Lucia, holding up a hand to show she would accept no alternative.

At the sound of the gate, they turned to see Luca bounding around the side of the house towards them. He was carrying a cardboard box, out of which something was seeping, leaving a trail of spots on his trousers legs and on the paving stones too. '*Gelato di marroni*!' he declared, holding up the box. 'There is a *ragazzo* who sells it on the next street. He gives it to me for free. For free! Can you believe this? He says to tell you all *benvenuto*!'

'*Benvenuto*? Really?' said Lucia, looking around with sparkling eyes. Her gaze lingered on Raphael. 'Did I not tell you?' her expression said.

'Was it a Pesagno van?' asked Leonard, who liked to keep a track of these things.

'Maybe.' Luca thrust the box at his mother, who held it above her head to see where the drip was coming from.

'I think it must have been Pesagno. Short chap, rather thick in the chest?' Leonard puffed out his own chest in imitation, but Luca had already turned around and was heading back up the path.

'I see what else I can find,' he grinned.

The gate banged behind him. Lucia set down the box on the table.

'I will write to your sister myself and tell her to come,' she said, looking at Leonard and licking the ice cream from her fingertips.

Leonard laughed. 'Because of the ice cream? They have

ice cream in Brussels too, you know, I'm not sure it will quite swing it.'

Lucia stared at him for a long moment. 'Because otherwise I will never forgive myself.' She turned and went inside to fetch some bowls and not long after, the Cansinos said their goodbyes and went home.

Walking back, Miriam hooked her arm through Leonard's, matching his stride as he pushed the pram. She enjoyed these moments of quiet companionship and she hummed to herself, feeling content. Even when she saw the baby had fallen asleep, she did not mind, although it meant he would be impossible to get to bed that night. She tilted her head, resting it against Leonard's shoulder, and leaning into him, the way she used to when they were first married and she would meet him off the train each evening. Then they had walked in silence too, as if conversation were an intrusion, and it was only once they were back at the house that he would tell her about his day and ask her bits about her own. She remembered how she had worried where the baby would fit in all this, about whether the love she felt for Leonard left enough room for another person. But it turned out that maternal love was different, that it was made from all the same elements but somehow took up another part of her, so that rather than being divided in her affections, instead she had more.

'I hope she doesn't write to her.' They were crossing the road near Woodhall's shoe shop, and stopped to look in the window. 'To Laura. She'll be furious with me, she'll think I've been campaigning.'

'I'm sure Laura would never think that.' Miriam was trying to read the price on a pair of tiny leather sandals. 'Can you see what that says, Leonard?'

'Already she thinks I fuss too much. She said so in her

last letter. Do you really think he needs them? Surely he'd never get the wear? And of course she's right, I *do* fuss. I can't seem to help myself. Though did you notice how restrained I was back there? Twice I closed that front door — anyone could have walked in — and each time one of them left it open again. I thought to myself: it's their house, they must do what they like.'

'They're used to having a concierge.' Miriam straightened up, turning away from the window. 'I suppose you're right. Their feet grow so quickly at this age. Come on, Mamma will be wondering where we've got to.'

'Leonard Cansino, concierge.' He grinned and took hold of the pram, lifting his elbow so that she should tuck her arm through his. They walked on, Leonard matching his long stride to Miriam's shorter one, the wheels of the pram making a purring noise on the smooth flagstones. The air was still warm, and the people they passed nodded and said "good evening" the way people do when the weather is fine. At the junction with Orchard Street they stopped, looking left and right, then lowered the pram off the kerb and hurried across, because cars came round that corner at such a speed. Safe on the other side, they slowed their pace again. 'That's what they're saying, you know.' Leonard batted at a fly which kept landing on the hood of the pram. 'What I said about there being no war, it wasn't just for your benefit.'

Miriam smiled. 'I didn't think it was.'

'Hitchens, the fellow's called. Nice chap. Got a bit more to him than most of the ones I have to work with. He reckons we'll just do another Munich when it comes to it, the French too, that no one's going to fight for Danzig. It's terrible, isn't it, but when he said that, I was so relieved.' Again he swiped at the hood. 'I'd never have felt like that before.'

Because she knew 'before' referred to before the baby, Miriam did not reply. She found such reckonings impossible, for she could no sooner remember what she had felt before she became a mother than she could recount a conversation at which she had not been present. This moment right now, walking along Burton Road with the sun on her back and Leonard's arm pressing hers, this was who she was. Anything else was irrelevant.

'And you'd have thought she'd be relieved too, having a boy of that age. He'd have to fight, young Luca. He'd be one of the first to go.'

'To go?'

'To war. Oh, no, I didn't mean—' He stopped, realising what she had thought. 'I was talking about him joining up, that's all.'

'Of course.'

'I'd never talk like that. So offhand about it all.'

'I know you wouldn't.' She glanced at him, nodding reassuringly. 'Fancy the Sutton boy being in the army, he seemed so young when we met him in Milan? I'd never have thought him old enough.'

'They're none of them old enough.' He steered the pram around a loose paving stone, thinking about this. 'Awful, isn't it. On the one hand I'd do anything to delay war, and then on the other, I'm thinking, if we have to have it, let's get it over quickly, before the likes of Teddy and our little man are of an age. Makes you wonder if that's what all the politicians are doing too — mind you don't catch your heel there.' He watched as she negotiated the uneven surface, frowning at yet more proof of life's dangers. 'Someone should see to that. There'll be an accident.'

'There will.' She squeezed his arm and allowed him to pull her around to his other side, away from the road. She was smiling, her cheeks rising up so that her eyes were narrow slits.

Leonard looked at her. 'What?'

'You were wonderful today, I was so proud of you.'

'Me?'

'I know how much you wish it was Laura moving in, but you didn't show it, not one bit. You made them feel so welcome.'

'You're the one that did that. I just showed up and drank tea.'

Miriam stopped walking, pulling on Leonard's arm so that he stopped too. She wanted to talk about this. 'I wish it had been Laura. I miss the children, even more now we have this little fellow. I should have loved for them to be living around the corner. Think what an example they'd have set for him.'

'They're good kiddies.' A look of pride came over his face. 'They're not like the usual lot you get around here, that's for sure. Though when Luca came back with that ice cream, I thought to myself, that's just the kind of thing Rita would do, wander off and charm some stranger into giving her ice cream!'

'He was so pleased with himself! And didn't Netta remind you just a little of Coco? She's not pretty like Coco, but there was something about the way she was with Lucia, so guarded and watchful. Coco's like that sometimes.'

Leonard smiled, rocking the pram. 'They're good kiddies,' he said again, but this time there was something sad in it, and Miriam glanced at him and pressed his arm.

'In any case, I think Lucia was really grateful. The look on her face when she arrived – did you see it? She looked so relieved, like she couldn't quite believe she was here. If ever you doubt you've done good in this life, Leonard Cansino, think of Lucia getting out of that taxi!' He began to protest but Miriam continued. 'I tell you, there could've been dead pigeons in every room and she wouldn't have cared. She wouldn't, I know it. I hope I'd be like that.'

'You would.' He clamped his elbow into his side so that her hand was caught there, squeezing it until he felt her wedding ring against his ribs. He meant what he said, she would be happy no matter the situation, it was the way she was. He remembered something his mother had said when they were first courting and he had brought Miriam home. 'She's like a child,' Estella had frowned. 'Whatever can you talk about?' But it was just that quality that drew him to her, that childlike capacity for joy, to look directly at something and see it only for what it is.

She was talking about the Ardittis again. 'They brought almost nothing with them, just those few suitcases. I'd assumed they were having the rest shipped over, like Laura did, but apparently once they left it wasn't possible. Did you see Raphael's face when Lucia was explaining? I felt terrible for him. He thinks the apartment will have to be sold, that they won't be given a choice.'

'It's the new laws.'

'Those poor people.' She shook her head. 'Laura has a lucky star, leaving when she did. A month or so later and she'd have lost everything.'

Leonard made no response. He was remembering how his sister had paid for all the furniture to be transported and then promptly given it away.

Miriam gazed at her husband with gentle eyes. 'Someone else you've rescued.'

'Laura? Hardly. It's Marco Balestra she listens to.'

'For day-to-day stuff, perhaps. And it makes sense, their lives are more similar.' She leaned forward to straighten the baby's covers. 'But you're the one she really relies upon. No, no, don't grizzle, I'm just making you more comfortable – Oh dear, I knew we shouldn't have let him sleep, how cross he looks!'

'Perhaps he's hot.' Leonard reached his hand to the baby's brow, provoking loud cries.

'Do you think so?' They both began to fuss over the pram, causing the baby to scream louder and the people walking past to stare disapprovingly. When everything had been rearranged, and the baby had become so agitated that Miriam had to loosen his collar for fear he would choke, they set off again, lurching forward as if fleeing some catastrophe. After a while the baby calmed down.

'Good pair of lungs, that's for sure,' said Leonard, an observation he had made many times before. He glanced at Miriam, whose cheeks were flushed and whose upper lip glittered with beads of sweat. 'Perhaps I should mention him at the depot. They're wanting a new siren.'

'It's because we let him sleep.' Miriam looked at him guiltily.

They walked on in silence, each lost in their own thoughts. Miriam was wondering how she would get the baby to bed, and Leonard was still thinking of when they first met. He was remembering how happy she was, how she would seize upon the smallest of pleasures. Even before he fell in love, when they were just getting to know one another, he understood that she was good for him, that she wouldn't follow him to the darker recesses of his mind, but would stand outside, in the light, waiting until he came back. She would say it was because she hadn't the same education he had, she hadn't read the same books. But it was more that there was a kind of purity about her. She was what was known in the cotton world as 'unspoiled land,' where the soil hadn't yet been depleted by overproduction. He bent and kissed the top of her head, and she glanced up at him. 'That's for nothing,' he said.

She smiled. They had turned the corner and were walking alongside the fields that backed onto the hospital. The hay had been mown earlier than usual this year, and the air was heavy with tiny black insects, descending like a cloud and getting under their fingernails when they scratched their necks or elbows. Miriam put the net over the pram then looked at Leonard. 'Am I covered?'

'You do have a few extra freckles.' He took out his handkerchief and dabbed at her face. 'Look, there's Mamma. She must have been watching for us.'

The door to Number Sixteen was open, and Estella was standing on the step, looking out at the street. She was wearing a long black dress and her hands were pressed against the frame, like a cormorant drying its wings. Leonard began to walk faster.

'Ah, there you are at last!' cried Estella, 'I've been worried sick.'

'I said we'd be late, Mamma,' said Leonard, pushing the gate open with the front of the pram. 'The Ardittis arrived today, I did tell you.'

'Not this late,' she glanced at the neighbouring houses. 'Opposite has been home for hours. He's been out twice now to check on me, you've had everyone worried. Is he all right?' She peered at the baby as Miriam lifted him up. 'I hope you didn't let him sleep. You'll never get him down tonight if you let him sleep.'

'I think I'll put him straight in the bath,' said Miriam, patting the baby's back, her shoulders bowing as she slipped past Estella into the house.

'Isn't anyone going to tell me about the Ardittis?' demanded Estella. Leonard was wheeling the pram around the side of the house. 'Did the husband come too? I heard he might not. I heard she forged his signature on the visa application. Apparently he knew nothing about it, he didn't even know she'd left Milan.' She had learned this from Bobby, whose gossipy letters were in the best Alexandrian tradition. She watched greedily for Leonard to come back. 'Was it all of them then? The whole family?'

'Of course. They loved the house, I think they'll be happy there. Miriam did a wonderful job, I'm longing for you to see it.'

'Did I tell you that I was courted by an Arditti once?' She watched as Leonard took off his shoes, picking them up and carrying them with him down the hall. 'He was terribly in love with me. It broke his heart when I married your father.'

Leonard was putting on his slippers. 'The one with the house in Heliopolis?'

Estella nodded, gratified. 'Mansion. It was a mansion, not a house. The staff they had, they had servants for jobs you can't even imagine.' She reeled off a list of possible employments, and Leonard, who had heard this many times before, nodded and said 'Who'd have thought?' so that she should know he was listening. 'He never got over me, by all accounts.' She splayed her fingers, with their heavy rings, and looked from one to the other. Above their heads the bath water roared along the pipes and Miriam's thin voice could just be made out, singing.

'I don't doubt,' said Leonard.

And, each satisfied that they had reached the required endpoint of the conversation, they headed into the dining room to listen to the six o'clock news.

CHAPTER 3

In the eight months since their wedding, a change had taken place between Bobby and Josette. Where before they had been quite separate, two individuals looking out at a varied and entertaining world, now their sights were fixed on one another. It was as if marriage was a belt they had tied around themselves, and with each passing day they buckled it a little tighter, their hips pressed one against the other, their noses touching, until there were no sharp edges, no distinguishing lines. Bobby no longer knew where he stopped and Josette started, no longer understood which were his opinions and which hers. 'Do we like this?' he would ask. 'Is this us?' And Josette would screw up her eyes and pronounce it one or the other, as if it could never have been anything else.

They spent the summer of '39 in Europe, first motoring through the Swiss Alps, then in Paris, where Laura and the children joined them for their last week. They were, Laura would confide to Marco, the most irritating of couples to be around, all private jokes and long looks, endless touching and questioning. They had a secret language they used between themselves, made-up words whose meaning was all too apparent, and Laura took to speaking in loud, shrill tones in the hope that they might too. They did not. In the end, she took the children off on their own, spending hours in the Musée de la Découverte, shopping for clothes in the Galeries Lafayette, seeing films they had already seen many times over. She said it was to give the newlyweds some space — it was their honeymoon, after all — but really it was for her own sake. Being around them made her churlish. She discovered she was not as generous as she had thought, that she did not delight in the happiness of others, but rather begrudged it. When she told Marco this too, he laughed and said 'Don't worry about it, everyone's the same,' and reminded her what Allegra had been like once. After that, she felt better.

On their last day in Paris they visited Dr de Perreira. Since Leonard's encounter in Milan, Estella had been determined to renew the acquaintance and had written to her 'cher Max' several times, begging him to visit them in England and lamenting their busy lives. In return he had invited her to lunch at his new apartment, with its private consulting rooms and views of Montmartre. 'Because I can just fly to Paris for lunch,' Estella grumbled, scowling at Leonard or the baby or whoever happened to be in her eyeline, as though it were their fault she could not dine in splendour with her important cousin. But in those last few weeks of August, when the newspapers were full of the impending crisis and even Leonard admitted it looked like war, she called her cousin and asked that he invite Laura and the children instead. 'Tell her to come home, *mi adorado primo*,' she pleaded, lapsing into the Ladino she often used with the 'old' family, '*el querer es poder*, please God.'

Dr de Perreira's apartment was in the 9ème arrondissement, on the first floor of a sandstone building with deep, single-paned windows and elaborate mouldings. At the last minute Laura had allowed the girls to stay behind at the hotel, and so it was just the newlyweds and Teddy who followed her across the Place Saint-Georges and up the cobbled street to the house. Josette and Bobby were in high spirits, their arms linked, their strides matched, for Josette appeared to have grown taller since her marriage too. They looked only at each another, and when Laura stopped to check a street name, or to point out something in a shop window, they would walk straight past. Three times she sent Teddy to bring them back.

The door to de Perreira's building was open and they took the lift to the first floor, Laura and Teddy going first since it was one of those narrow cages and Josette said it would crumple her dress. They stepped out onto thick carpet and Teddy had just turned and peered down the open shaft, calling to his uncle to press the button, when a young woman appeared in the doorway opposite them. She was extremely pretty, with black hair and wide-set grey eyes and a tiny mole above her top lip. When she smiled, dimples appeared in both cheeks.

'You must be Victorine,' said Laura warmly, for the doctor had spoken of his young housekeeper. ('*Victorine est très anglophile, elle nous préparera un festin!*')

'*Bonjour, Madame.*' She looked past Laura to where Josette was shaking out her skirt. '*Le maître* is delayed with a patient, he asks that you wait in his study.' She stood back so that they might enter, then led them along a corridor hung with prints and 'Diplômes de Medicine' into a luminous, lushly decorated room. A large desk took up one end, covered with papers and journals, and next to it, a leather ottoman, its surface dented in places. Glass-fronted bookcases lined the room, and above them, portraits in ornate gilt frames leaned out over their observers, as if straining for a better view. The most striking of these, a portrait of the doctor in his diplomatic uniform, would have been instantly recognisable to Leonard, for it was merely a younger version of the man he had met in Milan, down to the extravagantly curled moustache and the overbright cheeks. Laura, Teddy's hand held in hers, went and stood beneath it, gazing up and pointing out the doctor's medals.

'I said we were too early.' Josette stood at one of the windows, looking onto the street below. 'No one ever wants you to come when they say they do. Mummy would still be in her bath if people arrived when she invited them.'

'It's different here,' said Laura, still gazing at the portrait. She felt Teddy's eyes on her, and knew she had used that tone again, the one which had caused Coco to ask her if she liked Auntie Josette. She forced a smile and added, 'I'm sure he won't be long.'

Josette did not reply, continuing to look out of the window, her fingers picking at the tasselled edge of the curtains. Laura was telling Teddy about Ferdinand and Isabella, and how they had ordered the expulsion of the Jews from Spain. Cousin Max, she explained, was the first Jew to serve in the Spanish Army in almost four hundred years.

'We had cats named after them,' Josette interjected, turning to Bobby and smiling as she offered him this detail. This is what they did. They gave each other lessons about their past lives. 'Ferdinand and Isabella. They were strays really. Patch fed them.'

'Ferdinand and Isabella,' repeated Bobby, 'I love that. Don't you love that, Laura?'

Laura nodded and again Teddy glanced at her. 'Don't click,' she said, returning his gaze. He had brought his yo-yo and was clicking it inside his pocket, depressing the soft metal surface with his thumb and letting it pop back again. 'If you click then I'll put it in my bag.'

Teddy looked away. His mother had been snappy like this all week. It was why the girls had begged not to come today. 'She'll be all stiff and cross and we won't be able to move,' Rita had said, and it was true, that was exactly how she was being. But unlike his sisters, Teddy didn't mind. He squeezed his mother's fingers, still held in his, and after a moment she smiled and squeezed back.

Josette moved away from the window and came to stand near her husband. He was peering at the frames arranged on the doctor's desk, and she watched him. 'Anything interesting?' she asked, opening her purse and taking out a cigarette case, slim and gold, with her initials engraved on the lid. It was a wedding present from one of her mother's friends, and seemed as good a reason as any to start smoking. 'Anyone we know?'

'Who's this, do you suppose?' It was a photograph of two men in leather coats and berets, identical handlebar moustaches on their identically nonchalant faces.

'*Le prince et son médecin.* It's written on the back.'

'Oh yes, so it is. *Le prince et son médecin.* Must be that Bourbon fellow, what's his name?' He twisted it so that Josette could get a better look, but before she could respond they heard the sound of voices approaching along the corridor, a man speaking French and laughing, and a woman's reply. Laura turned around, gesturing to Bobby to put the photograph down, just as their host entered, his arms outstretched. He wore a red silk smoking jacket, knotted tightly at the waist, and narrow black trousers, and on his feet were Moroccan slippers, the toes of which curled up at a similar angle to his moustache.

'*Ma petite famille!*' He gazed around in delight, as if his guests were a mirror in which he might admire himself. 'So nice of you to come!'

'So kind of you to invite us,' said Laura, holding out her hand with sudden enthusiasm. The doctor seized upon it, cupping it inside his own two smaller hands.

'*Ma chère cousine.*' He pulled her towards him, his sharp black eyes peering at her face, 'I've been so looking forward to your visit.' He gazed past her to where Josette was shaking out her skirt. '*Votre maman est tres élégante,*' he said, and Josette giggled with delight.

'Actually, this is Josette, Bobby's wife,' said Laura, forcing herself to smile. This kept happening – in shops, at the hotel. People assuming she had four children and not three.

And every time she wondered, her brow furrowing, have I grown old?

'Of course, how silly of me!' said de Perreira, as smoothly as ever. 'Violette's daughter, I remember now. And how is your dear mother? There was a time when she and I — but that is for another day, I am forgetting myself. Victorine, champagne, we are celebrating!' He twiddled his moustache, his eyes following the housekeeper as she left the room.

'We were admiring your portrait,' said Laura, glancing at her brother. His gaze, as usual, was on Josette.

'Which one? Ah yes, the Sala. Do you like it?'

'Very much.'

De Perreira went to stand beneath it. 'Of course, I was younger then, barely out of the university. We all sat for him. His portrait of King Alfonse is considered a masterpiece.'

'You haven't changed a bit,' said Laura, 'I'd have known you anywhere.'

'You're too kind. Ah, here she is. Put the tray down here, *ma petite*.' He picked up a glass, the bubbles fizzing under his nose. 'I hope you are hungry. Victorine has prepared a feast, she wants to show you real French cuisine.' He paused, looking around with satisfaction. 'Quail!' He pinched the air to show how small they were.

'So lucky to have good help,' said Josette.

OVER LUNCH THEY DISCUSSED the latest news, the rumours of an alliance between Russia and Germany, the cooling of Soviet relations with Britain and France.

'Hore-Belisha's had to leave Cannes,' said Bobby, who had read it in the paper that morning. He paused to work a shred of meat from between his teeth. 'They say Chamberlain's recalled the entire Cabinet.'

Laura gave an involuntary shudder.

'Mummy adores Cannes,' said Josette, stretching her legs beneath the table so that her feet touched Bobby's. 'She says she could live at the Carlton. Darling, why didn't we go to Cannes, do you remember?'

Bobby began to say something about the heat, but de Perreira interrupted him. '*Il faut en finir*,' he said, because that's what everyone said in France that summer. Then, 'They cancelled the Furtwängler, you know.'

'At the Opera? I read about that.'

'*Quelle bêtise*, Herr Furtwängler is the very embodiment of Locarno. It is through men like this we will find reconciliation.' The doctor had clearly said this many times before, but the effect was nonetheless impressive, and everyone nodded and said yes, it was men like Furtwängler who would save Europe.

'Wasn't he given the *Légion d'Honneur* or something?' Josette had seen pictures of it in one of her magazines.

Bobby looked at her admiringly. 'Darling, however do you know these things?'

'I just do.'

'You're wonderful.'

'So are you.'

Laura kept her eyes on de Perreira. He was smiling, lost in thought as he nibbled the meat from a tiny thigh bone, and she told herself, I should be more like that. She waited for him to look over and then said: 'And what about Daladier's new ambassador to Spain?'

'The Maréchal?'

Laura nodded. Ask him about Pétain, Marco had said when she spoke to him that morning, I bet he's got a story or two, the Fascists love Pétain.

De Perreira gazed around the table, as if wondering which of his pearls to cast before them. Conversation, as he often told Victorine, was a science too. 'A wonderful appointment,' he said, shaking out his napkin. 'General Franco adores the Maréchal.'

'Marco says it's like Chamberlain sending a member of the Royal Family,' said Laura, adding 'Marco Balestra, you met him at the Carassos.'

'Quite possibly,' said the doctor. He met so many people. He sat back, his fingertips touching and making a roof over his round belly. 'Shall I tell you what is going to happen?'

'Will it upset me?' asked Laura. 'Because if so, I'd rather not hear,' and she laughed, as if she did not really mean it.

The doctor laced his fingers, his thick arms resting on the edge of the table. 'There will be a short war,' he said abruptly. 'There will be a short war, and when it's over you'll be glad of it.'

'Glad?'

'Think of it as the breaking of a fever.'

'I'd rather not think of it at all.'

'My dear child,' the doctor shook his head, 'in every illness there is a period of crisis, a moment when one must choose to live or die. This is Europe's.' He paused, an expression of serenity on his plump, satisfied face. Beneath the table Bobby tapped his foot against Josette's.

'You don't think it will all just blow over again? Like the last time?'

The doctor shook his head. 'We must put our faith in the Generals, the Generals will save Europe now.'

'The Generals and Herr Furtwängler,' said Josette.

Teddy looked at his mother. He sensed her moods the way other people sense weather.

'How brittle you are today, Josie,' said Laura.

'Am I? I don't mean to be.'

De Perreira smiled. '*Les chiens font pas les chats*,' he said. 'She's like her mother.'

'Like Mummy?' Josette beamed, delighted. She looked at the doctor with new interest. 'You were telling us about the Generals,' she said.

'I was.' He sat back in his chair, fists balled on his knees. The housekeeper had returned and was clearing the plates, and he watched her in silence, as if gathering his thoughts. 'It is perhaps indiscreet of me,' he began, when at last the table was empty, 'but I shall tell you a story.' He glanced at the housekeeper. 'Victorine has heard it before, *mes excuses, ma pètite*. I have a friend — let's call him *mon Général* — I've known him since his Syria days,' and he proceeded to tell a long and elaborate tale, the main intention of which was to reveal his acquaintance with General Gamelin, the French Commander in Chief. Everyone listened, rapt.

'And he too, your friend, he too thinks there will be war?'

Teddy looked at his mother, watching as she twisted her rings and made that face she made when she was worried about something but trying not to show it. Every day he listened to her asking a version of this same question, at breakfast in the hotel, of strangers in shops or on the street, her expression always that mix of regret and disbelief, so that he wanted to jump up and say stop, stop talking if it makes you sad, stop listening.

'*Mais bien sûr.*' The doctor smiled and embarked upon an account of a visit he had made to the Maginot Line, once again in the company of '*mon Général*,' describing the underground cinemas and the train tracks and a dinner of oysters and foie gras that would not have been out of place at the Ritz. 'They shall not pass!' he murmured, raising his small fist.

'They shall not pass!' echoed Bobby. He was stroking the cuff of Josette's sleeve, his long arm draped across the table, and she looked at her wrist pointedly. 'We should go,' he said, leaning back in his chair.

Teddy was instantly on his feet, and Laura laughed. 'Darling, do sit,' she began, but he blushed and would not look at her. 'Actually, I promised the girls we wouldn't be long,' she said, because de Perreira was now standing up too. Perhaps it was time to go after all. 'Coco will think we've been kidnapped or something.'

Chatter about the Weidmann trial and that poor Jean de Koven carried them to the door, but at the last minute Laura turned back, her hand on the doctor's arm.

'And will you stay in Paris? If there is a war?'

'*Evidemment.*'

'Even if they start bombing?' Teddy had run ahead so at last she could ask.

'They will never bomb Paris,' said de Perreira, smiling. He waved a hand at the stairwell, as if to say 'look how solid it is, look how beautiful'. He remembered something: 'Estella, she wanted me to tell you—'

'I know,' said Laura, more sharply than she intended. Then, softer, 'She thinks I should go home.'

The others were in the lift, Josette fussing with her skirt again, Bobby calling down to Teddy, who had taken the stairs. Laura let go the doctor's arm and smiled. 'Poor Mamma, it's so hard to have her children in so many different places.' And she thanked him one last time and turned away.

Walking back to the hotel, through the quiet, afternoon streets, Laura felt different. Catching up with the others, she slipped her arm through Josette's, saying, 'What a tonic,' because she really did feel better.

'Old rogue,' said Josette, 'all that "*ma petite*" business, I can't wait to tell Mummy.'

'But didn't you find him rather brilliant?'

Josette shrugged. And glancing at her, Laura thought, it's true, she is exactly like her mother. I never saw it before.

For a while they walked in silence and then Laura said, 'All summer I've had butterflies in my stomach. I've got so used to feeling anxious I almost don't notice it any more.

Not just when I read the newspapers or listen to the news, but all the time.' She stopped, her hand at her waist. 'But they've gone, the butterflies have gone.'

'That's the champagne!' said Josette, and Bobby agreed.

'Perhaps.' Laura dropped her hand, swinging it at her side in a manner that seemed uncomfortable.

Teddy had skipped ahead and was reading aloud a sign in the window of a bicycle shop: '*Chic velo phare porte bagages sonnette automatique.*'

'Well, in any case, I feel a lot better. He knows General Gamelin, imagine!' Laura gazed at the tall buildings with their finely wrought balconies and vaulted roofs, at the arched wooden doors with their glimpses of dappled, leafy courtyards. A woman was leaning out of a top floor window, pruning her window-boxes, the dry brown petals drifting on the breeze like old confetti. Pigeons preened in the eaves, and on the pavements people walked with their faces turned upwards, not looking for planes as they might have done, but enjoying the warmth of the sun. She sighed happily. 'I adore Paris, don't you?'

And Josette, whose heart, Laura was beginning to suspect, was hewn from the same stone as the pyramids, said, 'Of course. Doesn't everyone?'

CHAPTER 4

When the news broke of an alliance between Germany and the Soviet Union, Marco Balestra was napping. After a month in La Baule, he had begun to relax, and now most afternoons found him asleep in his room while Allegra had her treatments and the children played ping-pong or sat around the hotel. He would close the shutters and undress, then get right under the covers, and he was there when Roger Hallemans called by later that day to discuss their plans.

The two families had grown close that summer. The Hallemans had a villa nearby, just a fifteen-minute walk from the hotel, and the couples regularly met for cocktails or dinner at some restaurant. Odette Hallemans liked connections. She was not happy unless she was forging new alliances, making fresh bonds. When the Pact was announced and Odette decided they would stay on indefinitely in La Baule, she was determined that everyone else should do the same.

'I'm driving up first thing,' called Roger Hallemans from the next room, pouring himself a drink as he waited for Marco to dress. 'Up' was Brussels. 'Odette wants me to move the office. She thinks you should do the same. You don't want to be in the north if there's another war.' Marco came and stood in the doorway, buttoning his shirt. He was thinking about Laura; she would be back from Paris soon. He must telephone and see how she was.

'And you think there will be?'

'War? Almost certainly.' Hallemans was cleaning his fingernails with a cocktail stick, and Marco watched him, fascinated. There was a crudeness about his friend that no amount of success or good tailoring could disguise. Hallemans glanced up. 'Say what you like about Hitler, but he's a superb strategist.'

"Say what you like about Hitler" — How many times had Marco heard that recently. He turned away, going back into the bedroom and opening his wardrobe, gazing with satisfaction at the neat rows of bow ties. It was Wednesday. They always went to the Hermitage on Wednesdays. He would wear his blue polka dot.

In the next room Hallemans was still talking, now about the stock market, now about government loans, now about Marco's business again. As he spoke he poured himself another drink, and Marco thought: I hope he doesn't use all the ice.

'Are the girls meeting us there?' Marco meant their wives, both of them a long way from girlhood. If so then perhaps he would call by Sofia Carasso's on the way, see what she and Ezra made of it all.

'Odette thinks you should bring your sister-in-law here too. There are worse places to sit this thing out, and it would make matters easier with the business.'

Marco shrugged. The Hallemans' interest in his affairs both flattered and irritated him. 'Laura's plans are her own concern,' he said, wondering what Allegra would make of that idea. Relations between the two women were much better these days, Allegra seeming to have forgotten her earlier jealousies, often going out of her way so that Laura would feel included. 'See! She loses weight, she feels nicer!' Lucia Arditti had said when he told her, but could it be that simple? He picked up his jacket, carrying it through to the sitting room. Hallemans had opened the windows and was leaning on the balcony looking out.

'You weren't there the last time?' He turned around as

Marco approached. He meant Brussels, and he meant the last war. He shook his head, as if to dispel the memory. 'Take it from me, you want to get as far away as possible. Maybe you should take a villa. I could help you look for somewhere if you like.'

'Take a villa?' Marco leaned out of the window, looking to see if the Simca was there. Seppy had borrowed it that morning, he should be back by now.

'Allegra might like somewhere more *chez elle*. "A roof over my head and the children safe", they say, but they don't mean it. They want their things around them, their own table-linen and the family silver, their friends too.' Hallemans smiled. He was well prepared for this coming war, had been anticipating it for years now. 'Odette says we must think of it as a second holiday, that if everyone's around it'll be fun. Like last year. Now, how about a drink? Not much ice, I'm afraid. Melts so quickly in this heat. *Santé, mon ami!*'

Marco took his glass, looking at it thoughtfully. 'To your health, my friend,' he said.

◆　　　◆　　　◆　　　◆　　　◆

IN BRUSSELS, LAURA HAD slept late. They had left Paris the previous afternoon but had taken the wrong road, and by the time they got back the children were fractious and it had been hours before anyone fell asleep. Now, with everyone still in bed, Laura moved silently around the apartment, making coffee and enjoying having a moment to herself. She thought about telephoning Mamma to tell her they were home, and she thought about calling upstairs to ask Manu to move his car, as she couldn't get into the garage, and she thought about turning on the wireless and seeing if there was any news. But she did none of these things, instead carrying her cup through into the yellow drawing room and, like a cat, settling herself in a patch of sunlight by one of the windows.

In the villa opposite, the gardener was picking up rubbish from the front lawn, and Laura saw that foxes had been in the bins again. She had heard them wailing in the early hours, a strange, haunting sound like a woman in distress, but when she had got up to look, the street had been empty. Once, when Marco dropped her home after a concert, they had followed a vixen the length of the avenue, crawling along in Marco's Simca while the animal sauntered comfortably within the arc of the headlights. Marco had wanted to accelerate and drive the creature off the road, but Laura had stopped him. She caught his hand in hers as he reached for the horn, and held it, peering through the windscreen and wondering at such assuredness. Just before they reached the apartment, it had turned in at one of the gates on the opposite side and disappeared into the park beyond, and Laura had let go of Marco's hand and sat back.

'Once they start breeding you won't be so romantic about it,' Marco said. 'Someone should do something. *Figures-toi*, there's more of them in the city than the countryside these days!' ('*Figures-toi*' was what Marco always said when he was unsure of his facts.)

Laura shrugged and climbed out of the car. 'It was one fox. Until they built these houses, this was the countryside.'

'And in the countryside they shoot foxes,' said Marco, smiling at the neatness of his argument. He leaned across the seat, looking up at Laura as she searched for her keys. 'I'll watch you in,' he said, as she turned and walked towards the house. And he remained there, watching, long after Laura had gone, and the lights on the third floor were turned on, and then off.

THAT WAS IN THE SPRING, shortly after she got back from Bobby's wedding, when the city still felt like a foreign land to her. In the months since, however, she had grown more confident, and now she raced around much like everyone else, for life was full and there was always somewhere she needed to be. A stint on one of Allegra's committees had opened the door to a flurry of charity concerts and dinners, and her chimneypiece was packed with cards and invitations. In addition, the Carassos were upstairs, and so even on nights when she stayed home, Sofia would invite her in for supper, so that she was hardly ever asleep before midnight. The children were thrilled, for this was the Mammy they knew best, the Mammy who wore beautiful dresses and took time over her hair and face, and whom strangers turned to look at when they were out with her. So that recently, when she and Coco were driving and she was telling her about the vixen strolling in the light of the headlamps, Coco had grinned and said, 'She's like you. You stop traffic too.'

The lawn of the villa opposite was a neat, green square again and the bin back in its corner. Laura watched for a while as the gardener wandered up and down the path, snipping the dead heads from the potted geraniums, bending to pull weeds. It was almost a year since they had moved here and she had seen this view through all its different guises, but it seemed to her that this was her favourite. The trees were in full, brilliant leaf, the grass was greener than it ever was in Italy, and where before, beyond the houses, she could see a path or a bit of lake or the edge of the golf course, now such details were hidden. Nature had taken back the view.

She stood for a moment longer, then turned and walked towards her bedroom, where a telephone was ringing. Her silk housecoat, a gift from Isaac, was too big these days and she held the lapels as she walked, to stop it slipping off her shoulders. She sat down at her dressing table, sighed, then picked up the receiver.

'Leonard,' she said, for it was always Leonard at this time of the morning.

On the other end there was a pause. 'Actually, it's Allegra. Do you need the line?'

Laura laughed. 'No, no, not at all. Allegra, how nice!' She gazed at her reflection, leaning forward to get a better look.

'I wasn't sure when you were getting back,' continued Allegra. 'I'm sure you told me your plans, but you know how one gets sometimes. Well, how *I* get, anyway. I can't seem to remember a thing!' She hesitated, and Laura imagined her glancing around the hotel reception, smiling at the other guests. 'Did you have a lovely time in Paris?'

'Wonderful,' said Laura automatically. 'My brother was determined to see all the sights so we spent the week being tourists. And what a treat to be around newlyweds, they are as happy as can be—' There was a crackling on the line and as she waited for it to clear, she picked up a pair of tweezers and studied her eyebrows. Allegra was saying something about the news, but still she couldn't make it out, and she continued to contemplate her face. When at last the line cleared Laura gathered that the Pact everyone had been jittery about, and which was the reason for Leonard's frequent early morning calls, had now been confirmed.

'The French are mobilising,' said Allegra, 'I should think the Belgians are too by now.'

'I haven't seen anything,' said Laura, then stopped, thinking about Seppy and how frightening it must be to have a son so close to the age of conscription. How brave Allegra was, how matter-of-fact about it all. She felt that old despair slowly rising through her body, and she held her breath, waiting for it to pass. She remembered all the other scares — last September, March, as recently as May — and then she remembered what Leonard had said just the other week, that Hitler was not Germany and that once he had been dealt with, all of this would be over. She stretched out her legs, staring at them for a moment, then returned her attention to Allegra. She was saying something about reserving rooms in a nearby hotel.

'Rooms?'

'For you and the children. I know it's another long journey, especially when you've only just got home, but if you drive with Marco it'll be so much easier.'

'Marco is here?'

'Not yet, I shouldn't think.' Again the line crackled, and Laura waited for it to clear. 'So will you come? Odette and I were talking about it and we feel sure you should. It's so nice here, I know you and the children would be happy. Only don't delay, there's talk of evacuating the schools. Precautionary of course, and you don't want to get caught up in that.' She offered a number of further reasons, learned, as she put it, from people she knew who knew people who knew, and Laura smiled and said how kind it was of Allegra to look after her.

'Well we all love you,' said Allegra. 'We're worried about you.'

And Laura, to whom such attention was natural, nodded.

After they hung up, Laura sat for a while, her mind strangely empty. When the telephone rang again moments later, she ignored it, and when Rita came in to complain that there was nothing to eat, she ignored that too. Upstairs, she heard someone walking back and forth, and from the heavy tread she knew Manu must be in uniform, only boots would make that noise. She thought how hard it must be for Sofia, and then, because all mothers must do this, she imagined Teddy in his place and it seemed unbearable to her. And she wondered at the mess her generation had made of everything, failing to learn the lessons of the previous war and seemingly doomed to repeat them, and fear rose like bile in her throat.

She must act. She must decide for herself the right course of action, rather than always depending on Leonard or Marco or even Cousin Max. She remembered the photographs she had seen last year, of churches filled with women, hats bent, praying for peace. And then, quite unrelated, she remembered the dormitory they had made for the children last September on the drawing room floor at Moorfield Road. The two images seemed to conflate, so that thinking back now on that time she had spent in Manchester, Laura felt that the humility of those women praying became the humility of herself and the children, heads bowed, waiting to learn their fate. Then and there she decided to leave for La Baule.

CHAPTER 5

Two days later, Marco leading the way in his Simca, they joined the lines of military lorries and private cars snaking out of the city. Despite the King's insistence upon Belgian neutrality, the army had mobilised and on every corner and at every junction, men in uniform, with their leather gaiters and coloured collar patches, waited for orders to move off. Some smoked cigarettes, others chatted and called out to people they knew, but on all their faces was a kind of weariness, a wish that this could be over with. Laura, her eyes on the road, affected not to see, instead chatting about sailing lessons and tennis and how the hotel where Allegra had booked them rooms was owned by the same people as their old hotel in Cortina.

'It's *bershert*,' said Coco, who had learned this word from Leonard, adding 'Fate,' when Rita gave her one of her looks.

'Does it have a pool?' Teddy had his nose pressed to the back window, watching soldiers climbing onto the flatbed of a cart, two horses scraping nervously at the road with their metal tipped hooves.

'It has the biggest pool ever,' said Rita, twisting around in the front seat and grinning. 'It's called the sea.'

'It doesn't have a pool,' said her mother.

Progress out of the city was slow, cars bumper to bumper as they nudged through the suburbs to the west, and there were frequent pauses for military convoys or fleets of official-looking cars. In one, Teddy claimed to have seen Pierlot, in another, the Duchess Elisabeth, but no one believed him and soon they were on open roads and they saw only wheat fields, yellow-bronze against the summer sky. Laura kept her attention on the Simca, overtaking when Marco did, offering no resistance to his sudden bursts of speed, giving herself up to the journey. When they stopped for lunch just north of Paris, she was surprised to learn they were nearly half-way, for she couldn't help measuring it against travelling to England, and was quite sure they would be still stuck in Calais.

'How calm everyone is,' she said, glancing around at the other diners, the women in their best travelling clothes, the men going in and out to check the cars, a kind of triumph in her words. She remembered her conversation with Leonard the night before, how he had begged her to change her mind, foreseeing panic and disorder and barbed wire camps on beaches, like for the poor Spanish refugees. 'Allegra has booked us an hotel,' she had laughed, 'we shall be perfectly comfortable!' But still he had pleaded with her, until she had lost patience and reminded him that Manchester was hardly a safe zone and that he would do better to concentrate his worries on Miriam and the baby. And Mamma too, for that matter. After that he was quiet and when they hung up she had written him a long letter apologising for getting cross, which she still needed to post.

They arrived in La Baule as the sun dipped behind the promontory, the villas and hotels which lined the front tinted a soft blush pink. The tide was low, and the people walking at its edge left a trail, which moments later disappeared. Sailing boats drifted back to harbour and mothers stood with hands on hips watching them, while elsewhere fishermen in skiffs piled with nets and lobster pots were just setting out. Wirelesses blared from open windows, and strangers stopped to listen, shaking their heads and sharing theories of what was to come. And above all this the moon, half full, dawdled like a guest that has arrived too early, a faint orb in the pastel-coloured sky.

'Isn't this lovely?' said Laura, turning from the sea to the villas which looked out upon it. Narrow gardens divided them from the road, and trees grew at angles in the grey soil, their coarse trunks and umbrella-like foliage casting strange shadows. Teddy read aloud the names as they passed, some carved in stone beneath the roof, others painted fresh each spring, names like *Rayon de Soleil* and *La Plaisance*. Neighbours nodded to one another as they leaned out to close the shutters, folding their houses around them with especial care, since it was said a blackout was imminent. On the road, the cars which had been arriving all day, strapped with luggage and pieces of furniture, bunched up along the narrow pavements, engines running, as their owners searched for places to stay.

Ahead of them, Marco had stopped and was gesturing towards a chalet-style building high on the dunes above them. Tall pine trees, their lower branches sawn off at the trunk, surrounded it on all sides, and a narrow path led up to its entrance. Hotel les Pléïades.

From the back seat, Coco leaned forwards. 'What even *are* Pléïades?' she asked, resting her chin on her mother's shoulder and pressing down so that Laura winced.

Laura gazed at her in the rear mirror. 'I think they're nymphs. What a shame it's full, it looks rather nice.'

'The Pléïades were sisters,' said Rita, who knew these things. 'They were sad about their father.' She glanced sideways at Laura. 'So Zeus turned them into stars.'

Her mother nodded. Why must she always provoke? she wondered.

Marco had turned the Simca into a side street and Laura followed him, changing gears as they negotiated the steep hill which led behind the hotel. As they pulled up to the service-doors a man in a loose-fitting suit and bowtie came running out to meet them, moving dustbins and planks of wood to make space for the two cars. Marco grinned with satisfaction, stepping from the car and stretching luxuriantly.

'Good job, Reid!' he declared, continuing to make a series of flexing motions with his arms, 'I always know I can rely upon you. Don't tell me you were waiting for us?'

The man grinned, his hands thrust deep in his pockets. 'That boy of yours came by the casino. He said you were due this evening, and I know how you hate to leave the motor on the street.' He ran an appreciative eye over the car's insect spattered hood. 'I'll give it a going-over for you in the morning, if you like?' He glanced at Laura, who had come to stand beside her brother-in-law. 'I can do the both of them.'

Marco put his hand on the man's shoulder and gave it a shake. 'This fellow,' he said, turning to Laura, 'this fellow is my right arm.'

Laura smiled. 'You're English,' she observed, feeling the immediate companionship of exiles. The man nodded.

'The English love La Baule,' said Marco contentedly. Despite the long drive, he was in a jovial mood, and he began to expound upon the many virtues of the town, while Reid, without being asked, unloaded the luggage and took it inside. 'The developer's a big Anglophile. He wants La Baule to be the new Deauville, stuffed full with your English golfers. There's even talk of starting a charter route. Hallemans has been trying to get me to invest, but I don't think I will.'

Reid was back for another load. 'You can leave the other car. They're staying at the Bellevue tonight.' He glanced again at Laura. 'Right, shall we go in? We'll say a quick hello and then I'll walk you to your hotel.' Marco turned to the man with a grin. 'So Seppy was at the casino again, was he? That boy! I tell you, Laura, he's got lucky bones. He only has to look at a roulette wheel and he wins five hundred francs! It's true, isn't it Reid?' Reid said it was.

Marco led them around the front of the hotel, where wide, arched windows looked out over the bay and the sky above the trees was a deep purple. Hydrangea bushes with flowers the size of dinner-plates formed an undulating mass either side of the entrance, so that to walk up the steps was like crossing a moat. Fireflies glowed green in the cracks of the path.

'What do you think?' asked Marco, pushing open the doors and steering them into the empty lobby. He looked around, admiring the room as a stranger might, with its overstuffed chintz armchairs, the tasselled lamps, the piles of magazines and newspapers on low tables, all suggesting the good taste and obvious expense with which he liked to be associated. 'It's what the French call '*cosy*', that's the word they use.'

'It's lovely.' Laura glanced at the children. 'Isn't it? Isn't it lovely?' and they nodded. She turned back at Marco. 'Perhaps we should check in to our hotel. I should hate them to think we're not coming and give our rooms away. Just point us in the right direction. We'll find our way.'

'Absolutely!' said Marco, but rather than retreat, he flung open a door to their left, gesturing to them to follow. 'Wait till you see the view. It's impossible to grow tired of it. Of course, it'll be better in the morning, you don't really get a sense of it in this light. Here, children, stand here, do you see the little island out there? That's where everyone sails, sometimes there's dolphins.' Coco gasped, and he grinned at Laura, as if to say 'See what a good decision it was to come? How could you ever have doubted?' Then his eyes flicked towards the door through which they had just come and his face lit up. 'Aha! There she is, just the person I was hoping to see! I was wondering where everyone had got to!'

Expecting Allegra, Laura smiled and turned around, her arms lifted to embrace her sister-in-law, but instead she met with a tall, heavy-set woman with curly black hair and breasts that extended from her collarbone and her waist. She held a wooden stick from which hung that day's newspaper, and when she saw Marco she lowered the baton, so that it no longer seemed as though she were carrying a weapon.

'Laura, this is the famous Madame Michenet.' He leaned around Laura, repeating '*la fameuse*,' and winking playfully. This was the first Laura had heard of her, but she smiled anyway.

The woman tilted her head and it was clear that this was a game they played: he flirted, and she rebuffed. She held out a hand to Laura.

'*Enchantée, madame*,' she said, with the efficiency of someone whose job it is to be welcoming. She released Laura's hand, of which she had only touched the fingers, and turned back to Marco. 'Your wife said to tell you they've gone to bed. It's been quite a day. I was waiting for you so that I might lock the gates.'

'What an angel you are,' purred Marco. He took the baton and slid out the newspaper, folding it and setting it on the table. 'Madame and I are both night owls,' he explained to Laura. 'We have our little evening routine. Sometimes we enjoy a small brandy together as we set the world to rights.' He glanced towards the children, who were still gazing out of the window. 'Tonight, however, I must see my dear family to their hotel,' and he sighed, his eyes sliding back towards Madame Michenet. 'I don't suppose—?'

Madame lifted both hands to silence him. 'I cannot turn my guests out of their beds!' she said, and she shook her head, as if this were indeed what she had been asked. She looked Laura over. 'Come and find me tomorrow and I'll see what I can do. I'm not making any promises, mind.

These are difficult times and I must take account of my regulars.' She began snapping off lamps and closing curtains, so that soon the only light in the room came from the open doorway. Laura looked at Marco, who was smiling and buttoning his jacket.

'Didn't I tell you she was an angel? Come along, I'll walk you down there. Do you need anything from the car? Perhaps just take a small bag with the essentials. There's no point unpacking everything twice. I know, I know, you're not making any promises!' This last was to Madame Michenet, at whom he grinned as he urged the family out of the door. 'I'll be straight back,' he added. 'Be sure not to lock me out!' And his good-natured laughter accompanied them down the steps towards the promenade, where cars continued to crawl up and down the darkened road.

'You really mustn't trouble about the rooms,' said Laura, 'I'm sure we'll be perfectly comfortable in the ones Allegra found.' It occurred to her that perhaps Allegra would prefer a little distance, that her choice of the Bellevue had been intentional. She felt a sudden stab of remorse, as though in her haste to come to France, to avoid Manchester, to cling to the independence of her new life, she had acted thoughtlessly.

Marco stopped walking. 'Don't let all that nonsense about turning people out of their beds worry you, she'll have no problem if it's worth her while.' He made a rubbing motion with his fingers, to show what he meant. 'Not that I blame her, she has a business to run, after all. But it's why I thought you should meet her tonight, I didn't want someone else coming along in the meantime and taking your place. Now she has seen you, she will be sure to find something.'

Laura looked at him, not quite sure what he meant by this.

'She knows you're good for it,' he explained. 'Of course, she should have known that from me, but the French are a suspicious lot, always expecting you to do them out of something.'

'You seemed so friendly.'

'We are.' He yawned, covering his mouth with his wrist. 'The husband's nice enough too, you'll meet him tomorrow if you come for lunch. He takes care of the restaurant side of things. I've often thought that's a life that would suit me, running an hotel.' He yawned again, this time with his mouth closed, so that his jaw clenched.

'How funny you are.'

Marco looked at her, grinning. 'Come on,' he said, 'let's find your beds.'

On the third of September, Britain and France declared war on Germany and Miriam Cansino went to stay with her parents in St Anne's. Life would be easier out of the city, Leonard said, not to mention safer. And perhaps once they were settled, Mamma might be persuaded to go too. Leonard could take the train over on weekends off, and with any luck this crisis would be over before very long, and they could all get back to normal. In the meantime, Miriam should make the most of this lovely weather and take Baby to the beach. September had not been this mild in years.

But with the nights coming in, the wardens had their work cut out, and it would be some time before Leonard could get away for a visit. Even finding time to write a letter was a struggle, what with the training courses and the extra depot hours, and now this news that the ARP would be in charge of bomb disposal too. He never stopped, and so at least in that sense he was satisfied, for no one could accuse him of shirking his duty. Leonard was not a brave man. He could never have thrown up his life and run headlong into the fray, the way you heard other men did. His world was measured, controlled, as smoothly woven one part to the next as the bolts of cotton he watched coming in and out of the warehouse. His was an army of overseers — of worriers, he liked to say, not warriors. His battlefield was Darley Avenue, the back of the old hospital, those big houses on the Palatine Road who could always find one reason or another why the rules did not apply to them. And although it was often frustrating, and he would lose his temper and dole out penalties when perhaps a warning was more appropriate, he was proud of his work. These rules and petty fines were the only kind of heroism possible for Leonard. Had it not been for them, he would have felt the true force of his helplessness. Besides, disheartening as it was to have the same conversations night after night, to walk the same streets and knock on the same doors, already there were glimmers of progress. Such glimmers were small: a properly masked headlight, black-out curtains drawn mid-afternoon, a white handkerchief tucked into a hatband, drops in the ocean compared to what should be done. On his gloomy days Leonard barely noticed them, his attention on the tides that were rising all the time and would soon overwhelm them; but on good days those drops gave him hope.

And now, in these first months of the war, hope was the thing they all clung to. Let's hope it's over quickly, let's hope Russia is bluffing, let's hope he's overplayed his hand, let's hope he turns east not west. Estella, who spent her days pressed up against the wireless, offered up a new theory each evening, fizzing with enthusiasm and furious should either Leonard or his father demur. Her face painted to match her mood, smears of rouge warming her cheeks, she rose to the occasion with a glee only the truly melancholy can know. 'Thank goodness for Granny,' Laura said, reading aloud a letter from home, and the children would nod dutifully, because adults were always changing their minds about one another.

Without Miriam around, however, Leonard's mood was a gloomy one, and every day was a struggle against himself. His heart clenched for the young boys he saw on the platform each morning, unsteady beneath the weight of their rucksacks, faces tight with apprehension. He saw their families when he was on his rounds, women who flung open the door at the first knock, their expressions scrolling through all the emotions — fear, irritation, relief, settling to a cool politeness — because what was Leonard to them? When he pointed out a cellar window they had forgotten, they looked at him blankly, and he understood that an explosion had already taken out the heart of this house. At such times he made sure to be gentle, offering to take a look himself, perhaps sort it out for them. What else could he do?

At the end of October, when Miriam had been gone nearly two months, she had a letter from Leonard announcing he would come the next day. This had happened twice before, and then some crisis had prevented him, but this time he promised not to let her down. It was Hallowe'en and the wardens with young families had been given the night off, a gesture which amused Leonard, who could no sooner think of apple-bobbing than he could strap on a pair of wings and fly (as he wrote to Miriam). He would take the earliest train he could and get a taxi from the station. She must not even think of coming out in this weather to meet him. And if she 'phoned the office with a list of the bits and bobs she wanted, he would do his best to fetch them.

Miriam was delighted. She set about getting everything ready for his arrival, moving furniture about, putting away toys, lining the drawers with lavender paper so that he could unpack. She looked forward to having his things about, and had already decided that he must leave behind some shirts, perhaps a pair of pyjamas, which she could launder and have waiting for him the next time. It was important that this felt like his home too. Who knew how long this war would go on? Besides, she would hate for Baby to forget he had a daddy, which people said they could if you weren't careful. This was not something she would ever say to Leonard, it would only upset him, but she thought about it a lot. Such thoughts then led inevitably to Isaac, and to those poor children, and then that song Teddy loved would start playing in her head and she had to stop thinking else she would cry.

When Leonard arrived in St Anne's it was mid-morning. He was in good spirits, excited finally to be here, and he strode past the queue for the taxis and set off on foot. It was a beautiful day, surprisingly mild for the time of year, and he strolled along the seafront, swinging his suitcase and thinking about all the things they were going to do together. It was a relief to be out of the city, to forget his responsibilities for a brief while, and he smiled to himself, for the first time in many weeks feeling himself free of cares. The sky arched blue above his head, empty but for gulls and the occasional coloured paper kite, and the only sound was the breeze in his ears and the distant shrieks of children and dogs, almost indistinguishable one from the other. He stopped for a moment to tuck his ears inside his hatband, setting down his case and peering at the houses on the opposite side to see if he was close yet. An elderly gentleman in a bath chair, his lap piled high with rugs, was being wheeled across the road, and Leonard caught his eye and then saluted, for on days like this he understood that they were all connected, the old man, the children on the beach, he Leonard Cansino. This is our England, he thought.

Miriam's parents lived at the northern end of the promenade, and he walked purposefully, thinking of all the times he had visited when they were first courting. The houses were shabbier here, their large windows exposed to the full force of the Irish Sea, their once-bright woodwork faded and peeling. There were no trees or neatly trimmed hedges as there were at home, no green lawns or blowsy, dahlia-filled flowerbeds, and he remembered how surprised he had been when he first saw it. For a moment he felt a twinge of

something familiar. He had let her down. The thought
hovered for an instant, wings humming ominously, then he
batted it away, for he had promised himself he would be
cheerful. He threw back his shoulders, practised smiling, and
then a cry went up and Miriam flew at him from behind a
gateway, and her arms were around his neck and she was
laughing, and he was laughing too.

'I've been waiting for you! How long you've been!'
Her blonde hair was shorter than he remembered, and she
wore it loose, so that it blew about her face.

'I decided to walk. It's such a lovely morning.'

'To walk? But it takes ages from the station, you can't
have been that keen to see me!' She stopped, leaning away
from him as if to study him properly, her hands cupping his
face. 'Darling Leonard, you must be worn out. And carrying
that case too. Now I feel dreadful asking you to bring all those
things. Here, let me take it.' She turned, following his gaze as
he took in the front of the house. 'Do you remember which
window is mine? There, see? With the pink drapes. Wait till you
see how nice I've made it,' she added, for he was still staring
upwards.

Leonard nodded, allowing her to take his suitcase.
'Where's the little man?' He looked around for the pram.

'He's with Mother. She offered, she said it would be
nice for us to have some time to ourselves. They've all gone
out, you don't mind, do you?' She rose a little on her heels,
seeking his approval.

'Of course not.'

'He's been a bit of a terror recently. I think he's
missing you.'

'You mustn't let him wear you out.' The wind had
caught her hair again and he smoothed it away from her face.
How healthy she looked, with her pink cheeks and that
sprinkling of freckles she always got in summer, so delicate

they might have been painted on. 'Perhaps we could get a girl to help with him? Would you like me to ask around?'

She shook her head. 'He'll shape up once he sees his daddy.' She smiled. She did not really see Leonard as a source of discipline, but it was the kind of thing they said to one another. 'Come on, I've got the water boiling, you'll be ready for a cuppa.'

'I am.' He followed her up the path. 'You could do with a bit of fluorescent paint on this,' he said, stopping at the door and rubbing his finger over the escutcheon. 'I'll bring some next time I come.'

She nodded happily. 'I tell everyone you're in the ARP, you know, I'm forever boasting about you.'

'And they still speak to you?'

'Of course,' she said, quite seriously.

He looked past her at the familiar brown hallway, coats piled over the banister, a bicycle blocking the door to the parlour. He had been in that room only once, just before they were married, when the whole family had been invited to tea. He cringed at the memory, for Mamma had not behaved well, had sat there in all her finery complaining about a draught, about dogs barking nearby, about the fish paste sandwiches. 'Like the bloody Queen of Sheba', he overheard Miriam's father describe it.

Miriam led him upstairs, her hand on the small of his back.

'Don't worry that there's no blackout,' she said, when she saw him looking at the window, double height and made of dimpled, coloured glass, 'Dad's getting a man in next week to paper it up. In the meantime we've taken the bulb out on the landing, so we can't be accused of sending messages to German submarines.'

'But what if there's a raid? How do you see to get downstairs?'

'A torch.'

'A torch?'

'Covered with tissue paper, just like you told me.'

'I'm not sure I like the idea of you going up and down the stairs with just a torch. And carrying the baby too. Why didn't you tell me? I could have brought stuff with me and had that window covered up in no time. I shall worry myself sick thinking about it.' They were standing on the carpeted middle landing, at the door to Miriam's old bedroom. 'I should never forgive myself if you fell down those stairs.'

'I'm very careful.'

'Even so—'

She had been holding his arm, and now she squeezed it, a gentle pressure that he instinctively understood. 'I know you think I'm fussing,' he began, but now the gentle pressure was followed by a pleading look, and so with an effort he stopped himself. 'Am I 'Arping' too much?' he asked, using Bobby's word for his work. He smiled. 'Sorry.'

'You mustn't worry about us, Leonard. You have enough to worry about without adding us to the list.'

He nodded. But what else mattered more than them? The rest was duty, and while it was important, and the reason they must be apart, it amounted to a set of tasks, it did not require his heart. He wanted to tell her this, to explain that without them there, he struggled to remember the point of it all, but he was ashamed. Always, whatever he was doing, whomever he was talking to, he was reminded that he was one of the lucky ones. A few years younger and he would be in a training camp somewhere, practising gun warfare with a broom handle.

'I'll try.' He spoke lightly, with a hopefulness he did not quite feel.

She opened the door, wedging it with the suitcase. Over her shoulder Leonard glimpsed a neatly made double bed, the baby's cot on one side and on the other, a small table laid up for tea, with his favourite biscuits arranged on a cake stand, and a teapot he recognised as his mother-in-law's best Spode.

'I can push the table into the corner when we're not using it.' Her eyes were on his, trying to see it the way he would.

'But where are your clothes?' He could see a small chest containing the baby's, but nothing that would fit Miriam's dresses.

'I use the cupboard in the hall. The bed took up more room than I thought — it's new. I couldn't have you sleeping in my tiny old one, not with your back. Don't look like that, darling, I'm perfectly happy.'

Again that twinging sensation, that feeling of having failed her somehow.

He moved past her to stand at the window, holding back the pink drapes and looking out. 'What is it, due west? You must get lovely sunsets.'

'Oh we do, wait till you see them! I'm so happy you're here.'

He felt her eyes on his back, but he continued to look out of the window. To the left, the way he had walked that morning, he could just make out the tip of the pier, and he pressed his cheek to the glass to try and see more. He had a sudden desire to be back outside, to be anywhere but here.

'Is everything all right, you don't seem quite yourself.'

'Don't I?' His hat, a grey fedora Laura had given him years ago, had ridden up, seeming to perch on the top of his head like some pale, nervous bird. He pushed it down again, then said, 'I don't suppose there's a lunchtime concert on? At the pier? I think I read they'd started up again, we could walk over.'

'Now?' She was holding the teapot.

'If you felt like it.'

Whether she did or not, she set the teapot back on the table, glancing in the mirror behind the door and then fussing around for a hairbrush, her bag, something warm to put over her dress. Leonard watched, swinging his arms, then went out onto the landing and waited for her at the top of the stairs.

And what's the alternative, he asked himself, have them stay in Manchester? No, here's much better, it's only a matter of getting used to it, and he leaned forward over the banister, the pressure of the wood against his ribs settling him somehow.

'You look like you're about to throw yourself over,' said Miriam, appearing beside him, belting her jacket as she walked.

Leonard glanced at her. He was thinking about the races he and Bobby used to have as boys, draped over the banister like this, the winner the one who made it to the bottom without falling off. How simple it all was back then, how easy it was to be happy. He moved sideways, the banister sliding smoothly beneath his shirt.

'Will I bring an umbrella?' Miriam was peering at the sky, the coloured glass giving little away.

But Leonard did not answer. He leaned lower, his stomach pressing onto the rail, his knees bent. For a moment he hesitated, as if trying to remember what came next, but then he kicked off, lifting his feet and his shoulders at the same time and propelling himself downwards. Slowly at first, then faster, gathering speed as he flew around the turn. Behind him Miriam screamed, and he looked up, throwing himself backwards at the last minute, catching a heel in the carpet runner and stumbling the last few steps. 'How was that?' he gasped, feeling for his hat which had flown off.

'You silly, my heart was in my mouth!' Miriam shook

her head as she slowly descended the stairs after him. And he fusses about me falling downstairs, she thought to herself.

'I'd forgotten what fun that is,' said Leonard, looking around, his cheeks flushed from the exertion. 'Did you see where it went? Oh, there it is.' His hat had rolled beneath the hall table and he picked it up, smiling at his wife with a kind of triumph.

Miriam took his hat, dusting it with the sleeve of her jacket, then returning it to his head. 'What am I going to do with you, Leonard Cansino?' she said.

THEY FOUND A BENCH AT THE far end of the pier and sat down. The Pavilion was closed 'for the duration', according to a typewritten notice, but in the Floral Hall opposite they could hear the orchestra tuning up, and a single violin played snatches of Beethoven's Fifth, which seemed to be all anybody played these days. Beneath them the water lapped at the cast iron columns and girders, making a soft, sucking noise as it caught in the narrow channels, and children with nets and jam jars squealed. Leonard sighed and closed his eyes, and when he opened them again Miriam was walking towards him holding two ice creams, licking one and then the other to stop them dripping on her hands.

'Here.' She sat down, passing him one. 'Treat.'

'I could get used to this.'

She smiled.

'I could, you know.' He swivelled the cone, considering it from all sides, then bit the ice cream with his lips. 'Laura does a walk like this every morning. Did I tell you I spoke to her? She and Marco stroll right along the front, then have coffee on the terrace at one of those big hotels. He's not daft, that Marco Balestra, he knows how to look after himself, we could all learn a thing or two from Marco.

Why are you looking at me like that?'

'Because, Leonard Cansino, you can barely sit still for a morning, even now you're worrying about what's happening at the depot, whether there's some crisis you need to be seeing to. It's not a criticism,' she bounced her hand on his leg affectionately. 'It's one of the things I love about you.'

'I rushed you out. I did, didn't I? You'd rather have stayed in the house.' He thought of the table laid up for tea and his heart felt suddenly heavy in his chest, as if there were weights on it. 'You'd gone to so much trouble and I rushed us out. Will we go back?' He made to get up, but Miriam's hand was on his leg, pressing him back down.

'But I'm perfectly happy. Be careful, it's dripping, don't get it on your trousers.'

Leonard gazed at his ice cream. Miriam was saying something about how she had given one to the baby last week, how she had to change all his clothes afterwards, but it had been worth it just to see his face. 'Of course, now he screams every time we walk this way. All he wants is another one. Dad says he's like that beagle they used to have, only interested in where his next meal is coming from!'

'I'll be able to come over more now things are settling down.'

'We'd like that.'

'It's been hard for you all on your own, I should never have left it so long.'

'Lucia Arditti's thinking of visiting too, did I tell you that? I had a letter from her, she said she misses us popping in and out all the time. I miss my daily Cansinos, that was how she put it. Isn't that nice? I like being part of someone's routine. Like a nap or a cup of coffee.'

'Or indigestion.'

'She says she misses us, she wouldn't miss indigestion.' She leaned over the back of the bench and dropped the remains of her ice cream into the bin. 'It was a lovely letter. Almost as lovely as the ones you send me.' She brushed crumbs of wafer from the front of her dress, shaking out her skirt. She treasured his letters, was proud to have a husband who could express himself so articulately. Her replies were more perfunctory, written when the baby was asleep, and, she was quite sure, full of spelling mistakes. Sometimes she copied the whole thing out again before she sent it, as if she were still at school and would be marked on presentation; and at the bottom of every letter she always wrote, 'Please Destroy'. Which, naturally, Leonard never did.

'She said it looks like Daniel Sutton will be sent overseas.' Miriam knew Leonard took a particular interest in the young man he had met in Milan. 'His poor mother, it must be a terrible worry. I don't think I could bear it. He had a place at Cambridge, you know.'

'He can go when this is over.'

Miriam nodded. 'When this is over' was a phrase Leonard used a lot, a kind of catch-all for the many ways in which life was being diverted. He used it to reassure her about the big things, such as the house they dreamed of buying or the school they would send the baby to; and for the small things too, buying himself a new suit, planting those roses they had talked about.

'Yes, but when will that be?'

'Soon.'

'Soon?'

He nodded. But perhaps it was the way she sighed and looked at her hands, clasped neatly in her lap. Or her tone of voice, which had an edge to it, he thought, as if she did not believe him. Or perhaps it was neither of those things and this was something Leonard had been building up to all morning, for really, it made no sense that he should suddenly be so upset. 'What do you want me to do?' he demanded, turning to her. 'Lie to you? Make something up? This war will be over when it is over, like they all are. If I say 'soon' it is because that's what I hope. It is because 'soon' means I get to sleep at night, instead of lying awake wondering if you're safe, if the baby will remember me, if I've made the most terrible mistake by not coming with you.'

'But how could you come with me?' Miriam eyes brimmed with tears, for she could never bear it when he was angry. 'You have the office, you have the ARP—'

'—I'm thirty-three years old, men my age are going off to France,' he said, his anguish causing him to seize upon other grievances. 'I'm useful neither to my country nor my family, how do you think that makes me feel?' Miriam tried to speak, but he was standing up now, shaking his head as if he had water in his ears. 'How do you think it feels to see you living at your parents', to think of you carrying the baby down those stairs in pitch darkness with a raid on? To see you being so brave, when it should be me that's being brave —' His voice trailed away. He put his hand to his hat, which had ridden up again, feeling suddenly foolish.

'But you *are* being brave,' said Miriam, gazing at him with confusion. It wasn't in her nature to fight back. She was one of those rare people who can love without feeling they must also defend themselves. 'Every day you're putting yourself at risk. And for others, too. I only have to look out for myself and the baby. Sit down, Leonard, please sit down, I hate to see you upset like this.'

She had her hand on his sleeve, pulling him down beside her. A couple by the railing had turned around and were staring at them, and at first he thought she was embarrassed, that she wanted him to stop drawing attention to himself. But then he saw her face, with its look of genuine concern, and he did as she asked.

'Darling Leonard.'

He leaned forward, his elbows on his thighs, his hands clasped and hanging between his knees. He stared at his shoes, polished last night before he went to bed, and bit his top lip as he always did when he was upset.

'Darling Leonard,' she said again, pressing his arm. She waited for him to look at her, but when he didn't, she rested her head on his shoulder and she too stared at his shoes.

'Do you want to know what I did last night?' he asked, his tone gentler now. 'I taught a group of ladies from the WVS how to use a stirrup-pump. Two hours I spent, with a bit of hose and a tin bucket. And then I walked along Princess Avenue and had abuse shouted at me when I pointed out that Number Forty-Seven had forgotten to paint their cellar windows.' He smiled wryly. 'The language was blue even if the windows weren't.'

'How dare anyone shout abuse at you. I hope you fined him.'

'What makes you think it was a 'him'. In my now vast experience of being shouted at and called all sorts of names, I can tell you that the women are the main culprits.' He was holding her hand, rubbing his thumb across her knuckles and ring finger with its simple gold band. He had never been able to afford to buy her expensive jewellery, not even a proper engagement ring. Instead he had a given her an old emerald solitaire of his mother's, but Miriam was afraid of it getting lost, and so he kept it in his cufflink box at home. 'When this is over, I'm going to buy you that ring we always talked about,' he said, his thumb continuing to trace the bumps of her knuckles.

'I don't need a ring,' said Miriam.

'Well, I'm going to anyway.'

The couple over by the railings had lost interest, giving Leonard a last, baleful glance before wandering away.

Miriam watched them go, her mind elsewhere. She was thinking of the things she had wanted to tell Leonard, all the little stories and observations she had saved up over the last few weeks to share with him, but which now seemed trite. How could she talk to him about the problem she was having with her fountain pen, or how frustrating it was that all the shops were out of sticky tape, or the gas panic that had resulted from her sister taking a mustard bath. All of it seemed so inconsequential compared to what Leonard was experiencing.

'I think—' she said after a while, 'I think we have to try to concentrate on the things that are good right now, and forget about all the other stuff. Because there's lots of things that are good, you know.' She turned to look at him, her eyes searching his face for reassurance that this was correct.

'I know,' he said. With an effort he smiled, and she continued to stare at him, as if looking were a fixative that would cause his smile to set. At last she let him go, turning back to gaze at the sea.

'Just wait until you see the sunset from that window. You won't believe the colours of it.'

CHAPTER 7

Around this time, Daniel Sutton's regiment moved to Aldershot for rapid training. As Territorials they were a mixed bag, civilian and schoolboy officers drilling labourers and veterans of the Great War, but what they lacked in skill they made up for in enthusiasm, and the barracks was a lively, happy place. Army life suited Daniel; he liked the order of it, the rigour of the work, and he saw that he could do well here. He saw, in those early months of the war, what his life was going to be, and he was pleased.

At the beginning of January word came that the 51st Highland Division, of which the regiment was part, was headed for France. Daniel was on leave at the time, and when the telegram arrived his father led him to his study, where he sat him down and spoke of Mons and Ypres and the Somme. He spoke of the mud, the particular smell of the trenches, described the wisps of smoke that rise from a bullet wound and the 'marmalade' that results from machine-gun fire. Then he shook his son's hand and advised him to attach himself to B Echelon, since it is in Supplies that the real glory lies. It is also, although he did not say this, where a fellow is most likely to survive.

The weather that winter was grim, heavy snow falling across Europe and the west, as if the earth wished to cover its eyes from what was coming. Major Palmer left for France with an advance party, but it would be another two weeks before the regiment would receive their marching orders, rough seas and storms on both sides of the Channel making any move impossible. Among the younger men this delay was unbearable, for what good was all their hard work and training if the balloon went up before they even got there? Every day there were new rumours: that Hitler had tanks on the Dutch Water Line, that the Sixth Army were massing at the Belgian border. Even the regular officers could not hide their impatience, ordering surprise kit-inspections and dawn parades, just to pass the time. Only those who had seen war before, the older ones in the ranks, did not complain, because to them it was a reprieve.

Around the same time Daniel received good news. A report he had written had been commended by Division HQ and was to be used as a manual throughout the 51st. Such an honour was unthinkable, and even Colonel Smart, until then oblivious to Daniel's existence, sought him out for praise. Rumours circulated of a transfer to Brigade Staff; better still, that General Fortune wanted him at Headquarters. Daniel's star was on the rise and there was a new tone to his letters home, one of confidence, and (according to his sister) of self-importance too. 'How conceited he is,' Ruth observed, reading over her mother's shoulder. 'Not a word about us and how we are.'

'Oh Ruth,' sighed Mrs Sutton, 'be pleased for him.'

'You watch, he'll be a menace,' warned her daughter.

And there was some truth in this, for Daniel was ambitious, and success, as it often will, made him proud. He saw that with hard work and dedication he could be one of those brilliant young men people talked about, and this became his goal. He gave short shrift to anything that did not interest him, and at times he could be dismissive, even unkind. This was unintentional — he would have been horrified had it been pointed out — but it was impressive too, for such single-mindedness was rare. Second Lieutenant Daniel Sutton, it was agreed, was a young man who would go far.

◆   ◆   ◆   ◆   ◆

ON THE DAY OF THEIR DEPARTURE for France, Daniel woke
early. He had been charged with entraining the vehicles and
was worrying how they would get to the station, since it
was snowing again and the roads were black with ice. He had
put a call in to the RTO and was now sitting in the ante-room
of the Mess — which smelt of beer and last night's cigarettes
— flicking through the *Illustrated London News*. There was
more about Hore-Belisha's resignation, with the usual
speculation about feuds within the War Office and clashes
with the army Chiefs of Staff, and he was thinking what his
father would say.

He'd say it's because of the Jewish issue, Daniel
decided, imagining Mr Sutton's gloomy expression. Daniel
loved his father, but did not always agree with him.

'Thank you, put it here,' he said to the orderly who
had come in with coffee, and he reached over and poured
himself a cup, sipping from it as he continued to read.

From the corridor came the sound of animated voices
and two officers appeared in the doorway, removing their belts
as they entered and dropping them on a table. The taller of
the two, a broad, red-faced fellow, was recounting some
escapade with a woman, while the other man, shorter, was
grinning and interjecting comments. Daniel glanced up,
nodding coolly, then went back to reading.

'Not disturbing you, are we?' The taller officer, whose
name was Wilkinson, dropped into the chair next to Daniel,
letting his arms drape either side and gazing at him until he
looked up.

Daniel leaned forward to pour himself more coffee.
'Not at all.'

Wilkinson continued to gaze at him.

'Anything interesting?' asked the shorter man, pointing at the newspaper with his cigarette.

'What?'

The officer blew smoke rings into the air between them. 'Anything interesting in that thing?'

Daniel held out the newspaper. 'Take it,' he said, but the other man shrugged and looked away.

Wilkinson yawned, covering his face with his hands and rubbing energetically, so that when he took his hands away it was redder than ever. He thought for a moment and then announced. 'I'm starved. Let's have breakfast.'

The other man jumped up, crossing the room and calling for the orderly. 'What'll we have?'

'Full English?' Wilkinson rubbed his face again, then stood up, glancing at Daniel. 'I mean, full Scottish. Dining room?'

The shorter man shrugged amiably, and followed him towards the door.

Just then another officer came in. Lieutenant Gilbert Ross was slight, with dark eyes and a heavy brow and he glanced mockingly at the two men as they went out. Seeing Daniel by the fire, he strode over.

'Here's the laddie!' he said, grinning and pulling off his beret, which was thick with snow. He shook himself, unbuttoning his greatcoat and flinging it at the back of a chair. 'You look snug!' Like most of the officers in the regiment, he had lost his accent at boarding school, but still there was something of the Scots in it. 'I take it you've heard?'

'Heard what?'

'Move's off. Delayed 'til tomorrow.' He dropped into one of the high-backed chairs, which at any other time of day would be occupied by a senior officer, and stretched out his legs. His trousers, wet around the ankles, hung loosely on his gangling frame. 'Message from Simpers.' (Captain Simpson was the Regimental Adjutant) 'Wants a word, said to call by his office.'

'A word with me?'

'With both of us.' Gilbert pulled a face. 'Give us our new orders, I suppose.'

Daniel stood up, taking his beret from his shoulder-strap and crossing to the mirror to put it on. Gilbert watched him, twisting a loose button on his sleeve and making no attempt to follow. He nodded towards the dining room, where the two men could be heard laughing and banging the table. 'Laurel and Hardy are up early. Will I tell them the news?'

'If you like.'

Gilbert considered this. 'Don't think I will.' He grinned. 'Not after the way Wilkinson played last night, I swear he cheated. Where were you, by the way?'

'I had to finish some reports.'

'Och!' Gilbert leaned forward, rubbing his hands and holding them towards the fireplace where the embers of the previous night's fire still glowed. Out of all his fellow officers, Daniel liked Gilbert best, but aside from cards, they had little in common. Gilbert was impulsive, erratic even; his mind, like his pockets, was a jumble of random acquisitions, so that one never knew what he would bring out next. Even during manoeuvres he was unpredictable, ordering his men to do one thing and then changing his mind and demanding something else, and always at lightning speed. As a result his platoon regularly placed first in regimental exercises, for they were soundly drilled. But Gilbert was a loose cannon.

'Och!' he said again, looking at Daniel with his hooded eyes, amused at the idea of wasting a perfectly good evening working; he turned back to the fire, adding bits of kindling and coal until faint flames appeared.

'Come on,' said Daniel, nodding towards the door,

'better see what he wants.'

'Don't you want to eat first?'

'I've had coffee.'

'I need something. I'll follow you over.' He stood up, crossing to the bar and ringing the bell. 'Hell, never mind!' He grabbed his coat and ran after Daniel. 'Hold up! If I'm missing my porridge, you could at least wait for me!'

And they clattered down the hall and out into the bright white morning.

CAPTAIN SIMPSON WORKED AT THE other end of the building, in rooms attached to the Colonel's residence and intended for the Colonel's wife. When they entered he was sitting on a narrow sofa, holding a stack of papers and leaning forward as he arranged them in piles on the floor. There were boxes and files scattered on every surface.

'You wanted to see us, sir?' asked Daniel, pausing in the doorway. He waited until Captain Simpson looked up, then saluted. Gilbert did the same.

Captain Simpson had a round, flat face, which made him look younger than his thirty-five years. He was dressed in service uniform, including his regimental cap, but on his feet he wore black velvet slippers, embroidered with a crest. He touched his fingers to his brow. 'Ah yes! I do indeed. One moment.'

'No hurry, sir,' murmured Gilbert, looking sideways at Daniel.

They waited in silence, eyes raised respectfully, while the Captain sorted the piles of papers. When he finished he looked up again. 'You've heard the news?' He stretched an arm behind the sofa, feeling for his boots. 'Brig's been on the blower all morning, awful palaver.'

'Delayed, sir? Until tomorrow?'

'Quite.' He lifted a leg, folding his trouser around his narrow calf and pulling on first one boot, then the other. He was singing to himself, that French song everyone was always playing, '*J'attendrai, le jour et la nuit, j'attendrai—*' and evidently rather pleased about something. 'The thing is,' he said, as he fastened the last of the leather straps, 'something's come up. Bit of good news, in fact.'

'Good news, sir?'

'Rather.' He flexed his feet back and forth, so that his boots made a squeaking sound, then stood up. 'It turns out the Brig was planning a show for the new arrivals. The King coming down, royal inspection and so on. Cheer 'em up, seeing as they're not getting away.' He paused, glancing out of the window at the thickly falling snow. 'Only now we're delayed, it's us gets the benefit. Bit of a facer, eh, missing it by a day.'

'We're going to be inspected by His Majesty, sir?' Just last night Daniel had been reading his Customs of the Service booklet and wondering about the Ceremonies section.

'Well, there's the rub.' Captain Simpson picked up his regimental stick, gripping it with both hands as if it were the bar of a trapeze. 'The Brig still wants to get the vehicles off pronto. Ship's waiting, Navy's in an awful fidget. Of course, we could just draw straws, but I thought I'd have a word first, seeing you're both here.' He looked from one officer to the other.

'You need officers to go to the station, is that it, sir?' asked Daniel.

'To the port too. Vehicles won't drive themselves off the trains. Means missing His Majesty,' the Captain paused, his long fingers with their perfectly rounded nails, opening and closing around his stick. 'Rotten luck really. Kind of thing a chap remembers.'

Daniel nodded. He was thinking about his promotion.

He would soon be leaving the regiment, to make this sacrifice seemed especially noble. He raised his chin, 'It would be an honour, sir.'

Captain Simpson looked at Gilbert, who muttered, 'Ditto, sir.'

'Well that's jolly decent of you both. Jolly decent.' He smiled, something he did rarely, and which gave his face an odd, clownish look. 'Appreciate it. Won't forget. Right, best get on, lots to do if we're going to be ready for His Majesty. I'll leave you to tell your men. Hopefully they won't take it too hard. Other opportunities and all that!' He turned away and picked up a stack of papers, humming to himself as the two officers went out.

In the hallway Gilbert looked at Daniel and made a face. 'An honour?'

Daniel frowned. It sounded rather foolish now. 'I just meant—'

He stopped, for a man in overalls was hurrying towards them. It was Grimes, a wiry, good-natured corporal, who had once worked as a chauffeur for Daniel's father. Now he was a driver in HQ company and part of the convoy headed for the station that day.

'I just heard, sir, move's off.'

'Thank you Grimes, I know.'

Daniel turned away but the Corporal stopped him, grinning broadly. 'WO has a letter for you, sir, I think it might be the one you've been waiting for.'

'All hail, it's the blessed promotion!' cried Gilbert, throwing up his arms, and dancing the first steps of a reel. 'Corporal Grimes, remember this moment. One day you'll tell your grandchildren about it.'

'Shut up, Gilbert.' Daniel smiled. Then glanced at his watch. 'It'll have to wait now, I must see about the new schedule. Grimes, do you know if there's a car I can take to the station?'

'Oh, the self-control of the fellow, d'you see that Corporal? If it were me, I'd be sprinting across that parade ground, you wouldn't see me for dust. What is it they're making you? Captain Staff Officer isn't it? Gas Officer to the entire Division? To think we knew you when you were a wee Second Lieutenant!'

'Ignore him, Grimes,' said Daniel, the very mention of his commendation causing a flutter in his chest. 'Lieutenant Gilbert lost a lot of money last night, he's not quite himself.'

'Been playing bridge again, sir?'

'Poker, my good man, poker — bridge is for ninnies!' Gilbert put his arm around Daniel's shoulder. 'I'll make it all back tonight, don't you worry. Can't keep a good man down.'

'If you say so,' said Daniel, buttoning up his greatcoat. 'Right, I'm away to the station, have the Mess Orderly keep me something if I'm late back.'

'Be an honour,' said Gilbert, making a low bow.

Daniel pushed past him, opening the door and shivering as icy gusts blew along the passage. Snow was settling on the parade ground and the roofs of the barracks, and the sky was white and heavy-looking. Grimes followed him out.

'Will I come with ye, sir? Might do to take one of the lorries if the roads are bad.'

Daniel was already out of the door but he stopped and looked back. 'Actually, Grimes, that's not a bad idea. I could do with your advice on the flatbeds too, I'm worried they might be a bit narrow.'

'Aye, sir, we can always put couple of trolleys either side. It's only for getting on and off that you want a bit more width. Once they're up, those tanks could sit on a sixpence.'

'Hey!' Daniel and Grimes were walking away, but Gilbert shouted after them.

'What is it?'

'Will we get a couple of trolleys for our game tonight? Think how much bigger your head will be when you're SO, it's a tight fit even now!'

Daniel chuckled, glancing at Grimes, who was doing his best to keep a straight face. What matter if people thought him pleased with himself? 'Sarcastic devil,' he said, waving at Gilbert as they walked away. 'Come on, where's that lorry of yours? No time to waste!'

It was early evening when Daniel got back to barracks. He went straight to the WO's office to collect his letter, arriving just as the man was locking up, crates of papers stacked outside the door. 'Sarn't Major, I think there's a letter for me.'

'Ah, Lieutenant Sutton, yes sir.' The WO was small and blockish, with square hands and square fingers, one of which he now waggled at Daniel. 'What am I saying? No, I gave it to Lieutenant Kershaw, sir, he's dealing with it.'

'Dealing with it?'

'Marked 'urgent' it was, didn't want it getting lost in all them boxes.' He winked, a gesture which caused his eye to disappear into his face, like a finger pressed into wet clay. 'All ready for tomorrow, are we? Been polishing your spurs, I know you young fellows like to put on a show!'

Daniel nodded, not wanting to waste time explaining that he was leaving with the vehicles. 'I'll go and look for him, thank you.'

He turned and went out, heading for the Officer's Mess, where the men were always gathered at this time. Even though it had been a long day, and there were still things to resolve before tomorrow, he was in good spirits. Talking with the RTO that morning — a Staff Officer of the old school complete with cravat and suede shoes — he enjoyed the impression he had made on the older man; noticed how he nodded approvingly when Daniel spoke of his place at Cambridge, his expected promotion, his ambition one day to serve on the General Staff. 'Continuity of care,' the RTO had told him, employing a medical term he felt Daniel would appreciate. 'That's the secret in this business.' The phrase still rang in Daniel's head as he strode into the hall, 'continuity of care, continuity of care,' for the idea had resonated, and he looked about himself with new solicitude.

He found Lieutenant Kershaw sitting outside the billiard room. He had a stack of letters on the table in front of him, and was leaning over them, making slashing gestures with a black pen.

'You wouldn't believe what these dunces write,' he said, looking up as Daniel approached. 'Simpers is emptying the stores. Help yourself to a drink.'

He nodded towards the ante-room where Captain Simpson, his flat face shining and moon-like, was pouring champagne into tall flutes and passing them around.

'I won't, thanks. Still have things to do tonight.'

'Of course, you're off in the morning. Bad luck on that.'

Daniel shrugged. From the next room came a chorus of 'The King!' and a clinking of glasses.

'They're finishing anyway,' said Kershaw, without looking up. 'Smarty's ordered an early night, make sure everyone's fresh for tomorrow. Right, that's me.' He folded the last letter, pushing it back into its envelope and dropping it on top of the others. 'Better not get censor-duty for at least a month, I'll be blacking lines in my sleep. Were you looking for the game?'

'Game?' Daniel had forgotten about Gilbert's plan to play that night. 'No. Well, sort of. Actually, it was my letter I was after, the WO said he gave it to you.'

'Letter?' Kershaw yawned, his jaw creaking loudly, and began to rise. 'Signed and returned, like it said.'

'Returned? To Div HQ?'

'That was the idea.' Kershaw squared the pile of envelopes on the table, fixing it with an elastic band then pushing it inside the front of his jacket. From behind them came the clack of snooker balls being potted one after the other, and they turned to see an orderly in white gloves skimming balls across the table. 'I say, did I do the wrong thing?'

Daniel did not reply. Perhaps it was vanity, but all day he had been looking forward to walking into the Mess holding his commendation; had imagined the fuss everyone would make, how the other officers would crowd round and clap his back, how they would envy him. Now it might be weeks before he was given his transfer, and who knew where everyone would be by then? He frowned and glanced towards the ante-room, where the first bars of the National Anthem were being struck up.

'Might just stick my head in, are you coming?' Kershaw meant the game, was nodding towards the card room. Daniel shrugged, feeling churlish, but remembering his promise to Gilbert he followed the other officer along the corridor. From inside the room came the sound of cards being dealt, and Gilbert's familiar voice calling the possible hands.

They entered the room, the lights bright and glaring after the darkness of the corridor. Half a dozen officers were sitting at a green baize table, their faces intent upon the upturned cards, but only three of them were still playing. Gilbert, one of the three, was grinning, his fingers drumming the edge of the table, and looking expectantly at the two other players. A pile of coins and the odd note were heaped in the centre of the table, and every so often Gilbert glanced at them, then back at the two players.

Daniel quickly took in the hand. The last card had been dealt and there was little to show between the three players: Clayton, whom Daniel had known at school, had a pair of nines, Wilkinson a possible straight and Gilbert was queen high. If Clayton's hole-card was a nine, then he beat Gilbert;

if Wilkinson had the seven, the hand was his. But perhaps Gilbert had paired his queen? His dark eyes gave nothing away. Daniel smiled inwardly. How many times had he seen that look and folded? Or stayed in longer than he should, for it was the same look whether his friend was winning or losing. And tonight Gilbert had been winning, a stack of notes and coins in front of him, a handful of which he now cast into the centre.

'Five bob.'

Daniel glanced at Clayton, who was frowning, then at Wilkinson, his brow shiny with concentration. Surely Gilbert was bluffing, but in that moment he understood that the other two would not risk it, and he felt a kind of exhilaration, as if he were watching a magic trick being perfectly executed.

'Oh, you beauty,' thought Daniel, as the two men flung down their cards.

He stepped closer to the table, resting his fingertips on the green baize and watching as Gilbert gathered up his winnings. Wilkinson was complaining, demanding that Gilbert show them his cards, trying to whip the men up when Gilbert refused.

'Deal you in?' Clayton looked around as he shuffled, the cards gliding through his fingers. His eyes rested upon Daniel.

'Better not. I've got an early start.'

'Here,' Gilbert threw a threepenny bit into the middle of the table, 'I'll stand your ante. Jack's a dull boy, a few hands won't kill you. Deal him in.'

Daniel smiled. Gilbert always got like this when he played, bullish but generous with it. He pulled out a chair and sat down, looking behind him at the other officers, who had been drifting away but now drew closer.

'I hope you're feeling lucky, laddie.' Gilbert's head was lowered, his eyes glinting beneath the ledge of his brow.

'Luck's for amateurs,' said Daniel. He smiled, lacing his fingers at the edge of the table. Gilbert's bullishness was infectious.

Clayton squared the deck and began to deal. Daniel slid the first card nearer, shielding it as he lifted a corner. Four of hearts. He pushed it away, keeping his gaze on the table as the next card landed (seven of clubs, no help), then lifting his eyes and looking around.

'Ace bets,' said Clayton, nodding to Wilkinson.

'Shilling,' said Wilkinson, his red face more than usually vivid tonight. He had been drinking, as all of the officers had, and had that glazed, dull look some people get. Daniel had played with Wilkinson before when he was like this, and knew that if anything it added to his game. He was harder to read.

'Three to the ace, nine to the nine, two to the seven, six to the five.' Clayton glanced at Gilbert. 'Pair of nines bets.'

Gilbert grinned and turned to Daniel, and in his face Daniel saw the same casual audacity that had made him catch his breath earlier. His eyes were narrowed and his mouth, though turned up at the corners, had an animal quality, as if he might at any moment stretch out his lips and bite. But Gilbert was thinking only of the cards, and now he looked away, drumming the table with his fingers as he contemplated his bet.

He is completely alive, thought Daniel.

And perhaps it was the excitement of leaving tomorrow, of his letter finally arriving (even if he had not seen it), of the King inspecting the regiment (even if he would not be there). Perhaps it was being sober when everyone else had been drinking. But Daniel's felt his heart lift inside his chest, and he was filled with a sudden energy, so that he too wanted to drum the table, to curl his lips and bite.

'See your shilling,' he said, glancing at Gilbert, 'and — raise you another.'

'Oh ho!' Gilbert snorted and sat back, folding his arms and gazing around the table with a look that said, 'See, this is how you play poker.'

'With a two and a seven?' said Wilkinson. He rubbed his brow, scowling at Daniel through his fingers.

'With a two and a seven,' said Daniel, fixing his gaze on a point just above Wilkinson's hairline. For as long as there had been a regiment, there had been a Wilkinson in its ranks. Indeed, an uncle, Major Wilkinson, was in command of B Company. 'Any objection?'

'Your money.'

'It is.'

'Not for much longer,' grinned Gilbert.

It was true. Gilbert won that hand and the next one too. Clayton dropped out, offering to deal instead, and Wilkinson became increasingly bad tempered, commenting on everything and throwing his cards when he lost. Daniel continued to bet high, even when he had nothing, because what did it matter? They were going to war tomorrow, these were his compatriots, his comrades in arms; if he could risk his life at their side then what was a quid or two in spare change? Look at all of us, he wanted to say to them, look how brave we are, how selfless. His father had told him how the whole town turned out to see them off in the last war, waving flags and singing as they boarded the trains, many never to return. Not so this time; the RTO said entraining these days was a dull affair. But they could still rejoice in their own courage. They must.

'For Christ's sake, Sutton, what are you playing at?' Wilkinson was glaring at him across the table.

'Five card stud.' Daniel slid his cards towards Clayton. 'Aren't you?'

Everyone laughed.

'Raising like that. You had bugger all.'

'Which is presumably why you folded.'

'What the—' Wilkinson began to get up, his bleary face leering furiously at Daniel.

'Och, cut it out,' said Gilbert, batting the air as if Wilkinson were a fly that was bothering him. 'Play the person not the cards, right Lieutenant Sutton? Or should I say 'Captain'? Got his promotion today.'

There was a flurry of congratulations and Daniel grinned.

'Last hand?' he looked sideways at Gilbert. 'We've got an early start, remember.' There was to be no risk of tanks going out of the gate as the King came in.

'Tell you what, how about all-or-nothing Snap? Last man standing takes the pot?' Gilbert pushed his winnings into the centre of the table. 'Useless where we're going anyway, Frogs won't touch it.'

Daniel laughed. It was typical of Gilbert to spend all evening winning, then throw it away on a whim. 'Suits me,' he said, and Wilkinson, cheery again, agreed.

Snap was something of a tradition in the regiment. When the previous Colonel was in command — a man of noble Temperance stock — gambling in the Mess was frowned upon, with Snap and Clock Patience the only games to escape prohibition. As often happens, however, sins were merely transferred, and many an officer had lost his salary on a hard, fast game of Snap.

'Stand back now,' Gilbert instructed the watching men, spreading his arms at either side like an athlete on the starting blocks. 'Clayton, deal them out. And no peeking, Wilkinson, I've got my eye on you. Sutton, you clot, pay attention, this is serious stuff. Righty ho. Everyone ready? We're off!'

And they began to play, Gilbert setting down the first card, a seven, Daniel adding his on top, a three, Wilkinson, his thick fingers fumbling, landing a six. Round they went again, slowly at first, gaining speed, the cards like a wheel they were turning, or a pan being stirred. Each time it came back to Gilbert he went faster, his arm like a piston, his eyes intent on the cards. 'Come on!' he goaded, 'come on!' Because that was how you won. You created chaos.

The first pair went to Gilbert, the second to Daniel. The officers watching leaned in, cheering the players on, growing more raucous with every round. Gilbert won again, scooping up the pile, squaring the edges, baiting Wilkinson with a 'Keep up, keep up,' so that everyone looked at him and laughed. Daniel laughed too, his gaze constantly drawn to Gilbert, who had that same magical quality Daniel had noticed earlier, a kind of radiance that shone out of him. Faster they went, the cards blurring before their eyes, so that Daniel had the impression of birds swooping and falling. And at his side, Gilbert, ever quicker, ever more determined, shooting them down.

Wilkinson won a round, keeping himself in the game. Then Gilbert again. Nothing mattered but the next card. They were hunters, charging through the long grass, chasing down their prey. Daniel dared not blink. Around him the room became louder, wilder, all eyes focussed on the pile in the middle. It was a parlour game, they were grown men, but in that moment it was as if their lives depended on the next card, on the next call. Gilbert was hooting, lifting out of his seat, lunging left and right, always just on the periphery of Daniel's vision. A two from Wilkinson, an ace from Gilbert — each card brought a gasp, a catching of breath. *This is the one*, thought Daniel, his tongue pressed to his teeth, ready to shout, and he flung it across the table, watching for it to land. But he had thrown too hard and it missed the pile, skimming the green baize and disappearing off the table. An ace, was it an ace?

'Foul!' cried Gilbert.

Daniel, laughing, was bending his head, looking for where it had gone.

'Pick it up, you bloody Hebrew.'

The words came from nowhere. Daniel, one hand on the table, the other reaching for his card, was suddenly still. At first he thought he had misheard, but then so had everyone, for when he raised his head the room was silent. Only Wilkinson made any noise, moving around on his chair, snapping the corners of his cards, tutting. Daniel gazed at him, disbelieving, then slowly, holding on to the edge of the table, he stood up. His gaze never wavering from Wilkinson's bloated, drunken face, a tight, choking feeling in the back of his throat, he turned and walked out of the room.

And only when he was through the door did the spell break and the silence which had held the men release them again. Gilbert, cursing, slammed the table with his fist and jumped up.

'Och, wait!' Gilbert ran into the corridor, catching up with Daniel and grabbing at his sleeve. From the Mess came the voice of Captain Simpson instructing an orderly on the correct way to polish regimental plate. 'You shouldn't have just walked out like that. You let him win.'

'Let him win?' As if a stupid game mattered now.

'Let him get to you, I mean,' said Gilbert. 'He's a bloody fool. Ignore him.'

Clayton, who had followed Gilbert, nodded. 'He's drunk, that's all. Been like it with everyone.'

'It's not the same.'

'Of course it is.' Gilbert glanced towards the Mess. 'Come back. At least let's finish the hand.'

'No. It's late, I'm going to bed.' Daniel rubbed his

neck, slipping his fingers under his collar and scratching the hot skin. He smiled at Gilbert. 'It's fine.'

'But it's our last night.'

Daniel shrugged.

Gilbert, gazing at him, let go of his arm. 'He's a bloody fool,' he said again.

Daniel nodded. He felt his acquiescence — for that was what it was, better to name it — like a rope about his feet, tugging at him, pulling him away. From what? From a card game? Well, so be it, he thought, smoothing his sleeve where Gilbert had been holding it. 'See you in the morning,' he said. 'Set your alarm, eh? Don't want to have to wake you up.'

And he turned and strode away from them, his heels on the stone flags chiming like bells.

THE NEXT MORNING, DESPITE SIX inches of fresh snow and roads like glass, the vehicles were entrained for Southampton. Two days later, along with the rest of the 51st Division, the regiment arrived in France.

CHAPTER 9

As often happens in times of war, people everywhere looked about themselves and asked, 'who are you and what can you do?'. In Alexandria, now resident to thousands of Allied troops, they also asked 'and when are you free?'. Like gulls to mackerel (where the gulls wore Service Dress and the mackerel a little something she picked up in Europe) the drawing rooms and salons of the city were aflutter as never before. As Violette d'Araquy liked to say, 'one must do one's bit'.

But if the locals were hospitable, the weather was less so. The winter of 1940 was a particularly wet one in Alexandria, and the gutters of the Rue Fuad frequently flooded with rust-coloured rain, so that, leaving Baudrot or the Club, it was necessary to leap from the kerb to the car. Officers in khaki drill or white duck arrived for cocktails with hems ringed red, and soon laundry services and somewhere to keep a change of clothes were offered too. Now, when Josette called by the Rue Rolo, she found her bedroom stacked with kit bags and her mother and Clemmie playing host to a brigadier one day, an admiral the next, and various subalterns on leave from the desert in between. Despite having yearned for married life and a home of her own, Josette slipped with ease into this world of chatter and compliments, and soon it was here that Bobby came each evening to collect her.

Aside from the dimming of headlamps and the occasional air raid siren, wartime Alexandria had much to recommend it. There was the matter of martial law, of course, in accordance with the '36 Treaty, and a certain amount of censorship too. But if you avoided the area around Pompey's Pillar you could forget about the internment of German Nazis, some of whom had been to lunch just weeks before. Likewise the half a million Italian troops stationed in Libya and Ethiopia, because until Mussolini made up his mind and threw his hat in the ring, what good would worrying do?

At the beginning of February Bobby stopped by the d'Araquys as usual to pick up Josette. Philippe had kept to his word and done his best for his son-in-law, but competition in the cotton business was tougher than ever, and Bobby's heart was not in it. When a guest at one of Violette's lunches offered him a desk job organising supplies to the Canal Zone, Bobby was quick to accept. Now he bounded up the stairs in the pay of the British Army, and even Clemmie struggled to make fun.

Josette was on the veranda when he arrived, sitting with Mrs Patchett and two Royal Marines drinking lemonade. Bobby went straight to her, taking her hand and holding it in his as he grinned around the little group. He was feeling chipper, having received a letter from Leonard that morning and keen to share it with her. Usually Leonard wrote of missing Miriam, or Papa's ear, or how difficult it was for Mamma being alone all day, but in this letter he simply copied out large parts of a speech he had heard at the Manchester Free Trade hall.

'Listen to this,' he said, waving the letter at Mrs Patchett, who was knitting, and waiting until she looked up. '*Fill the armies, rule the air, pour out the munitions, plough the land, build the ships, guard the streets, succour the wounded, uplift the downcast and honour the brave.* Isn't that wonderful?'

'Churchill,' said one of the Marines. The speech had been in all the papers before they left.

'Uplift the downcast,' said Mrs Patchett, counting her stitches. 'I like that. What a way with words some of them have.'

Bobby nodded, squeezing his wife's hand. 'Listen, there's more: '*Let us go forward together in all parts of the Empire, in all parts of the Island. There is not a week, nor a day, nor an hour to lose.*' He stopped and looked at his wife. 'Doesn't that make you feel brave? "All parts of the Empire", that's us.'

'So it is,' said Josette, smiling.

'Makes me think I should be taking that job in Cairo,' said Mrs Patchett, looking meaningfully at Josette and clearly referring to a conversation they had had earlier. Josette frowned, gesturing to Bobby to put the letter back in his pocket.

'*Alors,*' she said breezily, and stood up, glancing around for her bag, '*on y va?*' Since Paris they often spoke to one another in French. She glanced at the Marines who were getting up too, adding, 'Stay there. Patch will look after you, won't you Patch?'

The older woman sighed and clicked her tongue.

They moved through the various rooms, gathering up Josette's things, picking up snippets of conversation. Someone had seen someone who had had lunch with General Wavell, and the talk was of base-camps and field-hospitals and an imminent invasion of Libya. Someone else, fresh off the boat, was bemoaning the cancellation of Ascot, and someone else still had seen Gielgud at the Globe, and wasn't he doing wonders for the Polish Relief Fund? To all of these they nodded and smiled, slipping out of the door just as Violette clapped her hands and said 'Turn!' — so that everyone turned and spoke to the person on their other side — which was what all the smartest hostesses were doing these days.

'What job?' asked Bobby, once they were outside and walking towards the Corniche. He was fond of Mrs Patchett and liked to keep up with her news.

'Nothing really,' said Josette, gazing past him towards the windows of a dress-shop. 'She's just got it into her head she should be doing war work. One of Mummy's pesky colonels put her up to it, going on about how they need English secretaries at GHQ. Suddenly Patch announces she's a dab at shorthand and dictation and all sorts, and he practically offers her a job. Is that real silk, do you suppose?' She peered through the grimy glass. 'Actually, I don't like the colour. Come on.'

She pulled him after her, their fingers interlaced, as they had been since Bobby first sat down on the veranda. Bobby was still thinking about Mrs Patchett.

'They really do need secretaries, you know. I get calls about it all the time.'

Josette narrowed her eyes, a habit she had copied from her mother, and he shrugged and stopped speaking. He knew better than to interfere in such matters. He pressed her fingers and smiled, turning back towards the sea. Their apartment, a wedding present from her parents, was in Chatby, but Josette liked to walk the first part home. She had an idea that people seeing them would assume they lived more centrally, an illusion she was happy to encourage. Now, however, she scowled and said 'Anyway, Patch is needed here.'

'She is?' Bobby was immediately attentive. It had been over a year since they were married, and even Violette, uninterested as she was, had taken to commenting. Just yesterday he had heard her say, 'I only had to look at Philippe!' and the corresponding nods from the women, and Clemmie's 'Ew, mummy, please,' made the context clear.

'I've got something to show you.' Josette was searching in her bag and he pulled her beneath the awning of a Greek grocery store, because they were blocking the pavement. Earthenware bowls crammed the open shelves, full of olives and cornichons and those briny sour onions people always avoid at cocktail parties. His gaze rested on a jar of marinated anchovies and he thought, remember this moment, remember where you were. She pressed something soft into his hands. 'What do you think?'

Bobby held up a knitted white tube with a large hole on one side. He looked at it in wonder.

'It's for the Finns,' she said, 'it's taken me ages, I kept dropping stitches and having to start again. Aren't you impressed?' She took it from him, putting her hand inside and wiggling her fingers through the hole. 'For their faces,' she explained, 'Patch has everyone making them, even Mummy.'

'For the Finns?'

Josette nodded. If she sensed his disappointment, she gave no hint. She rolled up the knitting and put it back in her bag. 'Yes, they're having the most awful time, did you know some of the soldiers don't even have uniforms? Just skis and lots of — oh, what's the word?'

'Word?'

'It's a Finnish word, it means 'fighting spirit'. Patch read it somewhere, she says that's what's foxing the Russians, they didn't know they had so much of it.'

'Crikey.'

Josette gazed at her husband, two lines appearing on her otherwise smooth brow. She saw how people watched her, how the likes of Mrs Gardiner and the Greek Consul's wife looked her over as if she were an experiment whose outcome was already assured. ('Cousins,' they said, and sucked their teeth.) And now he too was watching her, so that she wanted to wrench her hand from his and make a fist of it. But instead she said, carelessly, 'Perhaps we should buy some olives.'

Just then there was a blaring of horns and a car swerved across the road and up onto the pavement behind them. It was Clemmie, driving his mother's new Alfa Romeo ('My spoils of war', said Violette, having bought it cheap from a departing Italian). He slammed on the brakes, coming to a halt just inches from the front of the shop, then smiled serenely, his sunglasses pushed back into his hair. Beside him, grinning and half out of his seat, was Captain Webster.

'Ah! The magnificent Mrs Cansino!' Webster rested his elbows on the top of the windscreen, surveying Josette as he might a horse he was thinking of buying. 'And her dashing young husband. How splendid to see you both. We were just talking about you, were your ears burning?' He leaned a little closer to Josette, for it was she he meant.

'Only good things, I hope,' she said, looking at him through her lashes. Before she was married she would never have flirted, but now it seemed strange not to.

'Ah, that would be telling!' He lowered his voice, as if to share some great secret, but just then the owner of the shop, a small man in sandals that slapped as he walked, appeared in the doorway, shouting and gesturing to them to move the car. Webster considered him with distaste. 'All right, all right,' he said, then, 'Bloody wops, makes you wonder why we bother.'

'Webster's getting up a Concert Party,' said Clemmie, ignoring the interruption. 'Said I'd help him drum up a few acts. For a percentage of the profits, of course. Right, Webster?' He glanced at his friend, and Webster, whose attention was back on Josette, winked and said, 'Sure, sure.'

'Well don't look at me,' said Josette, 'I'm hopeless at that sort of thing.'

'Nonsense, you have a lovely singing voice,' said Bobby. The arrival of the car had forced him deep under the awning, and the blue and white fabric hung low over his forehead, like an enormous hat.

'Darling, I simply don't. Though it's sweet of you to say so.'

'Frankly, a girl could stand around reading the phone directory and the chaps would be entertained. Pretty face and all that.' Webster glanced at Bobby. 'No offence, old man.' He flashed him a smile, all moustache, then nodded at the seat behind. 'I say, do you two want to jump in? We were on our way to the club, got some sort of do on tonight.'

There was a 'do' on every night at the club these days, an antidote to what the officers called the Bore War. Josette glanced at Clemmie, who had lowered his sunglasses and was looking past her towards the sea.

'Another time, perhaps,' she said.

Webster peered at Bobby. 'How's that sister of yours? Laura, isn't it?' Clemmie slipped the car into gear and began to move forward, 'Tell her I was asking after her, would you? Ask her if she'd like to be in my Concert Party!'

'She's in France,' said Bobby, released from beneath the awning.

With a scraping of tyres, the car plunged into the traffic, narrowly missing the back wheels of a gharry and tipping Webster, arm raised in salute, back into his seat. 'Cheerio then!' he shouted, but the car was already speeding away, leaving in its wake clouds of red dust that Bobby wafted and made worse, until Josette told him to stop.

'She could have, too,' she said, once they were walking again. He glanced at her, waiting for her to continue. 'Laura. She could have played the piano.'

'She hates that kind of thing,' said Bobby, who knew Josette envied such talents.

'Yes, but she could have.'

'And so could you. I meant what I said, you have a lovely singing voice.' They rounded the corner onto the Corniche, walking on the pavement at the edge of the sea, where the waves made a ringing noise in the holes of the rocks. Instinctively he moved Josette to his other side, away from the road, then bent and kissed the top of her hair as they walked. Whatever else marriage had changed about her, it had not changed the scent of her hair — a mixture of roses and sea salt. 'Though I'd hate for you to be going off all the time. Those Barker girls were just in Mersa Matruh. I'd miss you awfully.'

Josette did not reply. Everyone was talking about Mrs Barker and her war effort. No doubt that was where Webster had got the idea. 'They'll be impossible to marry after this', had been Mrs Gardiner's comment, but Josette thought it only made them more appealing.

'So do you think she will leave?' said Bobby, after they had walked in silence for a while. He was thinking about Mrs Patchett again.

Josette shrugged. 'I hope not. I can't imagine her not being around, even if she is a bit of an old stick sometimes. Did I tell you she's after Mummy to give up her furs, she says they need them more on the Karelian Isthmus than she'll ever need them here. She's right I suppose, but Mummy was furious. Until she heard who else had given them and then she said maybe she'd think about her old rabbit. Or Daddy's raccoon. Oh! I've just remembered it.' She stopped, looking at Bobby and holding up a finger. '*Sisu*. That's the word I forgot.'

'*Sisu?*'

'Yes! The Finns have *sisu*! It means they can keep going even when everything's against them.'

'Fighting spirit. Like in Leonard's letter.' Bobby patted his pocket, delighted. He would use it when he wrote back.

'Guts!' said Josette, because that was the word Patch had used.

Bobby looked at her proudly, at her narrow face with its high forehead and pale lashes, at her small mouth, puckered now, pleased with herself for remembering. He thought of Clemmie driving off like that, and Violette, so busy with her colonels and her lieutenants that Josette was left knitting balaclavas on the veranda. '*Sisu*,' he said, smiling. 'I like it. It's a good word.'

CHAPTER 10

Upon the Division's arrival in France, Daniel Sutton was transferred to Base Depot near Saint-Nazaire. He was in charge of First Line Reinforcements, making sure the regiment had everything they needed, and had anyone asked him he would have said he was glad to be away. The incident with Wilkinson had left a bad taste, and besides, his promotion might come through any day, it was as well to get used to being independent. But as the weeks went on and nothing arrived from HQ, Daniel grew restless, and it was with relief that he received a telegram mid-April, recalling him to the regiment north-east of Paris. The Germans had invaded Norway and there were fears of an imminent attack on Belgium. If that happened he did not want to be stuck down here, away from the action.

ON HIS LAST DAY DANIEL WAS invited to lunch with the Depot CO, Major Fielding, at his hotel in La Baule. He was early, having hitched a ride in one of the supply lorries, and to pass the time he wandered along the front. It was a bright spring day and La Baule was at her most beautiful. It was as if the icy winter had refreshed her somehow, and, like a swimmer emerging out of cold water, there was a kind of glow about her. All along the Boulevard des Dunes, the stone villas, with their fretted balconies and slate roofs, gleamed in the sunshine. Knobbly pine trees, with branches like bent arms, stood sentinel behind low walls, their roots escaping onto the pavement beyond and causing fissures in the *pavés*. Housemaids, with hands more used to scrubbing steps or beating carpets, crouched over freshly dug flowerbeds, tucking the soil around the new plants as tenderly as they might settle a baby in its crib. Gulls drifted aimlessly on the warm breeze.

Glancing at his watch, Daniel turned back, arriving at the hotel just as a car pulled up outside and two officers jumped out, breaking neither step nor conversation as they strode inside. Daniel trailed them up the path, catching scraps of the usual subjects: the occupation of Denmark, the sea-battle off Trondheim, whether income tax would rise to ten shillings in the pound. Thinking they must also be reporting to the Major, he followed them into the hotel, but when he entered the reception hall they had disappeared.

'Is Major Fielding here?' he asked a servant.

The man pointed him towards the dining room, where a table marked '*Réservé Monsieur le Commandant*' had been pushed against the salt-speckled windows. Daniel glanced around the room, noticing the tablecloths, the neatly folded napkins, the handwritten menus in their leather books. After months eating his meals in the Mess, he had forgotten such things existed.

At the far end of the room were doors giving on to the garden, and Daniel wandered towards them, looking out over coarse grass, spotted with daisies and yellow moss. Glossy-leaved rhododendron bushes edged the lawn, and beyond, a line of wooden benches angled towards the sea. On one of these sat two women chatting, and as Daniel lingered in the doorway, they stood up and began to gather their things. The shorter of the two, her dark hair tucked behind her ears, turned and glanced up at the hotel, and as she did Daniel saw that it was Signora Balestra from Milan. He felt a jolt of conscience, for Lucia had written to him about the family being nearby, and he had promised to visit. He turned away, doubting that she would remember him, but as he did so the Major, his booming voice causing Daniel to snap to attention, came striding into the room.

'Good, good, you're here!' Major Fielding was a large, broad-chested man, with greying temples and a kind, not quite handsome, face. He looked the younger officer over, adding, 'At ease, we're not on the parade ground now.' then glanced past him towards the garden. 'Won't be a jiffy,' he said, pointing him towards the table, and he bounced out of the door, declaring, 'Madame Balestra, *bonjour*!'

Daniel watched in dismay. He moved towards the table, playing with an edge of tablecloth as he waited for the Major to return.

'How's the invalid? Feeling better I hope.' Major Fielding was following the two women back through the door, his attention on Laura.

'Miss Lucas is pleased with her, she says she can get up in a day or two.' The other woman nodded, pinning her hat, and Daniel saw that beneath her cape she wore the uniform of a British nurse. 'Are you sure you won't have a cup of coffee?' Laura asked, but the woman shook her head.

'Better dash,' she said, 'I'm Third Floor this week, Sister Rodes has a fit if we're late. Gastric ward,' she grinned at Daniel, 'mind you don't drink the water.'

Miss Lucas hurried out, calling 'cheerio' over her shoulder, and Laura, smiling, said, 'What a pet. I do hope I haven't got her in trouble.'

'Lieutenant, this is Madame Balestra,' said the Major, pulling out a chair and gesturing to Laura to sit down. 'Will you join us for a spot of lunch? This fellow'll be glad of civilised company, billeted like pigs they are.'

Daniel blushed. 'Guérande, sir. Not too bad.'

Laura was gazing at the young officer with curiosity. 'I feel sure we've met,' she said. 'In Brussels? Or Manchester, perhaps?' She shook her head, as if to dislodge a memory.

'Milan.' Daniel glanced at Major Fielding, 'Daniel Sutton. I was staying with the Ardittis.'

'Of course, the Duomo!' Laura seized his hand, holding on to it. 'Oh how awful of me — I'm usually so good with faces.' She turned to Major Fielding. 'Major, what have you done with that schoolboy I met? He's quite transformed!'

'Fine young officer,' said the Major, although in truth he barely knew him. 'Found him stealing my VMG locks, so invited him to lunch! What do you say, will you join us?'

'You're very kind Major, but I said I'd eat with Rita. Madame Michenet has made me a tray.'

'A tray! Didn't think the old bat stretched to room service. Asked her for a cup of tea this morning, know what she said? *'On dit bonjour.'* Just like that: *On dit bonjour.* Wouldn't give me a thing until I said it, damn cheek.'

Laura smiled. 'But it's nice, Major, don't you think, people being so polite to one another?'

The Major snorted. Everything about the French was starting to get on his nerves: their formality, their unfriendliness, the way you had to fill in twenty forms to get even the smallest job done. Sooner this war got started the better, might lick one or two of them into shape. He frowned, pushing at his cuff to see his watch. 'Where's that woman with our lunch? I swear she's working for Fritz, the way she torments us. Madame Balestra, ever wonder if she's working for the other side?'

'How impatient you are,' said Laura, laughing. 'Poor Madame Michenet.'

'Poor, my foot. Costing the Treasury a fortune these billets. And for what? A bit of black pudding and no bath!'

Laura looked at him disapprovingly. 'That's not Madame's fault, it's the new restrictions,' she said, but then she stopped, for she knew there was no point. This was why Marco wanted her to find a villa. He said the British Army always stirred up tensions, he and Allegra had moved out months ago. Laura might have gone too except that the weather then was so dreadful and none of the houses she saw were heated. Perhaps now it was getting warmer she would look again. She smiled at Daniel. 'What a shame Rita is ill, she would have loved to see you. Perhaps you might join us for lunch on your day off?'

Daniel explained that he was leaving the next day to return to his regiment and the Major, patting his chest for his cigarettes, declared, 'Day off? *Au contraire*, word is we're all on two hours' notice. Keep that to yourself, mind.'

Laura turned away, looking past the Major towards the garden and the sea beyond. The news that morning had been so cheery: eighteen enemy ships sunk, the Nazi fleet trapped at Oslo. 'Miss Lucas says it'll all be over by Christmas, that the Navy will win the war for us.'

'Does she, by golly?'

'She says they're going to entice the German fleet from its lair, then smash it.'

Major Fielding leaned forward, looking for a match. 'Bit of a red herring, if you ask me, this Scandinavia business. Western Front's the one to watch.'

Laura frowned, her gaze still on the horizon. People were always doing this, making you worry the moment you started to feel brighter about things. 'Well, I think the Navy are just splendid,' she said firmly. 'We can well say Britannia rules the waves now, can't we Mr. Sutton?' She waited for him to agree, then continued. 'Miss Lucas gets it from Sister Rodes, apparently her father-in-law's something big in the French military.'

'Ah yes, General Rodes. Thought the name rang a bell.'

'He says this will be the end of Hitler and his gangsters. Says we'll all be back to our old lives soon.'

'Hmmph.' Major Fielding lit his cigarette and sat back. 'Damn nonsense. That's the trouble with those old fellows, their hearts aren't in it. Had a Colonel like that once, got himself into frightful hot water.' He tapped his forefinger on the tablecloth. 'Take a tip from me, Madame Balestra — you too, Lieutenant — there's going to be a lot more fighting before this war's over, and no fear. This time we mean business.' He grimaced, and Laura, glancing at Daniel, thought of his poor mother and paled. Behind them the door to the kitchen swung open, banging the wall and bouncing back. 'Ah, here she is at last! *Bonjour Madame!*' He winked at Laura. 'Just about given up hope.'

They all turned as Madame Michenet sailed into the room, her starched apron sticking out from her waist like the prow of a ship. She looked around, her dark eyes making no attempt at warmth, then began fussily rearranging the place settings.

'Oh, I'm not eating, Madame Michenet,' said Laura, quickly getting up, and causing the men to get up too. 'We were just chatting. This young man is a friend of Rita's, isn't that a coincidence?'

Madame Michenet pursed her lips. She was fond of Laura, felt a certain protectiveness for the young widow, but was it really appropriate for her to sit around chatting with army men like this? Indeed, Monsieur Balestra had said as much the last time he was here. He had even mentioned Major Fielding by name, but Laura had laughed and accused him of *le snobisme anglais*, whatever that was. She picked up the chair Laura had been using and returned it to its place at another table.

'Do you play golf?' The Major was asking the younger officer. 'Links course, not too bad. Care for a game this afternoon?'

'I'm rather out of practice, sir.'

'That's all right, m'boy, we all are.' The Major turned to Laura. 'Where's that son of yours? We could play a threesome.'

'Teddy? He's at school, Major.'

'Shame, he's got a fine swing. I saw him whack a seven iron into a low tide, couldn't hit it better myself.' Madame Michenet set down a bottle of wine with particular force. 'My dear woman,' began the Major with annoyance, but Laura interrupted him, putting a conciliatory hand on Madame Michenet's arm and addressing herself to Daniel.

'Of course, you know Teddy, don't you? Coco too. Lieutenant Sutton did a little sightseeing with the children, Major — the Leonardo, wasn't it? You wouldn't recognise them now, they're quite grown up.' An air of sadness had crept into her tone, and catching this, she laughed. 'Coco's even had a perm. Rather dreadful at first, but she's improved now. Everyone likes her much better.'

'Damn good way of practising bunker shots,' said the Major, gazing through the taped-up window towards the dunes beyond. 'Till some busybody local complained: endangering *la voie publique*, he said. Silly fool. No sense of enterprise, these people.'

'You're impossible, Major,' said Laura. She looked at him fondly. How nice it must be to march through life as the Major did, paying attention only to the job in hand and knowing you were part of some bigger endeavour, some greater purpose. Marriage had felt a little like that, indeed in some ways the Major reminded her of Isaac. And in other ways, not at all. She pressed her hair, remembering she was supposed to be upstairs with Rita. 'Gentlemen, will you excuse me, I really must check on my daughter.'

'Lucky we're endangering anything, considering the state of our supplies, isn't that so, Sutton? Golf balls are about the best ammo we've got just now.' Major Fielding picked up the bottle of wine, ignoring Laura's attempt to leave and declaring, 'Rally round. A toast!' He poured three glasses, sliding them across the table. 'Your health,' he said, raising his glass and looking from one to the other.

'Looks like *la vie française* suits you after all, Major,' said Laura.

'Maybe. Mud in your eye.' They drank, then for a moment stood in silence, looking out at the sunny garden. A honey bee, the first Laura had seen that year, kept dropping into view at the top of the window, and craning her neck she saw the feathery tips of the new wisteria blossoms, not yet grown to their familiar, grape-like forms. Years before, a green stem had been trained along the struts of a wooden balcony, but now, gnarled and thickened, it had become the edifice itself, parts of it painted along with the hotel. Daniel, who had followed her gaze, was thinking of the wisteria on the house in Dundee, a mass of untidy green shoots but never any flowers. He wondered what everyone was doing at this moment, if his mother was in the garden, his father at the shop? His last letter had been weeks ago. A hastily scribbled note from Ruth, telling him about a tennis match she had played, about her mother volunteering for the WVS, about how everyone was riding bicycles these days.

Major Fielding refilled their glasses. 'Of course, it's War Office,' he continued, still thinking about the state of their supplies. 'Not our concern — no cause for *le cafard*, as they say. By Jove, really quite nice, this.' He peered at the bottle. 'Perhaps Madame's fond of me after all.'

'Or fond of your Mess account,' said Laura. She set down her glass. 'I really must go. I'll be good for nothing this afternoon and I promised the children we'd call by the Carassos. Sofia lets them use her gramophone.'

'Still *Boum*?' Major Fielding grinned.

'Still *Boum*.'

'We could do with a bit of that at the Depot, eh Lieutenant?'

'Bit of boom, sir?'

'Bit of boom!' repeated the Major, rather pleased with himself. Laura, her hand raised, was moving towards the door and he called after her. 'Will I see you for our usual *rendez-vous*, Madame Balestra? *Devant le* wireless, nineteen hundred hours? We can cheer on the British Navy.'

'And the French, Major.' Laura paused in the doorway. 'They say Admiral Darlan is being wonderful.'

'Your General again? Righty ho. Hurrah for England and France.' The door closed behind Laura, and Major Fielding, dropping into his chair and gesturing to Daniel to sit too, looked around impatiently. 'Now where the devil's that woman got to with our lunch?' He banged the table with the flat of his hand, causing the glasses and cutlery to jump. 'I'll give her *Bonjour Madame*. Nerve, eh Lieutenant? Talk about a blockade. She could teach Whitehall a thing or two!'

CHAPTER 11

U pon his return to the regiment, Daniel went to see Captain Simpson. Months had gone by since the letter from HQ promising his promotion, and yet here he still was, Second Lieutenant Sutton, no better, no worse. In addition, his manual was everywhere, stacked in crates at Base Depot, handed out to new recruits with their uniforms, even, he saw now, neatly displayed on the Captain's bookshelf. At the risk of appearing pushy — '*pas d'histoires*' the Brigade Liaison Officer had advised, loosely translating as 'don't fuss' — he hoped Simpers might put a word in for him and help him on his way. GHQ was now on the Maginot Line, under the command of the French Third Army and, if nothing else, a transfer would mean eating well.

Captain Simpson was at his desk when Daniel entered. New Leave orders had come through and his was the God-like task of deciding who went when, a duty he delighted in. His sleeves rolled, his narrow moustache twitching like the whiskers of a nervous rabbit, he was scribbling furiously on his blotter, every so often looking up and listening to a conversation going on in the next room. It was between the Colonel and the local Mayor, and on the subject of winter sports. Through the open door Daniel saw the Colonel, a founder member of the Glenshee Ski Club, giving a demonstration of the correct way to bend one's knees when slaloming, while the Mayor watched and offered comments. Captain Simpson grinned contentedly, waving at Daniel to sit down.

'Lieutenant Sutton, just the fellow.' He looked back at

his blotter. 'Twelve and a half percent of three four four, any thoughts?'

'Three hundred and forty-four, sir?'

'Yes, yes.' Captain Simpson squinted at him.

'Er — forty-three, sir?'

'Hmm. That's what I got too, well done, forty-three it is. About time, the chaps are ready for a bit of R and R. Not you mind, Lieutenant, you'll have to sit tight, we want to get the key men away first. So, if I send seven officers that leaves —' He was counting on his fingers, glancing at Daniel.

'Thirty-six, sir.'

'Exactly. Thirty-six ORs. Right, have the SM do the troop roster, Lieutenant.' He scribbled the order, holding it out to Daniel. 'Did you want something?'

'To ask about my promotion, sir.'

'Promotion, Lieutenant?'

'For my report, sir. It's rather a long time ago now, but my report won the Division competition—'

'—good show, well done you.' Captain Simpson was writing on a sheet of paper, muttering aloud to himself, 'Squadron Leaders, Technical Officer, Medical Officer, Squadron Sarn't Majors, is that everyone?' He looked up. 'What is it, Lieutenant? Get to the point.'

'Sorry sir. The thing is, I was to be transferred, made a Staff Officer, but it's been months now. I've called up GHQ but they say it's a Third Army matter, and, well, Third Army say the post's been filled.'

The Captain gazed at him blankly, his mind clearly elsewhere. This recent Norway business had got everyone jittery, it would do the men good to get back to Blighty for a while, see how normal everything was. 'My dear chap, sounds like you got the wrong end of the stick.' He stood up, moving towards the Colonel's office and quietly closing the door.

'Happens all the time with these Frogs, that's where the Liaison chaps come in. Ask that prince fellow,' — the Brigade Liaison Officer claimed direct descent from Louis Quinze — 'he's your best bet.' He sat down again, looking back at his list. 'Will I get Major Palmer away too? While we're still on Troop Training?'

'But that's just it, sir. It was Prince Murat who told me about Kershaw, sir, about his move.'

'Kershaw? What's he got to do with anything?'

'Apparently he was transferred to GHQ, sir.'

'That's right, he was, couple of months ago now. Bit of a mystery really, I didn't see him as the type.' He looked at Daniel, his moustache quivering in what was almost a smile. '*Un mystère*, as they say. Or is it *une*, I never remember?'

'*Un mystère*, sir.'

'Tricky, all these le and la, I can't see how anyone remembers.'

'No, sir.'

'Do you know, I think I will. I'll get Major Palmer away too. What's that then, eight officers? Better take off an OR, tell the SM thirty-five.' He held out his hand for the order, scrawling a thick five where the six had been and passing it back again.

Daniel folded the paper and slipped it inside the front of his jacket. 'The thing is, sir, it was Lieutenant Kershaw signed the commendation. You don't suppose he was promoted in my place?'

Captain Simpson eyed Daniel, chewing the end of his pen. He was not an unkind man, but there were moments when these young fellows tested his patience. 'Cock-up, you mean?'

Daniel nodded.

The Captain considered this for a moment. 'Highly likely. Of course, there's not much you can do about it now.

Should really have brought it up earlier.'

'I didn't know—' began Daniel, but the Captain interrupted him.

'—Gas Attack, eh? Colonel was just saying we need to brush up our Gas schemes, last drill was a shower. D'you think you might give a few lectures, seeing you're the expert?'

'Of course, sir.' Daniel's voice cracked. How would he tell his parents his promotion had been given to the wrong man? It sounded so implausible. He wished now he had never told anyone, he should have known it was too good to be true.

'Good show,' said the Captain, turning back to his list. 'Now, where was I? Ten days' leave. All right for some, isn't it Lieutenant!' He paused, struck by the look of misery on the young officer's face. 'I say, cheer up, it's not as bad as all that!'

'No sir.'

'Doesn't do to advance too fast. People don't like it.' The Captain's own career had been a slow, careful progression, one that was still very much under way. He leaned forward, his small eyes with their red rims fixing Daniel sternly, so that when Daniel looked back on this conversation he would remember it as a warning. 'Keep your head down, Lieutenant Sutton, work hard, that's how you get on in this business.'

'Yes, sir.'

The Captain's expression softened. 'Right, then. And thirty-five, not thirty-six, remember. Colonel's a martinet when it comes to his numbers!'

WITH MANY OF THE SENIOR OFFICERS home on leave, duties in the camp fell to the subalterns. In addition to the promised Gas lectures and Troop Training, Daniel was given responsibility for the Regimental Diary, and he spent his evenings trying to think of different ways of writing 'dull and overcast,' which it mostly was. But towards the end of the first week, the weather lifted, and instead of spending evenings in the Mess, the men would wander into town, playing boules in the square or sitting outside a bar, where wine was brought in pichons and beer served cold. Here they would discuss the news from Norway (not good) and debate when exactly Italy would come in, and Lieutenant Wilkinson, with whom Daniel maintained a curt civility, would make a nuisance of himself with the waitress, so that someone always had to take him home.

On the night the next Leave List went up, Daniel and Gilbert, finding themselves once again not on it, headed out of camp alone, borrowing bicycles and pedalling cross-country towards a swimming spot one of the ORs had discovered. Tomorrow was Whit Friday, and Gilbert had hoped to be going home, had even bought presents to take with him — saucisson, cheese, a bottle of the local Calvados — which were now in his basket to share with Daniel. The land here was reserved for intensive training, and where there had once been crops there were now the ruts and tracks of tank manoeuvres, causing the bicycles to rattle as violently as if they had been cobblestones. With the sun on their backs, the sky turning from blue to pink to flaming orange, they stopped to pull off their shirts, riding the last part bare-chested and shouting to one another above the clatter of wheels. Out of breath, laughing and shoving one another like the children they still were, they stripped off and ran down the bank into the inky black water, shrieking as the cold hit them with a slap. The riverbed was silty, their feet sinking to the ankles, and they kicked and thrashed until they were out in deeper water, where they lay on their backs and drifted in the current, looking up at the darkening sky. It was a new moon, only the thinnest edge of silver showing, like the blade of a scythe, and Daniel, floating dreamily, imagined the sky was a ripe wheat-field that the moon would mow. All around them they heard the chirrs and trills of evening, the lu-lu-lu-lu of a nightingale, the goo-ku of a cuckoo. Frogs in the soft grass of the riverbank croaked and clamoured, percussion to the songbirds' vocals, and an owl, silent but for the thump of its wings, flashed white against the canopy of trees.

'Just fancy, a whole summer of this.' Gilbert moved his arms up and down, churning the surface. 'Like a hot bath, this is. I'm not a bit cold.'

'Hitler weather.' Daniel was still gazing at the sky, and now he raised an arm, pointing. 'There's the castle, do you see? Up there, through the trees, looks impressive, doesn't it?'

Gilbert did not reply. He was watching the bats, looping above the water like bunting.

'The architect was beheaded. So he couldn't build one for anyone else. I've been reading about it.'

'Listen.' Gilbert craned his neck, his arms still working to keep him afloat. All around them the sound of clicking, like so many tiny snapping fingers. Daniel turned his head, hearing now the bats, now the sloshing of water, now the leaves rustling on their sap-filled branches, now the squeak of the cattails at the river's edge. A dragonfly thrummed past, keeping low over the water; moments later another one followed, taking the same line and then disappearing out of sight. Beneath their legs, fish twisted and turned, sometimes rising, sometimes drifting in the shallows. A fat trout broke the surface with a splash, surprising them, and they stopped floating and trod water, watching for it to do it again. A church clock tolled in the distance, a solid, heavy chime, not the clarion of an English bell but deeper, more noble somehow.

'Ten o'clock already,' said Gilbert, counting the peals.

'We've missed the news,' said Daniel. 'Should be something about Chamberlain.'

Gilbert rolled onto his stomach, his chin in the water like a crocodile, and began paddling back towards the side. Daniel watched him haul himself onto the bank, reeds and twigs snapping beneath his weight, then disappear beyond the ridge where they had left the bicycles. Moments later he returned, buckling his trousers, his shirt open over his bare chest, carrying the basket with their picnic. Sitting on the fallen trunk of a willow tree, its branches still green with leaves, he put the bottle of calvados between his knees and took out his penknife.

'Likely he'll be for the chop too,' he said, meaning Chamberlain, 'like the castle fellow.'

There was a pop as the cork worked free. He poured himself a glass and leaned back.

'And what's that?' he asked, pointing through the trees, to where a silver pinprick of light glowed in the dimming sky.

'That? That's Jupiter. It's always the brightest at this time of night. Mars should be around somewhere too.'

Daniel peered around, but the canopy of trees was too dense, and after a while he flipped over, tucking his knees to his chest and turning lazy somersaults in the water. When he bored of doing that, he kicked his legs and dived down, until his hands found the bumpy surface of the riverbed. Opening his eyes he saw only black water, but his fingers grabbed at the grit and silt, and as he rose again he brought a handful with him. He came up amongst the trails of chickweed and watercress that lined the riverbank, shaking his head to clear the water from his ears, and looking up to where Gilbert was sitting, just above. He had lit a pipe and the glowing embers cast shadows on his face, giving it a ghostly look.

'Here, catch!' He swung his arm, throwing the mud as if it were a cricket ball. Gilbert ducked and the mud landed in the ferny bank behind.

'Hey! Mind my brandy!'

Daniel laughed, gazing back at the river. 'What a place,' he said. 'Who cares if we never get leave, if we can come here.'

'We'll get leave,' said Gilbert. 'Simpers reckons end of the month. Can't wait. Never thought I'd miss Dundee, but I do. Miss my old mum. Miss my bed. Miss waking up to a cup of tea and bacon bap.'

'You get tea and bacon baps here.'

'Not the same.'

Daniel reflected on this. It seemed strange to him, the idea of missing home. He supposed that years of boarding school had knocked it out of him, for he felt none of the nostalgia Gilbert expressed. Indeed, on the rare occasion he thought of Dundee, of his parents and Ruth and the home where he spent his holidays, he mostly felt guilty. Guilty that he was missed, guilty that it was he who had been given all the opportunities, guilty, now he'd lost his promotion, that he might have disappointed them. He sighed, not wishing to linger on such thoughts, and Gilbert, imagining he was cold, reached down and helped him up the bank.

'This'll warm you up,' he said, pouring him a brandy.

Daniel found his clothes, pulling them on. then taking the glass from Gilbert and sitting down next to him on the fallen trunk. His skin burned from the chill water, and he had that hollow, light feeling which often follows vigorous exercise, so that he wanted to slap and stamp his feet. Gilbert was cutting slices of sausage, and Daniel picked them from the point of his knife, his fingers clumsy with cold. The night was quiet now, the only sound the rhythmic purring of the river, and for a while they did not speak. Above their heads the sliver of moon continued to rise, and, looking up, Daniel searched again for Mars. He was remembering a night at the Depot, not long after he had arrived in France, when Major

Fielding had ordered everyone outside to see Venus, Jupiter, Saturn, Mars and Mercury lined up one above the other. It could be fifty years, he said, before they shared the same sky again, and everyone had looked at him blankly, for theirs was a generation that lived only for today, that could not conceive of such a time. He turned to Gilbert, thinking to ask if he had seen it too, but as he did, Gilbert stood up, brushing himself off.

'Come on, best be getting back.'

A breeze ruffled the leaves overhead, then silence.

'Not yet,' said Daniel.

Gilbert shrugged, reaching for the Calvados and pouring them both another glass. Daniel continued to gaze at the sky, the vast stillness communicating itself to him, so that his thoughts quieted and he felt utterly calm.

'Why did no one tell me about Kershaw? I could have done something about it if I'd known.'

'Kershaw?'

'Him getting my promotion.' Daniel looked directly at his friend, his skin still stinging from the cold water, so that he felt strangely invulnerable. 'Surely everyone knew.'

Gilbert shrugged. Out of sight was out of mind in the army. 'You weren't here,' he said.

'You could have sent me a note.' Daniel turned away, his gaze fixing on the tightly coiled scroll of a young fern. Seahorses, his mother called them. Apparently when boiled, they tasted of asparagus. 'Was it because of that Wilkinson business? Is that why?'

Gilbert stared at him, bemused. 'I don't follow.'

Daniel did not answer. He thought of that last evening in Aldershot, the words 'Pick it up, you bloody Hebrew,' as vivid as if they had been spoken just yesterday. He sighed. The more he reflected on it, the more sure he was that it was his Jewishness — that old offender — which had scuppered his advance.

'I'd be on the Maginot Line now,' he said, aware of the pointlessness of the comment, but saying it anyway.

Gilbert leaned forward, patting the ground for his tobacco. 'Then you had a lucky escape, my friend. They live like moles up there. They'll all have rickets before the year's out.' He looked up, grinning as he struck a match, gesturing with his pipe at the river, the trees, the silent landscape. 'Besides, look what you got in its place. Maginot's got nothing on this.' He lay back, his arms extending either side of him along the tree-trunk, his ankles crossed.

Daniel looked at him, envying such ease, such ownership. Even Nature, it seemed, was there for Gilbert's comfort. 'Rickets?'

'No sunlight.' Gilbert yawned, his head dropping back, curls of blue smoke rising into the air between them. 'MO thinks it's a real problem.'

IT WAS JUST AFTER DAWN WHEN they cycled back to camp. Gilbert had fallen asleep, and Daniel, seeing no reason to wake him, had spent the night drinking brandy and smoking, listening to the creaks and groans of nature as he might have listened to the creaks and groans of a house. Now, as the first streaks of colour began to gather on the horizon, and the sun began its lissom ascent, they made their way through the narrow streets of the town, beneath the shadows of the castle, to their billets. Gilbert was in good spirits, standing on his pedals and surveying the bright morning, his head constantly turning this way and that, as if afraid to miss something. Behind him, heavy limbed and heavy headed, Daniel did his best to keep up.

'Will we see if Claudine's awake?' Claudine was the baker's wife, a pretty, round-faced woman, who might herself have been made out of dough. 'Maybe she'll take pity and give us breakfast.'

Daniel shook his head. If he was clever he could still get a couple of hours' sleep before roll call. He glanced up, the sky now a light mauve, swallows reeling above the shuttered windows. 'Bed for me,' he said.

But at that moment there was a loud scraping noise, and from the next street, rounding the corner at great speed, a Humber shooting-brake hurtled into view. Straight away they recognised it as the Colonel's, and they jumped to attention, bicycles clattering to the ground, their fingers pressed hard against their brows. But if the driver saw them he did not slow, the car flashing past and then disappearing, and they had just time to note the familiar head of Colonel Smart looking grimly through the rear window.

'Christ,' said Gilbert, gazing after the departing Humber, 'what's that all about?'

Daniel yawned. 'Who cares?' He climbed back onto his bicycle. 'Come on, let's go.'

'Not like him to be up so early.'

'Probably off on one of his jollies.' The Colonel's social engagements were a source of constant wonder.

Gilbert grinned. 'Breakfast with Lady Gort?' He bent down, pushing his trousers back inside his socks. 'At the Paris Ritz.'

'You mean the Crillon,' corrected Daniel. 'Only Americans go to the Ritz.'

Gilbert snorted and picked up his bicycle, kicking the pedals so that they spun. At the same time there was a crackling sound in the far distance, like thunder or a lorry tipping gravel, and Gilbert looking questioningly at his friend. 'Ack-acks?'

Daniel nodded. 'Probably Pontoise.' Recently the anti-aircraft guns had been going off at all hours. 'Natives getting restless.'

Gilbert squinted in the direction of the noise. It was a

cloudless morning, but there, above the horizon, black specks had appeared, followed by tiny brown and white puffs that fizzled and went out. He watched, fascinated, but Daniel had set off, his wheel veering left and right as he got his balance, and after a moment Gilbert followed. 'Who could sleep on a morning like this,' he mused, catching up as they passed the sugar factory. With its blue painted windows and arching roof, all of it glowing, it might have been a cathedral, and Gilbert, surprising himself, thought, 'God is everywhere, even in a sugar factory.' But to Daniel he said, 'How about a café Cognac? Start the day properly.'

Daniel laughed. 'Go to bed, Gilbert,' he said with affection. Off towards the north the sky was still crackling, but there were more trees here and the wood-pigeons mostly drowned it out. And he turned into the narrow lane that led to his billet, waving as Gilbert cycled on alone.

CHAPTER 12

In fact, sleep was to be elusive that particular day. No sooner had Daniel closed his eyes than they were open again, peering at the bristly face of Corporal Grimes as he leaned over his bed, urging him to wake up. A small dog was in the room too, whining and nipping at Grimes' trouser leg, and every so often the corporal turned and aimed a kick at it, cursing beneath his breath.

'Balloon's gone up, sir— ow!' Again the cursing, followed by more barking, then a loud stream of high-pitched French. This last confused Daniel, but then he sat up and found that the room also contained his elderly landlady, Madame Rouget, still in her nightdress, with rags waving about her curled grey hair, like some ghostly Medusa.

'Hell's going on, Grimes?'

'It's started, sir, Jerry's in Belgium!' He had picked up Daniel's discarded shirt and was holding it out to him. 'You're wanted at HQ, sir. Something about—' he glanced at his hand, where there were numbers written in thick black marker, 'Something about G1098, sir. Ouch! Bastard bit me!'

'Active-service scale,' said Daniel, swinging his legs out of bed. He grinned at Grimes. 'Basic allowances. It means we're moving up. Not that one, Grimes, a clean one! *Alors, Madame Rouget, ça y'est!*' He beamed at the old woman, who had caught hold of the dog and was dragging it out of the room. Her buttocks beneath the cotton of her nightdress were like two enormous hams.

'He's in Holland too, sir, causing bloody hell by the sound of it. Mind, now Winston's in charge — you heard about Churchill, did ye sir? Old Winston'll sort him out, right enough. Are these yours, sir?' He had picked up Daniel's boots, still spattered with mud from the river bank.

'Well, I don't know who else's they'd be. Leave them, Grimes, I'll do them.' Daniel prided himself on keeping his belongings neat, having Grimes in here was like having his mother poking around.

'Need a batman, y'do sir,' said the corporal, producing a handkerchief from his pocket and looking around for something to dampen it.

'Over there,' said Daniel quickly, pointing to a pitcher of water by his mirror. He was worried Grimes was about to spit on it. 'Really, Grimes, isn't there something more useful you could be doing?'

Grimes did not reply. The main thing he had learnt working for Daniel's father was not to pay attention when he spoke sharply. He never meant it, and the boy — hardly a boy now — was just the same. He turned his back, concentrating on cleaning the boots, polishing them with his sleeve when he had finished, and setting them down in front of Daniel. 'That's better.'

'And you're sure it's the real thing?' Daniel was buckling his Sam Browne, thinking of the Colonel in the back of the Humber, how serious he had looked.

'SM seems to think so. Goering — that's the fat one? — aye well, it's his lot mostly in their rotten Heinkels. Bombing everything, they are. Can y'manage, sir?' He had picked up a shoe-horn, but Daniel waved it away. 'Right then, will I run you up in the lorry? I've got it outside.'

'Thank you, Grimes.'

'Dump the surplus, that's what we've to do. Funny, all you hear about is what we haven't got, then next minute we're dumping what we have. Makes no sense.' He opened the door to the landing, listening first for the dog, then peering out. When he turned back he saw that Daniel had not moved, but was gazing blankly out of the window. Feeling the man's eyes on him, Daniel rubbed at his chin, as if contemplating whether he should shave.

Grimes smiled. He was remembering all the times he'd driven the boy back to school, watching in the rear mirror as his face grew paler the closer they got to their destination. Funny how so much about a person could change, so that they were almost unrecognisable, and then, bam! the years fall away and it's just a boy being driven to school. 'We've time, sir,' he said kindly. 'You know what these Froggies are like, they'll want their breakfast first.'

Daniel thought about this. It was true that any orders would need to come from the French High Command. 'No, let's go. No doubt you'd like something to eat yourself, Grimes, I hear it's rather good these days, since the QM brought in a local.'

'Fries his eggs in butter, sir. You never tasted anything like it.'

'I dare say. Perhaps that's what Fifi found so irresistible.'

'Fifi, sir?' He followed Daniel onto the landing.

'Madame Rouget's dog. She's usually such a quiet thing. So is Madame, for that matter.' Daniel looked sideways at the older man, his eyes laughing.

'Aye, I have that effect on all the ladies, sir,' said Grimes.

IT WAS ANOTHER FOUR DAYS before the Regiment moved up: four days of sorting files at HQ and offloading surplus stores; four days of sticking pins in maps to chart the enemy's advance, and then four days of moving them southwards; four days of waiting for the officers on leave in England to return, and knowing they would not; four days of glorious hot summer, during which war still seemed a world away.

On the evening of their departure — they were a late serial and it was almost midnight before they set off — the news from the front was so gloomy they were advised to disregard it. The Fifth Column, the Colonel assured them, was the real enemy. Think of all those imaginary parachutists they had been sent to investigate. When a passing civilian announced the surrender of the Dutch army, the Colonel lost his temper and had a man arrest him. He understood that battles are won as much by faith as they are by bullets.

It was a clear, moonlit night. They were to entrain at Evreux, and the convoy assembled on the main road north, tanks and carriers at the fore, troop lorries towing the 25-pounders following, HQ and supplies at the back. Officers on motorcycles wove up and down the line, measuring the distance between vehicles (eighty yards was advisable) and reminding the drivers to aim for a steady 12.5mph, because any faster over the *pavés* and it would damage the suspension. Once they arrived in Belgium, where roads were built from concrete, they might speed up a little. The men were excited: had you put a hand to their chest, it would have felt hot, like the grilles which covered the tank-engines. Boots tapped in foot-wells, fingers drummed steering-wheels or fiddled with route cards. Every so often a song would start up, usually in the back of one of the troop lorries, but quickly spreading down the line, '*Mademoiselle from Armentieres, parlez-vous?*', '*Roll out the barrel,*' '*Oh, oh, oh! It's a lovely war!*' Daniel, checking the straps on the last of the office trucks, raised his head to listen. 'This is it,' he thought. 'This is what we've been waiting for.'

And then slowly, axles grinding, men cheering, the convoy moved off. From where he stood at the rear, Daniel watched them snaking away, each single headlamp, veiled and tilted down, tracing a small blue circle on the black road, like beads on a necklace. Women in cotton frocks, shawls tugged about their shoulders against the night air, waved from their doorsteps and threw flowers. '*Vous vous battez comme des tigres!*' cried one of them, and Grimes, driving one of the 15cwts and waiting for Daniel to jump in, grinned and gave a thumbs up.

The journey was uneventful, along wide straight roads lined with impossibly tall poplars, their leaves making a shushing sound that the men, sleepy now, were happy to obey. Later, when Daniel tried to remember what it had been like before, this was the image he would return to. And although it was dark and he was at the rear, he would imagine every detail: the Colonel leading in his shooting brake, the tanks and the carriers strewn with flowers, himself, different then, chatting with Grimes. He would see Gilbert standing up in his hatch, Captain Simpson weaving around in the second Humber, Clayton rumbling alongside on a motorcycle, pointing out the cattle in the field and saying, 'Look, did you know cows grazed at night?'. He could even pick out Wilkinson, his thick frame hunched over the steering wheel, complaining about the truck in front, or how dark it was, his loud voice braying in the still, silent night.

CHAPTER 13

On the seventeenth of May, then, a full week after German troops invaded the Low Countries, the regiment crossed the border into Belgium. They were to head east towards the town of Ath, and Daniel, still in charge of the regimental diary, scribbled the route on a piece of paper so that he should remember it. The roads were heaving with refugees, a relentless tide of traffic coming the other way: mattress-topped motorcars, carts drawn by horses or mules, bicycles, people pushing prams or barrows, and all of it crawling along, weary mile after weary mile.

'Poor sods,' murmured Daniel. He was writing a report for Brigade about their missing equipment, files strewn across the seat. 'Easy over the bumps, can't you, Grimes?'

'Sorry, sir.'

Voices wafted through the open window — Dutch, Flemish, Walloon, French — and Daniel listened, picking up occasional scraps. Antwerp was burning; the enemy had broken the French line at Wavre; Italy was attacking Yugoslavia. Likely none of it was true, and even if it were, there would be little they could do right now. Daniel sighed.

'Another scorcher, eh, sir?'

Daniel looked at Grimes blankly.

'I'd put the fan on, sir, but I'm worried she'll boil up. Good mornink! Good mornink!' Grimes leaned out, grinning at a group of Dutch nuns and mimicking their polite greetings. 'Just like Draffen's, that'd be.'

'Draffen's?'

'Still see the D on the back panel, sir. Palmed us off with a right load of shite. What's the Froggie for knackered, sir?'

Daniel smiled, gathering up the files and tucking them beneath the seat. Draffen's were old rivals of his father's, something the corporal was well aware of. '*Crevé*, I believe.'

'*Crey-vay?*' He tried it out. '*Crevvay*. Thank you, sir, I'll use that.'

Progress was slow. The convoy stopped and started, stopped and started — every so often Grimes obliged to get out and drag aside some obstacle or remonstrate with someone coming the other way. From the height of the lorry, Daniel could look straight into the squat, redbrick houses that lined the road, and he wondered at the families who lived there. Was that breakfast laid out on the table, or was it some other meal, abandoned days before? Were the curtains drawn against the sun, or was it because the house was empty, the inhabitants long since departed? In one, a woman sat straight-backed on a chair, tears streaming down her face, on her lap a pillowcase into which she had gathered a few belongings. As the convoy passed she glanced up, catching Daniel's eye, but her expression was so wretched that Daniel looked away, ashamed. These people had been here before: they had built their homes on the ruins of other homes, dug their gardens on the mud and shell-craters left behind the last time the invader passed this way. For a long while afterwards he kept his gaze on the road.

And now, in amongst the cars and the barrows, soldiers began to appear. Some were in vehicles, horns blasting as they wove in and out. Others rode bicycles or hurried along on foot. There were French Colonial troops, with their distinctive yellow cuffs, Belgian infantry or artillery men, hatless and usually without weapons, even the occasional officer.

'*Vous allez où?*' demanded Daniel. The column had stopped again, and he leaned out of the window, waving to a Belgian gunner. The man's uniform was in tatters, his head bare.

'*On rentre pour s'organiser*,' said the man, the words thrown over his shoulder as he hurried past.

'What was that, sir?' asked Grimes.

'Pulling back to 'reorganise',' said Daniel grimly. He did not believe it for a moment, and was about to say so when a commotion up ahead interrupted him. Traffic had halted on an intersecting road and people were running into the fields at either side, screaming and throwing themselves into ditches. Daniel leaned forward, rubbing at the windscreen with his sleeve, and Grimes did the same. And then the screaming became louder, and it was coming from above them, a loud, piercing wail that seemed to split the sky, rip it apart as a knife rips through fabric, and they watched as a dark shadow hurtled vertically towards the earth. It was like an enormous bird of prey, its wings with their black crosses rigid at its side, talons outstretched. At the last moment, when it seemed that it must certainly crash, the nose lifted and they heard the crackle of machine gun fire and the whine of falling bombs, then the earth leapt up, once, twice, three times, columns of black smoke rising through the air. The lorry rocked on its axle and dust billowed in the open windows, and when it cleared, Daniel found he was holding his pistol and he was firing out of the window at an empty sky, pop, pop, pop!

He lowered his arm, slumping back against the seat. Grimes had set the wipers going and was splashing water from his canteen over the windscreen. He glanced over at Daniel. 'Could do with you on the Brens, sir,' he said. 'Didn't hear a single one.'

The pistol was warm against Daniel's thigh, and he

pushed it away, feeling foolish. It was true, the column had offered no defence. 'I should check the trucks.' Daniel put his hand on the door to open it, hoping his legs would support him.

'They're fine, sir. Not a scratch, I'd say.' Grimes nodded towards the wing mirror. Now the smoke had cleared, they saw the rear of the convoy stretched out behind them. 'Jerry needs his eyes testing, sir, missed us by a mile. Hold tight, we're off.'

The limber in front shuddered and rumbled slowly forwards, just as figures began to emerge from the ditches, sobbing and calling out to one another. Grimes slipped the lorry into gear, following slowly after, and Daniel watched as bicycles were recovered, motorcars started up again, carts and barrows set upright. A man was walking towards them across the field, stepping carefully over each furrow, in his arms a bundle, Daniel dared not look what. Nearer, thrown by the blast, a horse, a hole where its stomach had been, the road around it red and slippery. Suitcases spewing silverware, a birdcage, silk dresses fluttering from the window of an upturned car — everywhere Daniel looked he saw strewn the precious parts of a life, the parts someone had chosen to save. He turned back to Grimes. 'We should help them.'

'We are helping 'em, sir.' Grimes shifted in his seat, concentrating on the muzzle of the 25-pounder. 'Or we will, just as soon as we get there.'

Daniel frowned. He was thinking of the bundle in the man's arms: it must have been a child. He felt nauseous, and he closed his eyes, letting the breeze from the open window cool his prickling skin. Grimes chattered on, something about the Military Police and how they should never allow refugees onto these roads. 'Fast convoys, heavy convoys, one-way traffic,' he said, counting them off on his fingers. That was how things were arranged in the last war.

'Bunch of schoolboys, them Redcaps, that's the problem,' he said, leaning forward over the wheel. He glanced at Daniel. 'Due respect, sir.'

HQ WAS A FARMHOUSE OFF THE main Ath road. Here they learned that the rumours were true: that the enemy had broken through at Sedan, that the BEF were falling back, that disaster was imminent. A speedy retreat was the Allies' only hope, and to this end the regiment was ordered into position on the River Dendre, charged with keeping the bridges open for the withdrawal, then blowing them before the enemy could cross. This was text-book soldiering, and the men moved up with good cheer, glad at last to have their shot at Jerry. 'First party with the Boche!' the Colonel announced as the squadrons moved off, and the officers grinned and said things like 'Now he'll catch it!' and 'Soon show those Prussian bastards!'

Daniel watched as the last of the carriers disappeared around the corner. Brigade had promised the regiment more artillery, and he was to remain at HQ until it arrived, then accompany it up the line. In the meantime there was plenty to do, for the regiment had only one small-scale map for the area, and so he had set up a table in the garden and was making copies onto tracing paper. The sun warmed his back as he worked, throwing squares of yellow onto the grass and flowerbeds, and every so often he would look up and squint at the blue sky beyond the trees, at the birds which flashed black and white as they swooped, at the plumes of grey and orange smoke that moved back and forth like curtains on the horizon. Occasionally the telephone rang, and he would run inside to answer it, but mostly it was quiet, only the rumble of traffic on the road above and the clatter of distant artillery to accompany his thoughts.

Towards dusk, a Liaison Officer arrived with an order for the regiment to withdraw. Daniel radioed through to Captain Simpson, who was at Brigade, who passed the order to the Squadron Leaders in their positions on the river. The troops promptly retreated, but barely had they arrived back at HQ, engines softly turning over, men chatting and kicking their heels, when another order arrived sending them back again. All chaos ensued. The summer nights were short and it was three or four miles across open ground to their positions. With officers cursing and men scrambling for their vehicles, they moved off again, Gilbert Ross waving from his turret and shouting 'Conquer or die!' because that was Gamelin's *Ordre du Jour*.

'Situation's damnable.' Captain Simpson was at his desk when Daniel came back into the farmhouse sometime later. From this angle, with his flat face and rounded shoulders, he reminded Daniel of the seals that surfaced from time to time along the Tay Estuary.

'Admirable, sir?' He had misheard.

'Damnable, you fool, damnable!' He glared at the younger officer, his mouth working nervously and his moustache moving up and down like a sluice-gate. Daniel, chastened, made no reply, and after a while the Captain looked away. 'Still no sign of the artillery?' he asked.

'No, sir.'

'You've called Brigade?'

'Yes, sir. On its way, they said.'

Captain Simpson stood up and crossed to the window, the buckles on his boots making a tinny, jangling sound as he walked. 'If the enemy attack, we'll never hold,' he said, his voice small and unfamiliar. He looked back at Daniel. 'Have you thought about that?'

'Yes, sir.' A knot had been forming in Daniel's stomach all night. At first he had thought it was hunger, then lack of sleep.

Now he understood it as fear. On the desk was one of the maps he had been tracing earlier, and he gazed at it helplessly. The regiment were at the extreme right of the British front, with eleven bridges and some thirteen miles of riverbank under their guard. 'We could ask the Dragoons, sir.'

'The Dragoons?'

'On our left sir.' He pointed to the map. 'HQ is in Bouvignies, sir, it's only a few miles from here. They might lend us some guns — to stiffen the line, just till ours arrive.'

The Captain was silent. Silhouetted against the window, it was impossible to read his expression. But suddenly he was nodding, looking around for his cap, for the keys to the Humber. 'Come on, Lieutenant,' he said, grabbing the map and rolling it as he walked, 'what the hell are you waiting for?'

They set off north. Almost immediately, however, they became snarled up in the mass of retreating vehicles: troop lorries, ambulances, trucks carrying ammunition and petrol, armoured cars and tanks. And in between, filling the gaps like sand around flagstones, infantrymen, marching back with lowered heads, disbelief written in every weary step. The Captain pounded the horn, waving his stick out of the open window and cursing with increasing agitation, but it was to no avail, and the first streaks of daylight were starting to appear when finally they pulled up at a small farmhouse with a sign fixed to the wall: '4/7 RDG HQ'.

A sergeant was leaning in the doorway, smoking a cigarette and talking to someone inside, and at the sound of the car he straightened up.

'Can I help you, sir?' Captain Simpson was already climbing out, and the sergeant, noticing the insignia on the officer's cap, grinned and said, 'CO'll be glad to see you, sir. He was getting worried.'

Captain Simpson looked around, shaking the creases

from his trousers. The slow drive had distressed him still further. 'Is he here?' He looked past the sergeant towards the farmhouse. In the greyness of dawn, his cheeks gave off an unusually pink glow.

'Expecting him any minute, sir,' said the man. 'Will you sit down?' He pointed to a wicker bath-chair on the grass, glancing at Daniel and adding, 'Only one, I'm afraid. Don't know where they disappear to.' Inside the farmhouse a wireless was crackling, and the sergeant turned his head, straining to catch a few words. 'Best see to that. Won't be a tick, sir.'

Captain Simpson sat down, his head sinking briefly onto his chest then, with effort, lifting again. His eyes were dull but there was an elasticity about his features, so that it seemed possible that any emotion might present itself. He looked at Daniel, then at his wristwatch. It was 4 a.m.

Just then voices could be heard on the other side of the garden, and through a gap in the hedge appeared a man of medium build, with a ruddy complexion and neatly trimmed moustache. He wore riding-boots and tailored breeches and he walked with the wide-kneed gait of a man who has spent his life on horses. He was followed by two subalterns, and, hearing their approach, the sergeant put his head out of the door and said cheerily, 'Here he is, sir.'

Captain Simpson leapt to his feet, introducing himself and launching into a rapid and flustered account of his regiment's misfortunes. Daniel listened in dismay, thinking how much worse it all sounded when put like that — the missing gun-locks and shoulder-pieces, bridges not yet blown, troops barely in position, the promised gun-battery failing to arrive.

'We haven't even finished Troop Training,' he concluded, looking around morosely.

'Haven't finished Troop Training!' A guffaw from the two subalterns greeted this last, and Captain Simpson bristled, because what was funny about not completing their schemes? He began to protest, but then he saw that the Dragoon Colonel was grinning too, and he stopped.

'I'm afraid we're all in the same boat on that one,' said the Colonel. 'Listen to the ground, that's what I tell the men, the ground'll tell you what to do.'

Captain Simpson smiled weakly. He was going to have to get to the point. 'Sir,' he began, but the other man cut him off.

'You want to borrow some of my guns, is that it?'

Captain Simpson nodded. 'Just till our own arrive, sir.'

The other man considered this. 'Not as if it isn't in our interest, I suppose,' he said, thinking aloud. 'That right flank's been on my mind all night. What do you need?'

'Anything you can spare, sir.' Captain Simpson turned to Daniel, but Daniel had been distracted by the sound of shell-fire from the direction of the town, and was not listening.

'I'll see what I can do. Sergeant, is that sausages I can smell?'

'Yes, sir. Rabbit, sir.'

'Care for a spot of breakfast, gentlemen?' Daniel was still gazing nervously towards the town. 'There's plenty of time yet, Lieutenant, the enemy's just checking where we are, warming up the guns. Is the wireless back up, Sergeant? Can we get through to B Squadron, see if they can spare a platoon of Brens?'

'And perhaps some VMGs, if you had any going,' said Captain Simpson hopefully.

The Dragoon Colonel sighed. 'All right, we'll see about some Vickers too. And in return, you can do me a favour. There's a rumour the bridges aren't being blown, that the Frogs are buggering off without setting the explosives first. I need to know my flank is secure, that the bridges'll be blown when the time comes. You could check and let me know.

Understood? Can't have the enemy slipping over and getting behind me.'

'Yes, sir. Lieutenant Sutton here will see to it directly.' He turned to Daniel, adding, 'Perhaps you can borrow a motorbike, Lieutenant. I'll be needing the car to get back to HQ.'

'The sergeant will sort you out, have your breakfast first,' said the Dragoon Colonel, beginning to walk away. As an afterthought he turned back, 'You know what you're looking for, do you, Lieutenant?'

'We covered it in manoeuvres, sir,' said Daniel.

'Oh well, in that case!' The Colonel glanced at Captain Simpson, his cheeks bright again and his small teeth chewing at the corner of his moustache. 'Be just like in manoeuvres, won't it Captain?'

The regiment was now back in position. From A Squadron's HQ south of the main bridge, the town rose up like some enormous tapestry, each brick and tile carefully stitched into place, the colours vivid and sharp. Lollipop trees, unnaturally green, punctuated the stone quay, and below, reflected in the violet-brown water, upside down versions that wobbled with the current. In recent days, thousands of feet had marched these streets, but they were gone now, in their place the usual debris of a retreat: broken-down vehicles, discarded uniforms, petrol cans, stores, anything deemed too cumbersome to save. Men too — French, Dutch, Belgian, British — sleeping in doorways or stretched out along the towpath, every so often reviving and setting off again, so that to anyone watching it was as if the landscape itself had got up and walked.

Captain Hughes, or Hughie as he was known to his men, was standing on the south side, his elbows on the bonnet of a 3-tonner, field-glasses pressed to his eyes as he studied the opposite riverbank. Beside him, his foot tapping involuntarily, was Gilbert, and to their right, crouched beneath the truck, A Squadron's wireless operator, from whose lap came the occasional wail and crackle of a dying radio. They were watching one of their tanks move onto the bridge, Hughie hoping to get sufficient artillery across that the enemy could be kept in the north of the town. But just as the tank approached the bridgehead the skies erupted, and shells rained down from the far side, some pounding the cobbled street, others landing in the water, so that where before had been calm and sunshine, now was dust and smoke and wet black rubble. Windows overlooking the river shattered, the glass splintering in its frame, then slowly, prettily, gushing forward like the overflow from a gutter. Those who had been sleeping now woke up and ran for shelter, and on the bridge, the one still point in all this noise and panic, the tank rolled its sights and prepared to return fire.

'Tell 'em pull back!' said Hughie, dropping his field glasses as the wireless operator, whose name was Jenkins, shouted the order into his receiver. He glanced around, his hands thrust in his pockets and an expression of irritation on his face. 'We're too late,' he added, to no one in particular, and Gilbert, watching as the tank made its slow, lumbering retreat, nodded.

'At least we know he's there, sir.' The shelling had ceased, and Gilbert stepped out from behind the truck, gazing at the other side of the river with new interest. His beret had slipped forward, and his eyes seemed darker and more hooded than ever. At that moment a motorbike appeared on the road to their right, and the officers turned, watching as it pulled up alongside the truck. It was Daniel Sutton.

'The cavalry!' said Gilbert, grinning.

Daniel clambered off, feeling for the kickstand with the toe of his boot. 'I've come to check the bridges, sir,' he said, looking past his friend and handing it to Hughie. He liked the senior officer, all the young men did, since he was kind and took them seriously. 'Top Brass are worried they won't be blown.' He paused, clearing his throat. 'More guns on their way too, sir.'

Captain Hughes scowled, skimming the note and then passing it Sergeant Jenkins. Daniel waited, but when nothing was said, he asked: 'All right if I look at the bridge then sir?'

'Help yourself,' said Hughie, swinging his arm towards the river as if inviting Daniel to make himself at home. 'If you don't mind getting your head blown off.'

His mouth was set in a grim line, a nerve in his cheek flickering as he looked past Daniel towards his men's positions. They would have to pull back, give the enemy a bit of slack, then catch him as he came across. He turned, gazing towards the railway embankment to their south: that was probably their best bet. He communicated this to the WO, still crouched over his radio, then jumped onto the running plate of the truck, banging his hand on the bonnet and holding the windscreen as the truck swung round.

'What will I report then, sir?' persisted Daniel, running after the truck.

'Report what you like, Lieutenant. For God's sake, jump on if you want to speak to me. That side!'

Daniel did as he was told, launching himself at the other door as the truck swung around, and peering around the windscreen at Captain Hughes.

'Sir, the Dragoons want to know, if the enemy breaks through our lines.' He shouted in order to be heard over the roar of the engine.

Hughie glared at him in annoyance, gesturing towards the empty road. '*Have* they broken through?'

'No, sir. Not yet.', he wanted to say, but he did not dare.

'Well, then. Here, sergeant, stop here.' They were across the railway and Captain Hughes jumped down. He watched as Daniel jumped down too. 'One hour's rest my men have had. One hour in I-don't-know-how-many days, and half-rations to boot. All because someone in HQ took a message down incorrectly.' He raised an eyebrow. Clearly he blamed Daniel for the mistaken withdrawal last night. 'Do you not think you might be better doing something about that instead? Rather than wasting my time with stupid questions?'

'Yes, sir.'

Captain Hughes nodded. 'Right, then.' He turned away, looking back towards the town, and at the same instant the sun, which had been slowly rising, cleared the rooftops of the nearby buildings and filled the place in which they were standing with brilliant yellow light. Hughie lifted his chin, stretching his neck as a cockerel does before it crows. 'Right, then,' he said again, and for the first time that morning he smiled. If nothing else, this was going to be an interesting day.

WHEN CAPTAIN HUGHES LIFTED his chin and smiled, he forgot all the things that had been bothering him that night and he saw only this particular moment. He saw his men pulling back, setting up behind their new positions, he saw the tanks and carriers manoeuvring into the formation he had ordered, he saw himself, tall and broad-chested, and the respect he commanded from officers and troops alike. His big body, at times cumbersome, felt light as a feather, and now he stepped across the street and ran up the stairs of a nearby building, appearing at the upstairs window and looking out on the squadron's fresh positions. He felt excited, the kind of excitement one feels before a difficult exam or race, and his mind ran over all the possible variations of attack. He called down to Lieutenant Clayton, waiting on the embankment, and pointed out a Bren carrier that was too far forward, a slit trench with insufficient defences, a tank — Lieutenant Ross's no doubt — not yet buttoned up. Clayton hurried away to see to these, and Hughie remained in the window, his eyes narrowed and on his face an expression that only another soldier would recognise; the expression worn by a man who knows he will kill that day, that he will put every ounce of his strength to the task of taking other lives. He moved away from the window.

Below, feeling out of place, Daniel hurried back to where he had left the motorbike. Someone had moved it out of the way of the retreating vehicles, and he found it leaning against a tree, a horse chestnut with broad sticky leaves and white flowers, the lower branches broken so that Daniel had to duck beneath. He hesitated, looking past the knobbly grey boughs and deliberating whether to ignore Hughie's warning and check the bridge anyway. It seemed impossible that anything bad could happen when the sky was so blue, the air so still and peaceful. Indeed, gazing towards the bridge he saw there were people on it, workmen by the looks of it, sauntering across as if it were just any other morning. How normal they looked, going about their day. Surely, he reasoned, if the enemy were there they would fire on them, for that was what they did. He shuddered, remembering the man with the bundle, and to put the thought from his mind, he stepped out from under the tree and began walking towards the bridge. If he could just check the pilings, see whether the holes for the guncotton had been bored, then he would have something to report back.

'Sir! Here, sir!' It was Jenkins, the WO, crouched in a nearby doorway and gesturing frantically at Daniel to move off the road. Daniel looked at him in surprise. The workmen were over the bridge now, walking along the road towards the squadron's positions, and Daniel hesitated, glancing around. Behind him, at intervals along the embankment, field-glasses sparkled, every eye trained on the small group. There were perhaps a dozen of them, their boots kicking up the dust so that their feet were lost in a haze of white. And it was as if the town was holding its breath, for there was not a sound. Even the wood pigeons, that moments ago had been fussing and fretting their wings in the trees above, were silent. Daniel frowned. Why was everyone so twitchy?

The group were just a few hundred yards away when they suddenly scattered. Daniel was looking towards the embankment, saw the muzzle of a gun lift and lower, saw Captain Hughes raise his hand. What does he want? he wondered. Then the Brens opened up, the Vickers too, and the air so crackled and burst that Daniel, throwing himself down next to Jenkins, had to press his fists to his ears. After a minute or two they fell silent again, for the street was empty, the workmen had disappeared, but seconds later a pair of enemy horses were galloped over the bridge, halting so the traces could be undone, then turned and galloped back again. In their place they left a German field gun, its wheels rocking as mortars were sent screaming onto the squadron's positions.

'Bugger!' Jenkins fiddled with the buttons of his radio. With what little battery he had left he called for back-up from the other squadrons, pressing his headphones to his ears as he waited for a response.

With the same wonder he had felt for Hughie's raised hand, Daniel gazed around himself. Apart from the noise, which was excruciating, there was something rather beautiful about the scene before him. The shells from the field gun traced long, graceful arcs, oddly peaceful against the empty sky, and when they landed, the earth seemed to briefly embrace them, as though it welcomed the devastation. Likewise the bullets, round after round of shiny bronze bullets, zigzagging the air and reminding him of the green-gold beetles his mother got in her lilies. The little puffs of smoke given off by the Brens, the canvas sides of the lorries that billowed and snapped, the way the tanks moved forward and back and around, as though completing some complicated dance routine: all of it felt so correct, so choreographed, that Daniel could only watch in admiration.

'Not hurt are you, sir?'

Daniel shook his head. He could hear Captain Hughes somewhere, shouting orders, his voice audible even above the crash of shells and gunfire, as if it had a frequency all of its own. Daniel began to get up, holding on to the wall and craning his neck to see what was happening.

The enemy fire had intensified, German infantry were now running over the bridge and then splaying outwards along the towpath, moving either side of the field gun as a river moves either side of an island. The enemy was everywhere.

Jenkins stood up, pulling the earphones from around his neck and dropping them in the doorway. 'Battery's dead.' He rubbed his face, leaving dirty streaks from his forehead to his chin. 'We need to warn them up the line.'

Daniel remembered his promise to the Dragoon Colonel. 'I'll go,' he said.

Jenkins looked at the young officer with concern. In the last war he had been much the same age as Daniel, and he remembered his first contact with the enemy as if it was yesterday. Judging by the face of this young fellow, he would remember it too. 'Might be a bit hot up there, sir.'

Daniel nodded. He thought of Captain Hughes, and how harshly he had spoken earlier. Well, now he'd show him. HQ were always being blamed for situations not of their making, about time they were given some credit too. He would warn the Dragoons and then he would get back to HQ and warn them too.

'Know where you're going sir?'

'Thank you, yes.' Daniel stepped out of the doorway, looking for the horse chestnut tree where he had left the motorbike. Immediately, bullets rang out against the stone walls, and Daniel gasped and flung himself back again.

'Stay low, sir,' said Jenkins helpfully. 'Harder to get a sight on you when you stay low.'

'Yes, yes,' said Daniel, straightening his beret.

'And don't stop, sir. If you stop you're finished.' This last was spoken into empty air, for Daniel had set off, running at full tilt along the wall, his head down and his arms dangling at his sides. As he ran he imagined he was on the rugby field, that he was as tall and broad as Captain Hughes and that nothing could catch him, and before he knew it he was standing under the cool leafy branches of the chestnut tree, his breath coming in short rasps. It was a distance of perhaps a hundred yards, but he was as overwhelmed as if he had swum it underwater.

The motorbike retrieved, he returned to Dragoon HQ through open countryside. Behind him smoke rose in fat grey plumes above the town, and shells caused the earth to rattle and vibrate, but Daniel saw nor heard either. Blank-faced civilians stared as he roared past, and with each one he felt a stab of fear, remembering the workmen on the bridge. This was what they did, they made you feel they were everywhere.

When he reached Bouvignies, the sergeant who had made breakfast was in the garden, burning papers in a large metal dustbin. He looked up, smiling when he saw Daniel. 'Back so soon? What do you need now, sir?'

Daniel quickly related what had happened.

'Ah.' The sergeant replaced the lid on the dustbin and moved over to a table, where a map was laid out. He picked up a marker. 'So here, then?' he asked, pointing to a spot on the river. Daniel nodded. The sergeant stood back, scratching his chin thoughtfully. 'I hate to ask, sir, but you wouldn't just run up and tell the CO yourself? We've no radio contact and I don't want him getting caught by surprise.'

'Where is he?'

'About a mile north of the town, sir, top of the Tournai road. Have they tanks across?' Daniel thought not. 'Bit of time yet then, sir.' He picked up some papers stacked on one of the chairs, carrying them over to the fire. 'And tell him not to worry about here, I've got everything under control.'

IF THE DRAGOON COLONEL WAS worried about anything at all, then he was doing a good job of hiding it. When Daniel arrived he found him sitting in a deckchair on the river bank, reading a newspaper and drinking tea. A pair of earphones were draped around his neck, and every so often he would raise them to his ears and listen intently. When he saw Daniel, he lifted his cup and waved him over.

'The Sergeant said your wireless wasn't working,' said Daniel, before he could stop himself. He was annoyed that he had come all this way when they could just have radioed the message.

The Colonel was amused. 'I requisitioned a battery from a passing Gloucester, our need was greater. Tea?'

Daniel shook his head. 'I won't, sir. I just came to tell you they've broken through. The enemy. They've crossed the river.'

'Wondered if they had. Heard a commotion a little while back. That must have been it. Smith, bring another cup, Lieutenant Sutton—' he looked at Daniel, pushing his glasses up his nose. 'It *is* Sutton, isn't it?'

'Yes, sir.'

'Lieutenant Sutton's had a nasty morning.'

Daniel began to protest, but the other man held up his forefinger: his headphones were crackling and he put one to his ear. 'Well, you'd better push them back, Captain,' he said into the radio. 'And get a wriggle on too, we need to blow this bridge. You didn't see which way they went, I suppose?' This last was directed at Daniel, who shook his head.

'Well, I doubt it'll make much difference anyway. Rubber pontoons.' He nodded northwards, to where his other squadrons were deployed, 'Jerry's secret weapon. Clever, really.'

Daniel had no answer to this and the Colonel turned back to his newspaper, smoothing it with his free hand. He had had time to think this morning, sitting here waiting for the remainder of his troops to cross the river, and there were one or two things that were bothering him.

'No gas masks, Lieutenant, have you noticed that?' He meant the Germans. 'I've seen quite a few Jerry brought in this morning, not one of them carrying a gas mask. Makes us look rather stupid, don't you think?' He gestured at the detector band on Daniel's sleeve, as if it were Daniel's foolishness alone. 'You have to wonder what else we've got wrong.'

'I don't know that we've got it wrong, sir—' said Daniel, thinking of his manual and feeling a kind of protectiveness for the horrors it anticipated.

The Dragoon Colonel's headphones were chattering again and he put them to his ears, listening attentively. Daniel, thinking this was his opportunity to slip off, set down his cup and began to move away. 'A moment, Lieutenant. Something I want you to show you.' He was looking past Daniel, his gaze on the other bank of the river, his mouth, with its neatly trimmed moustache, open in anticipation. At last he saw what he was looking for. 'There they are. See, Lieutenant, there they are!' He jumped to his feet. 'Where's that sapper—?'

'Sir!'

'—good, on my order. Look, what a sight for sore eyes, eh, Lieutenant?'

Daniel looked and saw a column of British armoured cars moving slowly across the bridge towards them. In the foremost vehicle a young officer had stood up and was waving cheerfully, and when Daniel glanced at the Dragoon Colonel, he saw he had lost that languid, Sunday-morning air and was quite radiant. Men were hanging off the sides of the cars, their faces drawn and exhausted, and as the first car passed by, the young officer shouted something about all the troops being back on 'our side of the river'.

'Marvellous, sir,' said Daniel, assuming this was what he had been intended to see.

The Colonel did not reply, gesturing towards the bridge where the last car was just pulling off. He raised his arm above his head, nodded, and before Daniel could wonder what was happening, there was an tremendous explosion and, right before their eyes, the bridge sprang into the air, as if it had only ever been pretending to be fixed and solid. Stone, wood, bits of metal railing, all came crashing back down, most of it landing in the river, where it floated for a moment and then sank without trace.

'Want to know how to blow a bridge?' cried the Colonel triumphantly, as though the whole exercise had been for Daniel's benefit alone. 'Well, that's how, Lieutenant. That's how.'

Around this time Estella Cansino, taking a hot water bottle to Leonard's room, slipped coming down the stairs and fell heavily on her shoulder. Everyone was out, Solomon at synagogue and Leonard at an ARP lecture, so the new maid, whose name was Kitty, ran next door to Mrs Levy, who telephoned the doctor. When Solomon got back an hour later, he found Estella still as she had fallen, on the small landing, since the pain was terrible and she could not be moved. Only when Dr Friedmann gave her chloroform could they get her to the bedroom, but by then Solomon was beside himself and Mr and Mrs Samuels from opposite had to be called to sit with him. Poor Leonard, arriving home to such upset: Kitty sobbing on the stairs, Mrs Levy trying to get Estella into a nightdress, the Samuels, whose Vivian was in bed with German measles, running back and forth across the street. It was, as Leonard later wrote to Miriam, a most shocking experience.

And this in what was already the worst week of the war so far, when every day the newspapers screeched new disasters; when hospital ships were sunk and refugees bombed as they fled on open roads; when the enemy was headed straight for the Channel ports, and from there— well, everyone knew where they would go from there. It was a week when all that was safe and familiar must be reconsidered, a week of awakening, a turning point, during which the sun beat remorselessly down, and the skies were ominously clear.

Word of Estella's accident soon reached Palatine Road, and Lucia Arditti came straight round, appearing on the doorstep just as Leonard was heading out to the office. The shoulder had been set in splints that morning, and a bed made up on the drawing room sofa, so that Estella would not have the trouble of stairs. But nothing was right: the cushions too lumpy, the pillows either too low or too upright. And so instead, she was sitting in the window in a high-backed chair, fat tears glittering at the corners of her painted eyes. Kitty had the day off, Solomon was at one of his meetings, but it seemed that Leonard's absence was the most wounding, for she would not even say goodbye. How could a course on fitting new filters take precedence over his mother? What if she had a funny turn while he was gone? What if parachutists landed — they were being warned every day to watch out for them — and took her prisoner, worse still, slit her throat and left her for dead? All of this she thought and did not say, her lower lip trembling and her eyes turned glassily towards the window as he kissed her cheek. Reinforcements could not have been more timely.

'*Cotoletta*!' Lucia burst through the gate just as Leonard closed the front door, her long feet in their sensible pumps sending up waves of gravel. She set down a basket on the front step then bent to shake her skirt, so that air could circulate beneath. 'Everyone loves my *cotoletta*, we will have her better in no time. How tired you look.' She seized Leonard's face, cupping it with her hot red hands, 'What a good thing I came.'

'*Cotoletta*?' Leonard must have frowned, for she squeezed his cheeks reassuringly.

'Veal, mio caro, veal. I know how it is. What trouble I had to find it, you would not believe the fuss. Of course, in Milano you only have to snap your fingers, none of this 'shilling a week' business.' She released his face, turning around and gazing towards the street from which she had come. Apple blossom from next door's tree lay like icing sugar on the hedge and front lawn, and she smiled. 'But as I say to myself every day: Lucia Arditti, where would you rather be? Almost a year, can you believe it? And how nice everyone still is. Even Netta has her little friends. Of course, when Mr Halifax sees what a gangster he's dealing with—' She stopped, her hand to her heart as if to control its beating. 'But enough! I don't want to talk about it. And you so tired, poor man.'

Leonard, his briefcase pressed to his belly like a shield, opened his mouth to protest, but Lucia waved him away.

'Now off you go and don't worry, I will see to everything. Where is she, in her room?'

Leonard glanced at the window, where the back of Estella's head shone round and yellow, like the yolk of an egg. He was quite sure she had heard Lucia, but he knew she would not turn round while he was still there, she would not give him that pleasure. He felt a sudden pang, but not the usual pang of guilt or dismay, but rather one of irritation, so that his gaze hardened and he might have been looking on a sworn enemy. He caught himself, tried to soften it into something kinder, but Lucia, who missed nothing, was now tutting and pushing him towards the gate. 'Off you go, I'm sure you have many important things to be seeing to. What a sky! What a day it is!'

Leonard went. Talking to Lucia felt like standing on the service line and watching smash after smash go hurtling past him. He simply could not match her energy.

'And the lilacs! Make sure to notice the lilacs!' Lucia leaned over the gate, the iron finials pushing against her ribs, so that when she stood up there were dents in the front of her cotton dress. She waited until he had turned the corner and then looked back at the house. There was a kind of ecstasy about her, her chin lifted and her arms hanging loose at her sides, like Saint Sebastian but without the arrows. How nice it was to be able to help people. She had almost forgotten. And, wreathed in smiles, she charged up the path and in through the front door.

Estella had closed her eyes and was affecting sleep when Lucia entered the room. Leonard's departure — she had expected at least one more attempt at placation — had caught her off guard, and she was feeling aggrieved. Her eyes pinched shut, the blanket he had so carefully laid across her knees discarded on the floor, it was some time before she deigned to notice Lucia's arrival. When she did, she found her perched on the edge of the sofa, gazing at her in rapture.

'What a picture! Stay just where you are, don't move. What a young face you have.'

It was true. There was not a wrinkle on Estella's plump countenance, not even her scowls had left a trace. She lifted her chin a little higher, wincing, for her shoulder really was painful, and looked at Lucia with new interest. From habit she did not like the woman. She had never forgiven the family for taking Laura's house; and then there was all that fuss Miriam made last summer, always dashing round there with the baby, leaving Estella twiddling her thumbs and lonely. Leonard had talked to her about it in the end, and after that it was better, but Estella still felt she had been usurped. And now the famous Signora Arditti had popped up again.

'How kind of you to visit, I do hope you're not breaking any curfews.' It was blunt as an opening salvo, but important to establish positions.

Lucia gave a small squeak. 'My heavens, what a thought!' She bent to pick up the blanket, folding it across her own lap and then transferring it to Estella's. 'Although my husband says it will be any day, he will not be able to resist going in with Old Nasty now. Il Duce,' she added, in case Estella thought she meant her husband.

Estella nodded. 'Old Nasty' was a new one, she must remember it. Her eyes, with their carefully drawn lashes, slid to the basket. Leonard had made lunch before he left, but it was a mean little affair: tinned soup and yesterday's bread. Veal cutlets (Estella had ears like a cat, she heard everything) sounded much more appealing.

'Of course, a curfew is if we are lucky,' continued Lucia. 'More likely they package everyone off to a camp, like all those German cooks you hear about. My poor husband, he talks of closing the garage door *e finito*!' She laughed gaily and Estella winced. 'He doesn't mean it. We don't have a car, for one thing, although Luca's motorbike might just do it. Is the sun in your eyes? Would you like me to close the curtains, I can pull them half across. How's that?' Lucia jumped up and started tugging at the thick damask drapes. 'I'll not close them completely, such a shame when it's nice out. We should be in the garden.' She sat down again, her knees slightly apart and her big hands on their narrow wrists hanging in the space between. She might have been a sixteen-year-old girl at her first dance, so eager did she seem, so loose in her limbs.

Estella looked around impatiently, thinking about the cutlets. Butter or oil, she wondered? Perhaps she would use a mixture of both, like Laura's Nina used to do. She smoothed the blanket across her lap, momentarily lost in thought. People were funny about frying things in butter these days, especially now it was rationed, but Lucia Arditti was a law unto herself, everyone said so.

As if she could read her mind, Lucia sprung up again. '*Ma poi*, I almost forgot!' She launched herself at the basket, taking out a waxed butcher's parcel which she held towards Estella. 'I'm making you *cotoletta*!' She lifted a corner of the paper and put her nose just inside, as if it were a warm cake or a piece of soap, not slices of raw veal. 'In Milan I am famous for my *cotoletta*, I add a secret ingredient. Can you guess what it is?'

'Not anchovy, I hope.' In Italy they added anchovies to everything. Estella hated anchovies.

'To *cotoletta*?' Lucia laughed, shaking her head. 'Try again.'

Estella shrugged. She did not like guessing games, particularly when they concerned her next meal, and she pushed out her bottom lip, giving herself a sulky, disagreeable air.

'All right, I'll tell you. Cream, I add cream to the egg. An Italian would be horrified, they are so particular about these things. But I tell you, you'll never taste better *cotoletta* than mine, and it's all because of the cream.'

Estella thought about this. 'Cream?' she said, and she could almost taste it. 'I do like cream.'

Lucia beamed. 'I'll take it through, put everything in the cool? No, no, stay there, I'll find it!' She was already hurrying into the hallway, for Lucia could never do things at the same pace as anyone else. She always had to run at them, as if someone had flipped an egg timer and she had to complete the task before the sand ran through. Doors banged, as she tried first the cellar, then the cupboard where they kept the ironing board and winter coats. And then at last, 'Oh, what a charming little kitchen! What a treat!' She had found it, her exclamations muffled now, so that she sounded as if she had a bag over her head, or was underground. 'How funny these houses are, so much bigger than they look on the outside. Is it all right if I open the back door, let in a bit of air?'

Estella did not reply. She was looking out of the window, her attention caught by a young fellow with a bicycle outside Number Twenty-one. Rotterdam had fallen in a matter of hours, they said, because of young men like that

one dropping out of the sky on bicycles. Or something like
that, the news was so fantastical these days, it was hard to
know what was real and what was made up just to scare
people. She closed her eyes, feeling suddenly exhausted, then
quickly opened them again, checking he was still there. He
was. Probably she should open the window and call him over,
ask him what he was up to. What was it Churchill had said,
something about the comfort of sharing the peril? Well it
didn't feel very comfortable. Nothing did any more.

'*Eccola*, how are we?' Lucia burst back in, smiling
radiantly at Estella and looking her over as if she expected
some transformation to have taken place during her absence.
Estella glanced at her, then looked back at the street. Oh good,
there was Mr Tomkins, he'd soon know if there was anything
amiss, he was one of Eden's new Local Defence people,
nothing got past him. She raised her good arm to wave, her
rings sending tiny sunbeams bouncing around the room, but
Mr Tomkins was busy interrogating the suspect and did not
see her. Reluctantly she returned her attention to Lucia, who
was now by the fireplace, peering at the photographs Laura
had sent last summer — Rita and Coco with a little dog, Teddy
in his bathing suit — and making the same tutting noise she
had made when she shooed Leonard out of the gate. 'And how
is dear Laura?' she asked, emphasising the word 'is' as people
do when they think they know the answer.

'Laura?' In fact they had not heard from Laura in
over two weeks, not even a cable. 'Oh, Laura's fine.'

Lucia nodded, still looking at the photographs. One,
taken with another family, she picked up and brought over to
Estella. 'Such pretty girls,' she said, for it was easy to pick
out Rita and Coco, they looked just like their mother. She
pointed to a figure at the front of the frame, a young boy
with crooked elbows and hands pushed deep into his pockets.
'And this is her youngest? I forgot his name.'

'Teddy? No, Teddy's just behind.' Estella tapped her nail against a beaming, round-faced boy. 'Laura's very pleased with him. He was top of his class this year.'

Lucia smiled, her gaze still on the photograph. 'How funny people are,' she murmured. Earlier, leaving the house with her basket, Raphael had come after her and made her promise not to go upsetting anyone, to go sticking her nose, as he put it, into the Cansinos' affairs. She glanced up at Estella, her eyebrows raised like a second pair of hands. 'Imagine thinking about school at this time.'

Estella made a wagging motion with her fingers, so that Lucia understood she should put the photograph back where she had found it. 'I don't see what's funny about it,' she said. 'Laura takes the children's education very seriously, that's why she went to France in the first place.' She had spoken sharply, but she could see that Lucia was not the type to notice such things, and so she turned away, her attention once again on the street: the young man had gone and Mr Tomkins was quietly inspecting his roses, as he always did at this time of day. Another crisis averted.

'Of course, she must come home now,' Lucia continued, her head bent as she continued to inspect the pictures on the mantelpiece. 'She cannot stay in France, not with everything that's happened. They must all come, Marco and Allegra too, we have plenty of room. What a handsome fellow,' she had stopped at a snapshot of Bobby, 'and so tall. Why is tall so attractive?' She giggled, glancing at her reflection in the mirror and giving her cheeks a quick pinch. 'You wouldn't think it now, but my Raphael was tall when I met him. He walked into the room and I thought, look at that beautiful, tall man! Do you think he could be shrinking?'

'It's his birthday tomorrow.' Estella's eyes softened, as they always did when she thought of Bobby. 'I've sent a card, but Leonard thinks it probably won't get there, the situation being as it is. Thirty. I'd hate him to think we'd forgotten.'

'He would never think that.' She turned and peered once more at the photograph. 'Thirty. And so tall.'

'I know how these things matter to him,' continued Estella, picking at a thread in the blanket. Her mind began to wander, and after a silence she said, 'Do you have grandchildren?'

'Me?' Lucia glanced again at the mirror and gave her cheeks another pinch.

'Of course, you're too young. How silly of me.' A little make up wouldn't do any harm, might take ten years off the woman. Estella sighed, thinking it was the husbands she felt sorry for. She would never let Solomon see her without her face on. At the thought of her husband she felt a sudden rush of tenderness. What a state he had been in last night when he found her lying there on the landing. She couldn't remember seeing him so upset, not in a long time, not since Laura's troubles, when they were none of them quite themselves. It was a reassurance in a way.

'Shall I put a record on? A little music, then I'll go and cook.' Lucia had moved over to the gramophone and was sliding the pile of disks sideways as she searched for something she wanted to play. 'How about this one?' She held up a paper sleeve. '*Tornerai*'. People forget it was first a success in Italy.'

Estella frowned. She didn't forget. In fact, every time she heard it she felt she was back in the Casa Grandolini, with Laura shut away and the children dancing like savages in the dining room. She was about to protest but it was too late, the needle was already crackling, the room filled with the wail of that dratted violin.

'Carlo Buti, everyone forgets Carlo Buti.' Lucia was swaying to the music, her thin body surprisingly graceful as she moved back and forth across the rug. 'Il Duce must be furious at what a hit it's been, I hear it everywhere. There's a German version too.'

Estella nodded stiffly. Only the promise that the woman would go and cook once it finished made it bearable. She picked again at the blanket on her lap, thinking that Miriam never put her through such torments. What a shame Leonard had insisted on her staying in St Anne's. He said she and the baby would be safer on the coast, but what about the flying tanks, hadn't he read about the flying tanks? She felt down the side of the chair for her *Daily Mail*, left there by Kitty each morning. She had to hide it, Solomon wouldn't have it in the house on account of that dreadful Lord Rothermere. But of course it was Kitty's day off. There would be no newspaper today, and she withdrew her hand, letting it droop on her lap.

Outside the window a breeze had got up, and the apple blossom that before had drifted gently onto the hedge now blew in swirls and flurries. Kitty would have to sweep the path tomorrow or there'd be petals all over the house, no one ever took their shoes off these days. Estella glanced at Lucia's feet as if in proof, and Lucia stopped swaying and came and stood next to Estella's chair, gazing out of the window. 'It looks like it's snowing,' she said, and there was such wonder in her expression that Estella could not help but smile.

'It does, rather,' she said.

'We're so lucky, no?' Lucia leaned forwards, so that her forehead was pressed against the glass. Blossom had settled on the grass and flowerbeds, turned the black metal gate a merry polka dot.

'Lucky?' The music had finished and the needle clicked on the turntable, like a metronome counting down the seconds.

'Lucky,' said Lucia firmly. She straightened up, a red circle on her forehead where she had leaned against the window. 'As I tell my Raphael, we are all together and we are all healthy, please God, that's more than most people. Of course, he then says about internment, or these new Emergency Powers, or that no one wants fadeless cretonnes any more —' She paused, looking expectantly at Estella.

'The woman is quite, quite mad,' thought Estella. As if in agreement, her stomach gave a low growl, and for a moment neither woman spoke.

'*Cotoletta!*' declared Lucia, clapping her hands and making a quick pirouette. She strode towards the gramophone, lifted the needle and then launched herself at the hall. She had only gone two strides when she turned and came back, peering around the door and beaming at the other woman. 'With the smallest bit of cream, remember. Ah, just wait until you taste my *cotoletta!*'

CHAPTER 16

After their retreat from the River Dendre, the regiment withdrew across the border into France. All along the line, Allied troops were moving back, arriving in one place only to be told to withdraw still further, a dark mass retreating across the landscape. Communications were scarce, for as fast as lines were laid they were cut or lifted again, and so they took their news from the ruins around them, from the craters in the roads and the bombed-out homes, from the cows that retched and trembled in the fields and the bodies scattered amongst them that did not.

On the 27th May, the day the French learned of the BEF's plan to evacuate from Dunkirk, the regiment was bivouacked outside Cassel, some eighteen miles inland. Daniel had been up late, overseeing the refuelling of the carrier patrols, and he was asleep when Gilbert came bursting through the doorway of their tent just before 6 a.m. He was in high spirits, dropping onto the end of Daniel's camp-bed, then springing up again when it threatened to collapse. He had been out looking for fresh bread – a luxury since the enemy had crossed the Somme – and now he leaned forward and tipped a dozen small, hard rolls from his battle shirt.

'Hôtel du Sauvage,' he grinned, in answer to a question Daniel had not asked, 'Not today's, I'm afraid. The place was deserted. And I found these too.' He produced a tin from each trouser pocket, throwing them down with the bread rolls. 'Lobster, nothing but the best for us, my friend. Come on, come on, I've got patrol in ten,' and he grabbed a corner of Daniel's blanket, throwing it backwards so that Daniel, groaning in irritation, was obliged to sit up.

'What are you looking for? Leave my things, won't you.' Gilbert was rooting through Daniel's neatly laid out kit.

'You'll never guess who I saw while I was there — where's your knife, I seem to have lost mine? Go on, have a guess.'

Daniel leaned over, pulling his trousers from the hook where he had hung them the night before, and feeling in the pocket for his penknife. 'Here. Now put all that back and keep to your own side.'

Gilbert grinned. Grimes had offered his services as batman to both officers but Gilbert seemed to undo his work just as quickly as he did it. His pipe was sticking out from beneath his pillow, and he seized it and hung it off his lip. 'General Adam,' he said triumphantly, lisping on account of the pipe. He looked around. 'What d'you think of that?'

Daniel swung his legs out of bed, leaning forward and rubbing his head vigorously. He paused for a moment, his elbows resting on his knees, then stood up. Gilbert was outside now, his tall frame casting a long silhouette on the canvas roof. 'Was the General out looting too?'

'Not looting, foraging.' His face appeared once again in the doorway. 'There's a difference, you know, ask the Brig. Chuck me those tins, I'll open them out here.'

Daniel did as he asked, laughing. The regiment had been obliged to supplement their rations for days now, a source of much consternation at Brigade. 'So long as your conscience is clear.'

'My conscience is always clear.' Gilbert turned away, running his hands over his brand new battleshirt, still creased where it had been folded. (He had also stumbled upon Brigade's uniform stores, but this particular bounty he was keeping to himself.) 'I say, Sutton, did you ever see such a glorious morning?'

Daniel came to stand beside his friend, pulling on his jacket and looking out across the plains. On the roads, long lines of transport continued their slow progress north, the sun glinting off the roofs of the vehicles, so that it was like a beautiful, iridescent serpent winding its way towards the sea.

'Shame there's a war on, really,' said Daniel, taking one of the open tins and sniffing it. 'Are you sure this is all right?'

''Course! I'd have taken more but just as I was getting into my stride, General Adam walks in, followed by one of those gold-braided Froggies. I scarpered pretty fast, I can tell you. It's never good news when the brass hats show up. Grab the bread, would you?' He dropped down onto the long grass, yellow kingcups pressing around his legs, and continued to gaze out over the green, shining fields.

Daniel came and sat beside him, tipping the bread rolls into his lap. 'What time are you away?'

'O-six fifteen.' Gilbert checked his watch. 'It'll be another scorcher, no doubt. Doesn't half heat up in there, the lads were down to their undershorts yesterday. And all I get from Hughie, "Button up, chaps, button up!" I'd like to button *him* up.' As he spoke he was picking at the bread, using his thumb to hollow out the middle, dropping the small dry pieces onto the grass beside him. 'Wait until you taste this,' he said, glancing around for the open tin. 'Lobster à la Sauvage. My invention.'

Daniel grinned, leaning forward and lacing his boots. 'General Adam, eh? What d'you suppose that's about?'

'My bet, he's looking for a new HQ. He can't stay in Arras with Jerry on the doorstep. Y'know, perhaps I should have stuck around, offered my services on the General Staff? I could have had your old job.' He grinned, licking drips of lobster juice from his wrist, then held out the sandwich to Daniel. 'Here, wrap your chops around that. I tell you, I'm wasted in a tank.'

Just then footsteps were heard running along the path below their position, and seconds later Grimes appeared, his face shiny with exertion. He was in full battledress, his rolled groundsheet poking out either side of his head, his tin bowler wedged somewhere in between. 'Oh, you're up, sir!' he said, with obvious relief, coming to a halt just short of the two men's boots, 'Thought I might have to wake you. *Bon appeteet*!' he added, for Daniel was now eating his sandwich.

'Make you one, Grimes?' offered Gilbert, jabbing lobster into the middle of another roll.

'No thank you sir, I had m'breakfast.'

'I'll make you one anyway, you can keep it for later.'

'Thank y'sir.' Grimes flushed pinker, and scratched his nose. He looked at Daniel. 'Petrol lorry's by the White House, sir, Colonel wants us away early.'

'He won't eat it.' Daniel pushed the last of the roll into his mouth and stood up, looking down and smoothing the front of his jacket. 'Grimes here has a very limited palate, Bully beef's about as far as he's prepared to venture, am I right, Grimes?'

'I've a delicate constitution, sir.'

'You've a delicate everything,' said Daniel. The comment was meaningless, but somehow it had become a habit, this tone of mocking affection, and so he said it anyway.

'Tosh, you just haven't tried it, that's all.' Gilbert stuck out his tongue, licking both sides of the knife-blade, then snapping it back into its handle. 'Sutton, give me your handkerchief. I'll wrap you up a couple, you'll thank me when you're stuck in some petrol dump half starving. Crikey, is that the time? I'm off!' He jumped up, scattering tins and rolls. 'Anyone seen my pipe? I'm sure I had it a minute ago.'

Daniel nodded at the pocket of Gilbert's battle shirt, where the tip was just poking out. 'We'd better be away too,' he said, turning to Grimes as Gilbert hurried away, 'do you have the rendezvous?'

But Grimes did not answer. He was listening to something, his head tilted on one side as he gazed at the upper branches of a nearby tree. 'Hear that, sir? That's a golden oriole, sir.'

'A what?'

'Golden oriole, sir. It's a bird.'

'However do you know these things?'

'Just do, sir. There it is again.' Grimes made a warbling sound in his throat. 'Just where you'd expect to find one too,' he added, looking back at the tree, with its heart-shaped leaves and purple fruit. 'They eat the berries.'

Daniel shook his head. 'Indeed,' he said, and then he turned and set off down the hill, his heart light in his chest and his feet running away with him.

◆　　◆　　◆　　◆　　◆

THE REFUELING POINT FOR THE patrols was a small village south of Cassel. Daniel ate another lobster roll sitting on the steps of a redbrick church, then, leaving Grimes in charge of the petrol-lorry, wandered through the surrounding streets in search of a look-out. The village was deserted, the houses shuttered and their inhabitants seemingly departed, and after a while Daniel turned back, for the silence unsettled him. Coming back into the main square he found Grimes squatted beside the front wheel, making tea in a canteen.

'Thought I'd make us a brew, sir. I reckon they'll not be along for a while yet, might as well get comfortable.'

Daniel felt a flicker of irritation. Familiarity between the two men had bred, if not quite contempt, then certainly initiative on Grimes' part. 'Not until I've made a full recce, Corporal,' he said. He glanced up, since it occurred to him that the bell tower would have as good a view as anywhere. 'Stand to,' he said over his shoulder, and he strode towards the church.

From the belfry, birds scattering through the narrow arches as he entered, Daniel gazed out over the rooftops of the village. To the north, on the same roads he had watched earlier that morning, the retreat of the Allied armies continued, a constantly shifting mass curving around the slopes of Cassel towards the coast. And to the south, open countryside, the rippling wheat fields parsed with narrow roads, along which the convoy was expected to return. Daniel moved from one opening to the next, eventually coming back to where he had started, and watching as Grimes, below him in the square, stared motionless at something high above his head. Another golden oriole perhaps, and Daniel smiled, craning his neck and searching for it too.

And then he saw them: enemy bombers, wave upon wave of them, arriving from the west, breaking formation as they neared Cassel and then rising in spirals, like bees above a hive. Round and round they went, higher and higher, so that, watching, Daniel was bent almost double, his fingers gripping the brick sill. One by one they reached their peak, then turned and plunged towards the earth, the boards beneath Daniel's feet shuddering as if in anticipation. Daniel counted the bombs — ten, twelve, fifteen — the vibrations reaching him before the sound, so that after the first few he put his ear to the floor and he counted them that way instead. When at last it was quiet and he looked out again, the sky above Cassel, only moments ago sharp with morning, was a black simmering haze. He turned and ran down the spiral stairs and back onto the street.

'Looks like they got us, sir,' Grimes turned around as Daniel hurried towards him. 'Right above our positions, they were.'

Daniel nodded. He was thinking about General Adam. What if GHQ were still in the town?

'Oh, don't worry about them, sir,' said Grimes, when he expressed this. 'They'll have left pretty sharpish, they're not daft. Look out, here he comes again,' and he pointed to where more aircraft were appearing above the already blazing buildings. 'We're catching a proper packet!'

Daniel frowned, checking his watch, then walking past Grimes to where the sun lay in bold stripes across the middle of the square. Behind him — he did not need to look — the hill town was being pounded, each explosion soliciting a counterpart tremor that rippled through the silent streets of the village. After a while, Grimes came and stood at his elbow.

'Gives me the creeps, sir, this place.'

'Nonsense, Grimes.' Again he checked his watch. 'What time exactly was rendezvous?'

'Ten hundred, sir, but we're just to wait.' More eruptions from the town, only this time it was shell fire, and Grimes glanced round. 'Now that's more like it, bit of gunnery. Was wondering when the laddies'd wake up!' He affected a vaguely apologetic look, so that Daniel should not think him disrespectful. 'Not our lot, sir. Our lot are much quicker off the mark. That's the Heavies, sir, hear that? Jerry won't know what's hit him once he catches a few of those.'

Daniel did not reply. If they were firing the 18-pounders then there must be enemy tanks up there too, no one would use heavy artillery on aircraft. And Boche tanks meant Boche infantry — that was how their precious Blitzkrieg worked. Something hard settled in the pit of his stomach, and suddenly the deserted streets and empty buildings took on new menace. What if the enemy was here too?

'Feeling all right, sir?' Grimes peered at him.

'I'm fine,' said Daniel, though his skin tingled and a fine sweat had broken out on his brow.

'It's that tinned fish, sir. It's upset your system.'

'Don't be ridiculous.'

'I tell you sir, we're not used to it. Plays hell with the liver.'

'Do shut up, Grimes.' It came out more harshly than he intended, and straight away Daniel regretted it. He looked around, trying to get a grip on himself, remembering something his father had said to him that last day in his study. 'Your men will look to you to guide them, don't let them down.' He thought of the Dragoon Colonel reading his newspaper as he waited for his troops to cross the river, and the image calmed him, so that he turned back to Grimes with new resolve. 'How about that cup of tea? Then we can take turns on lookout. Like having the best seats at the Majestic it is, up there.'

'Right ho, sir.' Grimes took off his tin bowler, using it to fan his face as they walked back to the lorry. 'Milk and sugar, sir?' The regiment had been without both since the retreat, but Grimes always managed to keep a secret stash. 'I might have a biscuit for you if I hunt round — settle your stomach, right enough.' He grinned, forgetting for a moment the battles that were raging on the hills beyond. 'Good job I'm here, sir. You were never much good at looking after yourself.'

Daniel smiled, the terror that had lodged in his stomach easing slightly. 'You're probably right,' he said.

They waited in the village all morning and well into the afternoon, and still no sign of the patrols. From the bell tower they watched as the enemy massed around Cassel, mortars and shells screaming back and forth across the ramparts of the old town, the summer sky sparkling with A/A fire, vivid red beads which glowed against the blue and went out.

To the south, infantry and push-cyclists could be seen weaving across the plains, insects not men, scuttling around the slopes of the town until it seemed they would encircle it. At one point, when Daniel was on lookout, he watched as enemy tanks nosed their way into the gardens of the chateau where, just hours earlier, he and Grimes had collected the petrol lorry; black flecks disappeared into the outbuildings, scrambled over the beds of lilies and flowering beans, until at the last moment a troop of Bren carriers arrived, guns blazing, and drove them out again. Similarly the line of Panzers that emerged from the small wood abutting their own regiment's position: swastika flags draped from their turrets, they pressed forwards, temporarily hidden beneath the ridge of the hill, until, just when it seemed too late, the gun batteries on the hill suddenly came to life. One by one the German tanks were disabled, the screech and dull thud of the shells followed by a clatter of rifle-fire. And although even with his field glasses it was a blur, Daniel imagined it all. He imagined the gunner working the firing pedal, the bombardier calling out directions, the troop sergeant laying down next to the gun and taking potshots with his rifle.

When Grimes climbed the stairs to take over, Daniel was in his shirtsleeves, jubilantly pacing the floor: 'We got the bastards, picked them off like big fat pheasants — look, Grimes, is that us?' He meant was it their regiment's artillery.

'More likely the Gloucesters, sir.' Daniel looked disappointed, and so he added, 'Mind, I might be wrong. In any case it's quietening down, sir. Jerry's had as much as he can take.'

They watched together for a while longer. The sun, a soft peach colour now, was beginning its descent behind the hill, and with it the enemy seemed to have departed too, for the ground no longer shook and the air was still. Swallows made silent loops of the bell tower, as if binding it in some invisible thread, and the pigeons that had departed earlier returned and made cooing noises on the other side of the sill. The light, so sharp before, as if cut with scissors, became hazy, and Daniel lowered his field glasses and carefully cleaned the lenses with his shirttail, blinking as his eyes became accustomed to a shorter range. In the square below, the stony-faced buildings, once so menacing, glowed.

And then, as if they had been there all along, a column of tanks and Bren carriers appeared in the distance on a road parallel to the village. Moving slowly, their tracks raising barely a dust-cloud, they trundled at the regulation intervals like well-behaved schoolchildren returning from an outing. Some of the vehicles were damaged — carriers with parts of their armour blown off, a tank without its guns — and it was clear that the men had seen combat. Grimes gave a low whistle, and Daniel glanced at him, understanding that he was envious, that there was no heroism in waiting around this empty village. Indeed Daniel felt it too, and he looked longingly at the returning patrol, his eye running along the line until it landed on Gilbert Ross, recognisable even from here, leaning forward in his turret.

Daniel grinned at the sight of his friend. 'Come on, let's get back, Grimes. We can meet them at the chateau and fill them up there.'

'Right y'are, sir. After you, sir.' Tiny flies, of the kind that often precede a storm, swarmed around their heads, and Grimes followed Daniel down the stairs, vigorously wafting his hands. 'Wee buggers,' he said, as they climbed into the lorry, 'worse than at home.'

◆ ◆ ◆ ◆ ◆

IT HAPPENED JUST AS THE CONVOY reached Cassel. The forward vehicles had passed the chateau on the lower ridge, but as the rear moved up, the attack started. Enemy tanks hidden in a copse of trees began shelling the road and although the battery on the hill returned fire immediately, it was already too late. Gilbert Ross, in his usual place on the rim of the turret, had his head blown off by a well-aimed mortar. One minute he was there, biting on his pipe and joking with the driver, the next his body was being hauled over the front of the tank and rolled in someone's British Warm, the only thing there was to hand. By the time Daniel arrived with the petrol lorry, the worst of it was over.

They buried him that night in the chateau garden. As they lowered his body, still wrapped inside the overcoat, into the black soil, Captain Hughes recited lines from the *Rubaiyat of Omar Khayyam*, surprising everyone since he was not thought of as the type for poetry. Only when he reached *'nor all thy tears wash out a word of it'* did Daniel struggle, but there is nothing like the eyes of one's fellow officers to keep one composed. His best friend had been killed today. Tomorrow it would be someone else's, or perhaps even himself. That is what he thought then, watching numbly as the grave was filled and armfuls of long, hollow-stemmed lilies were heaped over the mound. Later, much later, he would understand it differently. He would understand his life as divided into two parts — one that preceded Gilbert's death, when everything was bright and there for the taking. And one that came after.

That night the fine weather of the last weeks finally broke and it began to rain. From their positions on the eastern slopes of Cassel the men looked out the next morning on a damp and wretched scene, water dripping from the trees overhead and coursing down the blackened banks. 'Well that's that then,' thought Daniel as the Brigadier splashed away, having ordered the regiment once again to withdraw.

He squatted down next to Grimes and started copying the route onto small cards: Cassel-Ryveld-Winnezeele-Groglandt-Oost Cappel-Rexpoede. The regiment were moving closer to Dunkirk, tasked with keeping the roads open for the retreat. 'If I die today,' he reflected, 'it will be in one of these places.'

With the same detachment he had felt burying Gilbert Ross, Daniel prepared for their departure, arranging for the last of the supplies to be packed and the vehicles lined up by the road. B Echelon were at the rear of the convoy, and Daniel, his trousers rolled, watched as the column slowly formed up. The rain, lighter now, had caused his hair to curl, and he smoothed it with the heel of his hand, his gaze occasionally straying to the chateau and its gardens. They were in for a bad time, the Brig had said: there was no longer any hope of victory, their job was to delay the enemy for as long as possible and pray that the perimeter around Dunkirk held. Daniel, who had not slept, changed into service dress.

They moved off in the early evening, a long, winding procession that included battalions of the Welsh Guards and the Royal Artillery. Daniel was in a truck with the RSM and Grimes, and the three of them took turns to drive, for the going was slow and they expected trouble. The roads were worse than ever, with civilians, pathetic in their distress, turning and following the retreating troops. 'Can't we shoo 'em back?' asked Grimes, and the RSM, hearing 'shoot,' looked surprised and said best not. And so they continued to weave around the laden farm-carts, to stop and wait while crossroads were cleared of broken-down motors or, in one case, a herd of cows. A distance of barely twelve miles, it took them all night.

Rendezvous was in the village of Rexpoëde, in a small square opposite the town hall, but when they arrived in the early morning, the place was deserted and Brigade nowhere to be found. Daniel, feeling anxious and wanting to keep himself awake, got out and wandered back the way they had come, the sun just rising and the day already warm. Birds were singing and the grass which edged the road was a glorious vivid green, so that Daniel, after a second night without sleep, felt himself in a dream. Retreating troops passed silently on either side of him: a platoon of gunners with no guns; a Bren carrier draped with bodies, some sleeping, others not so fortunate; a Colonel on a pushbike, the tyres making a slurring sound on the gritty road. Daniel saw them all and yet he saw nothing, for his mind was on the regiment, on what he would do if he could not find them, on where they could possibly be.

After what seemed like several hours — but in fact was about twenty minutes — a 3-tonner appeared in the distance, and to his relief he saw it was the ration-truck, with Captain Minton behind the wheel and the various tractors and lorries that made up B Echelon following behind. He ran towards it waving his arms.

'Sutton! Need a lift, is it?' The Captain, known as

Minty, grinned. Until a few days ago he had been a second lieutenant like Daniel, and wore his promotion lightly.

'I can't find the convoy,' said Daniel, his voice seeming to boom from somewhere deep inside him. 'They're not at the rendezvous.'

He stared up at the lorry, and suddenly it was as if everything was made of wax and slowly melting before his eyes. The handle of the door, the half-open window, the captain's face, with its neat moustache and freckled cheeks, all of it flickering and insubstantial, as if the atoms might fly apart at any moment. And the brightness. He had to squint, for the sheer colour of it made his skull tighten, made the bones of his face feel sharp.

'Come on, hop in.' Minty leaned across and threw the door open. Daniel's head was spinning. 'Hop in!' the other man repeated, and Daniel heard himself think *grab the handle*, then watched with curiosity as his hand reached up and did just that. Every movement he made — stepping onto the running board, sitting down on the seat — was preceded by a clearly audible thought inside his brain, *lift your foot, bend your knees*. It was as if everything that was usually smooth and automatic had been broken into single frames, like a movie played at the wrong speed, or one of those flip-book cartoons.

The truck started off again, lurching forwards, so that the usual accumulation of Penguin books and bits of food slid up and down the dashboard. Daniel stared, for nothing seemed real to him: not the dog-eared Agatha Christie novel, not the Kraft cheese melting in its tin, not the clay-like hands that held the steering wheel, every so often plunging sideward as they changed gear. He could feel himself seeing, feel his eyes swivel in their sockets, feel the thoughts as they announced themselves in his brain. Beside him, Minty was chatting away, but his words were garbled, as if he were speaking underwater, and Daniel was aware only of an enormous mouth, like a clown's mouth, with big red lips and black teeth. He closed his eyes.

When he opened them again they were back at the town hall. He was alone, and when he turned his head he saw that B Echelon had pulled in behind, arranging itself on three sides of the square. Troops milled around the front steps, stretching or brewing up, calling to one another in voices that sounded squeaky and far away. With an effort, Daniel sat forward: even his hair hurt.

'You're right, no sign of them.' Minty was back, leaning through the open door and feeling for something beneath the seat. 'Here, have a drop of this,' the hollow pop of something being uncorked, then a bottle pressed into Daniel's hands. 'You look like you could do with it.'

'Thank you. I'm quite tired.'

He lifted the bottle to his mouth. The whisky was warm, sliding easily around his mouth and causing the muscles in his face to twitch. He had an urge to smile, to laugh even, but he fought it, swallowing and leaning back against the seat. He took a breath, and then another one, and then another, each time finding it a little easier, as though some obstacle were being slowly pushed aside. His heart, punching at his ribcage like a fist, gradually stilled.

They waited there all day. Retreating troops continued to pour through the town on their way to Dunkirk, and enemy aircraft made frequent passes, but the action was for the most part elsewhere. Captain Minton, finding no trace of Brigade in the immediate area, decided they should press on towards the coast, and the vehicles were lined up on the main road, Daniel and Grimes leading off in the lorry. But barely had they left the town than they were stopped by a Military Policeman, his red cap glowing like a beacon: only ambulances and water trucks were allowed inside the Dunkirk perimeter, everything else must be destroyed.

'Destroyed, sir? How's that?' Grimes looked at Daniel uncomprehendingly. They were a cavalry regiment, the vehicles were their horses. 'That's not right, surely.'

Daniel gazed at him without answering. The clamour of earlier had quietened, but the world remained a jagged and dangerous place. He opened the door and leaned out, looking back along the line. One by one, directed by the MP, the vehicles were pulling off the road and onto a narrow track, and Daniel gestured to Grimes to do the same thing. Their place on the road was at once filled by other traffic, as water fills a dyke.

'But sir—' The older man, his usually animated face suddenly dull and childlike, looked in disbelief at the scene ahead of them. A large field, the green rosettes of young potato plants running in rows from side to side, was full of wrecked vehicles. Trucks lay nose down in the surrounding ditches; others waited patiently, engines running, as sugar was poured into their radiators, or men with sledgehammers set about smashing them. In one corner six Scammell tractors burned furiously.

Daniel climbed out, holding on to the door handle, and waiting as Grimes reluctantly passed down his belongings. The track beneath his boots gleamed sticky and iridescent, and when he looked he saw it was petrol, and that all around men were upending cans and pouring the contents onto the ridged field. Officers shouted above the noise of engines and hammering, 'Dump the stores,' 'Small packs only,' and voices murmured their replies, some polite, some not. Every so often something exploded.

Daniel set his kit on the grass verge and began to unpack it. Years of boarding school had cured him of sentiment, and he kept only what was most necessary: extra socks, a clean shirt, his toothbrush and razor, a sleeping bag. The rest he threw into the ditch. All around him men were doing the same, some changing into fresh uniform, one or two shaving, others spreading themselves out on the grassy verge and watching the planes high above their heads, as if they had nothing better in the world to do than this. Someone had tuned a wireless to dance music, and when Grimes returned from dumping the lorry, he was decidedly cheerier.

'Better than shooting 'em, I suppose,' he said, and Daniel understood he meant better than shooting horses.

They set off on foot in the early evening. From all sides came the constant boom of combat, and farms and cottages blazed in every direction. They formed up into pairs, Minty and Daniel leading, the men following behind, and did their best to keep a steady pace. But the going was slow: the road, as someone observed, like Dens Park on Cup Final day. And with Minty still on the lookout for Brigade, they were frequently delayed. Ahead of them, Dunkirk glowed red against the darkening sky, great columns of flames soaring above the blazing oil tanks, so bright they could have read a map by it. This is what hell looks like, Daniel thought.

Now it was midnight. Now it was dawn. Now it was that moment just before the sun comes up when the human spirit is at its most vulnerable, when men lie down on mountaintops, when life seems least precious. Daniel, who had dropped back and was walking with the RSM, drifted in and out of sleep, propelled forward only by the rhythm of those around him. To turn his head, to tighten his boots, to speak, required impossible effort, and so he did none of these. By some miracle the men stayed together, but had someone dropped out, joined the bodies in the ditches, sat down and refused to go on, Daniel would not have known.

'Nearly there now, sir.' Grimes fell into step alongside, his gaze on the horizon. Day was breaking, to reveal a thick pall of black smoke lying over the coast. They had seen it for days now, soon they would be walking beneath it.

Daniel nodded. It was the most he could manage, every part of him consumed with the single aim of not stopping. He had never felt so tired, never known the mental battle required to keep a body moving when it is no longer willing. In the course of the night he had discarded almost everything he carried. Now even a pair of socks was too heavy, and he threw them away.

The road wound on. They were to the east of Dunkirk, the marshy land on either side of the road flooded and brackish-smelling. Somewhere in the depths of his exhaustion, a memory was triggered. That last night of freedom, when he and Gilbert had gone swimming. He could feel the water cool on his skin, smell the moss on the river bank, the sweet musk of silt and rotting leaves. Time shrank away, or perhaps it expanded, for suddenly there was no present or past, only a kind of searing, thrilling consciousness. He was everything: he was the river drawn inexorably forwards, he was the road beneath his feet, he was a fish, a bat, that black-headed gull drifting on the air current, a smoke ring fading to nothing. The feeling of separateness, of the world as brittle and unreal, not only returned, it intensified, consuming every part of him so that he feared he might suddenly snap and disappear. Like the socks. Like Gilbert. Like the architect who built the castle by the river. Fine threads that bind and then release. Somehow he kept moving.

Daniel had no memory of crossing the canal, nor of the long walk towards Bray Dunes, with its pretty villas lining the main street and houses named after shells or seabirds. Nor did he remember how they ended up coming across the dunes, for all the men he spoke to afterwards had walked through the town, which made perfect sense when you looked at the map. But he did remember the silence. The silence of those vast sandy wastes, with the tufts of dry grass and endlessly sloping hills that blotted out the horizon and birds that flew up out of nowhere without a sound, not even their wings beating. It was a silence that seemed to fill every part of him, and yet at the same time, a silence that emptied him out. There was no wind and the sun blazed not from the sky, but from the sand all around, so that he walked with his eyes almost shut.

And then suddenly, without warning, they came over a last hill and the sea, flat and calm, greeted them with a roar of ebbing, lapping waves. Military Policemen on motorbikes wove up and down the beach, sand pitching around their wheels like surf, and a gentle breeze blew west, so that the smoke above Dunkirk never reached them. Gulls waded in the shallows, picking at bits of seaweed and empty razor shells, and the sky was a hazy, heat-filled grey. And everywhere, troops sitting patiently on the warm sand, sleeping or eating something from a tin, gazing towards the horizon where, if you squinted against the glare, the shadows of boats and troopships could be seen. For some reason, at that particular moment on that particular morning, there were no Luftwaffe bombing the beaches, no sudden Stuka dives onto the waiting boats, no screaming, bleeding men wondering why now, on this particular beach, it should be their moment to die. Later someone would tell Daniel it was because the RAF were there, patrolling the coastline so that they could make it safely to the boats, but Daniel did not see them either. Overwhelmed, he fell to his knees.

THEY WERE TAKEN OFF IN A matter of hours, rowed by dinghy to a minesweeper waiting further out. Daniel was led to the Captain's cabin, and while they were still waiting to leave, he fell asleep, waking again when it was late afternoon and they were just off the English coast. Instantly thoughts of Gilbert Ross, the regiment, the horrors he had seen and of those that were to come, filled his mind. He closed his eyes, but the pictures remained, and so he got up and went on deck. They were coming into dock at Ramsgate, a place Daniel had never heard of before, and he leaned over the railings with the other men, staring at the crowds of civilians lining the seafront beyond.

What are they doing here? he thought, gazing at the women in their summer dresses, at the men singing and waving Union Jacks, at the children tugging on their arms. Buses were lined up to carry the troops to the station, and as each set off, a cheer went up and people hurried alongside, thrusting chocolate bars and packets of cigarettes through the open windows. Daniel felt sick at heart. How naïve everyone was, did they not understand that this was a defeat? That the danger had now reached this very coast?

'Welcome home, we're so very glad to see you.' An officer in service dress, his buttons gleaming and his belt so polished that it resembled mahogany, stepped forward as Daniel descended the gangplank. 'You'll find everything is laid on. We'll soon have you comfortable. I expect you'd like a beer or something.'

Daniel looked away, at the harbour dark with troops, at the stretchers being carried along the quayside, at the pile of rifles on one end of the jetty and the pile of ammunition on the other. A woman in the same WVS uniform his mother now wore offered to call his parents, but Daniel could not remember their number, so he shook his head. Someone else offered a mug of cocoa, but he brushed them away. Another bus set off along the seafront, and once again the crowd surged alongside, waving flags and laughing.

'I don't know what they're cheering for,' he said, moving past the officer. 'I feel ashamed.'

CHAPTER 18

Sofia Carasso was giving a dinner party. A letter had arrived from Manu and she was in a mood to celebrate, for it is not every day one's son is decorated for bravery. In all the rooms of the villa people were busy, rearranging furniture and lifting rugs, moving chairs from one room to another, plumping cushions. Flowers, cut fresh from the garden, were thrust into vases — roses, poppies, delphiniums and clematis — and strewn around the surfaces. Deliverymen slipped in and out as if on pulleys.

In the midst of all this, Sofia, wearing pink satin beach pyjamas and a fur stole, stood at the dining table, writing the names of her guests on small, smooth pebbles. Each one she laid above a place setting, moving around the long table and frowning in concentration. Kasha, his big hands clasped to his chest, watched from the doorway.

'Haven't you something to do, Kasha?' she asked, when she had already made several tours of the table and it still was not right.

The manservant nodded, but remained where he was. 'He met Pierlot and General Denis, madame?' he said after a while, for Sofia had read him Manu's letter.

Sofia stopped what she was doing and smiled. 'Both,' she said, 'true patriots, not like that treacherous Leopold.'

At the sound of the doorbell Kasha went out. 'I'm not home,' Sofia called after him, her attention back on the seating plan. Husband and wife were sitting together, that would never do. Once again she began circling the table.

'Even to me?' It was Laura, her hair pulled back

beneath a silk scarf, in her arms a bunch of peach-coloured peonies. When she saw all the vases of flowers she laughed and looked disappointedly at her offering. 'I liked the colour,' she said, holding them out to Sofia, 'although it's the strangest thing, they have no scent at all. Perhaps you can lose them somewhere.'

'My dear Laura, how sweet you are. Look, Kasha, *pionyeh*,' and she gestured to him to take the flowers, looking back at the table. 'I thought I had it, but I moved one, and now it's all unravelled. It's the wives that give the most trouble, have you noticed that? Allegra Balestra, for example. Where on earth does one put her?'

'Oh, Allegra will be happy anywhere.'

'It's not her I'm thinking of.' Sofia drummed her fingertips on the edge of the table, chewing her lip in a new way she had. 'Why is it so many men have dull wives?' she wondered, with the assurance of a woman who could never be thought such. She picked up a pebble and exchanged it with another on the opposite side. 'How is Marco? Is he feeling brighter?'

Laura sighed, pulling off her head scarf and dropping it on a chair. The news of Belgium's capitulation had shocked everyone, but Marco had taken it especially hard. 'It's the office he minds most,' she said, then stopped, for it was the same for the Carassos. They too had lost both home and business. She looked around as Kasha came back, carrying the peonies in a tall glass jug. 'But tell me about Manu, is it true he got out at Dunkirk? Was it as dreadful as everyone is saying? His poor wife — Lise must have been beside herself.'

Sofia made a small tilting motion with her head. 'Lise?' The existence of her daughter-in-law seemed a constant surprise to her. 'I suppose she must. Here, Kasha, put them on the table. How pretty they look, did you trim the stems?'

'The florist wanted to remove the leaves,' said Laura, reaching out to straighten one of the blooms, 'but I think that's a shame, don't you? They look so nice through the glass.' She moved slowly around the table, reading the names on the pebbles. 'Lluís? Don't tell me you got Señor Companys?'

Sofia beamed. She had been trying to lure the exiled Catalan president all winter. 'I met his wife in the post office, we bonded over our absent sons.' She straightened a napkin. 'What a gathering of lost souls we will be, *un dîner des exilés*. The Hallemans are coming too, do you know Roger Hallemans?'

'Of course.'

'I'm never sure if I like him.' Sofia stroked her stole, 'I always find there's something slippery about him? I've put him next to you, I hope you don't mind.' She stared at the table. 'Now look at that, I have all women this end, that won't do at all. I don't suppose you saw Ezra on your way in. He's so much better at this kind of thing than I am.' She glanced towards the windows, which were open and gave directly onto the sea. A light breeze had got up, causing the shutters to rattle on their hinges, and for a moment Sofia forgot herself and imagined the scenes Manu had written about. The burning black sky, the ships bombed and machine-gunned from the air, the bodies — in the water, on the beach — some neatly lined up, others lying where they had fallen. He had been lucky, he said. He had been given permission to board a French destroyer. Others like him had been hit with rifle butts, knocked backwards as they climbed the rope ladder onto Allied ships, their Belgian uniform proof that they were not worth saving. She shuddered at the thought of it, and Laura, standing beside her, took her hand and rubbed it affectionately.

'I've had a letter from my brother,' said Laura after a while. 'From Leonard.'

'Dear Leonard, how is he?' asked Sofia. She barely remembered him, but the fact he had been to one of her parties inspired a certain affection. 'Is he still putting out fires, or whatever it is he does.'

'Air raid warden,' said Laura, smiling. 'Yes, he is.'

'He should come here. Everyone should come here, your parents too. I hope you've told them.' She was looking at the table again. 'I could just leave them.' She meant the women. 'After all, it's hardly my fault there's not enough men. What do you think, Larotchka?'

'I think it's all going to be perfect,' said Laura, letting go of her friend's hand and moving to stand behind one of the chairs. She was thinking about Leonard's letter — how worried he was about her affairs, how nothing she wrote seemed to reassure him. It was as if he wanted her to despair, as if only by suffering would she prove that she understood how bad things were. She sighed, picking up a silver spoon and turning it back and forth so that tiny sparkles flashed across the ceiling. This room always reminded her of the apartment: the height of the windows, the way the sun seemed to flood every surface, like liquid that had nowhere else to go. German officers would be living there now, that's what Marco said. German officers with their boots on, sitting on her yellow sofas, playing her piano. It gave her a pain in her heart just to think of it. 'The Avenue Louise is in ruins, did you know? A Belgian family were in the hotel this morning, asking Madame Michenet for rooms. Naturally I inquired about the Avenue des Nations, and they said it was untouched. How funny. Just one street away, and nothing.'

'I shouldn't have minded if it was bombed. Of course, I wouldn't wish anyone hurt, but the house itself means nothing. In fact, I think I'd prefer it.'

'You don't mean that.'

'Actually, I do. I never liked that house, and if we have to lose something, I'd rather it be bricks and mortar.'

Laura frowned and fiddled with a button on her dress. This was how everyone talked these days, making little deals, offering this in exchange for that. Who says we have to lose something? she wanted to ask, but she refrained. A noise in the corridor caused them both to turn around.

'Ah! There she is!' Sofia opened her arms as a small girl of about two years old flung herself into the room. She had red hair and skin that had been turned a soft gold by the sun, and her face was a mass of freckles. 'Mimi, say hello to Laura, Laura's helping with our pebbles.'

Laura smiled, watching as Sofia picked the child up and stood her on a chair. 'I'm afraid we're not doing a very good job,' Laura said. Like many mothers, she had little interest in other people's children. The little girl stared at her unblinking, her thumb in her mouth.

'Is *maman* sleeping?' Sofia removed the thumb, glancing at Laura. 'You've never known someone sleep the way Lise does, even Ezra finds it strange. I sometimes wonder if she has a condition. What do you think? Is there a condition where you sleep all the time?'

'Not everyone has your energy, Sofia,' said Laura. 'Besides, she's probably been worried about Manu. Worry is exhausting. What a picture the two of you make.'

Sofia looked down at the child. The thumb was back in, and once again she removed it. 'You'll get rabbit teeth,' she said sternly, 'and no one will want to kiss you.'

'Oh Sofia!'

'It's true.' Sofia bent down so that her face was level with Mimi's and bared her own perfectly even teeth. 'Everyone wants to kiss Sofia,' she said.

Mimi giggled and bared her own small teeth in return. Sofia laughed, and showered the child with kisses.

'Sofia, you're shameless,' said Laura, and the other woman smiled, straightening up and smoothing the front of her satin pyjamas.

'What were we talking about?' said Sofia after a while. She had set the child on the floor and was back to studying the seating plan. 'Oh yes, Belgians in the hotel. How is Madame Michenet? Still listening to her German radio?'

Laura flushed. It was Rita who had told everyone this.

'Oh darling, I'm not judging, Kasha's practically glued to Radio Stuttgart, says it's the only way to get any news.' She moved two pebbles, stared at them for a few seconds, then moved them back again. 'They've been dropping leaflets on Paris, did you hear? Manu wrote about it in his letter. Claiming they'll be there on Bastille Day to dance with the Parisian ladies.'

Laura winced. How crude it all was. She wanted to ask if it was possible, if this Blitzkrieg everyone talked about could indeed carry the enemy into Paris, but she had promised herself to be brave and so refrained. What was it someone had said to her the other day? '*Il n'y a pas de situations désespérées, il y a seulement des hommes désespérés.*' She must remember that when she wrote back to Leonard.

'Marco thinks he might have found me a villa,' she said, thinking to change the subject. 'I went to look at it yesterday, it's terribly nice. The owner's asking a small fortune, but Marco's sure he'll be able to negotiate, he says the French expect it.' She had resisted taking something permanent, had hoped they would soon return to Brussels, but these recent developments would add another two years to the war, everyone said so. 'We shall miss our sea view. We've been rather spoilt at the hotel, but it has the prettiest little sun terrace, I can quite see myself sitting out there with my coffee.'

'I should say you'll miss your nice Major too,' said Sofia, narrowing her eyes, and Laura smiled, because Sofia was always teasing her about Major Fielding.

'Actually I've hardly seen him.' This was true, for the officers now left the hotel before dawn and were back long after Laura and the children were in bed. She supposed that they were busy at the Depot, and Teddy, who was interested in such things, said it was surely the case, especially as the Major was in charge of ammunitions. But occasionally there was a note, pushed under her door or left for her in reception, suggesting a trip to the pictures when things got quieter, or offering some detail he thought the children might like — how the new Defiant planes had shot down thirty-seven enemy aircraft in one afternoon, that kind of thing. She was always a little cheerier on those days.

'I should have invited him, how silly of me,' said Sofia, reaching out and tucking a strand of hair behind Laura's ear. 'Especially with my dearth of men. Although I suppose we're just going to have to get used to that. What is it they say, Britain is fighting to the last Frenchman? Darling, don't look like that, I'm only teasing.'

'I know,' said Laura, shrugging. 'I'd better go, I left the children with their cousins. Allegra's got them rolling bandages for the Red Cross, she's wonderful how involved she gets.'

'Wonderful,' said Sofia, in that tone she always used when speaking of Allegra. Just yesterday she had seen that son of hers — Seppy, was it? — hanging around in front of the casino, not a care in the world. What matter that the Belgians had capitulated before he could be called up? Why should Allegra be spared Sofia's suffering, why should any mother? Sofia gazed at the table and felt a sudden release. 'Oh, that'll have to do,' she said, arranging the last of the pebbles any old how. She fretted too much, Ezra was always telling her so. 'These things always come out in the end.'

'Of course they do.' Laura turned away, looking through the open doors towards the sea. Voices carried on the breeze, carefree summertime voices, such as you always heard on

Sundays in June; children swimming or playing on the sand, mothers calling them to come and get a towel, stay in their depth, put a hat on. Children like Mimi, like her own three. She felt ashamed, sometimes, of how comfortable her life was, how easily she had sidestepped the darkness, found her way back into the sun. She thought of those poor people in the hotel this morning, of the wounded soldiers packed into hospital beds in the Hermitage or the Royal. Was it enough, she wondered, to roll bandages? Was it enough merely to witness the horror, to watch it on the newsreels, on the stretchers as they were carried off the hospital trains, on the faces of the men and women in the lobby?

'They came over the mountains, you know.'

Laura looked round. 'Who did? Sorry, I was miles away.'

'Señor Companys and his wife. In February, through four feet of snow, I'm hoping he'll tell us about it this evening. You wouldn't believe it to see her, she's the picture of elegance, not at all the hiking sort.'

Laura nodded. 'I must go,' she said again. 'Anything I can bring later?'

'Just your lovely self,' smiled Sofia. She came and stood in front of her friend, picking up Laura's scarf and gently tying it over her hair. Then she kissed her on both cheeks and watched as she stepped through the open doors and out into the warm afternoon.

And everywhere, beneath the arching blue skies of summer, people lifted their faces and felt glad. War was far away: it was a crackling cinema screen, a headline in a newspaper, a story told in a letter to be passed around at dinner parties. It was a dark presence at the edge of life, but it was not life itself. Not this life, this colourful, vivid, wondrous life, of sucked thumbs and peach-coloured peonies, of strangers who hiked over mountains and young men brought home from beaches. We must all suffer, people said, but they were not thinking of Herr Hitler and his Blitzkrieg, they were thinking of everyday things, such as why there were no rhum babas any more, or how their son was supposed to sit his Bachot. From the dunes of La Baule, to the streets of Alexandria, to the gardens and front rooms of South Manchester, people loved and fought and worried and felt joy, just as they always did. Because they were the lucky ones. Because now they were safe.

END OF BOOK ONE

British Military Glossary

Ack-ack / A/A *Anti-aircraft guns*

Adjutant *An officer appointed to assist the Commanding Officer (see below) with unit administration, often in the management of personnel*

ARP *Air Raid Precautions, a term covering the organisations dedicated to civil protection in Britain against air raids*

Batman *A soldier appointed to a commissioned officer as a personal servant*

BEF *The British Expeditionary Force. The name given to the British Army in Western Europe during World War II from 2nd September 1939 until 31st May 1940*

Bren *A British-made light machine gun used from 1935 onwards*

Brig *Brigadier, the senior rank superior to Colonel and subordinate to Major-General*

Brigade Staff *Nucleus of officers and support staff serving the Brigadier*

British Warm *A heavy woollen overcoat worn by officers based on the greatcoats worn by British Army officers in World War I*

CO	*Commanding Officer, in charge of a unit*
Echelon (A/B/C)	*A formation of units within a company of soldiers, often formed for tactical purposes*
Entraining	*Putting vehicles or artillery onto a train*
General Staff	*The officers attached to GHQ (see below), headed by the Chief of the Imperial General Staff*
GHQ	*General Headquarters, where the Generals and other officers coordinate operations*
MO	*Medical Officer*
Mess Orderly	*A soldier assigned to the mess (the canteen) as a servant*
NCO	*Non-commissioned officer. For example, a sergeant or corporal*
MP	*Military Policeman, member of the Royal Military Police, the corps responsible for upholding military law*
OR	*Other Ranks, personnel who are not commissioned officers*
QM	*Quartermaster, the officer in a battalion or regiment responsible for supplies*
RDG HQ	*Royal Dragoon Guards Headquarters*
Redcaps	*Nickname for MPs (see above)*

RSM	*Regimental Sergeant Major. There is only one RSM in a regiment or battalion. He is primarily responsible for maintaining standards and discipline and acts as a parental figure to his subordinates and also to junior officers, even though the latter technically outrank him*
RTO	*Rail Transport Officer*
Sapper	*A junior soldier responsible for tasks such as building and repairing roads and bridges, laying and clearing mines etc. Usually a private in the Corps of Royal Engineers*
Subaltern	*British army officer below the rank of captain, especially a second lieutenant*
SM	*Sergeant Major, the Senior Warrant Officer / WO (see below)*
VMG	*Vickers Machine Gun, widely used by the British Amy from 1912 onwards*
WO	Either: *Warrant Officer. An army rank senior to non-commissioned officer (NCO) ranks and subordinate to commissioned officers* Or: *Wireless Operator*
WVS	*Women's Voluntary Service, founded in 1938. British women's organisation which recruited women into the Air Raid Precautions (ARP) services to help local communities during World War II*

EUROPE
& THE MIDDLE EAST
AT THE OUTBREAK OF WWII

ALLIED POWERS

AXIS AND AREAS ANNEXED OR MADE PROTECTORATES

NON BELLIGERENT or NEUTRAL ON THE EVE OF WAR

Scale
0   50   100   200mi.

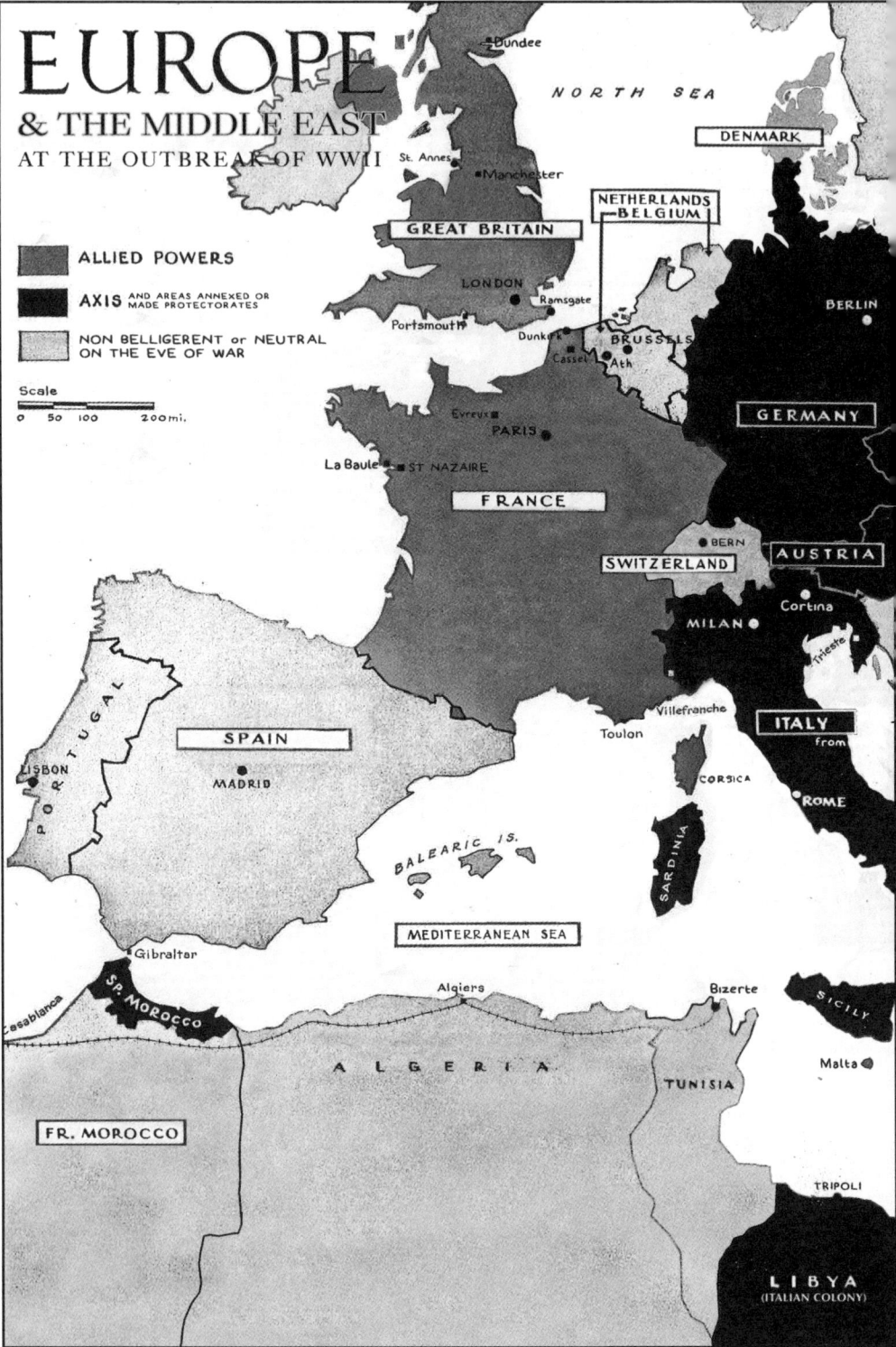

NORTH SEA

Dundee

DENMARK

St. Annes

Manchester

GREAT BRITAIN

NETHERLANDS
BELGIUM

LONDON

Ramsgate

BERLIN

Portsmouth

Dunkirk

BRUSSELS

Cassel   Ath

GERMANY

Evreux

PARIS

La Baule   ST NAZAIRE

FRANCE

BERN

AUSTRIA

SWITZERLAND

Cortina

MILAN

Trieste

PORTUGAL

SPAIN

Villefranche

ITALY
from

Toulon

LISBON

MADRID

CORSICA

ROME

BALEARIC IS.

SARDINIA

MEDITERRANEAN SEA

Gibraltar

Casablanca

SP. MOROCCO

Algiers

Bizerte

SICILY

Malta

A L G E R I A

TUNISIA

FR. MOROCCO

TRIPOLI

L I B Y A
(ITALIAN COLONY)

Map of Central and Eastern Europe, the Mediterranean, and the Near East.

Labels on the map:

BALTIC SEA
SWEDEN
LATVIA
LITHUANIA
DANZIG
EAST PRUSSIA
Tannenberg
MOSCOW ●
U. S. S. R.
WARSAW ●
POLAND
CZECHOSLOVAKIA
VIENNA ●
HUNGARY
RUMANIA
CRIMEA
BELGRADE ●
BUCHAREST
BLACK SEA
YUGOSLAVIA
BULGARIA
ADRIATIC SEA
ALBANIA
ISTANBUL
Dardanelles
GREECE
Corfu
TURKEY
ATHENS ●
CYPRUS
SYRIA
CRETE
BEIRUT ●
DAMASCUS ●
MEDITERRANEAN SEA
JERUSALEM ●
ALEXANDRIA ■
PORT SAID ●
CAIRO ●
EGYPT
(BRITISH PROTECTORATE)

Afterword

The story of the Balestras, the Cansinos, the Ardittis, the Carassos and the Suttons is true. That is to say, the family members, their various connections and the events that they experienced have not been changed, although all their names have. Whilst this book of course imagines their conversations and daily lives, much of what each of these individuals say and feel is to be found in their letters and postcards and in the recollections of their sons, daughters, nieces, nephews and friends.

Insofar as it has been possible, this story therefore seeks to present the truth about this intertwined group of people and their lives even if, inevitably, some of the facts are no longer accessible. And in doing so it is hoped that it preserves the essence of who they were and how their lives were altered by the events through which they lived.

S.K.F.

A NOTE ON THE TYPE

The text of this book was set in Caslon Classico, a typeface designed by the Swedish typographer, Franko Luin (1941-2005). It is based closely on the 18th century typeface Caslon, created by the great English typefounder William Caslon (1672-1766) who first cut this typeface in 1725.

His major influences were the Dutch Baroque designers Christoffel van Dijcks and Dirck Voskens. The Caslon font was long known as the 'script of kings', although at the other end of the political spectrum, the Founding Fathers of the United States of America also used it for the original printing of the Declaration of Independence in 1776.

Printing by FINIDR
Czech Republic